LAST TRAIN
FROM LIGURIA

Christine Dwyer Hickey

ATLANTIC BOOKS

LONDON

First published in trade paperback in Great Britain in 2009 by
Atlantic Books, an imprint of Grove Atlantic Ltd.

This paperback edition published in Great Britain
in 2010 by Atlantic Books.

5 7 9 10 8 6

A CIP catalogue record for this book is available
from the British Library.

ISBN: 978 1 84354 988 8

Printed in Great Britain

Atlantic Books
An imprint of Grove Atlantic Ltd
Ormond House
26–27 Boswell Street
London WC1N 3JZ

www.atlantic-books.co.uk

To Jessica,
with love

The paths to the past have long been closed,
And what good is the past to me now?
What is there? – bloodied flagstones,
Or a bricked-up door,
Or an echo that still can't be
Still, no matter how I plead…

'Echo' Anna Akhmatova

PART ONE

Edward

DUBLIN, 1924

August

EVEN BEFORE I CAME to my senses, I knew my sister was dead. In there, face down on the sawdust, behind the back bar counter. I was out here meanwhile at the bottom of the stairs, passed out on a mangy carpet. Our father's house. At least, this time, I knew where I was.

The carpet – piss, grease and stale ale – had been luring me home with its stench and after a while I persuaded myself to open my eyes. Into the darkness and the ticking of a distant clock, I managed to haul myself onto my feet. Remarkably steady. I noticed this immediately, how steady I was on my pins. And no hangover. Where was my hangover?

I tried to remember. For a long time nothing. Then the sound of a pot-boy wandered into my memory. Banging on the door of some room I'd been in. Calling time maybe, or reciting a message – singing it more like. The pot-boy's song ran so clear in my head, nasal and sweet, innocent and sinister, all at once. I could see bits from Harrison's pub, then Slattery's snug, and all the other dives and kips where I may have been over the past two days or more. Marble and wood; foot rails and slimy spittoons; a murmur of light; a hand made of jelly; the jabber of mouths through a gilt-edged mirror. Wherever I'd been, I was back here now anyway crossing over the hall to the door of the public lounge. Crumpled light on the glass. I stood for a while listening to silence, then, with a wary foot, pushed the door open. The house had been cleared; shutters down, night lights up, the oulfella asleep up in bed – I could hear through the layers of ceilings and floors, the growl of his snore dragging itself backwards and forwards.

Through to the back bar, I switched on the sidelights, then stepped behind the counter. And there she was. Dead as meat.

I tested the air with her name. '*Louise?*'

The sight of her blood. That so much could be contained in one body. Even a body as big as Louise's. An outrageous amount. Long splats across the bar counter, dots on the backdrop mirrors. A velvety puddle lay at my feet and from the corner of a ledge one flimsy string of it dangled in and out of a shadow. I looked at my hands and knew that they had done it.

How long I stayed there or what was going through my mind during that time I couldn't say, but the next thing I remember is kangarooing from my knees and making a dart for the far end of the bar. There, diving under the sink to unhook a bunch of keys, now scratching and poking through locks and bolts until I was in the oulfella's office standing before his safety box, one last long key in my hand.

My mind wouldn't budge. Three clanking sounds from upstairs got it going again; two short, one long. A crash of water, next a flushing chain – the oulfella. I knew his form: sleep for a couple of hours, then piss like a dog for a couple more. Finally he'd get fed up hoisting himself in and out of the scratcher and begin his nightly prowl. There was only one thing to do and that was get the hell out of there. I said it to myself as I opened the safe and stuffed a large manila envelope full of notes down the front of my trousers. *Get out.* I continued to say it as I stumbled back through the bar. I was saying it still as I lifted the bolt off the scullery door, cut through the backyard, skirted the barrels and crates, ducked under the clothes line taking a cold wet lick from a bar-towel across my face. *Get out, get out, keep going.* Then I was clawing up the back wall on all fours; grunting and

4

groaning like a wounded pig, knees and elbows knocking off brick, thighs grinding, squirming, struggling. And at last, I was over.

I picked my moment to drop. A spray of hot needles from the soles of my feet rushed into my head, blurring my eyes. I looked up at the back of the house and waited for everything to settle. Now I could see the various shapes of the windows, the slant of pipes and guttering, the sill that was beginning to loosen from the gable end. And a sudden bud of light, breaking softly into the oulfella's window.

Behind me a sound. I spun round and there was Mackey. Rising like a cobra rises out of his coils of cast-off coats, unwinding himself from a dirt-thick muffler and stretching out to me a long silvery tongue that was sticky with sleep. I nearly died at the sight of him. He stepped away from his filthy nest in the alcove of Quinlan's old coach house. Then, lifting his tilly lamp, pinned me to the limelight.

'Put that down,' I said.

A moment of mutual inspection followed under the piss-pale light. His overlit eyes glaring into me, and his head – oozing with long matted curls – for all the big size of him, still managed to look like an exaggeration.

'Mackey – put down the lamp.'

'*Pleathe?*' he said girlishly.

'Please.'

'Who put blood on you?' he asked me then.

I thought for a moment before answering, 'That's not blood, that's paint. Now put down the lamp.'

'Whatpaintwhypaint?'

'The cellar. I was painting the cellar. Keeps the rats away, you know yourself.'

Mackey squeezed his eyes up and gave one of his silent laughs. He lowered the lamp. By now the light in the oulfella's bedroom window was burning a hole in the back of my head.

'Here, Mack,' I began, 'you wouldn't lend us one of those old coats there for a few minutes?'

5

'No!'

'Ah go on, just for a minute. It's bloody freezing.'

'No! No no no no no,' he said, the massive curls shaking with his head from side to side.

I knew he wouldn't be quick enough for me. I was over to the coats, and had one dragged out of the stinking pile, before Mackey had time to think. I threw a 'So long, Mack,' back over my shoulder, as I ran to the top of the lane.

'Fuckarse!' he shouted when I was halfway there.

I turned into Church Street and daybreak was sniggering at me. It was jigging all over the orphanage brickwork and spinning a glint on the backs of seagulls making their way down to the river. I ducked into a tenement doorway to consider my options. There was only the one: the mailboat train. Somehow I would have to get myself to the station without being spotted, rat-scurrying from shadow to shadow.

By now the city was edging towards Sunday; church bells trapezing across the sky. Soon first worshippers would be crawling out of their holes. In any case what was I thinking of, hanging around here, blood on my hands and smeared into my shirt, the Bridewell prison only down the road? A child barked like a young dog in the tenement above. A woman's voice called, 'Ahhshh sleepsleep.' A milk cart rolled into a nearby street. The seagulls flew faster and lower to the ground. I looked up the broad long back of Church Street where a figure on a bicycle was taking shape. A shift-worker maybe, or the lamplighter getting ready to turn off the city. As the bicycle glided towards me, I pulled back into the doorway and waited for it to pass. When it didn't, I looked out again. There it was, a few yards away, coquettishly leaning against a wall.

The child barked again. This time a man let such a roar at it. The milk cart so close now, I could hear its every chime. I stepped out from the doorway and took a few long strides as far as the bicycle. Keeping my movements steady and smooth, I put one hand on the saddle and turned it onto the road. I cocked my leg over and pushed into the decline, through the ranting of gulls and the bells at full heckle; the sound of voices that could be inside or outside my head.

*

I kept my nerve well enough, until I got to the train station. There, standing before a heavy brown door, everything seemed to fall away, and I had no idea who I was, or where I was, or why I should be standing here in the first place. I could see abstracts of myself on the door's brass fittings and in the doorknob a round miniature of my face was lurking. Yet for the life of me I couldn't give that face a name. Across the brow of the door the word WASHROOM was painted, and over the coinbox a small sign said VACANT.

There was a rat-a-tat noise. By now it was so sharp and insistent that it seemed to be pecking right into my skull and I wanted it to stop, even for a few short seconds – just stop. I had the feeling then that I was an old man, perhaps confused, and easily irritated. I told myself, 'Relax, old man, wait, everything will come back in time.' Yet, when I looked at my right hand it was young. My other hand had gone beyond a tremble, jumping about of its own accord. I could see a coin in the pinch of its fingertips. Both hands were stained and heavily cut, which would at least explain why I was standing outside a washroom. I realized then that the rat-a-tat noise was the coin clacking off the door as my hand tried to get it into the brass penny slot.

Behind me an increased tempo of footsteps and a movement of slender shadows twitched like fish underwater. I thought that's what I was doing, standing underwater. I heard a whistle slash the air, another, and another. A long nasal voice began to call out. Numbers, I heard first. Then names. Names of towns. Destinations. A train station. Yes, yes, Amiens Street. The mailboat train. The mailboat.

Something tugged on the hem of my coat, and I froze all over, except for my left hand which continued to rattle away on the door. I looked down to find the ugliest child I had ever seen.

7

'What?' I snapped. 'Get lost, go on. Get.'

'It's only me, Mister. *Me.* 'Member me?'

'From where?'

'Only a little minute ago.'

I looked down at his bare feet, and he came back to me then as the scabby-toed paperboy. I remembered then, dumping the bicycle outside the station and edging my way through the usual hawkers and brassers, picking this lad out of the bunch with a tap on the shoulder as I passed him. I had crossed the road and slipped into Portland Lane where he had followed me like a lamb. When we got to the end of the lane, I told him I needed a service. He nodded. I began to open the top button of my flies and saw a sort of resigned dread come into his eye. Yet he still hadn't run, this ugly child, so scrawny he was held together by his own skin. 'For Christ's sake, it's not what you think,' I had snarled, pulling out the envelope of money.

Yes, that was it. The boy had bought me a passage and had found me a coin for the washroom. I had paid him an outrageous price. But then who was I to quibble or judge?

The paperboy reached up and grabbed me by the wrist, holding it steady, taming it. Then he plucked the coin from my fingers.

'Why are you still here?' I said to him. 'I thought I told you to go home.'

He fed the coin into the slot, and we both listened to it slide down the gullet and click. The boy held the door open with his foot. 'Your tickeh is in *dah* pocka,' he said, poking his finger to show, 'don't forgeh now. Platform wan. Five minutes.' I nodded, and he gripped my elbow. 'Stay steady,' he whispered. 'Steady.' Then he handed me a newspaper. 'For you, mister. For to cover your face.'

I was inside. White tiles and a rust-streaked sink. The echo of a slow-drip tap. There was a lump of soap and a thin, hard towel, shaving equipment I decided it might be best to ignore. There was a clothes brush and a nailbrush I could definitely put to use. And there was something in the mirror; but I didn't dare to look.

8

*

Before I knew it I was on the train, headed for Kingstown and the boat that would take me to Holyhead. I had made an effort to rinse the blood stains from my shirt in the washroom, and it felt like a cold second skin on my chest now. I could taste the dust that had risen off Mackey's coat since taking a brush to it.

As soon as I settled into the carriage, the missing hangover decided to return, making up for lost time with its full devotion. It caught me by the scruff of the neck and dragged me through fire and ice, fire and ice. It sucked every drop of spit from my mouth and then sucked the bones out of my fingers. It sat on my chest and gnawed at my stomach, it raged through every nook and cranny of me. Even my earlobes felt hot and sore. And I hadn't so much as a drop of whiskey. Why had I not thought to ask the paperboy? Usually whiskey would have been the first thought to come into my head. Now I would have to wait till God knows when and what state I'd be in by then.

It dawned on me, and with no small degree of shock, that I could forget about whiskey from now on. If I was to have any chance of surviving this thing, I would have to live the rest of my life on full and sober alert.

The door to the carriage snapped open and a blind woman was ushered in and introduced by a porter. She barely said good morning when he placed her opposite me, and I barely replied. A certain turn of her head implied conversation would be neither available nor welcome. This suited me fine. I would have preferred to have the carriage completely to myself, but I wasn't doing too badly, considering. Besides, the blind woman seemed to serve as a deterrent to other passengers. A face would come to the carriage window, beam when it spotted the vacant seats, take one look at my lady opposite, and push off again down the corridor. And at least she couldn't see me. Yet there was something unnerving about her marble eyes. Her straight, thin body. Those long, still hands so patient on her lap.

9

I looked out the window. The skeleton of an umbrella, caught between railings, was gallantly flapping one wing of black cloth. I kept my eye on it until the train heaved and began shoving into its own shrugs of smoke.

Resting against the window, nudging the train on with the side of my head, out of the station, through the rooftops, across the bridge and away from a city to which I now knew I could never return, unless to a hangman's noose. And every time I looked back into the carriage the marble eyes were on me. As if they could see every stain and thought in my head.

I was twenty-four years of age; a fool, a thief, a drunk – a hen-headed fucker in fact, just as the oulfella had often said. 'A hen-headed fucker, who ought to have been smothered at birth.' Now he could add murderer to my title. I caught my reflection in the train window, my mouth biting down on my knuckles, my eyes distorted. I felt as deranged as I looked. Anyone outside who happened to look up at the passing train would be bound to notice. I straightened myself up.

After Holyhead – what? Where could I go? I had lived in England for five long years of schooling and although I knew the place, and had learned to adapt to its manners, I had also learned to hate and distrust it. Besides I would be lifted there as easily as here. I needed somewhere further afield. Then Barzonni came into my mind. Because he was the only person I knew well who was living abroad, but also because he was the only one I could force into helping me. My old music master. I knew he had left Dublin in disgrace and gone back to Italy to start over again. I couldn't say exactly where, but surely any half-decent opera house would point me in the right direction? If I could persuade him (and with what I knew, what choice would he have?) to set me up with a reference, an introduction or two; some sort of a position. I had always wanted to see Italy anyway. And so somewhere between Ballsbridge and Booterstown, the first step of my future was decided. Italy.

As the train pushed past the end of the station wall a poster caught my eye. Edward VII puffing on a cigar. King Edward cigars. I tossed it around. Edward King. I had my new name. It was a start.

I was tired then, so tired. And my senses, which for the past few minutes or so had been almost too sharp to bear, were fast becoming indistinguishable, softening and tumbling into each other. So, although my eyes were open, I could see nothing. Nothing at all. But I could hear and feel the colour of blood.

Bella

GENOA, 1933

June

IT ONLY OCCURS TO her, the dilemma of her name, as the ship pulls out of Genoa harbour and the Italian voices on deck strike up their commentary of praise. The *bella* city behind them, the *bella vista* of the sea, the *bellezza* of Sicily waiting for them at the end of this long journey. That *bella* little girl in her *bella* little frock. Everything so.

Bella. She hears it over and over, flitting in and out of every sentence, so that for a few bewildering seconds it seems as if she is the topic of all conversations. But they seem to admire everything, the Italians. Then they admire each other. She likes that about them, their childlike ability to be constantly enchanted. Unlike the English, who so often need to be persuaded.

Bella closes her eyes. She hears the drum of footbeats along the upper decks, the yelping carousel of gulls, the many exuberant voices. Here and there she tries to untangle a conversation; since crossing the border at Ventimiglia yesterday, it's become an increasing anxiety. Childhood kitchen conversations with her father's ancient Italian godmother; faded textbooks from second-hand barrows along the Embankment; grammar classes in the Scuola di Sorrento on the Brompton Road; even recent nights spent in the translation of long dreary passages at the dining-room table – nothing, but *nothing*, could have prepared her for this extravaganza.

The thoughts of Sicily! Of not being understood, not even being able to understand; the child in her care; the rest of the household; and as for the notorious dialect? It could mean having to make a constant nuisance of herself with Signora Lami, asking her to translate this and that. And the Signora's letter had hardly given the impression of an approachable woman, never mind one who would be amused by a résumé that would turn out to be at best an exaggeration, at worst a bare-faced lie. ('I am pleased to say I speak Italian fluently and have difficulty with neither the written nor the spoken word.') What had she been thinking of, to claim such a thing? She would blame the dialect, that's what she'd do. Just until her ear accustomed itself to its new environment. She could say – *Mi dispiace, ma il… il dialecto…* No – *il dialetto…*

Behind her an old man begins to speak; a rusted voice, a slow delivery, and she is cheered to find she can follow his story with relative ease. He is telling a fellow passenger about the wedding he has just attended. His nephew's wedding, on the far side of Liguria, in a small hilltown called Dolceacqua – perhaps he knows it?

No, the companion does not, but has heard it is a beautiful place. *Certo è bello.* Most beautiful, just as the wedding was, the food, the weather, the olives, the church. And as for the wine of that region! Oh and the flowers. Everything. Everything. Except for, and unfortunately, the bride. When he says this there is a pause – a sigh from the speaker, a soft tut of condolence from his companion. Yet he will not say the bride is ugly, Bella notes, simply that she is not beautiful. *Non è bella.* But she has such a good heart, the old man emotionally concludes. So full of kindness. It is from here her real beauty shines, the heart. They will be happy, he is certain of it.

Of course they will, his companion agrees. Why wouldn't they be? Young, in love, living in Dolceacqua, most beautiful.

And she likes that too, the way they recognize it's not the bride's fault if she is no beauty, the way they imply she must nonetheless be loved, and made happy.

The faces on the dockside recede and crumble. The farewell hand-kerchiefs relent, and the brass band that an hour ago had caterwauled the passengers aboard plays fewer, weaker notes now. She is happy for a moment. That moment falls from her, is swished away to be replaced by another – this time one of dread. Far too conspicuous, she is, far too alone, here amongst these chattering strangers. And she must be careful of her back, already straining from days spent on rock-hard train seats, nights on inadequate mattresses.

The crowd thickens. Further up the deck there is an unexpected push and she turns slightly to see a fat boy barging through. His head, a curly black marker of his progress, pops up now and then, his voice a constant high-pitched chant: '*Voglio vedere!*' I want to see, I want to see.

People step back for him, pat his head, pluck his cheek, help him bully his way forward. This fat boy is now in charge of the crowd. When he shoves, it buckles. When he pulls at a coat or paws at a backside, there is indulgent laughter. Eventually she sees he has arrived at the railing just a few feet from her. He begins to scream angrily at the sea and appears to be hurling imaginary stones overboard as though he wants to somehow injure it. But in no time at all he becomes bored by all this. Then he starts roaring for his mother, '*Mamma! Mamma!*' and an affectionate '*Ahhhh…*' breaks out around him. Bella can't get over what a brat he is – God, say the Lami boy won't be like this.

'*Permesso! Permesso!*' The boy bounces himself off the railing and presses back into the crowd. This sudden movement causes the old man behind her to be pushed forward. She tenses her back. A snarl of pain runs down her spine and into her hip. '*Scusi,*' the man says; his voice, warm as an egg, sits for a moment in her ear.

She decides to go back to her cabin, turns from the railing and finds that after a few unsuccessful attempts the only way through is to raise her voice until, like the fat boy, she is shouting, '*Permesso! Permesso!*'

17

At last the old man and his companion hear her; they stand aside, create a sort of guard of honour consisting of old-fashioned walking canes and shoes so polished they look like glacéd cakes. They guide her through. She doesn't have to look at their faces to know they are studying hers. She passes, listens for a comment, a sigh or tut. But there is nothing.

*

The stink of the cabin! It haws its breath around her as soon as she steps through the door. Bella stays for a moment and considers the neighbouring cabins, doors pinned back by baggage or dressing stools to suck in whatever ocean air might happen to stray this way. But to leave the door open would be to invite full view of herself; nightgown on the bed, web of dead hair caught in the bristles of her hairbrush. Her mother's old alligator travel bag. It would also mean having to smile and respond to the greetings of every passer-by who, she had been startled to note, seemed to think nothing of stopping and staring right into an open cabin with a hearty 'Buon giorno!' She closes the door, then locks it. And sorry, now, that she exchanged Signora Lami's first-class ticket for a refund and a cabin such as this, with its grimy basin and cracked water jug. That monk-shaped stain along one wall. Shabby bed sheet and greasy head print on the pillow – pomade, she supposes.

Bella feels a little shaky, perhaps from hunger, but she is far too nervy now to go in search of anything to eat (at least in first class she could have rung for service). Perhaps it's pain? She rubs her lower back, considers taking one of the sachets her father has prescribed. But she knows the shape of pain, its sneaky ways, and knows that it is nothing now to what it might yet become before this journey's over. Hours to go. The rest of this sea voyage for a start; a stop-off at Naples to drop or pick up more passengers; then on to Sicily and the city of Palermo; a further two, maybe three hours cross-country before she would reach the Lami villa. She could be left in agony for days. She counts the sachets, only six.

Now at the travel bag, from an inner pocket she pulls out a pouch, which in turn gives way to another pouch – a long sausage shape wrapped in lace and secured at both ends by a twist. In her mind she calls this her money-tuck. Bella opens and spreads its skin of lace, exposing a stuffing made up of notes folded into each other, or notes grasped tightly around coins. Her fingers tip over the colours and faces of different denominations before taking her purse out of her pocket to remove the amount saved, so far, today. This she adds to and moulds into the pile. Rolling the sausage back into shape, re-twisting the ends, she bats the money-tuck between her palms for a moment before returning it to the pouch, within the pouch, and finally into the inner pocket of the travel bag. From the opposite side of the bag she pulls out a flask of water along with two biscotti and an apple saved over from breakfast. Then lays them on the cabin table beside an American magazine someone has left behind on the train, containing an article by G.B. Shaw and an exposé on the private life of Clark Gable – a hole gaping in the page where a fan has cut out his face. Steadier now, Bella picks up the portfolio of travel documents, flicking through until she finds her birth certificate inserted between the many pages of Signora Lami's directions. Anabelle Mary Stuart – shortened to Bella since childhood.

Into a basin half filled with water go a splash of cologne, two slow drops of lavender essence. Jacket and blouse removed, wrists cooling in water, she turns her head in the mirror and examines her face. Profile, quarter profile, front. Anabelle Mary Stuart. Mary Stuart maybe? Or does that seem to have a bit too much to say for itself? Anna then. Anna Stuart. Or what about Anne? Drop the 'e', even better the 'n'.

An – an indefinite article.

*

Signora Lami's directions had been nothing if not explicit.

They were delivered to Bella over a month ago in an elaborately bound parcel that turned out to be no less than a hatbox. It had puzzled her then, as she cut through the wrapping, noting the covering letter on Savoy Hotel stationery together with the index of instructions, train timetables, travel itinerary and a bunch of numbered envelopes; besides, if the Signora was staying at the Savoy, why go to this trouble, why not simply arrange an interview to give the instructions in person? It wasn't as if the Savoy was a million miles from Chelsea. And it would have broken the ice; after all, they would be living under the same roof in less than a month, and surely the Signora must have some curiosity about her son's future governess. Or nanny, or teacher, or companion or whoever it was she was soon expected to be?

The delivery boy, done up like a doll in Savoy livery, had shuffled on the doorstep while he waited for her to sign the receipt. Sniffing about inside his head, no doubt, for something to say that would take them both up to, and safely past, the moment that would decide his tip. Bella had been expecting the weather, the traffic, a newspaper scandal half-read or overheard. In the end he surprised her by blurting out, 'She made that many mistakes!'

'Who did?'

''Er…' He nodded at the parcel in Bella's hands. 'Wastepaper basket full up to…' The boy lifted his hand to his forehead as if he were the basket in question. 'Twice she sends for me to get more paper, I-mean-to-say-stationery. Twice. But when I come back like she says in an hour, all's right and ready to go.'

'Oh well, perhaps her English is not quite?'

'A fusspot is all.'

Bella groped through the coins in her purse. 'How long has Signora Lami been at the Savoy?'

'Fortnight, miss.'

'That long?'

'Leaves tomorrow, she does, miss.'

'Tomorrow – are you sure?'

'Oh yes, miss. For Sicily.'

She could see the boy liked the word Sicily, turning it over in his mouth, playing it between his small grey teeth.

'Where did you say?'

'Siss-a-lee.'

'I should send a reply.'

'No! She don't want none. Look it says so. There.' He pointed to the top of the receipt. 'Ree-ply. Not. Ree-quired.'

She had stood at the door for a moment, watching the doll-boy walk down to the gate where his little leg cocked over his bicycle. Within a few seconds he was at the end of the road, the bicycle plunging out onto the main road alongside a double-decker bus. She should have made more use of him. Another sixpence might have bought her a few extra brushstrokes. A shilling, a portrait, fully framed. How old was the Signora, for example? How fluent was her English? Was she calm, nervous, pretty, plain? Had there been a child with her? A husband? Did she have any callers? Had she dined in or out? And was it a suite or a bedroom where she had brimmed up the basket with her many mistakes?

Later, in her bedroom, Bella had spread the documents across the bed. First glance and she could already tell they would tolerate no deviation, and as for any untoward acts of initiative – well, she could put such nonsense straight out of her head. These weren't directions, these were *orders* and were even laid out on paper that looked like legal parchment. She read them again: 'Sit away from the window in this train. Stay in your cabin on that ship. Drink nothing that hasn't come from the hand of a waiter. Lock your door after dinner. In the street in Genoa neither look at nor speak to anyone – not even a priest.'

Really! It was as if she were a child or an imbecile. Nothing was permitted without the say-so of Signora Lami, from where, when and what she should eat, to the amount each porter should be tipped (a lesser amount the further she got from England, as it so happened). In fact, the only thing the Signora had omitted was a lavatory timetable.

Bella had picked up the bunch of envelopes. Each one numbered, dated and labelled with a more concise version of the instructions on the parchment. Inside was an appropriate amount of money to cover every situation from overnight hotels to taxicab fares. One envelope was stamped with the Thomas Cook logo. Bella had slit it open and looked inside. First-class tickets all the way. Father had certainly been right on that score – Bella was not expected to produce so much as a farthing from her own pocket.

She had rolled up the parchment, refolded the letter (which contained not the slightest hint of warmth or welcome), arranged the envelopes into chronological sequence and tied everything together with a piece of string. Bella had then slipped this package into a portfolio and shoved it into the back of the wardrobe, where it took up much less room and seemed to make much less fuss than it had done in the hatbox.

It was her father who had arranged the position, introducing the idea to Bella in early spring. 'I think it would do you the world of good,' was to become his recurring expression, as if he were talking about a day at the seaside or a course of cod liver oil. At first she hadn't paid the matter much heed – it was probably just one of his 'notions', as her late mother might have put it. 'Best ignored, soonest fizzled.' When the subject persisted it began to dawn on Bella that the poor man simply felt in need of a little reassurance – just enough to preserve the dignity of both father and daughter in their present arrangement. For her part, that she fully understood she was free to go if she so wished. For his part, that she insisted she would much, much rather stay.

And so she had humoured him for a while with soothing smiles and a little teasing. 'Yes, Father, I'm sure Sicily must be quite beautiful but I'm happy, thank you all the same, to stay where I am. And yes it must be lovely to wake each day-in-day-out to the sun – if not a little tedious.' She also gave the occasional chide. 'Oh, Father, now really. Stop it! Or I might just go off and leave you. And then where would you be?'

But what had started out as a flimsy notion had somehow solidified into a definite plan and one morning just before Easter there was her father, flapping a letter over his boiled egg and toast. 'It's marvellous news, marvellous, marvellous. And congratulations to you, Bella.'

'To me – why? Have I won something?'

'Such an adventure! A year or two in another country. Perhaps longer, she doesn't say how long you'll be needed, I'm afraid. Nor does she specify your duties. Never mind – all that can be ironed out when you meet Signora Lami.'

'*Who?*'

'Signora Lami. You remember? Bernstein in obstetrics recommended you.'

'Bernstein?'

'He's a friend of the Lami family. I believe he may even be related to her. Let me see now, I can't recall…'

'*Father.*'

'An opportunity like this doesn't come in every post bag, let me tell you. And you have the language. Well, as good as. I knew that mad old godmother of mine would come in useful in the end! Although it might be just as well to do a bit of brushing up before you leave. Early-to-mid May, she says. But you mustn't be impatient, my dear, by the time everything is organized you won't feel it going in. Now, about the Lamis; they are rolling in it by all accounts, so you'll want for nothing. There's the villa in Sicily and a summer residence on the Italian Riviera – *if* you don't mind – and God knows what else. There is also some German connection so you'll probably be popping off to Berlin or the like. You'll be mixing with the best, you know. So smarten up a bit beforehand. Streamline yourself – isn't that what it's all about now? Or so I overheard one of my nurses say. The boy, it seems, will be a cinch. Six years old, only child, meek as a mouse. Already has a nurse, a teacher and a music master too – good God! – so there can't be that much for you to do. The Signora speaks excellent English of course, and she's young, I think, much younger than the hubby – probably a bit of a story there. Lonely, I daresay, be glad of a pal such as you. She wants you to write a letter of acceptance, tell her a bit about yourself, include a résumé – better plump it up a bit. And hear this, Bella – she says that although the journey may be long and often tiresome, she will do her utmost to make it a comfortable one. First class from start to finish. From what I can gather, no expense spared. Absolutely *rrrr-olling* in it. And as for Italy – a country on the up, you know, now that that Mussolini chap has given them all a good kick up the backside. We could do with his like here, put the country back to work. Not that it need concern you. All that art and sunshine – what I wouldn't give to be young again! I tell you, Bella, you're a girl who knows how to land on her feet and no mistake.'

Bella could hardly believe it. 'Are you telling me it's all been arranged? That you have organized this behind my back?'

'Really, my dear, it's not as if we haven't discussed it.'

'But I thought you were joking.'

'Joking? Why on earth would I do that?'

'I just didn't realize you actually meant to go ahead and—'

'Well, you certainly led me to believe you were—'

'But I don't want to leave you,' she said. 'No. I *won't* and that's that.'

'Oh, don't you worry about me – I have my work and plenty of it. Besides, Mrs Carter will be here every day.'

'But it's not the same, Father. Mrs Carter isn't family. You'll be all alone. Coming home every night to an empty house. Nobody here. Always alone. I won't have it.'

Crab-like, his fingers pressing Signora Lami's letter into the table, he cocked his head a little to one side, looked at her, then looked away. 'Oh, Bella. I'm so seldom home, you know – between the hospital and my other commitments – well, let's be honest, my dear. It's you. *You* who are always alone.'

*

Bella knew exactly what she should do now. If there were any chance of getting the better of her father, she would have to learn from her late mother. What would Mother have advised?

She rested her forehead on the door her father had just closed behind him, then gave herself firm instruction: leave well enough alone for the moment. Withdraw, stay silent. Let him be the one to come back to the subject. Let him be the one to do all the talking until he has talked himself out of the idea. There is strength in silence, Mother would have said so. No surer way of unnerving a man.

Now. She would start by gently opening this door, stepping lightly into the hall, a slow easy turn for the stairs, pass by his study with neither remark nor glance, then continue on up to her room. Where she would remain until he decided to come around, first to his senses, then to her way of thinking. Yes.

But the more she thought of it! The way he had made the decision without her, the way he shrugged off any attempt to discuss the matter further; the way he kept making those awful jokes and jolly gestures throughout. Then the cold, cruel delivery of that last remark about her always being alone. Turning his back on her like that, then leaving the room, clipping the door shut behind him.

She snatched at the doorknob, twitched it open, then ploughed up the stairs shaking with rage. When she got to his study the door was ajar; she slapped it away from her. 'How could you?' she demanded. 'Father, how could you?'

He was moving about the room in his slow, efficient manner; pulling at shelves, plucking at drawers until he had constructed a pile on his desk: medical documents, sample bottles, pocket watch, stethoscope, a small narrow torch which he brought up to his face, switched on and eyeballed for a moment before switching it off again.

When the pile was complete, he immediately began to thin it out again, picking each item up and feeding it down into the soft leather gut of his big brown bag.

These were his props for the outside world. This was the bag that would carry them there. Bella knew the routine and knew that nothing would interfere with it. There was a time, long ago, when she would have been part of it. A house in Dublin then; a different desk. She was a child holding the bag open for him, lisping the title and purpose of each article.

25

She was going to be a doctor. They had both seemed so certain of it – why had it never happened?

She waited while he pulled his overcoat from the coat stand, shrugged his shoulders into it, slapped the creases out of his gloves, angled his umbrella out from the stand, and he still hadn't looked at her face. When he did speak to her, it was through the mirror while he fussed at his collar and stud. 'Listen to me, Bella, we moved to London for a better life, a new start – for your sake as I recall. We have been here more than seventeen years and well, your life is not exactly…'

'Not exactly what?'

'Well. Not what we hoped it would be. You're almost thirty-two, you know, and with your poor mother gone, and the trouble with your back resolved, and your other little problems well under control.'

'Father, please!'

'All right – there's no point in dragging all that up now, I suppose. What I'm trying to say is, there really is no reason for you to remain here day in, day out. You're in good health now and still relatively young.'

'I just don't understand it, Father.'

'Oh come on now, Bella, you don't want to be stuck with an old goat like me for ever.'

'But, Father, you're not an old goat.'

'Indeed I am an old goat. Please, my dear, it's for your own good.'

'I thought we were happy,' she said and began crying.

'Now let's not have any of this,' he said, turning around at last to face her.

She could see the back of his head in the mirror, the edge of his collar, the rind of thick skin over it, the line of his shoulders, the fall of his coat. It was as if somebody else was in the room with them. Somebody who had wandered in by mistake, from a crowded railway platform or some other populated and anonymous place. A stranger, bewildered and embarrassed to have found himself caught in the middle of this little scene. He was like a man who was pretending not to be there.

'I should be with you, Father. With you, here. I don't want to live in Sicily, in a strange—'

'That's enough, Bella.'

'Please don't make me go. Please. Please. *Please.*'

'Bella, stop it now, I said. *Now.*'

It wasn't until he raised his voice that she realized what she'd been doing, pulling at his lapels like that, sobbing and screaming, dribbling all over him. His hands came down and settled on top of hers, then in one strong steady movement, like that of an oarsman, he had lifted, pushed and dropped them away.

'Take control of yourself, Bella!'

She accepted his chair and the handkerchief too, offered at arm's length – not one of his own either, she noted, but from the box he reserved for hysterical female patients. Next she was clutching a glass, sucking at something he had concocted and mixed with water.

'Bella,' he said after a while. 'Are you settled now?'

'Yes, Father.'

'Are you certain?'

'Yes.'

'How do you feel?'

'Foolish.'

'Indeed.'

'I'm sorry, I'm just a little upset, that's all.'

'We'll forget about it now. But Bella, I have something important to say to you, and I want you to listen to me carefully.' He leaned a little way towards her.

'Yes, Father?'

'You are not my wife, Bella. You are my daughter.'

*

In the end Bella had decided to believe her father; that it was for her own good, a sacrifice was being made on her account. A sacrifice she must

27

respect. He was a father trying to prepare his only child for the future, it was as simple as that. One day she would find herself completely alone, no one to look to, nor care for. The few relatives they had left behind in Ireland would want nothing to do with her – nor would she make any attempt to contact them. Her father knew this just as he had known not to insult her with any pretence of a possible marriage.

She would be like poor Miss Vaughan who used to live across the road. A middle-aged orphan. In the meantime, what was wrong with striking out on her own for a year or two – if that was how she was going to end up? Alone in this house. But at least it would be *her* house, whatever little money remained, *hers* to spend as she wished. Not that she'd have to rely on her father's leftovers. She could make her own way. Take in lodgers perhaps, or become fluent enough in Italian to translate professionally. Or maybe even teach Italian – why not? Her father's study could be converted into a sort of classroom; blackboard set behind his desk, students placed at little tables round the edges of his silk Kashmiri rug. If that didn't suit she could always teach in a proper language school, where she could meet people, make friends, visit and be visited. She could live alone in this house one day as an independent woman, without fear of the rooms beyond the room she was occupying. Or fear of the street outside, because to go out into it would mean having to return to a house that had become her enemy. She would be more than just a name muttered by neighbours too polite to bring themselves to knock on her door. More than an occasional shadow at the lace of an upstairs window, or a pair of hands taking in a small box of delivered groceries every week. She would not lie dead for days on the flagstone floor of the kitchen. Nor be covered in a rough police blanket and carried down the garden path with Gilby's grocery boy mewling up at a constable, 'I knew it when she didn't answer the door the second I rung! She always answers straight off, she does. On other side, waitin' – see? – that's where she always is.'

She would not, *not* become poor Miss Vaughan.

*

The house grew alive around her and she couldn't seem to leave it alone, drifting from room to room, passing through the ghosts of her future: friends she had yet to meet; conversations she was yet to be part of; laughter. Everything became relevant. The mirabelle pattern on the dining-room wallpaper; the texture of a sofa, a cushion, a drape. Even ornaments that up to now she had either despised or simply not noticed, were mentally preserved. She would modernize this whole stuffy house, pull it apart, take it beyond recognition – streamline it. For days Bella felt a sense of elation and longed to get her new life in Sicily over and done with, so she could return to revise and relive her old one, as this other, independent person.

The sense of elation soon passed. One evening when she had just lit the study fire, and the aroma of the meal Mrs Carter had left in the oven was beginning to make itself known, a message arrived from the hospital. Her father would be detained overnight – again. Bella went down to the kitchen then, where she eased Mrs Carter's dinner out of the oven. She removed the lid – a casserole bulging with onions and smoked cod – and took it outside. She carried the dish down the garden path. Lumps of fish and half-raw potato spilled out, and her wrists flinched at the occasional spit of hot parsley sauce. When she reached the back wall, she tipped what remained of the casserole into a tin they kept there for next door's cat.

Returning to her father's study, she stood before the apothecary cupboard that took up most of one wall. It contained many and multi-sized drawers as well as several nooks and compartments, and had come from the widow of one of his patients, a pharmacist from Aldgate. It had always reminded Bella of a tenement building, a secret life held in each section, a different life each time.

She began, at first absent-mindedly, to open and shut the drawers. They made a clipping sound when they opened and a dry slight suck on the return. She did that for a time, opening and shutting: clip and suck,

29

her enthusiasm increasing along with her speed until both had slipped just a little beyond her control. Then she was standing on a chair stretching towards the drawers at the very top; clip, suck, clip, suck. Faster and faster, on and on. Clip, suck, clip. It was only after a very close topple that she finally made herself stop.

She was cold when she climbed back down. The fire had died and the room had grown dark except for a little street light through the window. Here she could see her father's consulting couch, the fold of a Foxford rug at its headrest. The couch, firm with horsehair and taut leather, would feel good on her back. She lowered herself onto it, pulled the Foxford rug up to her neck and lay down. Bella looked up at the window. She could remember her mother standing there, the evening after Miss Vaughan's body had been found, quietly weeping as she looked out on the street trying to find some sort of a reason.

'It's the English, you see,' she had begun. 'They make you feel like you're being forward when you're only trying to be friendly. They make you *ashamed*.'

'It's these streets,' she had decided then a few minutes later. 'Everyone trying to stay private when we're all on top of each other, looking in at each other, pretending we can't see.'

'It's these houses,' she had concluded. 'These awful Chelsea houses.'

Bella lay listening to the sounds of the surrounding rooms – the peevish chime of a clock, the sob and sigh of a water pipe, the whinge of an upstairs door Mrs Carter had forgotten to lock. She could hear no laughter, nor conversation from the future. There were only the sounds of a melancholic house. If she was to be honest with herself, it was a house that should suit her quite well.

*

Days went by and she couldn't shake off the feeling that if she went to Sicily she would never see her father again. Bella reminded herself that he was not an old man, although his exact age was unknown to her. There

30

had always been a slight awkwardness around the subject, probably because he had been some years younger than his late wife. Perhaps as many as ten. Judging by the date of the Hippocratic Oath framed on the wall of his study along with a photograph taken on the day, Bella guessed he must have been about twenty-four when he graduated from the Royal College of Surgeons in Dublin. This would make him now about sixty or sixty-one. It wasn't very old, but hardly the first flush either. In any case he would grow older. One day he would die. Perhaps be ill first, even linger. She found herself daydreaming about what it would be like to be his nurse, rushing to his bedside from Sicily on the summons of a telegram. In her daydreams his condition never worsened nor did he grow any older. He stayed much the same; sick enough to be infirm, well enough not to suffer too much. They would have years of that, her nursing, him being nursed. Her reading, him listening. Or fixing the blanket around his knees and bringing him invalid's soup; propping him up by the window on days that were warm, bucking him up on wet days when he might feel a little down. If a doctor came into the picture it would be to Bella he would address himself, drawing her into a hushed conversation on the far side of the door.

The daydreams passed, spat away by the rain on the window, or burnt up by the fire in the grate, and the feeling came back to her. She would not see him again. He would be dead before her return. She would find out, days after the event, in a strange landscape surrounded by people she didn't know. His habits and moods would all become lost to her, just as those of her mother had done. He would become a series of vague and disconnected impressions, impossible to remember, and therefore impossible to grieve. Instead of the house and its contents, she began to catalogue her father. She found herself, like a child, constantly trying to detain him with banal comments and pointless questions he clearly had no wish to answer. His work at the hospital had caused him to miss so many recent dinners that she took to rising early, sometimes as early as dawn, so she could breakfast with him. Just to be able to sit in his company, to watch his face, to hear his voice. To remember. She even made a special effort to eat a good breakfast, just to please him. But her efforts went unnoticed and her presence at the table seemed to irritate him. After a few painful attempts, she left him in peace to study his notes or read the first post. She told herself he was never at his best first thing in the morning anyhow; a man with so much on his mind.

She decided to make another attempt to visit her mother's grave, and even went as far as to order a wreath of flowers, drawing the florist into a lengthy consultation on the colour and shape of each bloom and throwing in a few reminiscences about her late mother, none of which were entirely accurate. But when the wreath arrived Bella couldn't bear the sight of it and threw it away. To escape the hawk-eye of Mrs Carter and make it blend into the rubbish bin, she had to first mutilate the flowers, then hack at the oasis that held them together until it crumbled to bits. How could she have even considered walking through Brompton cemetery with that absurdity in her arms, past endless terraces of gravestones and plots tended by love and grief, pretending to know or even vaguely recall where her mother was buried? Like looking for a house without an address. And even if she did manage to find the grave, how could she have imagined laying this insult down in the centre of what would have to be by now a shameful display of neglect, disrespect and trapped weeds?

Bella settled on a photograph instead, a portrait she couldn't quite look in the face. Her eyes instead recalled the plum-coloured coat, the curl of cream chiffon over one shoulder. She took the same scarf from her mother's chest of drawers, stood for a while with the drawer slanted in her hands, looking down into the intimacies of a life that had once belonged to her mother. Folds of silk, a book of Tennyson's verse. Stockings, a corset. The start of a Christmas shopping list, and a pair of yellow gloves warped to the shape of hands, now decayed.

She was shaking as she wrapped the photograph in the chiffon scarf and placed it in her mother's alligator travel bag. It was the first thing she packed for Sicily. The first physical acknowledgement that she would actually be leaving.

*

The luggage for Sicily labelled and waiting in the hall; clothes from former winters, in hope of future ones, moth-balled and boxed, ready for the attic. A few remaining days. Bella decided to pay a final visit to her father's old godmother, who lived in a nursing home in Piccadilly. Gummy by now and slightly deranged, the poor woman believed herself to be in a hilltown in Abruzzo, her days spent watching in the window for people long since dead, or waving out at strangers she suddenly recognized as her own. Not only had she lost her geographical bearings, but also her command of the English language, which, word by word, seemed to have fallen out of her head.

Bella knew, or thought she knew, that the old woman had once been to Sicily.

'*Madrina?*' she asked. '*Com' è in Sicilia?*'

'*Com' è? Perché chiedi?*'

'*Perché io vado in Sicilia.*'

'*Tu vai in Sicilia?*'

'*Sì.*'

'*Tu?*'

'*Sì. Com' è?*'

'*È come Africa.*'

Then the old lady started to laugh, a distant, spiteful sort of laugh that Bella found disquieting.

On the way home from Piccadilly a whim came over her. She would meet her father from the hospital. All that day she had been thinking of him, and how nice it would be to walk by his side for a while, be with him in public, away from the confines of the house, as an equal. A part of her also wanted to let him know that she had fully accepted her new life and was even looking forward to it. Her new life without him.

This was the hour when he usually took a stroll in the hospital grounds to clear his head, smoke a cigar and relax for a while before either returning to his patients, or, if his work for the day was done, returning home. She would accompany him either way, he would be pleased to see her, she was certain of it. Perhaps he would even invite her to supper. Nowhere too fancy – after all, she wasn't dressed – but somewhere friendly where they could chat. There was bound to be a place nearby favoured by doctors. He could take her there, introduce her to his colleagues, proudly, as he used to do, when she was a child and they went on little outings. He could say, 'This is my daughter, off to Sicily in a few days, *if* you don't mind!' Yes, he would get a kick out of that.

But the moment Bella climbed down from the bus and stood looking up through the trees at the long hospital windows, she was waylaid by shyness. Supposing she broke down when she saw him, started to cry again? Could she really trust herself not to make a scene? She decided it might be better to watch him first, allow a little time to monitor her reaction or, if needs be, compose herself at least.

She recognized the shape of him on the far side of the big glass door at almost the same moment as she noticed Mrs Jenkins sitting on a bench across the road. In fact she almost moved towards Mrs Jenkins, the widow of a doctor, who lived nearby and who had helped nurse her dying mother. Bella had sometimes felt her mother hadn't always been appreciative to this kind and pretty woman. Perhaps on occasion had even been a little rude.

She watched her father's shoulder push against the glass door and his head nod at a porter, who rushed to hold the door open. He was carrying his bag, which meant he must be finished for the evening, yet he wore no overcoat, no hat, carried no umbrella, despite the changeable weather and his fussy ways. He paused at the top of the steps for a moment, looked up at the sky, then descended before turning left, to take the pathway along the Fulham Road. He seemed smaller outside the house, his surgeon's suit old-fashioned rather than dignified, his legs somewhat shorter, the tails of his jacket a little too long. He was headed away from the hospital in the direction of home, but Bella knew where he was going even before he broke away from the path, veered across the road and doubled back under the trees.

He drew the tails of his jacket apart so he could sit beside Mrs Jenkins. They didn't touch. In fact no acknowledgement passed between them. They looked neither guilty nor innocent. And he certainly didn't look like an old goat. He looked handsome, in his prime, more than that, he looked like a lover.

A lifetime of whispers steamed up inside her head, strained whispers behind walls that had travelled with them from their old house in Dublin. Of course. There had always been a Mrs Jenkins. She had been there as her mother lay dying. In Dublin there had been another one. There always would be a Mrs Jenkins. That's what it had been about all along. An adult daughter was no good to this type of a man. She had simply been in the way.

That night saw the start of the money-tuck. Pulling the Signora's envelopes out of the portfolio as soon as she got home, opening each one and making a tidy pool of money on the bed, Bella began her calculations. Starting with the tickets. Why was it necessary to go first class – wouldn't second do just as well? What if she were to go into Thomas Cook's in the morning and ask for an exchange and a refund where possible? She could throw them some yarn about reduced circumstances and a sickly relative. A little less comfort, perhaps even a lot less for all she knew, but the reward would be in the refund – why not?

Next she examined miscellaneous expenses, subtracting what she felt might actually be needed from the amount the Signora had allowed. Adjustments could be made either way, as needs must and the journey proceeded, but already she could see a very encouraging start to her scheme. She began to feel better.

She was getting into her stride now, and with her mind alight with thrifty notions, went again to her mother's room. This time Bella moved without sentiment, going through every drawer, fancywork box or embroidered bag her mother had accumulated over her lifetime.

At first she took only those trinkets and jewellery bits that her father would be unlikely to miss, but then on second thoughts Bella decided to bag the pieces that would fetch the best price. What was he going to do after all? Follow her out to Sicily? Inform Scotland Yard?

Lying in bed, sleepy already, Bella closed her eyes and tried to look into the future. She could see as far as Sicily, silent and scorched as Africa. Beyond that another landscape, and beyond that a pulsing sciagraphy of shadow. The further she looked, the darker it became. Yet she couldn't say the darkness was ever complete. It allowed her to see that there was no horizon, that the landscapes would continue, one behind the other: they would never end.

*

Her father said he would skip the station. At his age he found farewells a little too much to bear. 'I will say one thing, however – if I may?'

'Yes?'

'Always remember, you are not a servant. Do you hear me now, Bella?

'Yes.'

'You are a surgeon's daughter. Remember that. And write, of course. Let me know how you're getting along. Lend a little excitement to my dull life.'

'Of course.'

'And you must promise to eat properly. Don't scowl, it has to be said, you know what you're like when… Well, if you say you're eating, you're eating. We'll leave it at that. How is the old back by the way?'

'Fine.'

'Good, good. Stand up now and we'll take a look.'

His fingers pressed along her spine, pausing sometimes to inquire, 'How's that? And that?' Then his questions trailed into a series of grunts. Finally he patted her on the shoulder.

'Keep up the exercises, maintain the curve, that's the trick. When you stand up swing into it, like so.' He put his hands on his hips and began to push himself forward, as he always did when he gave this little demonstration. 'Got it?'

She nodded and looked away.

'Off you go now. I'll miss you. But I'm sure I don't have to tell you that. Good luck, Bella. Safe journey.'

She thought there might be something else, an embrace, a word – something to give her courage. Anything at all. But already he was on the way back down the stairs.

Bella waited till he was in the hall again. 'Father?'

'Yes, my dear?'

She came down a few steps towards him and he turned from the front door, his coat over his arm. Then with a sad half-smile laid the coat down and held his arms out to her.

'Might I have some money please?' she said.

'Money?'

'Mmm. If you wouldn't mind.'

He put down his arms. 'Well, of course. I mean, but I thought I'd already given you—?'

'I'd like a little more. Just to be on the safe side. If that's all right with you.'

'I think I have maybe forty pounds or so in the safe. I could give you a cheque, I suppose?'

'Forty will be plenty, thank you. It's as I said, in case. If you could leave it on your desk before you go? Well, goodbye, Father, take care of yourself and don't work too hard.' She nodded, then turned and went back up the stairs.

*

Bella waited in her bedroom for the taxi to arrive. Through the rear window the garden was crawling with cats, and Mrs Carter, sweeping brush in hand, was staring bewilderedly down at them, as if trying to figure out what the attraction might be.

Bella moved to the front window. Down on the street early summer was showing: more people than usual, walking at a more leisurely pace, in paler clothes made of lighter cloth. Muslin on windows instead of heavy drapes; a dark red mat airing like a dog's tongue from one window down the way. Across the way, a housemaid scrubbing a step stopped and turned her face up to the sun. Bella let down the sash and leaned out to the smell of new paint and the gnashing of a gardener's shears.

And the one thing with which she would always associate this street, this borough, this time of the year – the Chinese wisteria: falling in clusters of pale-blue and mauve. Down the fronts and across the gables, through the railings and over the doorways, of all these Chelsea houses.

SICILY, 1933

FROM SHIPBOARD SHE NOTICES Signor Pino. His is the only calm figure down there on the dockside, the only one who doesn't appear to be either running to, or from, an emergency. Apart from the emigrants waiting to board the ship for America. They stand on the sidelines in dark, silent coppices; bags like dogs at their feet, clothes that are heavy and formal – what she imagines to be their funeral-best.

Pino wears jodhpurs and tall boots, like somebody waiting for his horse to be brought round. An urchin stands beside him, schoolroom slate held over a small, cropped head. As soon as the queue gives its first tentative shudder, the urchin makes a charge for the gangway, displaying his little blackboard to those already on the descent and accompanying them on their first terra firma steps, pushing the blackboard at them, pointing at its message, until he seems satisfied that it has been read and understood by all. Then, through similar urchins holding similar signs, he struggles back to the gangway and the next batch of passengers, to start the whole process again.

It takes her a moment to recognize the name chalked on his slate, Signora Stvart, the u drawn like a v in the Greek fashion. There had been

39

no need to worry about being Bella after all. Here she will be, like any other adult woman would be, simply Signora.

Under the slate, the child appears frantic, as if he is afraid he will never find her, and therefore, she supposes, will never be paid. She tries to attract his attention. But her gesture is timid, and his eye moves too quickly to catch it.

Bella turns onto the gangway and the heat is so sudden she feels almost molested; the thrust of it, the way it forces itself on her face and neck. She pulls back a few times, before finally accepting that from now on the heat will have a permanent hold of her.

And so down into a Palermo dockside morning she inches, keeping her eye on the queue ahead, as it lands and then splits to join other queues. Some are alphabetically arranged to facilitate baggage collection or custom clearance, others appear to have an official, if somewhat indefinite, purpose. At various points an officer pops up, black uniform and seagull gloves, turning a truncheon gracefully in his hand to conduct passengers out of the mob and into a line, until the terminal, as far as the eye can see anyway, is a tabulation of shuffling queues.

She steps off the gangway and, breaking away, waits for Pino. Bella sees that he has already spotted her, and is manoeuvring himself through the crowd, hip first and agile as a waiter. He is holding an old-fashioned veiled hat, and a pair of goggles sit on his head. When he reaches her, he gives a little bow, the goggles dip and she finds herself smiling into a pair of large, insectile eyes. His face lifts back to her and she tries to say something, something unnecessary, like to tell him that she is Signora Stuart and that he must be Signor Pino. But the noise on the dockside is dense, impossible to navigate and she can't even hear her own voice. She notes Pino nonetheless is following her lips with his eyes. She stops speaking. The impact of movement and sound is immediate and shocking: wheels, whistles, limbs, screaming machinery, brawling voices. In the distance a precarious sway of cargo, which, through her tired and distorted eye, seems to be aiming for the side of Pino's head. She resists the urge to push him to safety and turns her face away.

Hundreds of children; she has never seen so many. Squalls of them, barefooted and scrapping for attention. Bella concentrates on holding steady, as one after another they come at her. Each has something to sell – lavender punnet, rosary beads, bag of cherries or sugary bits, all shoved under her nose. Others seem to deal solely in promises: a cartwheel – if she'll only step aside. A song – if she'll only listen. A novena for the next nine Fridays to Sant'Agata of the mutilated breasts.

She thinks about offering her hand to Pino, but now his own hands, suddenly occupied, are no longer available: a click of his fingers and the children are dispersed as easily as flies. He passes her the hat; plucks the luggage docket from her fingers; claps his hand in the air three times for a porter; dismisses the urchin with a tossed coin; shoves the docket at the porter now stepping forward; tugs her alligator bag away from her – despite her best efforts to hold on to it – and finally beckons her onto the meandering but insistent path that he has already started to carve through the crowd.

They move towards the exit, past custom officials and immigration clerks, policemen and men in Hollywood suits. Pino greets some by way of a nod or a handshake, perhaps an embrace, pausing to do so without ever quite stopping. She can feel the eyes of her fellow passengers lift from their respective queues to watch her, unburdened and unquestioned, stroll by.

They come out through an arcade and the screeching of stallholders, the temporary comfort of shade. Pino rudders her along by the elbow until they are under a roaring sun and he is guiding her into a long leather seat. She is in the back of a car, a black open-topped car, the roof folded back like the hood of a pram, and she peering out like a baby. Behind her Pino is berating someone, and she is surprised by his voice, the weight of it first, then its anger, and not least of all, because she recognizes it as being his in the first place. She turns and yes, it is Pino, hysterical hands pushing a point at the porter earlier left in charge of her luggage. She feels afraid for the poor little man then, his body squashed and squared by luggage that does not belong to her. Slowly she looks away.

41

Now she's facing a nearby stall, a mound of ice spangled on a table. A young boy, brown and bony, crushes a cut lemon in his fist and twists his head to supervise the drops of juice falling over the ice. He keeps his other hand busy swatting flies away from, or plucking them off, the ice. There is a dog tied to the leg of the cart, a scabby-looking wretch, with ribs bursting to get out of its skin and a dry yellowish tongue. Now and then the boy touches the dog with his bare foot. Or he might break from his work for a moment to lower his hand so the dog can help itself to a lick.

She feels peculiar. Everything around her has become enlarged: the dog's enlarged tongue, the boy's elongated feet, even the flies on the ice seem to have grown recognizable faces, fly-eyes staring straight at her. She catches Pino watching her watch the boy and before she can prevent the misunderstanding, he is leaning over the door of the car, holding a shard of ice wrapped in a cone of brown paper. He pushes it at her, then gestures at the hat. She thinks he may be saying something about the violence of the sun. He tells her the hood of the car is broken and so she must wear the hat. He repeats this, word by slow word to Bella first, then for the benefit of the onlookers now gathering around, in a more rapid, almost apologetic version. Why can't the English signora understand? She must wear the hat! *'Deve mettersi il capello!'*

Already, the cone of ice is beginning to yield in his hand. He looks at it, then flings it to the ground.

A woman steps up, tells Bella to do what she's told, to be *brava*, put the hat on her head for the love of God before she is fried alive. Bella tries, but can't seem to get her hand to obey... She can see Pino is worried that perhaps she is going to faint. Somebody has said it: *svenire*, to faint. *'La signora sta per svenire.'* She wants to tell him there is nothing to worry about, that her body is solid, never so solid, here on this seat, as if it is nailed to it. It's her mind that's too light, trying to drift off like a balloon on a string that she has to keep pulling back. She wonders how to say in Italian, 'My mind is a balloon, floating off on its string.'

Pino climbs into the car, eyes abruptly blue. Almost at once he begins taking liberties.

'*Ex-cuse* me…' she begins to protest.

Her gloves give him no trouble, disloyally abandoning her hands in an instant. Naked hands. Now he is holding one of them and slapping her wrist. The voices of the little group close in.

'*Mi scusi*,' Pino says and inserts his index finger under the collar of her blouse.

'Please,' she says. 'No. You're not to. Don't. I said, no!' The top button leaps out of its clasp. 'I'll tell on you. I will tell. I'll scream.'

'*Signora? Signora?*'

The word signora comes and goes elastically from his lips and the blue has spilled out of his eyes and down his face. Her own eyes close. She feels him taking hold of her chin, shaking it from side to side. Her head fills up with smears of darkness and strands of electrified light. A man wants to know if she's eaten. Another one thinks they should call the doctor – after all, these English women with their thin bones and watery blood, anything might happen! A discussion begins – a *medico* is mentioned, a *Dottor Amalfi* suggested.

'That's right,' she says, 'that's absolutely correct.'

'*Signora?*'

'I am not a servant. I am a surgeon's daughter.'

Pino sighs, grazing her face with tobacco, cologne and something more pungent, perhaps garlic. He tightens his grip on her chin. '*Uno, due, tre*,' she hears him say, before a shock of ammonia goes hurling up her nose and cracks open her brain. Her eyelids snap, she hears herself gasp, thinks for a moment she might have been drowning and is being pulled up out of the water.

The hat rises from her lap and settles on her head. Shapes through a mist. The veil is rolled back and she can see the audience now; brown, battered, caps and shawls. And Pino, his face much too close to hers, his hand still on her shoulder. A sugary cake appears, a cup of coffee, a glass of water. A woman with a tray, a long white apron blotted with stains. Bella is urged to eat. You must eat, the woman is saying. '*Deve mangiare.*' Everyone seems to agree that all her problems will be over if only she eats. Even the children join in, chanting and clapping: '*Mangi, mangi, mangi.*'

Bella obeys. The cake is sweet, gushing cream and jam. The coffee is thick, black and bitter. The water, vile. Pino flaps a handkerchief, wipes it across her mouth and chin. She can feel his fingertips through the cloth; her lips yield and follow their touch. He brings the handkerchief down towards her dress where it hovers for a few seconds before he passes it to the woman with the tray who completes the job with a much rougher touch. Somebody offers her a new shard of ice. She takes it.

'*Sta bene, Signora?*' Pino asks.

She nods and then he is gone.

The next time she sees Pino, he is back by the mule station, hand leaning on the little porter's shoulder, both men smiling, talking, smoking, eating cake while they're at it, hooked tongues catching cream, hands reaching for tiny coffee cups on a tray held by the woman with the dirty apron. She blinks and they've disappeared.

Bella pulls a cushion into her back and settles into it. She leans her shoulder on the folds of the hood, sucks on the stick of citrus-sharp ice. Behind her she can hear the luggage rack being loaded and strapped, and for a second remembers to fret about her alligator bag, the pouch of money, the bits of jewellery belonging to her mother that she hasn't yet sold. Then her eyes close down.

She sees a terrace of blue-eyed mules. A woman in an apron with one mutilated breast. A dog with a scabby back. The dog cocks his leg, splashing yellow piddle all over a hill of ice. The woman walks towards her.

*

She misses the sullen shift of the sea, its curious muscularity, pushing everything on, giving the impression of always being in charge. The big black car too, ever decisive, following its own nose from Palermo to here,

44

barking and snorting at anything that had tried to get in its way, asking nothing of her, expecting nothing, only that she continue to drift in and out of sleep.

Now that she is responsible for her own mobility, Bella finds she's reluctant to move. Not that there is much to encourage her, here in this vast dim room, scarcely furnished.

A bed in the distance stands raised like a tomb, wings of muslin and a mattress obese with what would have to be goose feathers – even from here, she can see it won't offer much in the way of support for her back. Down this end, one dainty chair and a low lacquered table, the seat on the chair like a velvet lozenge which she wouldn't dare sit on. An enormous mirror on the back wall, her reflection skulking inside like a mentally disturbed neighbour at the window. Then the floor – a marble piazza. One large primrose-coloured rug in the centre. And that's it, really – no chest of drawers, no dressing table, not so much as a hook for a jacket, nowhere to lay out her personal belongings, nor indeed to hide them away.

*

'I shouldn't go unpacking if I was you, not till the Signora's 'ad a word,' the housekeeper had said on the way up the stairs, startling Bella with a shrill London accent that melted to honey the moment she had started to speak Italian, leaning over the banister to do so at a trundle of servants carting the luggage up from the hall. An English housekeeper – Bella had felt less alone then, thinking there would be at least one person to chat to. The housekeeper's demeanour and evasive eye, however, soon made it clear she was not the type to get chatty.

'Dinner's at seven. The Signora will see you before'and. Maria will come fetch you. I'll send the girl up with washing water.'

Through a pair of tall doors the housekeeper then retracted her string of servants, leaving the last, an elderly man wearing pale pink gloves, to clatter and clang his way out of the room. Bella hadn't been able to decide if she felt locked into her room, or out of the household.

Three hours to kill. Bella turns to the shuttered windows. Squirts of light through the slats. A warm cage over her face and hands. An infinite silence outside. She stays for a while listening for something to snag it. In the end she does this herself by dragging the iron rods away from their latches, then pushing at the shutters until the creaking gives way to a luminous rush. She passes through it, eyes blinking against a bouncing mosaic of yellow and gold.

Now on a terrace. How far she is from anywhere else in the world is impossible to know. Way beyond the perimeter of this villa there is a pock-marked mountain, a russet-coloured town cut like a dried wound into its shoulder. It could be ten miles away, or a hundred. There are other mountains besides, crawling all over the landscape, other villages and towns. Yet despite all that is available to her eye, nothing suggests the recent journey she has made with Pino. She may have been asleep for most of it, but for the last quarter of an hour or so, after waking and sensing they were almost there, she had remained bolt upright and alert.

Where has it all gone? The last few miles, the high gates they had finally passed through. The dogs that were silenced by a man with a stoop. The lodge where Pino had pulled in for a moment to take an oversized key from a child with an oversized head. The escort of cypress trees along the avenue; flowers that had looked as if they had been painted onto their stems. And Pino, his car. Where is all that? Bella looks down.

A garden built on descending terraces; balustrades and marble vases. Statues on a low wall in the distance. A fountain with a cherub astride some sort of fish. Closer to the house, a rigid parterre – hedges pruned and bent to someone's geometrical will. To her left hand a driveway turning into the villa. Surely this could only be the front of the house – it could hardly be meant for tradesmen? And yet. The way she had come in with Pino had also seemed like the entrance. There had been a loggia; wide stone steps to a large entrance hall, dark and mercifully cool.

46

Staircases and servants. The English housekeeper. Chandeliers. But a different driveway. A stand of Lebanon cedar to one side. A pond. The pond hosted by a large cast-iron frog standing on one leg. Another parterre – flowerbeds instead of box hedge, wrought-iron frill around the edges. A lawn with a trio of benches. She had been reminded of an English public park, had half expected to see men reading newspapers, women watching children, kites.

Bella walks to the end of the terrace, peers over the side of the balustrade; lemon scent and an orchard. She lifts her eyes and again there is nothing familiar in the landscape, not even the outline of a road, where a car might have travelled. Only haphazard fields and the tangle of wildflowers, dry brown mountains and arthritic trees.

She can remember leaving Palermo now, and how her mind had seemed to be swaying like a storm lantern, in and out of darkness. The skin peeling off the front of houses. Pink domes on the churches. Then nothing until... Scrub and the smell of almonds. A palsy of silvery leaves. Waking to terror on a road so steep she thought she was going to topple out of the car. Then despite the terror, falling back to sleep almost at once. Cobbled rooftops, brittle and cracked by the sun. Had she stretched her hand down over the side of the car she could have touched them; they would have crumbled like desiccated bones in her hand.

A large grass square. Pino had stopped and brought her a tin cup of cool water. Old brown faces under caps, playing something at wooden tables. A cupola of tree shade holding them in. Lemons falling out of trees. Limes. Waking again to more children again, jumping on the runner of the car. Pino reaching down to his side to pull out a whip which he lashed, or threatened to lash, at the children. She had tried to tell him to stop. The children dropping off one by one, screeching and jeering into the flurry of road dust. Two of them blonde, one ginger – surprising her.

Darkness again. Swirls of orange. Being thrown down sideways on the seat, now forward, now back. Pino leaning his arm over the seat asking if she's all right. Moving under an arch, leprous walls closing in on the car,

47

women hanging out of windows overhead, screaming across at each other. The noise deafening, suffocating, until sleep came again like a blessing.

On and off throughout the car journey, the noise from the dockside had slipped back to her. Coming out of the engine in a sudden yodel, in the scurry of pebbles beneath the wheels, on the nagging voices of goatherds they had passed along the way. Even the church bells that softly burst around her in some silent and airless town were accompanied by the sounds of the dockside. Then just before she had woken for good, the road had loosened and the car, taking a slight swerve, suddenly stopped. The back of Pino's head had appeared through the veil, a vast skirt of sheep wobbling around the car. Pino, lighting a cigarette, had remained quietly smoking even after the flock had passed into silence and stillness.

Silence and stillness. No sense of location. No sense of anything at all.

*

Bella feels herself jump as her attention is brought back to the terrace. A ratchety grinding in the garden below; mechanical, even a little musical – of course, crickets! Almost at once she sees a diagonal flit up the orchard wall. A lizard! She has never seen one outside of a cage or a picture book, nor heard the sound of so many crickets. It gives her a burst of childish pleasure. Now she realizes the extent of her journey, just how far she has come.

As the lizard slides into the lemon groves, she catches sight of someone moving through the trees. A slow figure, head covered and bowed, the dress full and black. The figure moves deeper into the orchard; foliage clasping around it masks Bella's view. Wads of greenery and pinpoints of light. The figure re-emerges just long enough for Bella to see it belongs to a nun.

She turns back into a room that the sun has filled up and a rug that has turned to gold silk. Nightingales around the edges. A glimmer runs through it. When she moves her head or takes a step to the side, the glimmer moves with her. She stoops and begins to stroke the silk. Warm

48

and soft, it seems to respond to her hand. She takes off her shoes and stockings, pulls the rug directly into the bank of sunlight and, carefully unfolding herself, lies down. Patting the rug with her feet and her palms, stretching her toes, Bella feels her spine settle into the carpet, the spread of the sun on her face.

High in the corner of the room sits an unlit votive, above it an elaborate cornice. On a faraway ceiling cherubs are dancing.

*

Maria has a deformed bottom lip. Sponge-like and purple, it droops towards her chin. Hair cut tight to a large head, face like cedar wood carved to the bone. She has huge hands, tough forearms and a pair of unfortunate legs, bandy as brackets. Were it not for the little rose-dotted dress, Bella would have thought her a man – perhaps a retired jockey. Walking with her now on the way to meet Signora Lami, there couldn't be a sweeter, more sympathetic guide – almost impossible to equate with the Maria of such a short time ago.

Bella thinks of the young girl who had arrived earlier with a basin of water, towels and a pot of lemon tea turned cold. The girl had found Bella, just up from her snooze on the rug, still in bare feet. Pretty little thing, hair tied back by a checked scarf, a child really, nine or ten years old. She had been completely taken aback by the sight of Bella's feet. 'Like marble!' she had gasped. '*Come marmo!*'

While Bella had prepared for her interview with Signora Lami, the child had remained, skipping about the place, devising little tasks that might delay her. She would hold the Signora's comb for her. She would lay the Signora's nightdress on the bed for tonight. She would brush the road dust from the Signora's jacket.

Lena, she had said her name was, not nine or ten, but thirteen years old. Far too small for her age.

She had been rubbing a cloth over Bella's shoes, head cocked, chattering her way through an extravagant story concerning a cousin and her

49

lover which Bella, although she could only understand bits, suspected was full of delightful lies. Then Maria had come storming through the doorway, shouting her head off. Something about Lena still being here instead of down in the kitchen. The further Maria came into the room, the more enraged she had seemed to become. After a few moments Bella began to understand this was because the silk rug had been left in the sunlight. For this the child had borne the brunt and all the blame; such lack of respect, exposing a valuable carpet like that, only fit now for the dogs to lie on. The Signora would be informed. Lena would be thrown out, she could live on the street in Palermo like the *puttanella* she clearly was. While Maria was dragging the rug out of harm's way Bella had tried her best for little Lena, explaining that it had been her mistake and not Lena's. But Maria didn't seem to hear. It was as if she couldn't even see Bella was in the room. Her bottom lip bouncing with agitation, Maria had marched over to Lena and, sticking her hand in behind the checked headscarf, taken a tug of hair in her fist. The child's head flew back, her eyes fattened with tears.

'Oh!' Bella heard herself say. 'Oh now. *Please!*'

Finally Maria noticed her, throwing her a look that implied if Bella didn't watch her step, she could very well be next.

*

Now walking through the convolutions of the villa, Maria seems to have completely forgotten the incident. Bella has to wonder if she can be quite right in the head.

She sees the nun again, praying again, as they pause at the open door of what appears to be a chapel. Bella considers asking Maria about the nun, who she is and why she is here. There is no doubt that Maria will be forthcoming. Since leaving the room and the weeping child behind them, her voice has been going in a non-stop canter of gossipy gems. Bella has gleaned this more from the expression in Maria's eyes, the emphasis of hands, the lowering of tone every time they pass a particular room, or servant, and has, in fact, understood little or nothing of what has actually been said. For all she knows, Maria may have already given her the story of the nun.

Inside the chapel the nun kneels in the centre of the altar rails. There is a full-sized candelabrum blazing on either side, giving her wings of jittery light. Her back so straight and dark and steady. Bella waits while Maria slaps her large hand into the holy water font outside the chapel door and collapses into a genuflection. Crossing herself and loudly whispering a passionate prayer, she finally staggers back up onto her little legs and starts yapping again, maintaining the tempo until they turn a corner to see, at the end of a corridor, the English housekeeper standing at a staircase. Then Maria, mid-sentence, falls silent.

The English housekeeper, by contrast, has nothing to say. When Maria hands over custody (or at least that's what it feels like) the most Bella gets is a nod. A few moments and many stairs later: 'Wait in 'ere please, the Signora shan't be long.'

Another vast room. Her mother might have described it as 'handsomely furnished'. For a house on Kensington Square maybe or a feature in *Household Miscellany*. Here it seems out of place, slight and absurdly lost, surrounded by too much height and space. A stage set in an empty theatre.

Bella wonders how the Signora should find her – sitting, standing, walking about? Then she notices the photographs arranged in sections along one wall and in little assemblies on occasional tables, sideboards and the top of the grand piano way down at the far end (where a whole regatta of silver frames appear to be crossing a sleek black lake). This might be the best option, to be found at the photographs – after all, why else were they there, if not to be admired?

After a few moments Bella begins to realize something odd about this little gallery. The photographs, taken in various locations and on dates chronologically arranged over several years, appear to have only one subject – the Lami boy. Here as an infant on a bed of lace; a blanket on the grass; held in the cradle of a woman's arms. She follows his progress, finding him now as a bigger baby, free of swaddling and filling into his own little shape – sitting in a bath bashing bubbles; trapped like an upturned turtle in a high chair waving a spoon; now lying back on the sofa holding one toe. A pretty baby, smiling and chubby, always obliging to the camera without ever seeming to be aware of it.

Older now, he stands on fat uncertain legs. Frame by frame the legs straighten and grow sturdy. They begin to change again, lengthening, thinning a little, while the photographs take on a different mood. Now he is posing, solemn and deliberate. And she thinks of the theatre again; the sort of publicity pictures that are found on the wall in the foyer or going up the Grand Circle stairs. The little archer; junior horseman; apprentice hunter buckling under the weight of a gun. The First Holy Communion boy, hands joined in prayer, rose leaves at his feet. At the piano in bow tie and miniature tails – the boy as musical prodigy. The latest picture shows him in fancy dress; an Indian prince, face gravied-up, moustache and turban included. A picture she finds no less or more contrived than any of the others – as if it were just another role out of many he has learned to play.

The fancy dress was the last to be taken, dated 1 April 1932 – *pesci d'aprile*. More than a year ago now. More than six years since the first picture was taken.

Apart from a dog here, a pony there, an impressive muster of white peacocks somewhere else, he is always photographed alone. Yet he can't have always been alone. In the picture at the piano a man's shadow leans over him and the man's hand – sea horse cufflink peeping out from under the sleeve of his jacket – is poised to turn the page of the music score. There is also the photograph taken when an infant in a woman's arms. But the shadow at the piano is incidental, and the woman holding the baby is firmly excluded. It's as if the camera wanted only the boy.

It hits her then that she doesn't actually know his name. How could that possibly be? She scours her memory, but there's nothing. All she can find is 'my son' in Signora Lami's letter, and 'your son' in her own reply. Yet she *must* have heard it somewhere.

Bella wanders down to the far end of the room towards the French doors, slightly parted. A narrow view of the terrace outside and a light breeze through the gap. She wonders if the missing garden could be out there, if she were to step out, look down – would she find it? She imagines herself for a moment, darting like a cuckoo through the doors, eyes pecking for glimpses of the cast-iron frog or the trio of park benches. She cranes her neck, straining to see through the side gap of the door. There are tiles on the terrace and a circle shape – a wheel. A sudden breeze causes a curtain gauze to shudder across her view. She waits for the curtain to move again to reveal – the wheel of a child's tricycle? Perhaps the boy is out there, too, having a shy, sly preview of her. (His name. She *has* to remember his name.)

Now a movement – a jolt. And the wheel edges a few inches, then stops. This is followed by another sound, an odd, insubstantial cough – a courtesy cough, as if someone out there wants to establish mutual awareness. Which way to move – if at all? Before she can decide there is more coughing – nothing courteous or insubstantial this time. A man's cough. Jagged and violent. Like a chain of angry howls.

Bella turns away from the French doors, and hurries back down the room to where the English housekeeper had instructed her to wait in the first place. Staying with her back to the terrace, facing the door she had earlier come through, she sits on the edge of the least comfortable-looking chair.

As it happens the Signora comes in behind her, by the terrace; brisk steps perfectly in time with the beat of Bella's heart. She is up off the chair in an instant.

'Please,' the Signora's voice says. 'Do stay as you are. Keep yourself comfortable.' She comes round to face Bella. 'I am Signora Lami – how do you do? Please forgive the delay, I'm afraid things have been, shall we say, rather hectic these past few days. I trust your journey has not been too arduous?'

'Not at all,' Bella mutters, taking a step towards the Signora, taking a step back again when she sees no hand is offered.

'Splendid.'

It is difficult to know which is more surprising, the Signora's formal, indeed almost comically regal, use of the English language, or her appearance. For a start, she's so young. Quite a bit younger than Bella, who up to now has been carrying an older Signora Lami in her head. She is also very good-looking. Although oddly dressed. Her hair – fair, possibly blonde – is pulled up and caught at the back in a covering that's not quite a wimple but much more than a cap. She is wearing a long navy skirt and a white starched pinny. In one hand she holds a large glass bulb, which after a few seconds Bella recognizes as being part of a breathing apparatus – the type she has seen from time to time in her father's study. It is then that it dawns on her – the Signora is dressed like a nurse. Of course.

'I've been admiring the photographs,' Bella says, because she feels by now she really ought to have said something.

'Ah yes.' The Signora's eye runs along the wall. 'My husband's passion.' She then goes over to a writing desk and moving behind it with the glass bulb raised in one hand, she uses her other hand to edge open a drawer. It drops and she stops it against her thigh.

'I must say your little boy takes a lovely photograph,' Bella says, hoping to hear his name in return for the compliment.

'Yes. He is a very handsome boy,' the Signora says, and begins rummaging through the drawer. 'Unfortunately he's not here. I sent him to our summer residence three days ago. In Bordighera – you know – on the Riviera – you would have passed it en route? It is cool enough today, thank goodness, but up to now the weather has – how shall we say? – been quite, quite ridiculous. Not very comfortable for him – you understand.' The Signora tilts her hip and hoists the drawer back up with her thigh, then closes it. 'You will like it there, Miss Stuart,' she says. 'I am quite certain. We are a small but friendly household. And Bordighera is very refined – many English are permanent residents, and others come as holidaymakers during the summer. There is even a season, almost like in London, from November to May, you know. My son is there now with his music master.'

'He's fond of music?' Bella asks.

'Rather.'

The Signora frowns and moves to the next drawer. 'Also his two cousins are staying there for a few weeks. Most entertaining, I'm sure.'

'That's nice for your son – someone to play with, I mean,' Bella says, hoping again.

'Hardly, Miss Stuart, they are older than me, the connection is through my husband's side. His first wife, you know. Yes. Americans. They have been *doing* Europe, as they would say, for the past few months. You know how Americans are. They like looking at things on a list. They wanted to come to Sicily, of course, but that was out of the question with my husband unwell.'

'I'm sorry to hear that.'

'Thank you, how kind. And so they remain in Bordighera. One of them, I can't recall which, broke something – her collarbone perhaps, so they have had to suspend their travels for a while. Playing tennis, I believe – we have a splendid lawn tennis club in Bordighera. The very first one in all of Italy. Do you play, Miss Stuart?'

'I'm not very good, I'm afraid.'

'What a pity. My son plays every day.'

'Oh, does he really?' Bella is beginning to wonder if the Signora actually knows her own son's name.

The Signora continues. 'Anyway, what I have arranged is as follows. You will rest until tomorrow and then you are to take the night ferry to Naples tomorrow evening.'

'To Naples?'

'In fact. I'm afraid it appears there is no ferry to Genoa until next week. So you will have to take the train from Naples. While there, if you don't mind, I would like to ask you to deliver a letter for me. It's rather urgent. I'm afraid I simply don't have anyone reliable to spare at the moment.' The Signora pauses and frowns at Bella. 'It will only be a question of taking a taxicab from the port and then back to the train station, Miss Stuart. You know, hardly more than half an hour.' She says this sternly as if Bella has refused the errand.

'Oh, of course, Signora Lami,' Bella says. 'Anything I can do.'

'Good.' The Signora almost smiles. 'That's settled then. Do you think you will require a lady's maid?'

'Well. I mean, I hadn't really—'

'It won't be a problem, the kitchen is swarming with girls, take a pick if you wish, although you will have to train her from the very first scratch. Some of them are frightful primitives, you know. Anyway, choose and then speak to Mrs Harding. She will be here in a moment to take you to dinner.'

The Signora reaches into the drawer and slides out a large envelope. Bella cringes slightly at what can only be another complicated set of directions.

'Everything you need is here. Now, if you'll excuse me, Miss Stuart, I must get back. You may have a stroll in the garden before retiring, but please keep to the garden at your side of the house. The one you will have seen from your terrace?'

'Ah, so there is more than one garden? I thought there—'

'Yes, my own garden is just outside here. I have designed it myself. In the English style, you know. But as our rooms are also on this side of the house I don't want my husband disturbed. Another time perhaps.'

'Of course.'

'If you need to know anything, you may ask Mrs Harding. Of course there is also Sister Ursula – her English is quite acceptable. One finds her about the place. Well, goodbye, Miss Stuart. A pleasure, all mine. No doubt we will see each other soon, in Bordighera.' This time she offers her hand and Bella takes it.

'I hope your husband feels better soon,' she says.

The Signora looks straight into her eyes. 'Thank you, Miss Stuart. But my husband is dying.'

When the housekeeper comes to take her to the dining room, Bella is still slightly dazed. Signor Lami about to die. The boy with no name sent away three days ago. He would have been leaving Palermo just as she was leaving Nice, their paths crossing on the way. Why had no telegram been sent to intercept her? It's not as if they didn't know where she'd be staying en route. A strange oversight from a woman as organized as Signora Lami, who, if her reams of directions were anything to judge by, had a higher than usual regard for the finer detail. A woman who dresses up as a nurse so she can look after her dying husband – for God's sake! – would surely know how to send a telegram. It was as if the inconvenience to Bella simply hadn't mattered. And now after coming all this way, to have to retrace her journey, almost as far as France. Except this time with the errand in Naples thrown in, just to complicate things even further.

The English housekeeper speaks, as if she's been reading Bella's mind. 'You know, we did send a telegram,' she begins. 'Actually we sent two. Both returned.'

'Really?'

'Oh yes, really. One to the train station in Nice. The other the station in Genoa. But it seems there was no Miss Stuart to be found in the first-class carriages of either train.'

'Oh?' Bella tries to sound and look surprised.

'P'raps you didn't hear them call your name?'

'Yes. That was probably it.'

''Appen they mispronounced it. Often do.'

'Indeed.'

They come into a hallway and Mrs Harding lifts a brown package from a chair. She says, 'Would you mind giving this to Alessandro please? He left it behind and can't be doing without.'

Bella accepts the parcel. At least she knows the boy's name now. Alessandro.

'Well, there's the dining room. Enjoy your dinner now.'

'Thank you. Oh, Mrs Harding?'

'Yes, Miss Stuart?'

'Signora Lami mentioned, well, actually she said that if I needed a lady's maid, one of the kitchen girls, and I thought—'

'And do you need a lady's maid?'

'Well, I suppose…'

'Put it this way, Miss Stuart, would you normally be used to a lady's maid?'

'No. But if the Signora… I mean, I thought perhaps Lena—'

'Lena?'

'Yes, she brought water to my room—'

'I'm aware of that, yes. But I'm afraid Lena is out of the question.'

'But the Signora said—'

'Maria would never allow it.'

'Is it up to Maria? Because quite frankly I feel she's hardly—'

'Maria is her mother.'

'Oh. I hadn't realized. Sorry – and her father?'

The English housekeeper ignores this question. There is silence for a moment. 'Did you have anyone else in mind?' she asks then.

'No. No, Mrs Harding, that's fine. I'm sure I'll be able to manage.'

'Very well, if you're sure. Safe journey, Miss Stuart. Please give Alessandro my best and tell him I shall drop him a line.' Then the English housekeeper is gone.

*

When Bella finally escapes to the garden, the heat has pulled back to a more considerate warmth. Everything else about the evening has intensified: smell, colour and above all else, the light, although it takes a moment to notice that she's been walking through liquid gold.

Her mind is stuffed with the trauma of dinner – how any one person could be expected to eat so much food in so many courses. And the servants, constant and overbearing as if they'd been instructed to report on her every mouthful. It had reminded her of the summer with the Johnsons in Margate, when her father had written that letter. Big fat Betty Johnson reading it aloud before dinner: 'Bella's appetite is poor, and deteriorates with excitement. She needs to be – I won't say watched, but certainly encouraged.'

At least in Margate the food had been recognizable. But here? A nibble or two of tough bread. A scrap from a slice of meat she had pulled around a plate for a while. The meat like raw rashers of bacon they'd forgotten to put on the pan. A fidget with a spool of spaghetti next, little snail-like creatures barnacled to the strands – the whiff of urine and ocean. That had been the last straw. She had thrown down her napkin, stood up and raised a determined palm. '*Basta*. No thank you. *Grazie. Enough.*' In the end all that had really passed her lips was perhaps a little too much wine.

Bella feels the weight of the wine now as she stands in the garden, staring down into a patch of grey pebbles. She shakes herself up. There's a walkway on the far side of the parterre sloping towards an archway pom-pomed with roses. She begins to move towards it.

Strange to be walking through what had, until now, been a distant view. Like stepping into an illustration in a book or sitting in the front row of the theatre; pencil lines and spits. Before, there had been a gorgeous compatibility about the garden, everything blending and flowing together. Now, up close and in this shortening light, each thing seems slightly disconnected. The water from the fountain like individual shreds of glass; the boy on his dolphin stands only for himself. The dolphin is a separate entity and doesn't even know of the boy's existence. Each lemon, leaf and blade of grass pushes itself forward as if it's the only thing that matters. Even the voices of the crickets seem different – harsher and slightly neurotic – and the slither of yet another lizard up another wall no longer startles or charms. Even so, Bella knows she has never been more physically aware of a place, and would give anything not to have to leave it tomorrow.

She turns to look back over the villa, locating her room at the gable end of the house, the only window not to have green shutters clamped to the wall. And there, the balcony she had stood earlier, looking down at this very spot, and the corner terrace where she saw the nun praying in the lemon grove. She turns away from the house and continues, passing beside a long low wall lined with terracotta urns and marble vases through air that is pampered with lemons and roses.

The archway turns out to be a pergola, longer than expected and much lower, so that she has to stoop through a tunnel of musty odour to pass to the other side. Coming out she lifts her head for light and air, and is surprised to find neither. The air remains ripe, the light dull. Her eyes adjust. Bella almost screams. After a few seconds, a short nervy laugh comes out instead. She is in a statuary. For one foolish moment it had crossed her mind that these figures might be real men, standing around in a large circle looking at each other. She feels like an intruder in a doorway who has stumbled on and silenced a conversation not meant for the ears of strangers. Some of the figures look so real. Naked or near naked men. The prime of manhood in fact. Robust legs and high tight rumps. One of them with a shoulder blade slightly turned as if he is preparing himself to throw a discus. There are cushions of muscle moulded into his long back, a strength and grace to every turn of his body. Vitality. It is hard to believe that should she lay her hand on his back, all she would feel would be cold and stone.

She reaches her hand towards him, then pulls back. She does this several times, before beginning to trace his shape with her palm, starting at his shoulder, drawing down the length of his spine, over his rump, down the curves of his legs. Bella steps into the circle. And now she is standing like a child in the centre of a game she can't quite grasp. Immediately she wants to get out again, but can see no way through. There is only the stout round thigh, the ready hand, the determined foot. She notices now, there have been a few attempts at modesty: a fig leaf or a swatch of loin cloth. One figure covers himself with his hand, a gesture that seems more obscene than modest. She reminds herself that these are statues and that she has seen such statues before in art galleries or books. They are not real men, with their hairless bodies and pretty bunches of harmless fruit. They will not harm.

As the light continues to deteriorate, she looks up at their faces. She sees eyes that are blank and blind, mutilated profiles, noses corroded to stumps on faces riddled with cancer. Amputees. She is certain that if she remains here, the statues will begin closing in. Her legs are dizzy, her head hot and weak. When a space appears between two figures, Bella closes her eyes and rushes through it.

Out now, on a corridor shaped by high-hedged walls, she passes Roman centurions, Grecian maidens, a private party of nymphs. There's a monumental stairway ahead, leading under a stone archway. The archway is decorated with a grotesquerie of faces. It is not the way she came in, but is the only way she sees out.

Almost dark. In what appears to be a forgotten orchard, branches claw out at each other, rolls of overgrowth are dense on the ground. A stench, vaguely yeasty, like a gust of air through the street grating of a public house. Beneath her feet windfalls yield and squelch, sometimes with a squeak. Bella tries not to imagine she's trampling on mice. She makes for the wall, stays with it until an overdrop from the house lights shows an iron gate. She passes through and is back on civilized ground.

The outline of the house is sturdy with shadow. Only the rooms above the loggia are open and lit. From here a chevron of light drops over the balustrade down on the parterre. She's in the wrong garden – she sees this at once; the lawn, the benches, the cast-iron frog, menacing now under a cuff of light.

Bella slips over to the trees at the side, sneaking along a pathway that winds through them and which she prays may keep her hidden until she finds her way back to the other side of the house. Something catches her eye then, a movement on the terrace. It takes a moment to accept that the woman up there could possibly be Signora Lami. Hair loose and long, a

61

sheet wrapped around her, bare arms and shoulders suggesting that she is otherwise naked. But it is the Signora. Bella sees that now, as she moves into the corner of the terrace to where an old man sits in a bath chair. Bella tells herself not to look, but her eyes keep returning to the terrace. She is afraid or unable to move away.

The Signora draws the chair out of the corner towards the French doors then stops at the threshold, where the light of the room settles about them. Signora Lami then goes into the room to return almost at once with a cushion and something which she hands to the man. The cushion drops from her hand and she kneels down beside the bath chair. The old man then begins brushing her hair. Bella wants to see his face. But he keeps it bent over his task, and the balustrade allows her to see only the hand drawing the brush over the hair, and the hair responding in sprays of fili-greed light. Even from here she can see the hands are ancient, as if they've been dried and salted. Yet there is nothing feeble in their movement, one hand firmly working the brush, the other smoothing and calming the hair back into place.

After a time the old man leans towards the Signora and says some-thing. She lifts herself towards him, raising her arms, and the sheet slips down a little. Now her arms are around his neck and his old hands are splayed on her naked back. They embrace for a while and speak to each other; the words fall softly and although they are not decipherable to Bella she feels the tone is one of comfort and love.

The Signora stands and pulls the sheet up, wrapping it around her body, tucking it into place. She moves behind the bath chair, twists it on its wheels a little, so that they are now both facing the garden. The chair takes a slight backward dip before they reverse into the room, allowing a momentary view of Signor Lami, his thick silver hair, his thin, fine-boned face. A face that is ready to die.

Edward

BORDIGHERA, 1933

June

THE DARK REMAINS FOREIGN. Everything else I've grown used to: food, smells, sound, speech, even the heat. I wake in the night and still have to think: is this France or Italy? (One time it was Baden-Baden.) But I always know straight away: this is not Dublin, this is some other place.

Only once did I make the mistake; years ago now. About six weeks or so after I'd left. In a long low café, bleaker inside than out, where I had ducked in out of the rain. The place was packed but without conversation. There was only the deafening bicker of delft and cutlery; the chomp and slurp of jaw and tongue; a howl at a passing waiter. I looked over the room: greasy moustaches and filthy paws holding sticks of bread like weapons. And the wine. Carafes all over the tables. More of them in a row on top of a nearby counter, alongside which a boy with an urgent face was pacing. When a carafe was emptied, it was thumped off the table, and the boy, hopping to attention, replaced it.

I had little difficulty talking myself into it. My bones were damp and I was hungry enough to want the scuttery stew that a fuzzy-haired sow was slopping out, table to table, from a bucket held to her hip. The rain slobbered all over the windows. I sat and stared at it for a few moments and considered resisting. But what was I to do in a place like this, amongst men like these – ask for a glass of milk?

I could smell it at a distance. Rough, red, almost black. My hand shaking slightly with lust, I reached for it.

Later I woke and there was a hot concrete block on my head. My brain was screaming and my gut swaying in that old familiar way. I got out of bed and made for a door that I was sure would lead me out to the landing and down the side stairs to the outside jacks of the pub, where I could puke away without anyone hearing. Every step of the way was there in my head; past the oulfella's room, my sister's room, the rooms that had once belonged to my mother. I was fiddling with the knob of the door, wondering what was the matter with it, how it had managed to shrink, when a voice from the bed asked what I was doing. French, I thought it was – and could only hope it didn't belong to the fuzzy-haired sow.

'Jacks,' I muttered.

'*Jacques? Qui? Qui est Jacques?*'

I opened the door and stuck my head in. A hum of lavender and must. A faint and sweetish sweat. Shoe leather and naphthalene. I was in a wardrobe, gulping on its stagnant air. Not much I could do about it now anyway. Hot vomit lashed out of my mouth, across coat sleeves and dresses, and down on a row of shoes, splashing in and out of their appalled little mouths.

'Animal,' I heard the voice say. 'Filthy pig.' This time it spoke in English.

That was in Lyons, I think. Lyons or maybe Valence, one of those pointless French towns anyhow. They had all become the same by then. Girls with thick ankles, a cathedral overstuffed with bricks, men with exhausted eyes. Everything crawling along: feet, wheels. Time. And still not a whiff of Barzonni.

A long-ago story. Now that's what I like. It's the sort of thing I hope to find when I wake like this, in the middle of the night, when only a story will steady my mind back to sleep. And it's always in or around the four o'clock mark; a long stretch till daybreak. I used to find the absence of drink cruel at this hour. I used to think, How am I supposed to live the rest of this night, minute by minute? The rest of this stinking life? But you grow used to whatever you have to grow used to.

Not that I don't, from time to time, slip.

The drink. The trick is not to shit on your own doorstep. Put up a fight, but if you have to give in, then travel away. Like one of those married men with a weakness for boys. Get on a train and keep going. That's what I try to do anyway. Then find a rooming house. A rooming house where nobody cares; a bar, and if needs must, a brawl where nobody matters. Satisfy the need, overfeed the need, wear it out till it weakens and goes whimpering back to its corner. Only keep in mind that it never quite dies – that's something I've learned the hard way.

My mind. A scavenging vulturous thing, tugs maggots out of the darkness. It pecks and tears, but will not settle. It skips from this to that. It skids. I say, Stop it now, stop for fuck's sake, if you'd only calm down. Show me a nice slow story.

Here's one I like: the Barzonni story. Naples, late summer, 1925. Walking away from me, down the Strada di Santa Lucia, where, after over a year of searching, without letting it be known I was searching, I had finally caught up with him. A year of hanging around stage doors in the hope of a glimpse; of buying drink for scene-shifters and carpenters in the hope of a hint; scouring the notices for private tuition in every half-cocked music academy from Torino to here. And there was the bastard, jumping onto a tram, folding himself into the herd and disappearing round a bend in the road.

The air went out of me, and I more or less collapsed arse first onto the ground. There was a low dockside wall at my back where I stayed with my head in my hands until the lightness went out of it and I could stand up again. I leaned my foot on the parapet of the wall and smoked a cigarette. On the far side, the wall dropped fifteen feet or so to a quayside. A shanty town down there, made up of iron sheets or old sail cloth held to the wall by long poles. Fishermen roaring at each other in an uncrackable dialect.

A little girl aimlessly wandering, bluebottles fussing around her head. Directly below me a woman was boiling some foul-smelling thing in a pot. Another woman plucked at rags on a clothes line. On the steps a beautiful, filthy young woman crunched snails between her teeth and dropped them in a bowl she was holding in the hammock of her skirt. A bare-arsed toddler was having a shit in the corner. A dog cowered nearby and waited for his chance. The toddler screaming at the dog, '*Via! Via!*' The stink of outdoor poverty. Of shit and woodsmoke and fish gut. In the background, the beautiful bay was beaming. And I thought to myself, Christ, this Naples.

Up here, at street level, the *scugnizzi* were prowling for tourists and other fools. Behind the backs of two strolling priests, sailors and prostitutes gave each other the eye. Disconsolate, I walked back to my digs off the Toledo, a tall narrow house, divided into any amount of cells, walls rotting from the outside in, and where even the landlord appeared to be on the game.

I found him again. As it turned out Naples was not large, merely compressed. A few days later in the Galleria, he sat at the table next to mine, outside a café. I could hardly believe it. He was that close. I could hear his every move, the soft click of his starched shirt front when he lifted his hand to salute an acquaintance, the irritation of his coffee spoon drilling his cup, ticking off the saucer. I could even hear the fucker breathe.

I kept my face behind the newspaper, now and then lifting it as if to glance at the passing crowd. Each time my eye picked out something else: the diamond ring on his little finger, a pigskin wallet on the table, the cufflinks shaped like sea horses. I looked up at the great glass belly of the Galleria ceiling and began to sweat. I felt sure its black iron framework was a cage about to drop down on me. Footsteps and voices were beating into my head. I stood up, threw the price of the coffee down and walked away across the marble tiles. After a moment I recovered myself and stopped under the canopy of the *tabaccheria* – I had waited too long to bottle out now.

Face to the window, as though studying the gift display, I remained until I saw through the glass his reflection skim over mine.

For two days and a night, I was his dog. When he went into the flower shop to buy his buttonhole, I was outside having a sniff at the boxes of lavender. When he went into the barber's, I snoozed in the sun on a bench across the road. I even pissed when he pissed, taking my place at the far end of the men's latrine on piazza del Pebliscito.

The following evening when he slipped away from the after-theatre crowd, I was behind him. We turned into streets that rose as they narrowed, deserted but for the occasional slither of a cat. Past stair-alleys and side-slits and the windowless *bassi* where people lived like mules behind stable doors, and where in the uphill darkness I could have easily lost him, were it not for the tap of his ridiculous shoes.

I would have liked to have been able to catch him red-handed at some boy or another, the way I had caught him years before in Dublin. Except this time I wouldn't be threatened into silence. Just as I would have liked to have smashed his face into the tiles earlier on in the public latrine. But I had to think of my future. If he was to be any good to me, then I needed him in one piece, secure and respectable; a man of substance, not of shame.

I can still see him going through that doorway in Naples, me stepping up behind him, tapping him on the shoulder. In the half light, the way he turns and gives me one of his frowns. I can see it dawn on him after a few seconds that it might be me, but…? He is put off by my beard and general appearance. I am far from the fresh-faced boy he last saw in Dublin and almost a year on the run has done my appearance no favours.

In the end I had to help things along by letting him hear my voice. I said something like, 'What's the matter, Maestro Barzonni – don't you recognize your old pupil?'

'You?' his voice was hoarse, his eyes alarmed, and I wondered if perhaps word had come through from Dublin that my sister had been murdered and I wondered if perhaps he thought I had come all this way to kill him too. 'How is it *you*?'

I shrugged good-humouredly and smiled. He took his eyes off mine just long enough to glance over my shoulder to the street outside, then behind him up to the door at the top of the stairs, where a lamp was burning and there was the muffled sound of radio dance music. Then he looked back at me.

'You're looking well,' I said. 'Prosperous anyway. I see you still wear the sea horse cufflinks my mother bought you.'

'What are you doing here?' he whispered.

'Living like a rat,' I snarled.

*

That was 1925. Eight years from then to now. How far I've come. Naples to Sicily to Bordighera. Much shorter coming back up, I'd have to say, than it had been going all the way down.

I lie on my back in this foreign darkness and remember such scenes so vividly I can actually see them. I see other things too, other people, from further away. Mother on the sofa poised for conversation with a stranger. The oulfella rubbing a cloth into the counter, big ruddy face softly wobbling from exertion. Customers come and go, day into night, but the cloth, like his conversation, rubs the same small area. And I see Louise. Her face a younger version than the oulfella's. Slightly less red perhaps, less fat, but it's his face she's wearing. I see her as she used to be when we were children, the heft of her hammering me to the wall with her massive hip, her face radiant with hate. The two of us scrapping like dogs throughout the house. Even when left to practise duets at the piano we wouldn't let up, pinching, biting, punching, pulling; disguising our squeals of pain with louder playing. She was always the stronger, the more resourceful fighter. Hard to believe, in the end, I would have got the better of her. Louise alive. Savagely alive. And that's not how I want to see her.

The day before yesterday. Out in the morning, promenade all to myself, by a whispering sea. The air was for the moment cool and I must have walked a long while because when I came back through Bordighera, the

market men had given way to old men and housewives. A few bureaucratic types were headed for the station and children in fascist uniforms
quacked around me at the newspaper stand.

I came into Tonino's café, still thinking about the housewives, with
their fine big arses and dark damp eyes, their tired little early morning
sighs. A stranger at the counter was talking to Tonino. From Albenga, I
heard him say. I sat down in my usual corner, cracked open my newspaper and felt the first whack of coffee hit my chest. Tonino was called to the
telephone and the stranger started speaking to me. We had a pleasantly
impersonal conversation about the headlines mostly: Hitler, and Spain,
Roosevelt, people shooting each other on American streets. The world was
a terrible place, he said, no law, no respect. Thank God we Italians have il
Duce to protect us!

He had taken me for a fellow Ligurian and I realized then that it had
been a long, long time since anyone has asked where I'm from. I started
to become afraid then. Of what? I don't know.

There was nothing remarkable about the rest of my morning, but
each little turn of it seemed somehow significant. I made my way up the
slope of the corso d'Italia, returning nods and good-morning smiles as I
received them, then bought a few oranges from Marco's. Next door the
barber waved his razor through the window at me, and jokingly threatened my whiskers. I went to his door, pulled the beads aside and lobbed
an orange in. He deftly caught it and laughed like a child. At the top of the
corso an elderly couple sat on a bench. He asked me for the time, and when
I stopped to check my watch, they both waylaid me with competitive little
tales of their individual ailments. The old man had sweets wrapped in
shiny paper in his pocket. As he spoke he opened the wrapper of one and
handed the bare sweet to me as if I were a child.

I came back to the house and stood for a while at the window, looking down at the garden. I opened the window and stepped out onto the
slight balcony. There was birdsong and butterflies – the usual. The dog
down the road with the baritone bark was hard at it. From the kitchen,

71

first rumours of lunch already on the air. I had a full free morning ahead of me.

I stayed there in the main house, read, listened to the radio, stared into space. Then I came down and picked up the lunch tray Elida had left for me on the hall table. I walked through the garden down to the mews, had my lunch, lay on the bed, may have even snoozed. When I got up, I sat at my piano.

My fingers flawlessly moving – there is something to be said for this sober life – anything else faded. I stayed like that until Elida came to my window and called out my name, her voice hacking up to me that it was time to collect Alessandro from tennis.

*

I have this in my head: if I could only see my sister, just once more see her, then I could find peace. Maybe even sleep a whole night. Or accept a morning like the one before last without being afraid it could be pulled out from under my feet. But I'd have to be able to see her, exactly as I last saw her – dead and smothered in blood. It doesn't really make sense this yearning for a bloody sister-ghost. But that's what I have in my head.

PART TWO

Anna

DUBLIN, 1995

April

TODAY I TELL HER Ginger Rogers has died. 'You remember poor old Ginger?' I say, as if she were an oulone who used to live down the road. 'Died last night, heart failure – according to this. Born 1911, that's a few years younger than you – and you're still battling away.'

These one-sided conversations. I'd forgotten how much of a strain they can be. Not that there's really any other kind in a hospital like this one, or that anyone pays a blind bit of attention. But I've been told to let her hear my voice, and so like it or not, that's what I do. They're big on the voice in here. It always comes back to it. Sometimes I think it's all that they have.

She's gone downhill since my last visit six weeks ago, a long time, considering. At least then her eyes would often be open, on a good day even make contact. The odd grunt or nod of the head in response to something I'd say so that there had been times when I'd been able to convince myself that she'd actually been listening to me. Now it seems she just sleeps all the time.

How easy it is to slip back into routine and before I know it I've given her the weather report (last night's rain, today's sun doing its best to squeeze through)' and I'm scanning the ward for something to comment on. The least little shift would do, a vase moved from here to there, say, or a new pair of slippers under a bed. But the passing of six weeks has gone unmarked in here and I find nothing noteworthy or new. Except for Mrs Clarke's vacant bed and I'm hardly going to comment on that.

The newspaper now, I don't mind so much – to read a bit out, throw in a comment or two, read another bit again. The wider world and its familiar strangers – it takes the onus off us both somehow. And it keeps her in touch. Or so the little blondy nurse never tires telling me. 'You never know what's going in there,' she'll often add with a knowing nursey wink.

I turn over the pages, quickly decide there's no need to go bothering her with Rwanda, Bosnia or OJ's trial. Then I go back to Ginger, this time reading the obituary aloud.

I've always quite liked this time of the day – this hour of adjournment in the ward's routine; feeding time over, afternoon medication just kicking in. In a moment the junior nurses will start to slip off for a sneaky smoke or a cup of tea. And it will seem like I was never away.

'You go on,' I'll say to them. 'I'll give you a shout if there's any excitement. If anyone jumps up like, and starts doing a jig.'

In fairness to the nurses they've never asked me to keep an eye on things, nor would they dream of it. It just sort of happened. I offered one day, then I offered the next. I always have to offer. Unless the staff nurse is on, in which case I'll keep my mouth shut.

Three nurses. Through the bars in a high-set window, I watch their caps slip into the frame, then wag and nod. Pokes of smoke rise and fritter. Only the tallest one shows the nape of her neck, and her hair which is corseted into a dull-orange bun.

In here, meanwhile, a lull begins to drift over the beds like a mild dust you can almost see, and all those little hidden notes that an hour ago would have been bashed aside now come into their own. The shuffling slippers come and go (that's Mr Carroll, who can't stop walking about). Mrs Lyons plays with her rosary, muttering obscenities as if they were prayers. Snores and groans sway and stutter. Under the covers old secrets are whispered. A lengthy fart purrs down the line. And through it all I can hear my voice, wandering up and down the ward, like something lost.

'Virginia Katherine,' I say. 'That was her real name. Did you know? Virginia Katherine McMath – at least I think that's how you pronounce it. Married five times. Can you imagine? *Five* husbands. One's bad enough,' I say.

As if either of us would really know.

It all comes full circle. I put the paper down for a moment and that's what I think. Full circle. We start off in a nursery and we finish up in one. Babies again. If I last long enough I'll be one too. And what will any of the in-between matter or mean in the end? The way I've lived my life so far, the way I'm feeling now, about this woman in the bed, the man who's recently left me, the meeting in a few minutes' time with the registrar of this mental hospital and whatever it is he has to say to me. A big fat ugly wrinkly baba, that'll be me. I'll open my gummy mouth when I want to be fed or when I want to gibber. I'll shit in my nappy when the urge takes me, and no other urge will concern me. I'll finish my days in a place such as this. Sexless and therefore free. Where it makes no difference if the genders are mixed in together, or even mixed into each other, come to think of it (hairy-faced women, men who could do with a bra).

If the shuffler sometimes shows a flop of willy through his pyjama slit; if the ex-reverend mother goes out to the toilet with one plump tit peering like a plucked chicken out the front of her nightie; and if genteel Mrs Lyons wants to mutter her obscenities – well, who's going to care or even half notice?

'Eighty-three years of age,' I say. 'Imagine? Proud of her pins till the end. You'd leave her in the ha'penny place, so you would. Age-wise and leg-wise. You'd knock her sideways.' And so I continue for a bit, stretching poor Ginger's legs this way and that, until they've become an exhausted subject. Well – you have to be saying something.

Yes. In the slow passing of hospital time a simple gesture can take on a sense of exaggerated purpose. The refilling of a water jug, say, or finding a vase for the ugly flowers I've brought from the garage shop down the road. Folding the newspaper over, taking it across to the table in the middle of the ward in case one of the nurses wants to have a look at it later. Going down the ward and into the visitor's toilet – now that's an expedition in itself. When all this is over it's usual to feel at a bit of a loss.

I stand looking down at the table in the middle of the ward. It's a kitchen table, red Formica, chipped black around the edges, and has been donated, like most of the furniture in here, by a charitable sort, or, as I'm inclined to think in my more cynical moments, the sort that's too tight to pay for a skip.

I come back to the bed and force myself to look at my grandmother's face. It's a different face to the one I left behind a few weeks ago, no longer scribbled with wrinkles and lines. Fuller since the stroke, you could almost say fat, and pink. I can't get over this. It makes me want to laugh out loud, to say, 'Would you look at the big fat pink face of you, Nonna!'

She looks so *well*. Now that she can no longer swallow and it's the intravenous drip, rather than herself, that's responsible for feeding her. Here's something else – without the power of her throat muscles she can no longer cry. At least that's all over, that constant crying. That awful constant dry-crying. Jesus! At least I'll never have to listen to that again.

All in all, and absurd as it seems, in some ways the stroke has been good for her.

Between the pink and the fatness and the expression of peace, traces remain of what has come to be known as 'the incident'. At least that's how it was described to me on the phone when they finally tracked me down in London: 'I'm afraid there's been a bit of an incident.' And that's what they've been calling it ever since. 'The stroke was most likely the result of the incident.' 'Certain tests had to be carried out on foot of the incident.' That's the sort of thing I've been hearing. What I haven't been hearing are the finer details: the whys, wherefores and, most intriguing of all, the how in the name of Christ could such a thing have happened in the first place?

Regarding the incident, this much I do know: it bruised her face and it broke her arm. It left long scratches and cuts all up her legs and across her knees. It fucked up her new hip. Despite all this damage, it has to be

78

admitted that for a while there before the incident, she was a total rip. And since it, apparently, has been a complete 'sweetie pie'.

I lean towards my grandmother. 'Nonna,' I say, 'I take my eyes off you for a few weeks and look at all the trouble. What are we going to do with you at all?'

I sit back and try to remember the other Nonna, what she was like before all this. But I can barely recall her younger face, which ironically looked older than the face she now has. I can only seem to get back as far as the nursing home where she lived for a year or so before she was sent here. Where we both thought she would end her days. A far cry from this hole, it has to be said.

She'd picked it herself, after first checking out God knows how many other homes. '*Now* this is it,' she had said. 'This is the *perfect* place.' Then she had proceeded to make all the arrangements, financial and otherwise. I couldn't get over her forking out that type of money or that she had that kind of money to fork out. Not that she'd ever denied me anything, but it had been scrimp and scratch all the way with Nonna, and I had often got the impression that spending money gave her a pain in the stomach. Not this time though. This time she couldn't whip out the cheque book quick enough.

She had seemed almost happy there, in her perfect nursing home. A veranda in summer where she sat like a memsahib on her bamboo chair, occasionally smiling and nodding at other people's conversations. The lawn to look at, trees to contemplate, the sound of water. An occasional party in the main drawing room – some eejit in a dickie bow telling corny jokes and banging on an electric keyboard. But still. A bright bedroom all to herself, and her own radio, although she always preferred to sit in silence. She was treated as a pet there, was, I believe, almost loved. They liked her neatness, her soft green eyes, what they saw as her acquiescent disposition. Of course they got over that soon enough.

They tell you to do that in magazines and care advice brochures, they say – try to remember your loved one in happier, more positive times. Try

79

to choose one or two things a day your loved one used to enjoy. It's interesting I think, the way they always use that expression 'loved one' – an undertaker's expression – like they're acknowledging that he or she has already died.

The buzzer goes on the door of the ward, and I hear Thelma coming out of the office to answer it. Thelma, a sort of nurse's aide, is a bit on the simple side. I suspect she may be a former patient, shoved in here a long time ago and for not that much of a reason. The door is unlocked and I can hear Thelma's loud excited whispers from here. A voice I recognize – that of the bunty little staff nurse – is admitted. The door is then locked again with a touch more ceremony than usual, and I can't help wondering if this is for my sake.

I get up and stretch my arm to tap on the window. The geometric line of starched caps falters and breaks apart. One startled eye turns towards me, like the eye in a shying horse. I give the nod that says, *The battle-axe has arrived, girls, better get yourselves back inside.*

Bunty's voice comes into the ward. 'Oh!' she goes, when she sees me (as if Thelma hasn't told her I'm here). 'Oh, long time no see, indeed.' She breezes by and it could be a snarl or a smile on her lips but either way I sense disapproval. When she comes back there's a stack of files in her arms. 'So', she says, looking down at the suitcase beside me on the floor, 'are you moving in – or what?'

'I was in London,' I say. 'I came straight from the airport.'

'London!' she goes, as if I'd said the moon. 'Imagine that now – business or pleasure?'

'Neither,' I say and for some reason find myself standing up.

She barrels off up the ward and I feel myself boil up with rage. I long to shout after her, to say something like, 'Here, you – I have my own problems, you know, I have my own life. And what about all the other weeks, days, hours, when I was the only visitor in this kip? I didn't hear you asking too many questions then!'

I imagine her stopping in her tracks, turning to look at me, the drop of her fat little mouth, a slow blush pushing north from her chest up her neck. Then just as she's getting ready to move off again, I hear myself continuing: 'And another thing – I wasn't the one who left the door open. I wasn't the one who let her escape. I'll be speaking to the registrar shortly by the way, and can't wait to hear what he has to say about that!'

In my daydream Bunty lowers her eyelids, her already red enough face darkening to a guilty purple. In reality she couldn't give a fuck, while I stand like a fool watching her move from bed to bed, fussing and fixing, checking on charts, yapping at patients – there she goes. Even those who are sleeping or in other ways beyond listening will be addressed: briskly, loudly, a touch of tolerance bordering, it has to be said, on genuine kindness. As she always does at the start of her shift and again when it comes to an end, the way a primary school teacher might speak to her pupils at the start and finish of the day.

It was never my idea to put her here in the first place. I sit back down and remind myself of this now, as I used to do every time I came up here for the first year or so. This was not my idea. It was that other place wanted rid of her. The so-called 'perfect place'. A few weeks, they had assured me, a few tests, a rest. That's how they got around me.

The truth was they just couldn't put up with her. Couldn't have her sullying the atmosphere of their veranda with her carry-on and dry-crying. Couldn't have her pacing the halls and landings, leaving the echo of that one repeated phrase in her wake, 'I can't, I can't. I'm not able. I'm not able.' On and on, she just wouldn't stop saying it. Until eventually they had stopped asking, 'Not able to what, darling? What are you not able to do?' But most of all they couldn't have her disillusioning the well-heeled relatives that their money had been wisely spent. She had simply become bad for business, I suppose.

Behind me there's the squeak of shoes and I turn to see Bunty. 'You have an appointment to see the registrar, I believe?' She looks amused. No, more than that, she looks as if she has to restrain herself from bursting out laughing in my face. The brazen cheek of me really, a mere mortal, to question the hospital authorities. Bunty obviously finds this a scream.

'That's right,' I say.

'It'll be Mr Brook who'll see you. Do you know Mr Brook?'

'No.'

'Oh, a lovely man! I can't begin to tell you. Actually he used to treat your grandmother, when she came here first. You know where to go then?'

I stand up and nod and go. Thelma is waiting to let me out. 'Here,' she says, 'you missed it! All the excitement your nanny caused. The police and all. You want have seen the state of her when they brung her back in. Ah you missed it, you did.'

I can never stand at the mouth of this corridor without remembering the first time I stood here. I can never look down the icy length of it without feeling that way again. There was a doctor with me – come to think of it, the last time I spoke to a doctor in here. He walked with me a little way, Doctor Ian Coyle, not an unusual name, but I had difficulty holding on to it just the same and had to keep glancing at his badge. He told me they had decided to keep her in.

'You mean for more tests?' I asked.

'No. I mean, indefinitely.'

'But I understood, I mean I was led to believe, anyway, you know, I thought – is she not going back to the nursing home?'

'I'm afraid not.'

'But I was told—'

'They just wouldn't be able to manage her.'

'But I can't leave her here. There has to be some place else. I mean not *here*, not this awful place…' I was crying a little then, and he said that he was sorry. We came up beside two brown plastic chairs set by the wall and sat down. I remember noticing how young he was then and that he reminded me of one of my honours art students. Earnest and brave, a bit of a swot. He pulled his chair closer to mine; no aftershave but two kinds

82

of soap. One wholesomely scented, probably from his mother's bathroom. The other, that pink disinfectant stuff in the square bottle by the sink in the ward.

He allowed me to smoke, even went as far as to fashion a little ashtray for me out of a piece of card he had in his pocket. He was very kind. 'Senile dementia,' he said. 'Your grandmother has senile dementia.'

I said nothing and after a moment he began to tell me a story. It was a third-hand story, told to him by the nursing home's GP, who had been given it by the nursing home matron. A condensed version of which was now on file. He told it well, soft-spoken and slow, so that his words became pictures almost as soon as they left his mouth. And I felt I was there, watching my grandmother in the dining room of the nursing home – the 'graciously appointed dining room overlooking the gardens', as the prospectus would have it. I could see her, standing up suddenly and lifting her plate from the table. The plate still full of dinner and her bringing it across the room to the French doors. Passing through them, going down the few steps sideways. Pressing her hand into the food, digging her fingers in and shoving it off her plate. I can see it falling, heavy and dark, stain-ing the velvety lawn with its bulk. And her coming back into the dining room, sleeves covered in gravy, spills all down the front of her dress, laying the gravy-streaked plate back on the table. Nobody paying all that much heed, until suddenly she starts making grabs at the plates of the other res-idents. *Pandemonium.* Old greedy eyes going into a panic, arthritic hands clutching their plate rims, shaky voices calling, 'Help! Help!' Staff from all corners swiftly arriving, my grandmother becoming violent, biting a nurse's hand.

'So you see…' he concluded.

'Yes, thank you, doctor, I see.'

We arrived back at the ward where I signed the committal papers for St Ita's hospital, Portrane, and had one more look at a heavily sedated Nonna. Doctor Ian Coyle was still chatting gently, not that I was really listening. I couldn't stop thinking of the episode in the nursing home, not least the idea of Nonna wasting food, wasting anything. Nonna, who would turn a jam jar inside out to get the last little smear out of it.

'Are you sure, doctor? Are you certain there's no other solution?' I had finally asked.

'You know, sometimes, Anna, quite simply, there isn't.'

That first day. Two and a half years ago – maybe more. After finally finding my way back to reception, I had stood outside the main door trying to pull myself together with a cigarette, before attempting the long drive home. Two young men stood a few yards away from me. The tall one wore a suit that was too small, the short one wore a suit that was too big. It had crossed my mind that maybe they should swap. After a bit of shuffling and huffing the tall one approached. 'Herehaveyegotasmoke-haveya?' came rattling out of his mouth. I noticed he had beautiful teeth.

I gave him a smoke and he skulked away. The short one then decided to chance it. Picking his way over to me, he held his hand open and flat, as if I were a horse in a field he was trying to corner, and against his better judge-ment at that, I placed a cigarette on his palm and he went back to his mate.

I had heard the lunatic cries from the sectioned wards off the corridors while I'd searched for my grandmother's ward. And I couldn't say the ward, when I did find it, was the prettiest. Yet I was more affected by this pair than anything else that day. It wasn't really any one thing about them, apart from the stupid suits, nor the fact that they were so young. It was their near normality that had got to me. Everything about them, from their eyebrows down to their feet, seemed to be only slightly askew, yet it was enough to make everything wrong. Like a room where the pictures hang crooked. Maybe it brought it home to me what sort of a place this really was. This place where any one of us could end up. This place where my grandmother would have to die.

*

And now, two and a half years later, on the way to see the registrar, I stand here again for the umpteenth time and still have to think about which

84

direction to take. As I look down the first long corridor running away from me like a dim country lane in the middle of nowhere, I try to understand how she managed it. At a stretch, I might be able to accept that she got herself out the door of the ward – if the keys were left lying around or someone had carelessly left it unlocked. But I just can't begin to imagine how, in the dead of night, she found her way not only out of the building but also off the hospital grounds.

I am baffled and appalled. I am angry. I am nothing short of impressed.

Moving towards the registrar's office. A silence you could swim through. I also notice, not for the first time, that unlike other hospitals, no smells linger in these corridors, and it occurs to me now that the numerous draughts have probably sucked them all out. So bloody cold. A bolt of ivy that has slithered through a hole in the glass of a window has now curled down to the floor. I can't remember this from six weeks ago. The chocolate-box pictures on the wall are buckled from damp and there's a bucket with rainwater still in it, set under a leak in the ceiling. Patches of pointless heat hit out from the occasional radiator along the way. And my footsteps, which started off self-consciously slow and restrained, have, in my hurry to get this over with, increased their speed and impact until they're banging out a Gestapo-like rhythm, and I am almost running.

The minute I set eyes on Mr Brook, I start whingeing. I can see the spread of my letter on his desk, my points and questions numerically arranged. The hand is heavier than usual, the lines waver, despite the several attempts to get it just right, and I can't even remember what those questions were now. It was supposed to have been a controlled sort of a letter. Designed to let these people know they weren't dealing with some fool to be fobbed off with a few watery excuses. Nor was it written by an indifferent relative who couldn't really give a shit when it came to it. I had flattered myself that this was the letter of an intelligent woman, a woman with no reason to feel guilt or remorse. A secondary school teacher in her thirties, for God's sake, well used to dealing with tricky customers.

And here I am blubbing like a baby and saying how sorry I am before Mr Brook even has time to open his mouth.

He brings me to a chair and I sit down, then he perches himself on the corner of the desk right in front of me. He passes me a pluck of tissues from a box and I notice his hand shows a slight tremor. He waits for me to compose myself. An elderly man, handsome and small, he takes his hand away from me then and folds his arms over a hand-knitted jumper. His trousers, although clean and pressed, bear the shadows of old stains that haven't quite shifted. His shoes are canvas, and he looks as if he's forgotten to shave. When he speaks his voice is frayed, his manner a little uncertain. He holds my hand and speaks to me as if I were a child. I duly oblige by behaving like one, sniffling and politely nodding so that in the end I'm only short of holding my arms up to him and calling him Dada.

He tells me about Nonna and how she'd been found. It was in the train station in the neighbouring village of Donabate, in the early hours of the morning. Wandering up and down the platform clutching an old wet cardboard box she'd found somewhere, probably in a bin. By the time the police were called she was already injured, covered in blood, although not as bad as it looked in the end. Arm broken of course, hip more or less banjaxed, blood all over her legs. Even so, she wouldn't let go of the box.

He releases my hand and, leaving his perch, goes to the other side of the desk. 'Anna,' he says, 'you express certain concerns in your letter – isn't that so?' He leans down to the letter rather than picking it up and I can see him reread, as if to remind himself.

'Oh please,' I begin, 'it doesn't matter now. Really it doesn't. I'm sorry I sent it at all.'

'My dear girl, you were quite entitled. And I'd just like you to know before we go any further that this sort of thing will never happen again. Never.'

He begins to tell me about a new electronic security system, soon to be installed, involving secret codes and a button panel. As he speaks his fingers move as if already on the panel, his expression slightly bewildered as if he's trying to understand how such a thing could be possible.

'Yes. If you forget your number then it seems – hard cheese. You have to go home.' Anyway, it means at least only a staff member can open the door. He tuts, then half laughs, closing that particular subject. Then, folding the letter, he slips it back into my grandmother's file.

I glance at the file. Not all that thick, considering. A whole life boiled down to a few flimsy pages; a few shameful incidents recorded. I wouldn't mind getting my hands on it, but haven't the nerve to ask.

'Anna?'

'Yes, Mr Brook?'

'We should probably talk about the tests now, and yes, my dear, you are quite right, it was without your consent. Now let me just explain why. The nature of her injuries being, well... You see we were concerned that a sexual assault may have taken place. Awful to think that such a thing could happen, but in fact not long ago, and not too far from here either, an elderly lady was sexually assaulted. Perhaps even by a patient in this hospital. The perpetrator was never found, I'm afraid. Anyway I'm glad to tell you no sexual assault took place. But, quite simply, we couldn't locate you, and therefore I made her my ward – this is the usual practice when no relative is available to a patient. Because you see it's imperative to act quickly in cases of sexual—'

'Please, Mr Brook,' I say. 'Please, could you not keep saying that, I mean – even if it didn't actually happen could you not keep saying it?'

'Which dear? Oh yes, of course, Anna. I am sorry. Look, why don't I get us some tea?'

I wait for him to ring a bell, or go to the door in the wall and call out to a secretary, but instead he moves to a corner of the room and lifts a small electric kettle from a tray. He removes a dead plant from the sink before filling the kettle.

'You were brought up by your grandmother, I believe?'

'Since I was eight anyhow. After my mother died in a car accident.'

'Ah, wasn't that unfortunate for you,' he tuts, as if it were down to some sort of carelessness. 'Was your mother an only child?'

'Yes.'

He goes to the wall and plugs in the kettle. Then turns around, smiles and nods as if he's only just seen me. 'And your father?'

'He worked away from home most of the time so Nonna, my grandmother, took care of me. He died last year – cancer.'

'I'm sorry to hear it. And what do you do yourself, Anna? Are you working?'

'I'm an art teacher in a secondary school.'

'Ah, that's very good. Tell me, do you have anybody else in your life at the moment, a husband? A boyfriend?'

'My partner and I just split up, that's why I was in London.'

'He works in London?'

'He's an artist. He can work wherever he likes but yes, now he likes London. I was over there because I was trying to… Well, I don't know really what I was trying to do.' And I begin to sniffle again.

'These artistic types, eh?' he says and rolls his eyes wearily before turning back to the tray. 'Still, a lovely girl like you won't be long about getting a replacement.'

I listen to the rattle of cups.

'And your grandfather? Is he dead a long time?'

'I never knew him. He died in the war, in Italy. It's where they met.'

'Ah, he was Italian? That explains it.'

'What?'

'She was speaking Italian, in fact the guards at first thought she was a foreigner. She used to speak it now and then when she came here first, and of course *nonna* is the Italian for grandma – am I right?'

'Yes. But no, he wasn't Italian, my grandfather. He was English. English. I've always called her Nonna, I don't know why, really.'

'I see.' When he turns back around there's a carton of milk in his

88

hand. 'Were they married long, Anna?' He lifts the carton to his nose and sniffs.

'No. Only a short time, I believe.'

'Ah I see. Was your mother adopted, do you know, Anna?'

I can feel my heart tighten like a fist. 'Is that what you found out, that my mother was adopted?'

'You weren't told anything yourself on that line, Anna?'

'No.'

Steam from the kettle blooms behind his head and I wait to see what's next. He turns away from me again and makes, then pours, tea. 'No thoughts at all on the subject, Anna?'

'No. To be honest Nonna is – was always very private. But I feel if my mother had been told, I would have been. Certainly my father would have said something.'

'And he never did?'

'No.'

'Well, I suppose in the old days people often kept that sort of thing quiet – do you take sugar, Anna?'

'No.'

'Oh good. He smiles, turning back around. 'Because do you know what? I don't think we have any.'

I don't want smiles or apologies about sugar, I want him to come straight out and say whatever it is he's trying to say.

'So, Mr Brook, are you telling me that when you examined my grand-mother you discovered she'd never given birth – is that it?'

'Well, yes but…' For a moment I feel as confused as he looks. He passes me a cup of tea and waits for me to accept and taste it. Then he takes a short breath. 'What I'm telling you is, not only did your grandmother never give birth, but she was never sexually active. I mean, never. As far as I'm aware.'

'But she was married?'

'Indeed.'

'I don't understand.'

He shrugs, then, priest-like, lifts, lowers and then joins his hands. 'The marriage was never consummated.'

Next he is standing up and I can see it's time for me to go. 'Anyway, Anna, I just thought you ought to know. Now I am sorry for all the upset, but at least she's safe, your poor old Nonna. At least there's no more distress.'

'Yes.'

He picks up his coat from the back of the chair and begins walking me towards the door. 'Again, I apologize.'

And again I say it doesn't matter. Even if I'm still not quite sure what the hell either of us is talking about.

I stand outside the office watching Mr Brook go to the reception area where a taxi driver, tucking a newspaper under his arm, steps up to him. There is a familiarity between the two men, and I get the impression that the driver has been waiting since dropping Mr Brook off. I can imagine Mr Brook saying to him, 'Wait here – would you? It shouldn't take long.' I look at the door of the office; heavy varnished oak, the title THE REGISTRAR painted in black across the top panel. Not even a proper Christian name, as if it's a movable post, allowing registrars to come and go, to be dragged off the golf course, or out of retirement without even needing to shave, when and as they're required. And I can't help feeling that somehow I've been duped.

I return to the ward to collect my suitcase. Standing at my grandmother's bed, I have an overwhelming urge to touch her, more from curiosity than affection. Her hand seems the obvious choice. But her right hand, along with her entire right side, is guarded by drips, and there's no way past the wigwam of wires. Her left wrist is plastered from forearm to just over the knuckles of her fist, squeezing her hand so that the delicate bulbs of her fingertips are bunched together like something dainty in a vase. The plaster of Paris is a lovely job, a confectioner's job, smooth and white and careful. It gives me an adolescent impulse to take a marker pen to it. For a second I see the black gleaming letters trail from its nib; three words and a question mark. I try to decide how I'd arrange them, these adolescent words that have come into my head – in a bracelet around her wrist, or one word beneath the other in a column. Either way, my question would be the same: WHO ARE YOU?

*

When I get home the nine o'clock news is just coming on the telly. I stand at the door while the light from the screen jitters into the darkness, and the voice of a newsreader speaks to me. I can't believe it's been on the whole time I've been away in London. Then again, since the day Hugh left I don't think it's ever been off. I'd even made a little nest on the sofa in front of it, because it was less painful to sleep out here than in the bed we had shared. It had been the last thing I saw at night, and was waiting for me each day the moment I opened my eyes. Even while I slept it was there in the background slyly inserting its images into my head. How else would they have got there – the bland-faced professor and his quantum physics; the black-shawled Mexican dodging bullets up the side of a mountain? And now in my absence it's been twittering away into the empty rooms of my flat. Suddenly I hate the bloody thing, I want to kick it over, I want to bash my boot heel right down through its glass and into its guts. I pick up the remote and switch on the silence. Then I go up to the studio. Hugh's studio, originally supposed to be mine. The best room in the flat of course, a converted attic accessed by a pull-down stepladder. I haven't been up here since before he left, a long time before that even, come to think of it.

I'd forgotten how much I liked it up here, how it had clinched my decision to take this flat. It's the skylights really; the way they throw light out in the morning across the long bare floor. Or even now, at this hour, the way they contain the night sky. The smell of wood and paint and turps; I'd forgotten all that.

I think about getting the long pole and opening one of the windows. I imagine how it will groan and yawn and yield. Outside there will be a glimpse of a black Georgian roofline. The sky will be diluted to mauve by the city lights, and the traffic, muffled by distance, will sound like the ocean. But then I remember I've left the pole at the bottom of the stepladder, and it feels too far to go all the way back down.

The room is dusty, but not untidy – he hasn't left enough of himself behind for that. What he hasn't taken, he has boxed and pushed under the eaves. 'I'll be back for the rest,' were the last words he said to me. 'You needn't bother your fucking arse, you stupid prick,' had been my dignified reply.

So that was that then, after all the years together, that was the end of it. I knew he wouldn't be back. What he had taken that day was all he had wanted. The boxes had somehow been meant to soften the blow. Some day I might go through them; for the moment, however, I imagine them to be a conman's ruse – a folly, stuffed with newspapers and bricks.

I move across the floorboards, stretching the width of this large house, smeared with years of paint and effort. There is something odd about the whole scene: the empty space, the dribbles of electric light from the bulbs hanging out of the rafters. The few carefully located props. And it occurs to me then, yes that's it, it reminds me of one of his paintings. I am walking through one of his paintings. All the more forlorn then, the dirty mug on an old kitchen chair in one corner; the twisted empty Marlboro packet on the floor; the can of Coke beside it, with one last cigarette butt squeezed out on its lid. And a tweed jacket humped over one of the boxes, the sight of which leaves me winded with grief.

I come back down, sit on the last step where I wallow awhile, bawling my eyes out. Then I stop, and begin to think about Nonna.

PART THREE

Bella

BORDIGHERA, 1933

July

UNDER THE AWNING OF Bordighera train station, Bella waits in the shade. Behind her a porter builds a small wall of luggage and she can hear the snail train potter off towards France. When she looks again the porter has disappeared without his tip, leaving an address tag pinned on the luggage: '*per Villa Lami, via Romano, Bordighera.*' All she needs now is a driver.

Outside the station, a row of heavy-headed ponies attached to carriages and traps; further along, noses to the shade, a quartet of vacant taxi cars. There's a chubby blue bus parked at an angle in the middle of the square. No sign of a driver in any case. No sign of life at all. Apart from the ponies and the devotion of flies all around them.

She stays for a while looking over the piazza, for a moment loses all sense of place. The buildings, ornate and often shabby, their fragile balconettes like strips of black lingerie. To the right, a group of squat palm trees. Over the way, more palms; longer, leaner, shaggier; big unruly heads gawking into the second-floor windows of a darkened *pensione*. A newspaper kiosk, boarded up. An ice-cream cart, abandoned. Four large flat-faced cacti growing from a trough just behind it. Like a queue of deformed children, she can't help but think. The café down the way is closed, chairs folded and decked against the wall.

Bella lifts her alligator bag from the rest of the luggage, crosses the piazza to a wall smeared with layers of scraped-off advertisements. Over a door a crucifix appears in an alcove, the face on the Christ gaudy with painted make-up. It hardly seems like a town on the Italian Riviera, a few miles from Monte Carlo or Nice. More like Mexico, she imagines. Or Cuba even. Some half-remembered place once seen in the dark of a picture house. Heat, dust, absence. The meandering snore of a swollen fly.

An avenue facing the station seems to offer the only way off the piazza. She pushes her eye up its considerable length, the slight dingy downturn that takes it to, and then over, a crossroads where it begins to widen and lift into the sunlight. It stretches on for a time, and only seems to stop at all because a large white hotel, backed up by a burly hillside, appears to be blocking its way. The air seems as if it might be cooler up there, the buildings and palazzi solid and clean like slabs of ice cream. There would be cafés with shaded terraces. People who spoke English probably. English people, even. Tall glasses of something cold and sweet. But she is too afraid of leaving the luggage unattended, of getting lost and being found some- where foolish, of missing someone who might this very moment be on the way to fetch her.

A double-faced clock stands on the corner of the crossroads. Bella checks her wristwatch and finds a different time by over an hour. She remembers the clock above the train station and, taking a backward glance, reads yet another time again. Somehow, she needs to know. She decides to go as far as the crossroads clock to consult its other face and there, caught between time and four corners, they find her.

The American cousins. Coming down the last few yards of the avenue. Equal height but different builds. One a little on the plump side. The other perhaps a bit scrawny. Two mousey-brown heads of hair, crimped to the ear. Four bare legs. The plumpish one sends down a wide overhead wave.

The thinner one, who at first appears to be carrying something, a baby or perhaps a small white dog, turns out to have her arm in a sling. Both dressed for tennis, even though the one with the trussed-up arm couldn't possibly have been playing.

The plump one says her name is Grace and insists on carrying the bag. 'They'll send the rest on up,' she says, clearly used to such matters taking care of themselves. Then, putting her arm through Bella's, she draws her over the crossroads, onto the avenue.

The other one is called Amelia. 'So how do you like Bordighera?' she asks. 'Seems a little sedate, wouldn't you say? Well, don't go fooling yourself, it's that time of day, the Italians snoring off lunch, the English on the beach, braising themselves to death. Just you wait another hour or so – see how sedate you think it is *then*.'

Bella, between the sisters, on an avenue that is proving steeper than expected, inclines her head from one to the other, smiles when it seems the right thing to do, finds herself frequently unsure of their accent, the speed of their delivery and their forthright manner (if they could really be saying what she thinks they are saying). They laugh quite a bit, particularly Grace. Sometimes Bella finds herself laughing along, without knowing quite why.

'Have you seen the Musso wallpaper?' Grace begins.

'I'm sorry – the which?'

'You know? Mussolini?' Amelia explains. 'Il Doo-che! You better get used to *him*, let me tell you. Radio, newspapers, movie reels, you name it, every which way your ears or eyes go – there's baldy old Ben-ee-toe. And as for the market place! His picture is pasted over every inch of wall, I swear it. Hardly a seam – wallpaper, practically. It's like a Mussolini parlour down there. I wouldn't mind if he was anything to look at, but he's rather awful – don't you agree, Miss Stuart? Don't you find him unattractive? By the way must we call you Miss Stuart?'

'Well, Aunt Lami would probably—' Grace begins.

'Oh God. Aunt Lami, let's not even think about *her*.'

Amelia carries on in a tired, distracted voice, turning her hips stiffly as she walks along, breaking here and there into a short sideways glide, like a coquettish child, Bella thinks, or maybe one of those new sporty-type film actresses. In fact the whole experience is beginning to remind her of the pictures, which is the closest, up to now, that she's ever been to Americans.

'She's not our real aunt of course,' Grace explains. 'The first wife, Aunt Josephine, was. Mother's sister – you know.'

'Quite a looker too,' Amelia says. 'You won't be surprised to hear. They met when old man Lami was staying in New York in one of Dad's hotels – Dad's an hotelier, you know. They fell in love, as the saying goes, and he took her back with him to Sicily.'

'Mother never forgave him,' Grace says, 'and then poor old Josie died.'

'Only gone five minutes,' her sister continues, 'when he took up with *numero due*. Well, the less said there… Except for this – I don't think she ought decide what we may or may not call each other. Wouldn't you agree? After all, we are not children. If my guess is right, we are all, in fact, a little older than our dear Aunt Lami. Worse luck. I certainly won't be asking you to refer to me as *Miss Nelson*! You've met Aunt Lami of course, in Sicily? And we'll be expecting a full and frank on *that*, let me tell you. Odd little item, isn't she? Of course, he's going to die soon. Wonder what'll happen to her then? For all we know he's gone already – was he still alive when you left? Would one notice at his age, I wonder? We would have had a wire if— at least one would hope they'd have the courtesy to wire if. Oh, please don't think I'm callous, I certainly hope you don't think that. It's just, well, we don't really know him. In fact, we don't know him at all.' Amelia finally stops and joins in with her sister in laughing like a horse.

Bella nods and smiles and tries not to look too bewildered. Around them the afternoon begins to stir. Shutters fall open on upper terraces. Out of dark interiors onto glaring pavements, shopkeepers cart baskets and crates. A waiter comes out of a restaurant rolling a tabletop like a wheel before him. Behind, in the doorway, an old lady sits, folding napkins and frantically smoking. Deanna Durbin coos out of a wireless. Bella notes the avenue is called corso d'Italia.

'You must forgive my sister.' Grace struggles to speak. 'She gets a little—'

'Overexcited? Overwrought? Over-easy?' Amelia suggests.

Grace exclaims, 'Oh now, that is en-*ough*.'

'You may as well know – it's why I'm in Europe,' Amelia continues. 'To calm my exhausted nerves.' She throws the back of her free hand up to her forehead and pretends to almost faint. 'Anyhow now that we've got my collarbone to worry about, my nerves are quite forgotten. Forty days, I'm told, before I can travel. These Italian doctors certainly know how to make something of nothing. Not even as far as Monte Carlo. I can't tell you what a bore it all is.'

'Pay no attention,' Grace insists. 'She just loves it here. You ought to know Amelia is this month's Bordighera Beach Miss. Oh yes, this is her actual title. In the afternoon the beach clubs hold pyjama party competitions – quite the hoot! My sister's picture? All over the wall of the Kursaal club. I mean, talk about il Duce! She is wearing this hat—'

'Oh, must you remind me!'

'Well, you were the one who entered, dear.'

'Now, that's only because I was drunk.'

'For which you only have yourself to blame.'

'Thank you, Grace, I am aware.'

On the corso. Lamps and trees in perfect alignment, the pavement tiled like an outdoor floor. There are English names over some of the shops: Good English Cakes. Real English Tea. And two French shops; one selling hats, the other artists' requisites. Outside the barber's, a poster shows this week's cinema attraction – *Detectivi Crek e Crok, Laurel e Holiver*.

'Now, had Aunt Lami's English doctor been here, my sentence may well have been lighter,' Amelia resumes, 'but he left a few weeks ago for Egypt. The English colony have to have their own doctor, you know – don't trust the Eye-ties – in fact they have to have their own just about everything:

church, clubs, shops. Frankly, I don't know why they don't just stay at home and turn up the central heating! Anyhow, the new English doc hasn't yet arrived. Unmarried too, or so it seems, with all his own teeth and hair by the way, so we can expect quite a stampede there! So now you have it, forty days, just like Jesus in the desert. Mother wants me home. Dad says it's best to stay, though he does have his concerns given the present political situation, I mean *anything* might happen at almost any moment – don't you agree?'

'Oh please,' Grace says. 'Please just let's not go into all that again – I swear, once she gets started on politics.'

'Oh Grace, really, everybody knows Europe is, well, in foul mood – is that a discreet way to put it? And anything *is* liable to happen. Except nobody wants to talk about it. So long as we all continue to pretend – we can continue to bask. And bask cheaply, at that. Oh, all right I'll stop. Not that Anabelle minds, I'm sure. It is Anabelle, right? Yes, I made it my business to find that out. Actually, I peeked at your papers when they arrived the other day. Or rather I peeked at the envelope with the official *Prefettura*'s stamp on.

'My papers?' Bella asks.

They pause outside the *tabaccheria* where a man softly sweating is cranking at the hinges of a canopy. He bows, mutters, '*Buona sera*,' and takes a long low look over the girls' bare legs. Both his greeting and his greedy eye go ignored or else unnoticed.

'Oh, you have to have papers for just about everything these days in Italy,' Amelia explains. 'Aunt Lami would have arranged it. You can't go to the ladies room without your precious *documenti*. Otherwise, whooooof, they kick you right out on your you-know-what.' Here Amelia lifts her leg into a high kick that almost makes her fall over and Bella is sure she hears the tobacconist gasp.

She feels the squeeze and pull of Grace's linking arm, the nudge of her elbow. Her mouth, wide with laughter, releases a smell of something warm and eggy, which Bella tries not to taste. Unlinking her arm and falling back slightly, she pretends to fix her shoe. When she catches up with the girls, arms folded firmly to her chest, they are still howling loudly. She is beginning to wonder if they've had a few drinks.

They near the top of the *corso*. Real fruit trees on the street! Bella wishes she was alone. She looks up to see clutches of small soft oranges. Over a wall, a swag of beady green olives. On the corner two men dressed in black fascist uniform gossip like housewives, and fuss at intervals over a little girl with Shirley Temple hair. She can see now the large white hotel recede and a street begin to open out on the perpendicular: via Romano. An open-top tram edges across it, a woman on its upper deck, holding a black umbrella against the sun.

Tall, narrow gates between pillars. The pillars topped with an urn of chipped stone grapes. A short pebble path to a few curved steps to a front door. The house, the colour of ivory with shutters of glossy green, set at an angle, making it look slightly askew, as if it has come off its thread. A comfortable garden, trees, bushes, and the same cerise blossoms that appeared to have been flung at random all over Bordighera. High stone boundary walls. One shouldering a lane which runs back down towards the sea and the town centre. A layer of trees just inside the walls: olives, figs, chestnuts, the – already by now – inevitable palms. A solid three-storey seaside villa. Nowhere near as grand as the house in Sicily. Far grander than anything she's ever been used to. Bella crosses the gate into Villa Lami.

On the way in Grace leans through the open front door and bowls the alligator bag across the polished floor of the hallway. Then she comes back down the front steps to order tea, which she does by shouting through a low window around the side of the house at somebody named Elida. A few minutes later a tray is passed through.

There is a well-positioned table in its own patch of shade near to the front of the house, marked out by vases of cacti and mandarin. But the cousins head off in the opposite direction, Amelia leading, Grace carrying the tray, away from the house, down a bumpy slope, towards the bottom of the garden. Wild roses and broom. A sudden curved wall of bamboo. A recurring glimpse of a building through the trees as they approach the back boundary wall – a garage with living quarters above; outdoor iron steps at the side. A few feet away from it Bella asks, 'Who lives there?'

Amelia turns with a silent 'shhhh'.

Bella notices then the chime of the tea tray in Grace's hands and that for the past few moments neither cousin has uttered a squeak.

Now in the lower garden, the wrought-iron table shows etches of rust, and on the ground a chain gang of ants traipses across the droppings from a former meal. A book has been left out to rot in the grass, and on a windowsill a dirty glass holds a slurry of rain-soaked cigarette butts. Bella asks after Alessandro and is told he is playing tennis at the club. She asks what time he is expected home and is given a shrug and a change of subject. She asks what time dinner will be, and she is told, 'It all depends.'

No sooner seated at the rusty table than nothing will do Amelia but wine. 'Oh, you must forgive us – what can we have been thinking of!' she declares, as if Bella has already made a strong complaint on the matter. 'Tea? Forget it! It's wine we need, to celebrate your arrival. To celebrate new friendship. Prosecco I think would be most appropriate. Wouldn't you agree? It's not champagne of course, but so what? Back home it's against the law to drink alcohol – you've heard of Prohibition, right? Much too embarrassing to even discuss. It's quite the novelty to be able to drink here. Well, without looking over one's shoulder anyhow. Prosecco is easily my favourite – what do you say, Anabelle?'

Bella says nothing.

Grace waits a moment and then: 'It's probably a little early, dear. Oughtn't we at least finish having our tea?'

The garden, the short clips of the villa she's managed to spot on the way, the haphazard routine of the household, all lack the pull of Signora Lami's domestic rein, so apparent in the house in Sicily. It isn't a question of neglect as such, Bella decides, more a sense of carelessness. Like a household run by grown-up children. She is beginning to see what the Signora had meant in her letter, by her son 'needing structure to his day'. And Bella feels easier in herself somehow, leaning back in her chair and looking around. At least now she has a function; a right to be here.

Overhead an umbrella of broad-leaved foliage, a scent on the air; deep, sweet. She thinks – almonds, a touch of thyme. She watches Grace chatter and serve, she watches Amelia smoke and sulk and gulp her tea.

A short while later Bella looks up to see a woman appear through the clearing. Her large frame – black hair, black clothes – pours like ink over a bright spread of mimosa. There is a basket of washing in her huge hands and she is walking in their direction, shouting. But her voice, which seems way too old and laboured for her big fresh face, is aimed somewhere above and beyond.

'Ah, Elida,' Amelia begins, the second she sees her. 'Now. Thank goodness. What we need here is some wine, for Signora Stuart, you understand, to welcome her – *Pro-secco*. Chilled, of course. I happened to notice a hefty box of ice was delivered today and took the precaution of storing a bottle or two inside – don't thank me, ladies, you're welcome. And so *Pro-sec-co*. *Per favore*. Please. *Grazie*. And *pre-go!*'

Elida doesn't acknowledge the cousins in any way, although she does allow Bella a little curtsey, and a laryngitic '*Signora*' before moving on, even as Amelia is still addressing her.

Grace begins to snort into her hand. Her sister, leaning back in her chair, continues to call. 'Elida? *Prosecco?*' But Elida has already disappeared. 'Well, I like that! Was she making a point of *ignoring* me?' Amelia asks, laughing at the idea. 'My God, that woman. Insufferable. Do you know what we call her? Queen Kong – that's what.'

Then they are off again, chattering, screeching. Telling Bella things she has no business knowing, things she can't help wanting to hear.

The music turns everything. Notes from a piano falling slow and cold, like first snow. There is something acrobatic about it, a touch of the circus ring anyhow, and for a moment she thinks it could be a piece by Debussy, although it turns out to be neither amenable nor decisive enough for that.

It silences the American cousins anyway. It lures other sounds out into the open. A water tap running in a nearby garden; a motorcycle lowing on the street outside. Crickets, birds, insects. She can hear them all now. The sip of tea on Grace's bulbous lips; the fidget of Amelia's fingers on the sail of her arm sling. And the notes, dripping through the overhang; individual, abstract, each one perfectly formed and independent of the other. Each one desperate to reach the one that went before it, to escape the one coming from behind.

'Who was that?' Bella asks when it stops.

'That? Oh, that was the English maestro. Edward King,' Grace says, glancing at her sister.

When Elida comes up from the rear of the garden, she is swinging the empty washing basket in her hand. She resumes shouting, pitching and forcing her voice, head lifted towards the place where the music has been playing. Her words struggle and crack as if they are crumbling in her throat. Bella feels like standing up and shouting on her behalf, whatever it is Elida seems to want to shout so much.

'*Maestro? Maestro? Aspetta Alesso.*'

After a moment a man's voice comes back. '*Arrivo,*' it says. '*Arrivo subito. Elida, cara mia. Arrivo. Arrivo. Arrivo!*'

When Elida passes again, she is smiling.

*

She leaves them in the garden, the cold sweat running off their bottle of Prosecco which, in the end, Amelia has to fetch herself. Grace doesn't appear to mind too much. Amelia, on the other hand, seems to take it almost personally.

'I should really be going,' Bella says, closing her hand like a lid over her barely touched glass.

'Don't you like it?'

'Oh yes. It's lovely, really. But I'd like to meet Alessandro.'

'Oh, don't worry about him. He's at tennis, I told you.'

'Yes, but still.'

'Grace – will you please explain? Edward will be going to pick him up soon. Unless he's gone already – has he? I mean I didn't notice him come out, or anything – did you?'

'He most likely went the other way. That door in the back wall? Well, it's been fixed up.'

'Oh? You never said.'

'Was I supposed to?'

'Of course not.' She glares at her sister for a moment, then returns to Bella. 'Where was I? Yes, they almost always stop for ice cream. They may even go and listen to a band on the promenade, they often do. Could be at least an hour. More. You've got plenty of time. We can all have a cosy dinner later on together, you'll meet him then. Edward too. He won't go anywhere without Edward by the way, except to his precious tennis lesson. Why not relax, help yourself to a cigarette.' A box of Turkish gold-tipped is pushed across the table.

'I don't smoke.'

'Goodness – but how you do show us up!' Amelia pulls the box of cigarettes back and redirects the neck of the bottle from her own glass to Grace's, then back again.

Grace says, 'Of course, we understand if you'd prefer to freshen up, Anabelle. You must be quite exhausted. All that travelling! Would you like me to go with?'

'No, please stay. I'll find my own way. I need a rest, and to unpack of course before Alessandro—'

'Well, if you're sure that's what you want. But you know Amelia is quite right. They do take their time coming home. Edward prefers to walk now, while the Italians are taking their *passeggiata* – which is what they call this before-a-dinner walk thing they do, in case you don't know. The English tend to come out a little later and he says they give him a headache with their constant twittering. Isn't that amusing, not to say a little unpatriotic?'

Amelia looks up. 'He said that? When did he say that?'

'Oh, he mentioned it to me once.'

'Really?'

Bella begins to rise from her chair. 'Just the same. I should… First day and all that.'

'And all *that*,' Amelia sneers, her eye following the latest surge of Prosecco expanding in her glass. 'By the way, he's called Alec.'

'I'm sorry – who is?' Bella asks. She waits for Amelia to take another pull of her cigarette.

'His mother prefers if we call him Alec. Not Alessandro, which she thinks an ugly name. And I must say, I quite agree. He's called Alec. Al-ec. Not Alessandro.'

'Oh. I didn't know.'

'Well, you do now, Miss Stuart.'

*

Whatever he is called, he's a beautiful child. Much more striking than the photographs in Sicily had allowed. And yet if she were to attempt to write his face into words, it would make for plain reading. Eyes: smallish and slanted, an unusual turquoise colour. Mouth: full, the top lip having a lift to it, shows the first squeeze of grown-up teeth through his gums. Hair: dark blond, thick and all over the place, despite the obvious efforts that have been made to control it. Face: full, cheeks pinkish, dashed with tiny freckles; skin lightly tanned. He might have been just another cute little boy. Except for his eyes. They are not the eyes of a child, but they are what make him beautiful.

By the time she gets to meet him it's past eight o'clock. He is waiting for her on the terrace just off a room Elida had called the library, although apart from an atlas, a few French fashion magazines and an ancient German–Italian dictionary, there is little to merit the description. It's across the way from Bella's bedroom, which is a manageable rather than small room, with a good window seat, an accessible English bed and practical furniture. There is also a small balcony with a view over the less-tended side of the garden.

The library, by contrast, is a large, silent room of polished wood and honey-coloured walls. Light comes down from three high windows. More light falls in by the large balustraded terrace. The furniture is of a high, if incompatible quality, as if over the years the room has been used as a last resort for unwanted pieces. It gives it the look of a bric-a-brac shop. Around the walls, hideous oil paintings: bug-eyed women in eighteenth-century dress, men with long wigs and improbable chins. Bella likes it in here. She likes the shape and the sense of space, the parquet floor that seems to suck in, then dribble out, reflections from all quarters. And she likes especially the brand new Philips wireless set in the corner – the single nod to the modern world.

'The library,' Elida hoarsely announces. 'Here is the room of the work. Your room with Alesso.'

'Thank you, Elida, that's lovely.'

'Only for you and Alesso.'

'Yes, I understand.'

'And for I also too. And Rosa.'

'For you also?'

'In the English lesson.'

'Am I to teach you English, Elida?'

'Yes, the Signora is say it. And Rosa.'

'Oh? She never mentioned it to me.'

'The Signora is say it,' Elida repeats, this time a little defensively.

'Of course, I'd be delighted.'

'Not for the misses. This room.'

'The misses?'

'The misses America. Not for them.'

Alec is holding a view of the sea on his shoulders; the blue grey light of an endless twilight. Behind him the dark outline of a fisherman's church, and beyond that a headland jutting into the sea. She can see the

107

flicker of citronella candles along the shelf of the balustrade, down in the garden, on the terraces and windowsills of the houses below. She can taste it, as the mosquitoes might taste it, sourly on the air.

He is dressed in a formal little man's suit of white linen, a soft white cap which he removes as soon as he sees her, the hair beneath popping on release, his eyebrows and eyes lifting as if to follow the course of each tuft. Later she will recognize this as the moment, the gesture, that made her love this little boy.

Bella holds out her hand to him; he looks at it warily, then nods.

'*Piacere,*' she says, returning the nod. She notices his eyelids flutter. '*Mi chiamo Signora Stuart.*'

He is staring at her, or through her, a funny expression in his eye. What they are expressing Bella couldn't guess. Arrogance, she thinks one moment, shyness the next, a mixture of both it seems to her then. Maybe he is just being inquisitive. She wishes he'd at least say something.

'*Sono di Londra, Inghilterra,*' she continues.

He looks down at his feet.

She is slightly irked to find herself so unnerved by this six-year-old child, with his formal, if not necessarily good manners. Somewhere in the back of her mind there is a stored snippet of advice: an ignored child will eventually come around. She decides to pay no attention to him, to act as if all is exactly as it should be. She walks over to the balustrade and, pulling in an appreciative breath of evening air, gestures at the view, which is fast filling up with an absurdly extravagant sunset of saffron and rose. '*Che bella questa vista – è vero?*'

He winces.

'*Non è vero?*' she persists.

He opens his mouth as if he is going to say something but almost at once closes it again.

She turns her back to him and waits. Soon it will be dark. Specks of electric light are already breaking out, down the hillside, over the town and in a carnival string along the part of the seafront which is visible from here. A tornado of evening starlings against the horizon fall in and out of formation. From the palm trees, fingers of shadow across one corner of the terrace. She can hear them fidget and wag.

When she turns to look at him again his left leg is trembling. The poor child is making strange with her – that's what it is. Bella wants to put her arms around him or to reassure him in some way, but anytime she even looks as if she might step in his direction, he recoils. It must be the accent, she decides then. The child can't understand what she's saying. Of course! She must put more into her accent.

'Alessandro?' she begins, pressing and rolling the syllables while rehearsing a few apt sentences in her head, along the lines of – *I am your friend. I will not harm you. Please do not be nervous.* She hunkers down to him, places her hands gently on the top of his arms and looks at him, this time using the name Elida had used. '*Alesso, senti. Sono la tua amica e spero che—*'

She feels him stiffen in her hands. His eyelids quiver for a moment and his eyeballs roll white. Bella, with a slight shock, releases him. Then he speaks. 'We are not permitted to speak Italian here, Signora,' he says, with the slightest stammer. 'O-only English.'

His words are stern but his young boy's delicate voice takes the chill out of them. She almost laughs in his face.

'Oh yes, of course. I apologize,' she says, straightening up and taking a step back.

'Mamma says.'

'Indeed.'

'I do speak very good Italian.'

'Well, of course.'

'To P-Papa sometimes. And the men in the tennis factory for making the rackets.'

'Yes, I see. The men in the tennis—'

'And the people in the town. But not the English ones.'

'No. I suppose not.'

'When I write to P-Papa it's English although… Italian sometimes. And always English for Maestro Edward because…'

'Yes. Yes, that's perfectly all right. I understand. Completely. And you speak English very well indeed – Alec. Is that what you would prefer me to call you – Alec?'

He makes a gesture, half nod and half shrug. Then his eyes take another alarming flip.

Bella decides to concentrate only on keeping the conversation in motion. 'I have just come from your Mamma in Sicily. It's very warm there.'

'Yes, Signora.'

'Too warm for you, I understand? Me too, I must say. Much better here. Although still very warm compared to where I live. I've come all the way from London, you know. In England. Queen Victoria was an English queen; she stayed here, I believe, in the hotel down the road. You must show it to me one day. Yes. But of course she's dead now. Now her son is the king. His name is George.'

'Yes, Signora.'

'Yes. Well, anyway. Alec, I just want to say, to you, that I hope we will be friends. Good friends. Very good friends indeed. In fact—'

'Only the servants speak Italian here,' he says.

Before she has a chance to answer him, he is walking away.

Bella feels she should say something. At least leave some mark of authority on their first meeting. Have the last word then, if nothing else. But there is Elida suddenly in the doorway, a huge tray in her hands.

Bella calls after him. 'Alec? One moment please, if you don't mind, I'm not quite…'

There is no response until Elida, turning her head slightly, sends a hoarse bark over her shoulder.

He comes back at once, and stands before Bella, one foot turned slightly in.

'Have you eaten yet, Alec?'

'I had dinner with Maestro Edward.'

'Here? You had dinner *here*?'

'No. At Damilano's in town. Maestro Edward said we should leave you to my cousins.'

'I see.'

'But then we saw them on the terrace of Bar Atu with the other Americans and they say they are having dinner later in the casino.'

Elida steps forward with her tray. 'Signora. I have for you. You want in the dining room or here is good?'

'Thank you, Elida. Here will be fine. Very well. Goodnight, Alec.'

'Goodnight, Signora.'

'Please come and see me after breakfast in the morning.'

He bows again and starts for the door.

'Yes, Alec, because you know tomorrow we must start lessons.'

'Yes, Signora.'

'Very well, you may go now,' she says, even though he is already well past Elida and halfway down the landing.

*

Tomorrow comes and Bella waits. After breakfast, after lunch, and still no show from Alec. Elida delivers her meals to the library without being asked to, but it suits Bella well enough not to have to deal with the American cousins. Or to have to acknowledge in any manner the way they sneaked out to dinner the night before without a word. A slight, no doubt intended, but one she hadn't felt at all. She had woken just before dawn to the racket of their drunken homecoming, and although she hadn't been able to make out what they were saying, Bella felt sure she had been the butt of all that hooting and neighing out in the garden, in the hallway and a little later on the stairs.

Some time after lunch, when Bella finally hears them go out – this time with a conspicuous absence of laughter or chat – she comes downstairs in search of Alec. He is in the kitchen with Elida, the two of them chatting away in Italian. Elida shelling beans from curly pink-mottled pods, Alec low to the table, drawing into a copybook. Behind them a young girl bent over a trough-like sink is belligerently scrubbing pots.

He jumps up when he sees her, making Bella feel she should rise to the occasion, and so, adapting a tone from a long-ago teacher that she can only hope sounds convincing, she proceeds: 'Alec? I thought we agreed to meet after breakfast?'

'Yes, Signora.' He pushes his chair away with the back of his legs. Face soft and red, eye evasive, he stretches over and closes the cover of his book, then starts to vigorously scratch the back of his head.

Elida, as if she too is being scolded, rises and, taking the bowl of beans from the table, moves out of the kitchen towards the pantry, tipping the girl at the sink with her elbow as she passes. The girl starts, gives a little grunt, then, pressing her wet hands down the front of her greasy pinny, slips out after Elida.

'Well, Alec – what have you to say for yourself?'

'After breakfast I play tennis.'

'Tennis?'

'Yes, Signora. I have a lesson with the tennis coach but sometimes in the afternoon I play with the Maestro.'

'I waited for you all morning, Alec.'

'Yes, Signora.'

Bella is aware of Elida and the girl cowering in the pantry. She can hear a wet recurrent sniff from the girl's nose and the occasional furtive ping of a bean dropping into the bowl.

'Come with me please, Alec. We need to speak about this.' He follows her into the hall. 'What time do you finish tennis?'

'At eleven.'

'Very well. I want you in future to come to me straight after tennis. Shall we say half past eleven?'

'Yes, Signora.'

'Good.'

'Except.'

'Except what, Alec?'

'I don't arrive home till midday.'

'All right, midday then – is that agreed?'

'Yes, Signora. But—'

'But what?'

'Lunch is at midday.'

'Oh yes, of course. Well after lunch then.'

'Yes, Signora. But after lunch I have to rest.'

'To rest?'

'Yes, all children in Italy have a rest in the afternoon. And because I have asthma Mamma says I must never forget it. Or I could die at once.'

'At once? Well, we certainly wouldn't want that. And what time do you finish your rest?'

'At half past three.'

'In fact you should be probably having it now this minute?'

'Yes, Signora.'

'This afternoon, at half past three, the moment your rest is over, I want to see you in the library. Do you understand me?'

'Yes, Signora. But I have to ask Maestro Edward.'

'Alec, we must fit our lessons in. That's why I am here.'

'I have to ask Maestro Edward.'

'Why?'

'Because we have piano lessons.'

'Every day?'

'Always. After my rest.'

'Well, when do you have your other classes – you know, arithmetic, that sort of thing?'

'It depends.'

'On what does it depend, Alec?'

'When the private tutor, he can come.'

Bella walks away from him across the hall to the open front door. She stays for a moment looking out into the afternoon silence through a gauze of yellow heat. 'When does he come, this private tutor?'

'It depends, Signora.'

'On what, Alec?'

'If he is busy in the public school or with the other private pupils.'

'Other private pupils?'

'In Italy there are many private pupils.'

'They don't go to school?'

'Only for exams and later to look for the results on the wall to see if they are promoted to the next class.'

'I see. Well, what does he teach you, this tutor?'

'English and classics and history and geography and arithmetic and military and—'

'I'll just have to have a word with him then – what's his name?'

'He doesn't speak English, Signora.'

'I thought you just said he teaches you English?' she says, coming back to Alec who is standing like a little statue at the bottom of the stairs.

'Yes, but he doesn't speak it.'

'Well how? Oh never mind. Look, I want you to come to me straight after piano this afternoon. I'll speak to Maestro Edward. We must set out a timetable. Do you know what a timetable is, Alec?'

He mulls this over for a moment. 'I know what a table is. And I know what time is.'

'Are you making fun of me, Alec?' she asks, rather hoping he is.

'No, Signora,' he says and begins scratching his head again.

'*Un orario*.'

'Yes, that means a timetable, definitely,' he agrees.

'You better run along now and have your rest. Go on. Oh! I almost forgot, I have something for you from Sicily.'

'You brought *me* something?' he asks, his eyes brightening and making her regret that she hadn't thought to bring some little toy or trinket.

'I'm afraid it's not from me. It's from the housekeeper, in Sicily.'

114

Suddenly he is a different child, hopping on and off the first stair, face flushed and urgent, voice aching with the sort of emotion that could easily turn to tears. 'Nollie? Nollie sent me something? My nature books! Is it? Is it?'

'Well, it certainly feels like notebooks. I didn't open it of course, but—'

'Did she show them to Papa? Did he write something in? Did he? Did he?'

'I don't know, Alec. She didn't say.'

'How many did she send for me? I will need many for here, for all the different things in Bordighera to draw for my Papa.'

'Calm down, Alec. Why don't we go up to the library and open your parcel and see?'

'But I must have more crayons, Signora. Because I have to fill the book with pictures for Papa. And pencils for writing the informations. The crayons now are not good, Signora. Only this size.' He makes a pinch of his fingers and, bringing them close to his eyes, squints.

'That small? Oh dear,' Bella tuts.

'The green is no more. And no black left in the box because when you colour the palm trees mostly is green and black and some brown but I have a little brown left because I yellowed the sand. But then I need more yellow because sometimes the sky—'

'Alec, Alec? Stop – don't worry. We'll get your new crayons for you. We'll get a whole new box of them just to be on the safe side. You can show me where to go. We can go together. Would that be a good idea?'

He nods a few times, smiling into her eyes in a way that makes her think: I have you now, my boy.

As they start up the stairs, she holds out her hand for his. He turns his face away, shakes his head fiercely and, placing one hand on the banister, stuffs the other into his pocket.

Then Edward.

Alec sees him first, dropping his head back to look up through the

115

stairwell, roaring out at the top of his voice, 'Maestro! Maestro! Nollie is sent the books. She is sent them. You are right.'

Bella looks up and there is Edward, leaning over a banister at the top of the house. 'Good news. Glad to hear it. But, Nollie *has* sent them. Nollie *has.*' He casts down a friendly half nod, a sort of a wave. 'And you must be Miss Stuart – shall I come down or are you—?'

'We're on our way up, actually.'

She waits on the return outside the library, Edward coming down the top flight of stairs, Alec charging up to meet him halfway, ranting away about Nollie and his crayons and his parcel from Sicily. Edward takes the stairs slowly, pausing to make an occasional curt remark over the din. 'That's quite enough now. Control yourself, there's a good chap. We are none of us deaf, if you don't mind.' He has a clipped English accent.

She tries not to look at him until he is standing in front of her offering his smooth long-fingered hand. Fortyish, she thinks. Maybe a bit younger. A little aloof. Stern. Perhaps even cold. A bit of a martinet maybe. Attractive enough – which might explain what the American cousins see in him. But not the child.

'I was coming to look for you,' she says. 'We've been trying to sort out a timetable.'

'I know you have, Miss Stuart. I couldn't help overhearing.'

'We are having a little difficulty getting organized, I'm afraid.'

'Just to say, Miss Stuart, what you've been told about the private tutor is true – not a word of English, never turns up anyway and really is a most terrible teacher when he does. I believe the Signora is hoping you'll be his replacement? I'm to arrange it, books, curriculum and so on – that's if you don't mind – he needs to pass exams in October, otherwise he won't be promoted. He has just failed his June exams, and rather spectacularly at that.'

'I see.'

'The system is a little complicated for private pupils but you'll get the hang of it. Also there is a further curriculum which Signora Lami herself has devised, as she feels the state education lacks in some quarters. Now, as to what he says about the piano lessons – completely untrue. I'm much more flexible than he makes out, as is his tennis coach. It's the Italian in him, he can't help it. If he's not ducking and dodging work, he's blaming the other chap. He is your typical *furbo* – if you are familiar with the term?'

'I'm not.'

'Don't worry, you will be.'

'I see.'

'Now, if you'll excuse me, Miss Stuart, I have something rather urgent I really must attend to. Nice to have met you.'

'Yes,' Bella says. 'And you.'

'Oh, and apologies for last night. Dinner – well, it was a misunderstanding on my part.'

'Please, don't worry.'

'However, we are available tonight. Half past seven suit?'

'Yes, fine.'

'I should warn you the Nelson sisters won't be joining us – a dance in San Remo, I believe. So there will only be myself and Alec for company, I'm afraid.'

'Oh, I think I can bear that.'

'Bear which, Miss Stuart – our company? Or the absence of the sisters?'

She thinks there might be a glint in his eye, and almost laughs, but decides on second thoughts not to risk it.

A few minutes later Bella, from a landing window at the opposite side of the house, spots Alec and Edward down in the garden. Alec, with the parcel under his arm, is tugging at Edward's jacket and appears to be earnestly explaining himself. Edward nods in response. So much for his urgent errand and so much for Alec's afternoon rest, she thinks. She is about to leave the window when Edward suddenly pounces on Alec and picks him up. Then he abruptly turns him upside down, letting him slip through his hands with a jolt before catching him by the ankles and

117

starting back towards the house, the child dangling close to the ground, the parcel falling out of his grip onto the grass. She can see Alec's open mouth, his eyes disappear up into his forehead, his hair like a hedge falling off his crown. Bella opens the window slightly and moves to the side where they can't see her. She listens to Edward laughing down into his chest, Alec screaming with joy.

'So you can't find any time for your lessons, eh?' Edward is shouting.

'No!'

'And you say you've looked everywhere, have turned the place upside down, in fact?'

'Yes!'

'So, now you're upside down yourself – what about that then?'

'Nooo,' Alec roared.

'Are you sure you've been looking properly?'

'Yes!'

'Have you looked in the grass?'

'Yes! There's nothing.'

'Not even an hour or two?'

'No!'

'A few minutes then?'

She takes a peek out and now he is swinging the boy, like a pendulum.

'Any luck yet?'

'No! Maestro, *noooo*.'

He swings him harder. 'Oh, come on now, you can't be serious, there must be some time, somewhere down there.'

'Yes… I find it. *L'ho trovato, l'ho trovato*.'

'*Bravo. Allora – uno, due, tre*.' Edward turns Alec the right way up, and lets him slide down on the ground. 'You will make out a timetable with your woman – what's she called? Miss Stuart – anyway she sees fit. Is that understood?'

Alec gives a slight stagger and breathlessly laughs. 'Yes, Maestro.'

'And we will work our piano lessons to suit that timetable?'

'Yes.'

'And you will not use your asthma as an excuse again. Especially as it's the wrong season for it. At least wait till September to chance it. *D'accordo?*'

'*Sì, d'accordo.*'

'*Bene. Bravo.* Now come on, what are we waiting for? Let's rip open the parcel and see what Nollie has sent.'

*

A few weeks later, Signor Lami is dead. Bella is the first to be informed, a privilege which surprises her, as much as it irritates the American cousins.

She is out on the terrace with Alec, one as bored as the other as they struggle with Signora Lami's supplementary and somewhat random curriculum. Today's suggestion in her Topic for Vocabulary Expansion Programme is the architecture of Sir Christopher Wren. Born in 1632. Son of the Dean of Windsor. Built St Paul's – after twenty minutes over a fat old-fashioned textbook stinking of book must, this is about all they've been able to establish.

The instant she hears Elida's croak – '*Signora Stu-arteh, al telefono, prego*', – coming up from the garden, Bella knows it has to be bad news. But she presumes it will be for her. My father, she thinks. In the time it takes her to go down the corridor, the three flights of stairs, she has forgiven him everything. He is dead, she keeps thinking all the way. My father is dead. That's all.

As she comes in sight of the telephone table, she slows up her step and begins to consider. But supposing he's not dead? Supposing he is merely ill, infirm even? What then – back to Chelsea? To be his nurse? She realizes then that she does not want to leave Alec. Nor this house, nor Bordighera. She does not want to leave Elida or Rosa the daily help who has started to become her friend. Nor the deaf mute kitchen maid with her constant head cold and violent mannerisms. Nor Cesare, the bandy gardener with his halitosis breath. Not even the American cousins, who have in their own peculiar way been keeping her entertained, or at least on her toes. Nor Edward. All of those people, who after a few short weeks have made her feel more at home than she has ever done in Chelsea or even as a child in Dublin. She does not want to go back to London to nurse a stranger.

But it isn't her father's housekeeper on the phone, nor, for that matter, Mrs Jenkins. Not even his secretary or one of his hospital colleagues.

'Signora Lami? Have you bad news for me?' Bella asks, surprised to hear her employer's voice, but still convinced that the news has come from London via Palermo.

The Signora is to the point. 'My husband is dead.'

'Your husband?'

'In fact. This morning.'

'Oh I see. Of course. Your husband. I'm very sorry to hear it.'

'Thank you. Now, Miss Stuart, I'm afraid I will have to ask you to give the news to Alec. I don't think he should hear it on the telephone and it would not be good for him to come all the way to Sicily expecting to see his father alive and then to see him not so, but quite dead in a coffin. To arrive to a father's funeral – a terrible thing for a boy. So. If you wouldn't mind?'

'*Me?* You want *me* to?'

'Yes. Unless you think it would be appropriate to wait until you arrive here? Then I could tell him in person, I suppose. But how would you feel about that, Signora Stuart, the journey here, Alec looking forward so to seeing his father, talking about him all the way, on the train, on the ship, in the car. How would you honestly feel?'

'Well, I don't know what to say to you, Signora Lami.'

'The funeral will be in a few days. So it would be best if you start as soon as possible. I apologize that I am not in a position to organize your schedule – you will have to make your own details, I'm afraid.'

'Please. Think nothing of it.'

'When you board the ship at Genoa you may ask the purser to send a telegram and Pino will meet you in Palermo. But? Very well. Perhaps?'

'Yes, Signora Lami?'

'Perhaps I *should* prepare him. But it would mean asking you to look after his grief on the journey.'

'Yes. Of course. I will do that, of course.'

There is silence for a moment, then the Signora speaks again. 'I have made my decision now, Signora Stuart. I will tell him myself. I'm quite sure that's the right thing to do.'

'Yes, Signora Lami, of course. He's in the library, I'll just go and—' But when she turns around Alec is standing behind her. Bella holds the receiver towards him. 'Your Mamma wants to speak to you, Alec.'

He takes the phone slowly and looks into Bella's eyes as he speaks to his mother. 'Hello, Mamma... I'm very well, Mamma... Yes, I can be brave... Yes, Mamma, I'm listening.'

His eyes bulge with tears. His bottom lip begins to give. She sees his leg shake and the tic she had noticed the first evening begin to jitter on his eyelid. Bella steps nearer. He turns his back sharply on her and begins pushing his voice down into the receiver.

'No, Mamma. I want Edward... Mamma please, yes, I know she is. I do. But—'

Bella moves out to the front steps. Elida has come round from the kitchen garden, a bouquet of basil held to her stomach, the green juices staining the grip of her fingers. They look at each other, then Elida, bowing her head, makes a sign of the cross. The echo in the hall lifts Alec's whisper. They can hear him inside pleading, crying – heartbreakingly trying to do neither. Bella knows he is worried about hurting her feelings or indeed disappointing her in some way because he would prefer Edward to go with him. If only the poor child knew how glad she would be not to have to go all the way back to Sicily.

By now Amelia and Grace have turned up, in their large foolish hats, backless tops and wide-legged trousers which they called pants, flapping like banners anytime they take a few steps.

'What's happened?' Amelia asks. 'Oh my God – is it?'

Alec comes out to the steps. He lifts his sleeve to wipe his eyes, then leaves it there to cover his face. 'Mamma wants to speak to you.'

'To me, dear?' Grace asks.

He shakes his head behind his arm.

'To me then?' Amelia suggests.

'To Signora Stuart.'

'To Signora Stuart?' Amelia repeats.

Alec nods and Grace moves to put her arm around him. 'Poor old Alec,' she says. 'Poor little sausage.'

'I am not a sausage,' he shouts, elbowing her out of the way, then running down the steps through the garden towards Edward's mews.

When Bella picks up the receiver the Signora is already speaking. 'And so in this case Edward may take him.'

'Yes, Signora Lami.'

'I think it will make much more sense. In fact I've decided now that would be best. Will you make the necessary arrangements, Miss Stuart? And please write everything down carefully, in case Edward forgets. May I please ask you to at least do that?'

*

Grace goes with them to the funeral in Sicily. Invited or not – Bella doesn't know, nor does she ask. 'It has,' Grace says, 'been decided that the Nelson family really ought to be represented and as such a journey is obviously out of the question for poor, indisposed Amelia, naturally, it falls upon me.'

A last-minute announcement, leaving time for neither discussion nor deterrent, Grace simply arrives in the hall with her baggage just as Edward and Alec are about to leave for the station. Clearly disgusted to be left behind, poor, indisposed Amelia decides not to come along to the station to see them off, 'seeing as how I'm such an invalid and all'. Then she huffs off to her room.

Alec seems to be holding up well enough, although his face is so pale the freckles seem to hover over rather than rest upon his skin. All morning he has been complaining of feeling cold, in spite of a heat so solid you could take a bite out of it, and in the end Bella has to put a coat on him. At the station Edward goes to buy the tickets, and Grace goes to buy a magazine and 'candies'. Bella steers Alec into the waiting room.

There is only one other person inside, a middle-aged woman fussily knitting in the corner. Bella, without quite knowing how, instantly identifies her as one of the dotty English brigade. Or 'the English Dots', as Edward calls them. She sits on the far end of the bench. Alec, kneeling on the opposite bench, begins to study a poster on the wall. The poster is for the *Balilla*, an organization for boys which, as far as Bella can make out, involves uniforms, badge-earning and outdoor adventure. Not unlike Powell's Boy Scout Movement in fact, except the Italian version seems to demand constant praise and gratitude to Mussolini. *I Figli della Lupa*, or the sons of the she-wolf, advertised here look to be about the same age as Alec. A camping holiday is to take place next month, enrolling in a few days' time at the Casa Fascista. Anyone who loves their country as much as they love their Duce is invited to enrol with the squadron leader.

She watches as Alec traces one finger over the outline of each boy, as if he were drawing them, their faces and hands, the pots and pans sticking out of their knapsacks, the cleavage of a lake between two mountains behind them, the tepee of sticks blazing in the campfire to one side. He is bored, she thinks. He should have more to occupy his life than Christopher Wren and tennis with ageing ex-pats. Worse, he is lonely. He should have friends his own age. Proper company. Not just Edward and Elida and me.

Out on the platform, two men are easing a floral tribute up against a wall. It is jammed with scarlet chrysanthemums and is as big as a tractor wheel. Another hefty garland appears at the waiting-room door, a man's voice behind it shouting, '*Permesso*.'

It passes right under her nose, the destination clearly marked on a label trimmed with black ribbon, along with Signor Lami's name, many titles and honours. A third tribute in the shape of a globe brushes the outside window. The woman knitting in the corner sighs. 'This country.'

'I'm sorry?' Bella says.

'Everything has to be an exaggeration. I mean, *everything*. Even death. Honestly!' she finishes with a roll of her eyes.

The waiting room starts to fill up. An old woman first, dressed in a black serge suit and a black silk turban hat. Tall and thin as an anchovy, a gold-tipped walking stick in her hand which glints and taps over to Alec. The woman speaks slowly, her words stretched and dry, so Bella can translate almost every one of them. She says she can remember Alec's grandmother. Remember, in fact, when his grandfather built the villa on via Romano in her honour and name: Marcia Lami. A wonderful woman. Beautiful inside and out. A personal friend of the late Queen Margherita no less. They used to call on each other regularly when Her Highness was in residence at her summer villa on via Romana. 'I hope you know that, young man,' the old woman concludes. 'I hope you realize that you have this blood in your veins, as well as any other.'

By now Alec has climbed down off the bench. The old lady steps back and others come forward speaking in the careful manner of sympathizers. A man with an attaché case who works in the bank. A woman who says her grandmother used to own the ice-cream shop across the road when his father was a boy. A nun from the local orphanage, who first praises the family's kindness, then pats out a prayer on the back of his hand. They continue to come and go with their condolences, until Bella can no longer tell one from the other, and the English woman, somewhat alarmed, stands up and begins stuffing her knitting into a bag. She fumbles her way over to Bella like someone being chased by a dog. 'I'm most terribly sorry,' she mutters. 'I had no way of knowing, the poor child. I'm so ashamed. My name is Mrs Cardiff, by the way. Please do forgive me. I mean, had I only known.' Then she is gone.

Bella watches the circle of sympathizers close in on Alec like a gate; throwing hugs on him, lavishing his face with kisses. When there is a shift in the crowd she catches sight of him, his shoulders twisting this way and that. She sees his eyes flutter like butterflies, thinks for a moment that she hears him call out her name. 'That's enough!' she shouts then. 'I mean – *basta!*'

She breaks through and pulls him away, then, pushing him ahead of her, brings him out to the ticket office to look for Edward. The queue is long. A woman at the top is holding the ticket-seller in some sort of a heated dispute. Edward stands behind her reading a paper, while behind him again the rest of the queue begins to fidget and groan. Then all eyes seem to turn to Alec. Here and there a hat is pulled off, a head bowed, a sign of the cross made. The boy is shaking all over. She pushes him on, until the queue is behind them and they are in the far corner, near the news-stand.

Bella doesn't know how to comfort him. She wonders if she should risk touching him. He allows Edward to rough and tumble him, and Elida, as long as it's in a functional way, to comb his hair or tidy him up before he goes out. He allows any of them to hold his hand to cross the road, help him on or off the tram, undress or dress him at the beach. But any need-less contact, anything approaching affection, and he always pulls away, if not exactly upset, then certainly irritated. She has noticed this about him.

She kneels down on the floor beside him and, with Elida's method in mind, takes to fussing. Hair, collar, coat, jacket, anything that is attached to him. She remembers the English woman then, and, removing his arm from his coat, reaches in and slips the black band off the sleeve of his jacket. She puts the coat back on, fixing the band on its sleeve where it could be seen and understood by all. At last his shoes. Lifting one of his feet onto her lap, Bella unties and reties his shoelace. Then, patting her thigh, invites him to place the other foot up. All the while she mumbles a few sensible words. 'Now you be a good boy, and make sure you eat something on the train, give it time to settle before the boat, you know, in case the sea is rough, and let Edward know if you feel in any way sick, and I've packed your new crayons and some copybooks, a story book too in case you want to read. And cards, Edward and Grace will play with you. Snap. You like Snap – what do you call it again, *Rubamazzo*, isn't it?'

He nods vigorously, his hand for balance pressed on her shoulder. She can smell the cologne Elida has used to plaster his hair into place, the lemon soap on his face and neck, his vanilla-flavoured breath. She can hardly look him in the face, but notices just the same that his lips are tightened as if he is trying to swallow everything back, but that his eyes at least are steady. She reties the second lace and says, 'There now. We're all set.'

He seems to pounce on her then, throwing his arms around her so that Bella has to steady herself to prevent them both from toppling over. She can feel the squeeze of his thin arms on her neck, a few sobs stirring in his chest, the thump of his heart against her arm, the pulse of his warm little body forceful yet fragile in her arms.

After a while, she opens her eyes to Edward's hand on Alec's arm. 'We better get going, Allo,' he is saying. But Alec clings on, shaking his head and sobbing into her neck. Edward gets down on one knee and leans closer to Alec's ear – 'Don't want to miss the train now, do we?' he says. 'You won't let me down now, will you? There's a good chap – I'm relying on you now, you know I am.'

They stay for a moment, the three of them hunkered and leaning into each other. When Edward finally coaxes Alec away and lifts the child, openly sobbing now, up into his arms, Bella stays on her knees. She starts to her feet then, dizzy-legged, confused, hardly able to see a thing. Until Edward's hand again leans down to take her by the arm and help her up. Faces everywhere, a woman crying to herself. A man with his hat held to his chest. Grace in there somewhere, mouth agog.

Out on the platform, the sounds of a station: whistles, bells, doors clapping into the distance. A woman with a hamper of squabbling chickens pushes her aside and asks Edward for help in boarding the train. He puts Alec down, who immediately takes Bella's hand.

They walk further down the platform, searching for the first-class carriages. By now the wreaths have grown into what amounts to a small hill of funeral flowers. A priest splashes them with holy water as the porters pass backwards and forwards, loading them onto the train. A group of young Blackshirts come trick-acting down the platform. They stop when they see the priest, the flowers, the black band on the arm of Alec's coat. Then, one by one, they drop down into a genuflection.

Bella helps Alec board the train and stands for a while on the platform looking up at the window at their three faces: Edward, inscrutable; Alec, dry-eyed now but still pale and stunned with incomprehensible grief; Grace, the cat who got the cream.

*

When she gets back Amelia is still in her room and has quite needlessly – as far as Bella is concerned anyway – left word not to be disturbed.

Bella goes up to the library; a room she has come to regard as her own. She has brought her few bits to it – three framed photographs, a shell-covered box, a silver Indian message holder on a stand, found years ago in a Hampstead antique shop.

She has made some adjustments. At first just a here-and-there tweak, a mirror removed, a few cushions brought in. But since Cesare has shifted all the unwanted furniture to another room, she has gradually rearranged the remainder into sections – one for schoolwork; another for sitting; one for her own private office; another close to the view, where she sometimes eats meals, alone or with Alec. And a day bed she keeps by the terrace door, for snoozes on hot afternoons. It has come to feel like her own apartment.

The photographs are of her family; her mother, plumpish in the first stage of pregnancy, making her look younger and prettier than she really would have been. Another of her parents, standing at a monument near the hospital where her father used to work in Dublin. He, matinee-idol handsome, her mother, by comparison, pinched and plain. Although both seem happy enough. The last picture shows all three of them, outside the tearooms in the Phoenix Park. It isn't a good photograph, but the only she had been able to find of them as a family. Her mother and herself seated on a bench, her father standing behind them. In all, a surly over-dressed trio, recalling any other vaguely unhappy Sunday afternoon.

Bella stands at the library table looking down at the scatter of Alec's nature books and sketch pads. He has a good hand for a child his age, an eye that seems to understand colour. At least, she thinks, as she runs through the pages, he seems to know the world isn't composed of flat blocks, but of colour shaped by weight and light. Colour that moves. He sees light and shade in everything. Red in a night sky, blue in the grass. He sees depth. Or he acknowledges it anyway, even if he hasn't yet found the knack of capturing it.

She picks one book up, flips it open on a drawing of a place she recognizes. The garden of the Bicknell Library where they had spent an afternoon last week. All the details are there: the wide-armed African palm, the arcade with its soft fringe of mauve flowers, the bush of ox-eyed daisies. And the stone bench where they had sat, drowned in shadow. At the side of the picture is a man, woman and child. Over each head hangs a name: 'Maestro Edward. Signora Stuart. Alessandro P. Lami.'

In the picture Alec is wearing a striped sports shirt, just as he had done that day. She had pressed it for him herself. She is wearing her navy dress with the red flowers and collar. He even remembered which shoes she had on. Everything just as it had been. Except for one thing – Edward had not been with them.

She closes the book. From lower down the stack she pulls out a nature copybook and drops it open on a page: a group of palm trees on the capo near the old town. Underneath he has written:

Papa – I hope you know all days Bordighera gives her palms to the Holy Father to make his house in the Vatican beautifuler. It is a big house, that is why Bordighera must have always palms. I know one is the Jericho palm like in the Holy Land and one is the Roman Palm. I will know the other names soon when I find my book of botanico.

I love you Papa. I sorry I made noise to your headache. I promise I am good. I hope you get very well. Please let me back if I am good always. Your loving son called Alessandro P. Lami.

p.s. When this book is full I ask Maestro Edward to post back to Sicily for you to write in the space here I leave for your message to me.

*

Amelia tells her about Signora Lami, one evening out on the *passeggiata*. A few days in an empty house and they have fallen into each other's company well enough, once Amelia is over her sulk that is, and it has been established that Bella will not be substituting Grace as her Prosecco-swilling partner. In any case Amelia has her own holiday friends for night-time excursions or the occasional cruise to Alassio or a spin in somebody's roadster up and down the Riviera: wealthy Americans mostly or middle-aged English toffs en route to smarter places.

They have some meals together, but as neither is all that interested in food these are rare or at least brief occasions. Otherwise it is the evening walk, then on for an *aperitivo* at Bar Atu where they sit on the terrace both watching and waiting, unashamedly, for one or more of Amelia's cronies to happen along and claim her.

This allows Bella to leave. Home to a tray in the library, or a café she has found near via Lombaglia, run by the elderly Luzzati couple and frequented by English Dots. There the food is simple, the plates small, and, as Mrs Cardiff has pointed out, 'There is no obligation to be seen making a display of enjoying oneself.'

Bella is always pleased to do the *passeggiata* with Amelia but equally pleased to leave her, which is just as well, she often thinks, seeing how she has never once been invited to stay.

In light of the collarbone injury, Bella had offered to help Amelia dress or take care of more personal matters but had been told that make-up and hair would be taken care of by a girl from the English hairdresser's who knew about such things, and as for other, more personal matters, Elida, as a servant, would be better suited. If this means Amelia doesn't regard Bella as a servant, it certainly doesn't mean she looks on her as a friend. Since that first day in the garden, it has been 'Miss Stuart' all the way.

Sometimes Amelia doesn't come home all night. Once she arrived still drunk at half past eight in the morning, her dress soaking wet and the side of her face dirty and scratched. Another time there was a bruise on her neck the size of a half-crown, which Elida, with much disgust, identified as a *succhiotta* – or a love bite, as it took Bella a few minutes to work out. About Amelia's behaviour Bella asks no questions and makes no comment, although she can't help feeling that for someone with her arm in a sling, Amelia leads an impressively active life.

Amelia tells her about Signora Lami at the end of the hottest day so far that summer – the hottest since before *la grande guerra*, it said on the radio news. All morning Bella has been trailing the shade around the terrace, the afternoon lying on the sofa in the shuttered library listening to the wireless and dozing off. Later she sat in a bath of cold water and read magazines, only pulling herself together when she heard Harriet, Amelia's twice-a-day beautician, arrive with her box of tricks.

By now the others have been gone almost a fortnight, while the Signora settles her husband's affairs. At first Amelia had fumed at their prolonged absence, but lately she seems to have settled down. In any case, earlier that day, a telegram had arrived saying they would all, including Signora Lami, be back in Bordighera by the weekend.

'Well, thank *Ch-rrist* for that!' Amelia had said, right into Bella's face. 'Might at least save me from dying of boredom!'

The evening has taken the edge off the sun and the beaches and promenade are starting to fill up again. Children and dogs, old men and cyclists, recently arrived holidaymakers reeling about with shocked boiled-pink faces. The Italians, as always, taking it slowly, men strolling with their hands clasped behind their backs, women with arms folded; all tirelessly debating dinner possibilities: the how and what of each little morsel, the where – if it's a question of choosing a restaurant.

At one end of the promenade the notes of a brass band bounce like audible midges. At the far end, from the Kursaal's *thé dansant* salon, comes the subdued whine of a string quartet. Young women, slightly tipsy, and therefore, Bella assumes, probably American, come out of Damilano's wearing beach pyjamas and hats shaped like cones. Bella waits to see if Amelia will address them. But they are given no more than a cursory once-over and a disdainful blast of cigarette smoke as they pass by.

She is in a peculiar mood, one Bella hasn't seen up till now. Amelia, whether buoyant or slightly angry, always tends to be at least energetic. But today she seems quiet. Bella puts it down to her arm, which has only that morning been released from its sling, and is sore and weakened, so that Amelia has to hold it up by the elbow as they walk along.

On the beach opposite the Hotel Parigi a sideshow has pulled in a large crowd. A man sits on a high chair, facing the promenade, the sea at his back. He has a ventriloquist's dummy on his lap. As they near they see the dummy is supposed to be Adolf Hitler. Adolf Hitler as a baby with his little moustache and a rattle in his hand. He wears a nappy and a bonnet with a swastika on the front, which he keeps trying to pull off, and the man keeps trying to put back on. He is shouting and crying for his '*Mutti*' to change his dirty nappy, but she has, it seems, run off with a Jew. '*Ein Jude!!!*' the baby howls. '*Nein! Nein! Nein!*'

The man tells him yes and what's more a musician.

'*Un musicista?*'

Yes, the ventriloquist says – with a very large trombone.

'*Un trombone grandissimo?*' The baby is inconsolable.

The beach is in uproar. Even from the sea, rowers in their boats have edged back in to listen. All around, the sound of laughing voices: French, American, Italian. Behind, Bella hears a cockney cry out, 'Go on, Aydolf, show us wot you've got then.'

Only one group is quiet. Young Germans who had been lolling on their beach towels a little way from the sideshow. They begin, one by one, to pull themselves up, and, brushing the sand from their costumes, walk away from the beach and down along the promenade in high-headed silence.

Amelia watches them go. 'Of course, she's a Jewess, you know,' she says, the *ess* hissing slightly on the end of the word.

'Who is?'

'Aunt Lami. Not that I give a hoot, I mean. Dad is a little different. He says it's not that there's anything *wrong* with them per se, it's just there's always trouble when they're around.'

'What sort of trouble?'

Amelia steps away from the spectators. 'Shall we start back?' she suggests. When Bella catches up with her she continues. 'We get a lot of German businessmen staying at our hotels, you know. Dad hears things. Shall I tell you a little secret?'

'If you want to.'

'We went to Berlin, Grace and I, in May. Although we weren't supposed to. But we were in Switzerland anyhow, so what the heck. While we were there we saw a lot of rather odd things. They have these rallies – oh, nothing like the pathetic little parades you might see here. These take place at night-time, people carrying candles, searchlights all over the sky. Thousands and thousands of people. It's sort of Busby Berkeley, military style if you get my meaning. It can be quite affecting actually, like a religious fervour, almost. Maybe not religious but – I don't know – triumphant, defiant; they're like people who have won a war they didn't even have to fight. We were there when they burned all those books – although we didn't actually see that. Students burning books. I mean, you have to think about that. They even burnt Helen Keller's books – you know? All you had to be was Jewish to get thrown in the fire. Or disagree. There's been quite a few anti-Jewish measures there – did you know?'

'No.'

'You won't say we were there – will you? I mean Dad would simply go crazy. Worse, he'd stop our allowance.'

'I won't, but—?'

'To be honest, Miss Stuart, there was a man I was rather sweet on, who had stayed a few weeks in our hotel in New York. We'd had a thing. A German, in the automobile business. I followed him. Talked Grace into coming along. She'll go nuts if she knows I've told you.'

'Oh?'

'It wasn't a very good idea anyhow, I'm afraid.' She gives a small hurt smile.

They come up alongside the pavilion. The instruments spark and spear against the last of the sun. The band is playing something Bella knows is by Puccini, although she can't remember the name.

'And by the by, she's not Italian,' Amelia says out of the side of her mouth.

'Who's not Italian – Aunt Lami? I mean, the Signora?' Bella asks.

'No. Not at all. She's German. Both parents Jews, although her father was a Baron von something or other. She spent quite a bit of her child-hood in Turin, where a lot of wealthy Jews live, you know. I believe she may have gone to school for a while in England. She's in love with England anyhow, as I'm sure you've probably noticed. Thinks it gives her style, I suppose. A lot of Germans are enamoured by the English. Fellow Aryans. Of course, that may soon change. Do you know, Miss Stuart, I feel about ready for an aperitif now – what do you say?' She moves off again and Bella follows.

'Yes, there's quite a bit of anti-Jewish feeling in Germany right now. I'm not sure I approve, to tell you the truth. Certainly not when it becomes legal. Goodness, Miss Stuart – your face! I'm sure there's nothing to worry about here unless – you're not one by any chance?'

'What? No, I'm not Jewish.'

'Well, that's all right then. But of course, you're not thinking of yourself, are you? That German man I fell for – know what he told me? He said the Italian Jew is almost impossible to pick out. That Mussolini has allowed them to melt into society. Unlike in Germany, where they stick out like sore thumbs. Here it's a needle and haystack scenario. Even their names sound Italian. They way they look, and behave. Apart from Rome, where they live in a ghetto – but that's just the poor ones, right? Otherwise they could be anyone, anywhere. Well, I mean, you didn't figure on Aunt Lami? Now if this were Germany, you'd know she was a Jewess all right. If this were the United States, come to think of it. The Lamis couldn't be in a safer place. Although – who knows what people will do when it comes to it? That aria the band is playing, by the way – isn't that? – ah yes, '*O mio babbino caro.*' My dear old dad, or something. God I can't bear it. Bad enough when it's played well!'

They come up to Bar Atu, and the waiter ushers them to what has become their usual table. Amelia lays her elbow down, takes another cigarette from her case and orders a bottle of Prosecco. 'How old would you say I am, Miss Stuart?'

'I don't know. Twenty-six or…?'

'Thirty-two actually. Grace is thirty-four.'

'I would have thought you younger.'

'How sweet.'

'I'm thirty-two,' Bella says, because she feels it is expected.

'Yes, we guessed you were thereabouts. So now, three old spinsters. That's what we are. Three old spinsters in Europe. Do you think you'll ever get married?'

'I don't know. Well, no. I don't suppose I will really.'

'No. I don't suppose I will either.'

The waiter arrives with the Prosecco, and they stay silent while he pulls it out of the ice bucket, then pops the cork. He looks at Amelia here and there as if expecting her usual flirty banter. But Amelia doesn't look at him. She lifts her glass and takes a sip.

'Grace may do – marry, I mean – she's got the ability to make herself agreeable and that's all most men want really. Aunt Lami of course will go again, I have no doubt. Do you think Edward is in love with her? I mean, I can't guess why else he sticks around.'

'I really wouldn't know.'

'Well, if you don't then neither do I.'

They sit for a while in silence, watching the sea darken behind the passing crowd. Amelia finishes her glass, reaches out for the bottle then seems to change her mind. 'Do you know, Miss Stuart – I don't feel much like staying out tonight. I think I'll come back now – if it's all the same with you.'

PART FOUR

Anna

DUBLIN, 1995

May

MY GRANDMOTHER BOUGHT ME this flat. About four years ago. 'Anna – guess what I'm going to do?' she had announced one day when I called her. 'I'm going to buy you a flat!' I was sure there'd been some sort of a misunderstanding, that she hadn't realized money would actually have to be handed over.

'Nonna,' I said, 'it costs an awful lot of money to buy a flat, you know.'

'This is the 1990s, Anna, you don't have to live in hope that a man will put a roof over your head. You should have your own independence. May as well have it now, rather than hanging around waiting for me to snuff it.'

I had been living with Hugh at the time, for about six months, and had been seeing him a little over three years. We lived in what he called 'deepest suburbia', as if it were a jungle. It was a bungalow, which he hated – picture windows and a utility room, kids screeching on a swing in the garden next door – but which I quite liked. The day after the phone call, when I arrived for my weekly visit to Nonna, she had the kitchen table layered with brochures and property pages, and her face stuck in a notebook that was fast filling up with comments and itemized lists. This has always been my grandmother's way: impetuous and organized at once.

She had it all figured out: 'Now. What you want is this – a place near work so there'll be no more sitting in traffic, you want a bright room where you can do your bit of painting. A studio, yes. You want a location that's on the way up, so you'll get value and space for your money – not some pokey hole that thinks it can charge what it likes because it's in the the right area. Oh, and somewhere big enough to take in a lodger, in case things ever get tight. But not so big as to cost a fortune to run. How much are you paying in rent at the moment?'

'I'm not actually.'

'Oh? So does that other fella pay it then?'

'No. He has the house on loan from a friend who's living abroad.'

'He certainly has the knack of landing on his feet. I'll give him that.'

Nonna had never taken to Hugh. It wasn't that she had officially barred him from her flat, but I had known after the first time I had brought him, not to bring him again.

'He's married, isn't he?' she had said the minute he left.

'Separated,' I said, 'but he'll be getting a divorce soon.'

'Will he indeed?'

'He's English, you see, and—'

'Yes, I gathered that. Children?'

'Two.'

'Oh, now that's very nice, I must say.'

'Yes, they're nice kids.'

'You've met them then?'

'Yes,' I had lied.

'Separated – you say?'

'That's right.'

'Since when?'

'Oh, ages ago.'

'Before you met him?'

'Oh, ages before that,' I lied again.

Three years on and she had long ago stopped asking questions about Hugh's family, settling instead for the odd swipe whenever the opportunity presented itself. She still referred to him as 'that other fella', but I no longer bothered to correct her; besides I thought if she was serious about buying the flat, the less said about Hugh, the better.

The day we went to look at the flat, Hugh had been using my car, and as Nonna seemed to begrudge him the least little thing, I told her it was in for a service but that I'd be happy to pay for a taxi. She wouldn't hear of it. The more buses the merrier, as far as she was concerned, to get maximum value out of her bus pass. We bused it to the estate agent's office. Then we took two buses to her solicitor's, and another one to her bank. I remember being a little surprised that she was known by name in both places.

Later that afternoon, in a big Georgian house on the rougher side of town, myself and a young estate agent had watched her, an elderly woman of uncertain age, a wiry little dynamo in fact, only slightly bent at the bony shoulders, skitting through rooms, sniffing and poking, pointing out various attributes and faults with her walking stick in a way that made me realize this wasn't her first inspection. Then she told the estate agent to let down the ladder for me and I was ordered upstairs to take a look at the attic.

'Do you like it?' she called up to me.

'It's very nice.'

'Yes, but do you like it *enough*? That's the question,' she said as I came back down.

'I suppose.'

'Is the light good?'

'Lovely.'

'Ah, for God's sake, Anna – could you paint up there?'

'I could certainly try.'

'*Brava!*' She nodded and smiled. Then, turning to the estate agent, 'Now I'm not going to waste time dragging offers back and forward – you've told me the asking price, and now I'm giving you my offer – the *only* offer, mind. Would it be possible to get in touch with the vendors today?'

He looked baffled, even a little put out, as if he'd been robbed of something and couldn't figure out how – or, for that matter, what.

We stood then, the three of us out on the street looking up to the top of the house where Nonna had decided my new flat would be. Across the way, two winos were sitting on the steps of a derelict house, taking turns to swig on a bottle. A teenage mother, pushing a buggy, screamed at her crying toddler to 'shut the fuck up'. At the end of the street a few dodgy-looking customers were pinned to the corner.

The estate agent was speaking louder than he'd done when we were indoors, as if he was doing his best to keep our attention on the house, and away from the street itself. I, too, was beginning to have serious doubts about the area. My grandmother only noticed the house.

'Now you make sure that other fella pays you rent,' she said, nodding a greeting to the winos as we walked back towards O'Connell Street to catch the last bus of the day. 'Let *him* be the lodger – that's what you do.'

'I will.'

'And don't let him near that studio. That studio is yours. He has his own place to paint – did you tell me?'

'Yes, he has a studio near the docks.'

'And who gave him that, I wonder?'

'It's a government scheme, Nonna.'

'Right. This will be a whole new start for you, Anna, see that you make the most of it. And whatever you do, don't go putting his name on any documents. Do you hear me?'

'I do.'

'I'll have a word with my solicitor, just in case.'

'You don't have to.'

'Well, I will anyway.'

We continued down North Great George's Street; grids or bars on all reachable windows, chains wound round the steering wheels of cars. An empty bottle of Marie Celeste sherry stood by the kerb, a pancake of dried vomit a little further down.

She paused when we got to the end of the street, looked back and with a sweeping gesture, 'Majestic, I suppose you'd have to call it. Just look at the workmanship. You'd never get that sort of workmanship today.'

'Do you not think, Nonna, that it might be, you know, a bit on the rough side?' I asked with a cautious tip of my head towards the middle-aged corner boys who were now staring in our direction.

'Ah, what's wrong with you, Anna? They're only passing the time of day having a chat. No one's going to murder you. And besides, haven't you that other fella to protect you?'

The very mention of Hugh warmed me. I knew he, at least, would love this street. He would find it 'interesting', 'edgy', 'raw'. He would find in it a source for his art; a place to invite his artistic friends without the shame of respectability. In those days I couldn't see my own hand in front of my own face, unless it was through Hughie's eyes.

'My father used to work near here, you know. Long years ago,' Nonna said.

'Did he? I didn't know that.'

'Oh yes. The Rotunda Hospital, down there. Some of his patients were from around hereabouts. Salt of the earth, as they say. Whatever that's supposed to mean. You know, I was reading this article on the future of Dublin and, well, things are on the up, you know. This is the time to buy. Definitely.'

I laughed at her earnest little businesslike face. 'You're full of surprises, Nonna,' I said.

'No more than yourself,' she had curtly replied.

*

I must have been dreaming about that first day with Nonna; my new start. I wake up thinking about it anyway, but before I can indulge in yet another lament for lost things, I become aware of something. Or someone.

143

I open my eyes and he's here again. Hugh – in our bed; his back to my back. I can feel his warmth lying in the space between us like a child or a family pet; some live, loved thing anyhow. I can hear him breathe, see the turn of his shoulder from the corner of my eye. I am so overcome with joy I nearly vomit up my own heart.

I talk myself down – after all, no point in getting too excited until I know the terms and conditions. What if it has been a one-off shag, 'for old time's sake'? What if he gets up in a few minutes, says how great it's been seeing me again, returns the keys, laying them gently on the table by the door, wishes me well, then leaves to go back to his wife and kids in London? In that case I will let him go without a scene – of course I will. No crawling or whining, no threatening to tell the wife or smother the children. And absolutely no name-calling. This is what I tell myself. On the other hand, what if he *wants* to come back to me? Well, he needn't think I'm going to make it easy for him. Although I doubt I'll make it that difficult either.

I don't know what time it is but the rain-grey light of early morning lurks over the bedroom. The state of the place. I've really let it go to hell and I wonder if he'll comment on it and what he'll say if he does. 'I always knew you were untidy, baby, but this really exceeds all…'

Baby. He'll call me baby.

The lamps in the sitting room outside have been left on and through the frame of the opened bedroom door, the flotsam and jetsam of a night that is beginning to creep back up on me. There's a plateful of fag ends on the arm of the sofa and I notice the curtains haven't been drawn and that on the far window there is something white and rectanglular stuck onto the pane. A pair of wine bottles on the kitchen counter I recognize as being 'this week's special offer', from an all-night grocery on Dorset Street. On the corner of the coffee table, a silver takeaway carton with a dribble of sauce down its side. And it comes to me now, the Good Garden Chinese and the bland bored face of the owner when he called out my number and I lifted my eye and unstuck my mouth from a clammy drunken snog,

144

before getting up from the leatherette seat to collect and pay for the order.

There are clothes on the sofa, clothes on the floor. I can see from here – my jeans, one of my socks, my knickers. One Doc Marten cherry-red boot. All this happens so quickly; a matter of seconds – from the time my eyes open to the time they land on the boot. I wish they hadn't, not so soon anyhow. I wish I could have held on to the moment just a bit longer.

I lie listening to the rain needling the windows, or soft shuffling on the rooftops and flat-roofed extensions that deform the rear of these houses, until I can't put it off any longer. Turning slightly to look over my shoulder, I find the wrong hair on the wrong-shaped head lying behind me; one gold stud earring, a gold chain around the neck, a signet ring on the hand hanging over the quilt. I slide out of bed and wish I could die.

Plucking my clothes from the floor, I trip over myself to get into the bathroom. I don't even consider wasting time by having a shower, and to go looking for clean clothes – if there are any clean clothes – would mean having to go back into the bedroom, naked, and I'd just as soon go naked out onto the street. I get back into my dirty knickers and jeans still damp from wine spilled all over them, by me or somebody else.

When I'm dressed I go into the sitting room, begin bashing about, then I move behind the counter to get stuck into the kitchen presses and drawers. I'm looking for paracetamol or a bottle of Rescue Remedy, something to ease the pain that is hopscotching inside my head. At the same time I'm looking for a way to wake up whoever it is, in there, in my bed. Just to get it over with, to get him out of my flat, that's all I can think about now. I hear the bed creak and a voice through a forced yawn calls out, 'Any chance of a cup of tea out there?'

He is on his side, resting on one elbow. I come to the doorway, arms propped with laundry I have no intention of washing just now, but which I hope lends me a busy, preoccupied air. He flips the bedclothes back, stands, stretches and walks buck-naked across the room. 'Back in a minute,' he says, giving his arse a quick dry scratch as he passes. I know him. Christ, I know him.

145

Shay. Shay something or other. Good-looking, mid-twenties, years younger than me anyway, full of himself from his stupid little fringe to the oxblood-polished toes of his 14-hole Docs. I know that he sometimes works in a pub off Gardiner Street where Hugh used to drink when he wanted peace and quiet, in other words a cure. A run-down dive that nobody goes into, owned by a bachelor publican in a nursing home, one disinterested relative living abroad just waiting for him to croak it. The manager, a piss-head on the fiddle, leaves this Shay in charge when he's off on one of his benders.

I also know that he's from the flats where a lot of my students live, which is how I know he has a child – no, make that two children – although he didn't stay with either girl beyond conception. I can't remember if he's the same Shay who has a sister in the nick for drug-dealing. And I can't believe I've been stupid enough to let him into my bed.

What I can remember, now, is dropping into the pub for a drink yesterday afternoon on my way back from visiting Nonna in hospital.

*

Empty house, apart from one old man at the far end of the room sitting under the television shelf. The old man, muffled up to the ears, here and there muttering about the cold. The smell of burning dust from a two-bar electric fire nearby him.

The light in the pub was a dull, watery brown except for one fluorescent tube behind the bar and a trim of unseasonable Christmas lights over a rusted mirror. I sat at the end of the counter, only meaning to stay there as long as it took for my drink to arrive, when I could fold myself into a corner, hide for a while behind my newspaper, wait for the dregs of the day to pass. It's so much easier to go home when it's dark. But straight off the barman had started chatting to me, and bit-by-bit I began chatting back. Before long he was giving me drinks on the house and helping himself to whiskey. He had seemed nice. He was funny anyway. He was all right, I suppose. Better than sitting on my own, muttering about the cold.

It grew dark and I was still there. He started making cocktails, dancing and wagging his arse in a rumba up and down the bar. He rolled a joint, the two of us hysterical at my efforts to inhale and hold it down into my chest. The old man began giving out yards, 'Ah what's goin' on down there now what's going on now, wha', wha' wha'?' Until the barman – now Shay – brought him over a pint and a small one.

'Right, Mick, that's a little present for you now, on the house. But keep it to yourself. OK for a piss are you? Sure now? Well, just give us a shout if there's a change in the weather.' It was only then that I noticed the old man was in a wheelchair.

An occasional customer had wandered in, always alone, never staying for more than one drink. Single men on the way back from the country looking for something to blur the return to one of the run-down bedsits or seedy B&Bs that seem to lie behind every second door around here. At some stage three girls out on the rip stuck their heads in the door and screeched at the shock of an empty pub. And we listened to their voices roller-coasting up the road, then fading away. It was so quiet after that.

By now the old man had fallen asleep and from a notebook hanging on the wall, Shay called a number and told someone on the other end of the phone that their father was ready for collection.

Shay Foster. His youngest brother is a student in my junior cert class, he had told me.

'Oh, that's just fucking great,' I had said, drunk by then. I was well drunk.

'I won't say a word,' he promised.

'Actually, he's not bad, your little brother, quite good, by the way. I should tell you that. Has a bit of talent. He could do something with that.'

'Like you, do you mean?' he had asked.

'Oh Christ YES – just like fabulous me!' I had thrown back my head, followed by my arms and had nearly fallen off the stool. He caught me on the way back up, grabbed the back of my head into the palm of his hand and stuck his tongue into my mouth.

'Not too young for that though – am I?' he had said, then asked if he could call me 'Miss'.

*

Now here I am, timid in the doorway of my own bedroom, listening to him pissing like a horse in my bathroom. There's no sound of a flushing chain or a tap being turned on – it's a no-frills piss he might take on the side of the road. Not that I can blame him for skipping the formalities – considering the mess that's in there. He comes back, boyishly jumps into the bed, pulls the pillows around him to form a little grotto, then clasps his hands behind his head.

He's looking me over. The cross on his chain is winking at me, a bunch of black hair pops out from each oxter, although his chest, bare of hair, has obviously been waxed. I imagine he probably thinks he's done me a big favour. He may even be deciding if he should do me another one before he gets going. Or then again, he may be thinking of an excuse to cut out now. But I get in there first.

'Shouldn't you be going to work?' I ask him.

'It's Monday,' he says.

'Don't barmen work on Mondays?'

'Not this one. Not this Monday.'

'Well, I'm going to have to ask you to leave, anyway,' and he frowns slightly as if he doesn't quite understand. I spell it out for him. 'Actually, I'm expecting people. Guests. For lunch. You'll have to – you know – go.'

'You wouldn't be tryin' to get rid of me now?' he says. 'You are – aren't you? Jaysus, that's a good one all right.'

I turn back into the sitting room.

A few minutes later he follows me in. He's buckling his belt and looking around for the rest of his clothes. 'Would it be all right if I finished getting dressed first or would you prefer me to do it out on the street?' He's pretending to be funny, but I can see he's annoyed. He steps on some-thing, winces, then lifts his bare foot – the stub of a spare rib is stuck to his sole and there's a deep pink bruise on the carpet. He flicks the spare rib off, finds his socks and boots, then makes a space on the edge of the sofa by pushing anything that's on it over the cliff and onto the floor. It's a gesture of contained anger.

'Look,' I begin, 'I just need you to leave because I'm expecting guests and would appreciate—'

His hand lifts to stop me. 'Don't talk to me as if I'm some fuckin' kid in your class.'

'I didn't say you were.'

'You're forgettin' somethin', love – you asked me back here. Not the other way around. And I'm goin', now, soon as I'm ready. So just spare me the friends over for lunch on a wet Monday morning bolloxology.'

He begins working the bootlace through the eyelets of the boot, his movements sharp and impatient. He lifts his head at intervals to survey the room and I can see his cold eye taking everything in. The dirty dishes piled in the sink, the towels on the floor, the dust, the grease, the plastic bags filled with rubbish that goes back a lot further than last night. And the multitude of empty Rescue Remedy bottles, little dark bodies and yellow labels, like big dead wasps all over the flat.

'So tell us – these mates of yours – are they pigs? Or maybe rats? Because to tell you the truth I can't see anyone human eatin' in here. Like what a kip. Jaysus! No wonder your man fucked off back to his wife.'

'Fuck you,' I say. 'You little gurrier, get out. Go on. Get.'

He stands up presenting his bald chest to me.

'Ah now, that's not what you said last night.' He puts on his shirt, flexing and jutting his neck and shoulders as he does. 'And don't fuckin' call me a gurrier. Who the fuck do you think you are anyway? Bleedin' slapper.'

He's raging now, and in a way I don't blame him. Last night we were equals, there had been talk about art and books. He had said it was nice to have someone to talk to about that sort of thing. Now here I am looking down my nose at him, and calling him names to put him back in his place.

He picks up his pretend airman's jacket off the chair and finally heads for the door. His face is red now, his jaw tight. But he keeps grinning at me like he couldn't care less. 'You weren't a bad little ride, all the same,' he says, 'for an oulone like.'

I open the door and stand behind it.

'Ah, what's wrong? I'm only tryin' to give you a compliment. Though I suppose come to think of it, it's not much of a one. Sure I'd ride anyone. Everyone knows that.'

'Get out,' I snarl.

Suddenly he's back in the room, lunging towards the window where he lifts the white shape I noticed earlier and I see now that it's a page from my sketch pad. A drawing.

'Souvenir.' He grins and rushes through the front door again.

'Give that back,' I say.

'No way I'm giving this back, love. This is worth a fortune to me.'

'Give it back now. Or I'll call the guards.'

'Would you do that? Would you? Then I suppose, in that case, I'd have to give it back.' He holds the drawing out to remind me.

'Please, Shay, please give it back.'

'Please,' he whines at me. 'Oh, she's remembered her manners now, has she? Well, she can fuck right off on her high horse, because I'm keeping it.'

He's down the first few steps of the stairs. 'Tell you what I will do for you. I'll tell me mates where you live. And that you're gagging for it. You know, they could drop round next time they're stuck. The end of a night like when all the young ones are gone. Or here, me little brother and his crew. You'd like that, wouldn't you? And I'm sure they'd be happy enough to oblige. You could draw them an' all. They'd love that, they would.'

'Are you threatening me?' I call down to him, rushing to lean over the banister. 'You little bastard, are you threatening me?' I'm screaming now, he's shouting back. We're calling each other other names. The word 'slapper' looms larger than most. He's laughing and I could fucking kill him, I could fly down those stairs after him and punch him right in the face.

Before he turns out of sight he gives me the finger. Then winks. 'Thanks for the ride, love. It was great.'

I see my neighbour Tony then, on the way up the stairs. Tony hesitates and appears to be deciding if he should go back downstairs or continue on up to his flat. Shay sees him and stops. 'Ah, sorry about that, bud, sorry about all the noise. But to be honest, I'm a bit hurt like, you know. She takes me home, fucks me brains out and now she's throwing me out in the pissin's of rain. Terrible, isn't it? And she draws this when I'm out of it. That's me, there. A nude study. Signed and all it is. Like I feel abused nearly – know what I mean? Like taken advantage of. *Violated*, in fact. Violated, yeah, that's the word I'm after.'

Tony presses his back to the wall, and waits for Shay to pass him. I want to run back upstairs and lock myself into my flat but I can't seem to move. There's Tony on the flight below, carefully placing his dripping umbrella in the corner by his door. His morning *Irish Times* sticking out of his Centra bag, the white of his doctor's coat showing under his rain-stained Burberry raincoat. He waits until he hears the front door of the house slam, then glances up at me. 'I've been up all night,' he says, 'I really don't need to come home to this.'

Then he pushes his key into the lock and opens the door of his immaculate flat, where his immaculate boyfriend will be waiting in their chrome and marble kitchen with the coffee gurgling and everything so fucking perfect and clean. He looks up at me with a mixture of pity and disgust. 'You know, Anna, you should really be more careful of whom you invite into your home.'

I come back inside and my hands are shaking. I find my handbag, and in the side pocket a Rescue Remedy bottle with a few drops left, which I lower onto my flattened tongue like a sacrament. I notice my purse is looking thin, and when I give it a feel, almost empty. The same goes for the fridge. I open the door and the stark light shows me: one full lemon wearing a Juliet cap of white mould, a few out-of-date jars and bits of God knows what, wrapped in tin foil, so old it has begun to desiccate. By some miracle there's a full bottle of soda water in the shelf on the door and slipping two paracetemol into my mouth, I go at it like someone who's just crossed the dessert.

I think of the drawing. Pissed, stoned, showing off, I had insisted on doing it last night. Him in the nude, his dick a lewd exaggeration. And signed of course, I had to have signed it. I begin sobbing with rage. I would willingly suffocate myself to stop that sobbing but no matter how hard I press my hands against my mouth I can't keep it in. Finally I do stop. I have to calm down. There is something I need to find. I don't want to name it yet, or think about it even, but I have to look for it and I have to find it.

I ransack the flat, tear the bedclothes off the bed, pull the cushions off the sofa, search everywhere and anywhere we may have been. By now I'm way beyond crying and have resorted to a deranged chant of *fucket oh fucket oh God please no fucket.* I go back to the bedroom, look through every inch of it, under the mattress, under the bed. I shake out the sheets, reef the pillowcases off the pillows, peer into their every corner. But still there is nothing. I can't find it. Maybe he's flushed it down the toilet. I go in and look for a few moments down at the frothy lager of piss he's left behind him. Or maybe it never existed.

I know I had it off with him, and can remember every mortifying second of going through the false, fancified motions of drunken sex. But I can't remember if he used a condom or not. I'm not on the pill. Hugh had a vasectomy years ago, so there's never been a reason to.

I give up eventually, sit on the floor, my back to the wall, the Golden Pages open on my lap, trying to get the alphabet to settle down in my head so I can find the name of a surgery. At least I can deal with the pregnancy worry with the morning-after pill. I will not even think about the HIV question, I will put that completely and utterly out of my head.

Then my eye catches something. I crawl to the sofa and shove it aside.

There. There it is. And so I sit back down on the floor of my filthy flat, with my splitting head and my near empty purse and the memory of the way that little prick has spoken to me, and the face on Tony at the door of his flat, and the thought of the drawing being passed around with the rumour, through the school, the neighbourhood. And I thank God with all my heart for this pink sausage skin under the sofa. This sad little sack of obsolete snot.

PART FIVE

Bella

BORDIGHERA, 1936

May–October

SHORTLY AFTER HIS FATHER's death it had been decided that
Bordighera should become Alec's permanent home. 'Less isolating,' was
how the Signora had put it. Three years on and as far as Bella can see,
Alec remains as isolated as ever, rarely mixing with other children except
during the high-summer season when the beaches and tennis club are full
of visitors and there is often someone needed to make up a tournament
or game. Otherwise he is usually alone, and as a result, Bella sometimes
thinks, just a little odd. He never mentions his father, which she finds a
little worrying. He still reads the letters they sent to each other through
his nature books – at least Bella has often come across one or more of
them under his bed. She also suspects that Alec may occasionally write to
his dead father, but has never been able to bring herself to open a notebook to see this for herself.

When Alec come across a possible friend he often frightens the child
with his zeal, wanting to be with them every minute of the day, suffocating them with attention and gifts smuggled out of the house (she caught
him one time, with a Swiss army knife belonging to Edward stuck up his
jumper). His only real friends are Martha and Lina Almansi, two little

black-haired girls from Turin who come to Bordighera on their annual holiday for three weeks every September. Inclined to the overstatement themselves, they take Alec's neediness in their own sweet, dramatic stride. He lives for September, becoming almost sick with excitement as the date of their arrival nears, then growing quiet in himself for a week or so after they leave. In between there are letters; pages from him filled with funny drawings, which the sisters seem to love. And they write back. To Bella's mind this means as much as all the hours of play. It keeps him in touch with the outside world. More importantly it makes him feel wanted.

The difficulty is in filling his day. Weekdays have lessons of one sort or another, meals, a walk, a game of tennis, and bedtime eventually comes round. Weekends tend to drag. All the more since they've stopped going to the 'Fascist Saturday' parades.

She used to love the parades; the truth is she often misses them. Their childlike exuberance, the way the whole point seemed to be the party afterwards. Boy scouts trying to keep their minds on the job, little girls sweet in white socks and capes. Old men showing off medals from battles they could barely recall. Officers and vanguard, *Cavalieri*, *Alpini*, all in their own way magnificently absurd. She used to stand on the sidelines with Alec, and wish in her heart he could be part of it. For a while she had hinted, then, as her position in the household had become more established, broached the subject with Signora Lami. Until Edward had advised her to drop it.

'She will never allow him to be part of the *Balilla*,' he had said.

'But what harm can it do?' Bella asked. 'It's only the boy scouts and if the child is lonely?'

'She would prefer him to be lonely than Italian. Haven't you noticed yet? She thinks being Italian is beneath him.'

'I thought it was just the fascists she disapproved of?'

'Fascists, Italians – it's all the same now, I'm afraid.'

In the end Bella had conceded. It would probably be best for Alec anyhow, she decided, to stay on the outside looking in. By then she was beginning to realize how he could be affected by strangers and crowds.

And so under a sky bloated with flags and fascist insignia, Bella would choose the most suitable spot, moving onto the next corner or doorway, at the first sign of a crush. The streets and *piazze* of Bordighera chiming with footsteps, Alec waving his flag and screaming his lungs out as each section filed by. '*Eia, eia. Alala! Alala! Evviva il Duce! Evivva il re! Evviva l'Italia! Duce! Duce! Duce!*'

The swagger of a dignitary here and there. A priest or two thrown in for good measure. Altar boys holding relics overhead: Santa Teresa, San Giuseppe, Madonna of the various locations. Mussolini, of course, just like any other saint, only better. And the band always that little bit ahead of itself, that little bit out of tune, while the air crackled with children's voices singing '*La Giovinezza*', Alec joining in, word perfect. He had been as enthusiastic as the best little *fascita* in town, his hand darting in and out in a Roman salute. His mother would have had a fit – had she ever been there to witness it.

Roll calls and speeches at either end, the whole town out to escort a single minor official to the train station or maybe to welcome a mob of poor children to Mussolini's fresh air colony camp. Whatever the reason it always ended the same way. Food, wine, dancing and high humour. Never a dark hint or a cross word. Apart from a rare squabble usually caused by a greedy hand or a jealous heart. Just another Italian excuse to get dressed up and go out to a party. The Day of the Faithful put a stop to all that. Since that day last December she can no longer enjoy such occasions, nor does she find they make suitable entertainment for Alec, especially as an outsider looking in.

Signora Lami, meanwhile, has continued to come and go; Germany, occasionally France or England. Whenever she visits Bordighera it always seems to be en route to, or from, one of these places. She comes for the whole month of December, stays for the fireworks on *capodanno* and goes off again on her travels come the second of January. She also spends the month of June in Bordighera. After that it depends on her somewhat mysterious schedule – which of course is never explained nor discussed. For almost three years, this has been the case.

Then, one morning towards the end of May, a telephone call is put through from the Signora. It starts with the usual blast of domestic instructions, then the Signora reminds Bella that she will be arriving next month and would like everything to be organized, also that the best guest room be made 'up to scratch'. She does not say in whose honour.

'Can you please tell me, Miss Stuart, what are my son's chances for promotion in next month's exams?' she goes on to ask then.

'Not bad, he's been working quite well lately. Algebra has been a bit of a problem again but Edward has—'

'Excellent. Please inform the authorities that he will no longer be an outside pupil, but that we will be sending him to school next term.'

Bella is sure she has misheard. 'School? Do you mean everyday school?'

'Yes, yes. Everyday school.'

'As in the state school, Signora?'

The Signora gives a slight tut. 'Miss Stuart, I really don't know. This is why I am asking you to research all solutions. What is available to him – this is what must be ascertained. I will make my decision when I arrive. If he passes his exams and is promoted next term it will be to the *scuola media* – are there many such schools in Bordighera, do you know, Miss Stuart?'

'I have no idea.'

'You can find out. Yes, indeed. Oh, and make inquires also about the *Balilla*.'

'The *Balilla*?'

'Yes, yes, you know, the Wolves, or the Musketeers or whichever is for his age group just now. One of the fascist youth brigades anyhow. The Sons of Italy, whatever they are calling it. You have seen them I'm sure – you go to the parades, I believe?'

'Not for a while, no.'

'Ah yes. The Day of the Faithful put you off, I understand?' The Signora gives a little laugh here before continuing. 'Well, you must overcome your reservations. Apply for him to be a member of the *Balilla*. Nothing too boisterous. Perhaps he could join the band? He is musical enough I suppose. Ask Maestro Edward if he can teach him a few suitable pieces on the flute or some portable instrument anyhow. Nothing requiring too much blow, with his asthma, also I don't want his cheeks becoming over-developed and spoiling his looks. Like Rosa's son, you know, the trumpeter?'

'Very well, Signora Lami. So that's state school? And the *Balilla*?' Bella asks.

'Oh yes, and Sunday mass. Do you take him to mass, Miss Stuart?'

'Well, no.'

'You are not religious?'

'No. But in any case I'm not Catholic. I've taken him occasionally to the Anglican church. And sometimes Elida brings him to mass.'

'Forgive me, I sometimes forget I am not the only non-Catholic in Italy.'

'I can take him if you like.'

'Excellent! He has made his communion you know. Rotate the churches, I wish him to be seen in all. However, as there is a Lami pew in the Magdalena – in the old town, you know – you may favour that a little more than the others.'

'So that's the *scuola media*, the *Balilla* and Sunday mass?' Bella asks again, just to be certain.

'Yes, yes. In fact, Miss Stuart, it is time Alec Lami went out to the world!'

*

On the first day of June the Signora arrives with Signor Tassi by her side, and gradually the complete turnaround regarding Alec begins to make sense.

Gino Tassi, the lawyer from Naples. Bella recognizes him at once as the man she delivered the letter to when Signor Lami was dying. If he has any recollection of their previous meeting, he keeps it to himself.

Bella finds him a pleasant sort, with a friendly, handsome face. Early forties or thereabouts, much younger than his predecessor anyhow – if this is what he intends to be. And he certainly seems to please the Signora, who has become quite giggly and frequently pink, causing Bella and Edward to exchange several amused glances. Alec, on the other hand, and despite Tassi's best efforts to woo him with presents and jokes, shows indifference. At best he responds with a chilly politeness, at worst he behaves as if Tassi simply doesn't exist.

The most surprising thing about Gino Tassi, in relation to the Signora anyhow, is how thoroughly Italian he is: mannerisms and dress, love of food and comfort, the way he turns the charm on for almost any female to cross his path. And not a word of her beloved English language ever passes his lips, nor does he show the slightest interest in learning to say so much as 'hello'.

Should the conversation turn to English the Signora translates for him and he responds accordingly with a smile or a gesture of sympathy. Otherwise they speak Italian 'for his sake', as Signora Lami apologetically puts it, as if it is a sacrifice that has to be made.

'So! Miss Stuart, have you succeeded in finding a school for my son?'

The Signora finally gets around to asking this question a few days into her stay, when she invites Bella to go with her to the tennis club to meet Alec. Signor Tassi has decided to stay behind and write postcards in the garden. Edward, as usual, is stuck to his piano.

'Well, Signora,' Bella begins, 'the difficulty is finding a place for him. The numbers are up considerably this year, it seems.'

'You have said who he is? His father? His grandmother?'

'They know who he is, Signora. Everyone does. But it seems many private pupils now want to be part of the regime.'

'Yes, it's certainly how Signor Tassi sees it. He advises it indeed most strongly. He thinks it is a very bad idea to be otherwise. That it can be read as disloyalty. I suppose one must at least be *seen* to make an effort. Do you have a solution, Miss Stuart?'

They come in by the Anglican church, passing through the narrow laneway into the club. Behind the high-ivy wall comes the steady tick-tocking of tennis practice. Bella follows the Signora along the side margins to the further court where Alec is playing. They sit on a nearby spectators' bench.

'No solutions, Miss Stuart? This is not very like you!'

'Well, there is one possibility. But again, there are difficulties. St George's in San Remo – it used to be the English school? Well, it's been revised as an Anglo–Italian venture. Boys and girls from all over the world. Mostly from the diplomatic circles. Italians too, of course. It's not quite a state school – there are fees involved. But it is recognized. In fact the pupils must be enrolled in the *Balilla* and participate in patriotic ceremonies. I went to see it – do you know Villa Magnolie? Well, it's a lovely villa really, terraces, gardens, classrooms – very modern. And there's an impressive art studio too, which Alec would love. The problem is transport. The train station is too far and is a stiff uphill walk anyhow, which would be bad for his asthma, although he does seem to be growing out of that. But in any case the buses are just not reliable enough. It would mean he could often be late, and well – you know how upset he gets about breaking rules.'

'In fact.'

The Signora says nothing for a few minutes, just watches her son run around the court. Sometimes she returns a bow or a wave from another spectator. Then she resumes. 'Would you say, Miss Stuart, that this St George's is merely making a bow to fascism rather than giving it a full embrace?'

'I think it would be fair to say that, yes.'

She returns her eye to the game. 'He's really not very good, is he? I mean, considering the amount of time he spends playing, and the coaching of course. He's extremely awkward – wouldn't you say?'

Bella feels a slight stab. 'Well, I wouldn't say that. I mean he is only nine years old, Signora. And he knows we're here, which is probably making him nervous. He's usually much, much—'

'He is almost ten, Miss Stuart. Could he be a boarder, do you think?'

'A boarder?'

'Yes. You know, I had always intended for him to go to a boarding school in England when his age was right, but I changed my mind. Do they allow boarders in St George's?'

'Yes, but I don't know if…'

'You don't know if it's a good idea, Miss Stuart – is that what you are saying? You don't know if he will be *able* for it?'

Bella looks away.

'You worry about my son, Miss Stuart, I think.'

'No. Of course not.'

'It means, at least, you love him,' she sighs. The Signora slaps her hands on her lap and stands up. 'Do you think we might refer to this St George as – San Giorgio? With perhaps the emphasis on the *fascista* element?'

'Oh yes, the prospectus is full of all that, actually.'

'Excellent. Call him in, would you?'

Bella walks along the side of the court towards Alec. The coach is shouting instructions, and Alec stumbling behind a racket that appears to be far too big for him. She hooks her fingers in through the wire, then waits until he catches her eye and comes running.

Later that evening Alec is told, 'My dear, we have some news for you.'

'Yes, Mamma?'

'From next term you will no longer be a private pupil. You will be going to school with other children. Would you like that?'

'I don't know.'

'Good. You are to go to school in San Remo. San Giorgio's it's called. Also you will be joining the *Balilla*. Won't that be fun? Miss Stuart has been very clever and arranged it all for you.'

'Will there be uniforms?'

'Of course there'll be uniforms! This is Italy after all – there are always uniforms!'

'But how will I get to school, Mamma?'

'Miss Stuart will take you.'

'The last time we went to San Remo we had to wait and wait, and the autobus was so late and—'

'There will be no need to worry about the autobus. Goodness no. We will buy a motor car! Can you drive, Miss Stuart?'

'I'm afraid not.'

'Never mind, you can learn. Tomorrow we will go to San Giorgio's and book a place for Alec to start in October. Then we will find someone who can teach Miss Stuart how to drive. So we will have a female chauffeur – a *chauffeuse* as the French say! Are we not a modern household after all? And when Miss Stuart learns how to drive, we shall buy her a car – what do you say, Miss Stuart?'

'I don't know what to say,' Bella laughs.

It is not the only news Signora Lami has to break during her holiday. Her next and final *bomba* comes the day before she goes back to Sicily. They have just returned from lunch in the old town of La Pigna, walking all the way back to Bordighera, the Signora in her lemon dress, turning heads on every street and café terrace along the way. Signor Tassi, in cream linen, looking as if he could burst with delight.

Then tea in the Bordighera tearooms is proposed, which Edward tries to squirm out of, just as Bella has been considering staging her own 'bit of a headache'. But the Signora is determined to 'make a day of it' as she seems to have done of so many days since her arrival. Boat trips and picnics; carriage jaunts and car hires; Monte Carlo, Menton, Nice. The Hanbury Gardens; jazz suppers and tea dances. They've had the lot. Not to mention clay-pigeon shooting, tennis matches, golf games, hill-hiking and a very close call in the trampoline competition, which mercifully they'd been too late to enter. There have been awkward dinners with guests the Signora appeared not to know all that well. Afternoon teas in the garden where the saucers and spoons seemed to do all the talking. That her companion should have a full and varied holiday seems to have been the order of each day. Even if it often appeared that poor Signor Tassi would rather sit on a terrace or stroll through town, watch and be watched, nothing else to do otherwise but prepare his *bella figura* for the *passeggiata*, and soundly sleep between meals.

Now, after speaking mostly Italian for days, and eating lunch in a *trattoria rusticana*, the diners with gingham napkins tied round their necks like babies, and the sight of so much food making Bella's stomach crawl, it seems funny to be sitting on the lawn of the tearooms, at a table stiff with white linen and teacups, listening to English accents all around, talk of cricket and the Henley Regatta.

'You are quiet today, Miss Stuart,' the Signora says as she pulls off her gloves. 'Have you something on your mind?'

'I'm fine, just a bit of a head—'

'I am glad to hear it. I thought perhaps you were worrying about something. Or perhaps your back was giving you trouble?'

Then Bella, without thinking – or as she would decide later, without taking account of the wine she'd had at lunch – blabs out, 'Actually, I had a letter from my father yesterday. He's coming over in August.'

'Really? Here to Bordighera?'

'Yes, on his way to the Olympic Games in Berlin. I was just thinking, my God, I haven't seen him in over three years.'

'But how lovely, Miss Stuart. Which date in August?'

'The first week, I think. Just for a few days.'

'Perfect! He must be our guest.'

'No,' Bella says.

'No?' Signora Lami laughs. 'What's the matter, Miss Stuart, don't you like your father?'

'Of course I do, it's, well, I mean, you're very kind but he'll be staying at the Hotel Angst, it's all been arranged.'

'The Angst? But that's only down the road. He may just as well be with us. You must write at once and tell him to cancel. Tell him I insist absolutely that he be our guest.'

'Actually Signora, he'd probably prefer the Angst. You see, he'll be on his honeymoon.'

'He's to be remarried! Oh my dear! Congratulations. Who is he to marry – do you know?'

'Yes I do. Mrs Jenkins is her name, she's a widow.'

'How lovely for him. How lovely for you all.' She turns to Signor Tassi and translates.

'Ahhh,' he beams, stands up and, taking Bella's face in his hands, kisses her on both cheeks. '*Auguri, auguri.*' When he sits down again he leans into Signora Lami and, heads together, they exchange a few whispered words.

'We may as well tell you our news now, as later,' Signora Lami laughs. 'We are also to be married! And we hope, if it can be arranged, in August. Can you believe it? August of the second weddings, we shall have to call it!'

Signor Tassi reaches over and takes her hand, then they both bashfully laugh.

Edward is the first to pull himself together, offering his hand and congratulations. Bella quickly follows. Alec, flicking through a deck of cards, appears not to have heard a word.

'Well, Alec?' his mother says. 'Have you nothing to say to your mamma?'

'No, Mamma.'

'Well, to your new papa then? Have you nothing to say to him?'

Alec stands up and, stepping up to Tassi, flings the cards at him. Then he juts out his neck and, opening his mouth as wide as it will go, silently growls at him, a look of hatred and hurt on his face.

The table falls silent for a few painful seconds, each one avoiding the other's eyes until the Signora speaks. 'You may take Alec home now, Miss Stuart. I believe he must be overtired. In any case I don't wish to see him again this evening, or for that matter before I leave Bordighera.'

*

At the beginning of August Signora Lami, now Signora Tassi, hosts a house party over several days to celebrate her marriage. A small private ceremony has already taken place in the South of France. No guests from either Italian household were invited, not even Alec. Signor Tassi's elderly brother, along with a cousin of the Signora's from Turin, were the only witnesses.

It made better sense, the Signora would later explain, to marry in France where there was less red tapes and fewer *bustarelle* to slip under the bureaucratic table. Nobody likes to ask why red tape and bribes should be necessary in the first place – after all, the Signora has been a widow for over three years. It is left to Rosa in the kitchen to utter the phrases 'mixed marriages' and 'godless France'.

After the civil ceremony in France, the witnesses having been dispatched, back to Naples for Tassi's elder brother, and in the case of the Signora's cousin, to a watercolour painting course in Cap Martin, the honeymoon began. The first two nights were spent in the Hotel Negresco in Nice, which the groom had loved, but the bride found a little vulgar. Then another few days on a yacht, which had delighted the bride but occasionally caused the groom to be sick over the side. The yacht took them up the coast from Nice to Portofino and then returned them to Bordighera.

*

As they dock a photographer is waiting, along with the house guests, heavily armed with flowers and good wishes, as per the Signora's instructions.

From Naples, the Tassi family – another of Gino's brothers, a widower, and his three adult sons. All high-spirited, hungry and fond of a drink. From Switzerland, a middle-aged couple that say little but smile all the time. A buck-toothed man from London, eager to discuss and observe fascism at any opportunity, and who refers to the British fascist leader, 'Sir Oswald Mosley or *Tom* – as he is known to his closest friends.'

A few local residents are also present, none of whom Bella has ever seen or heard of before. Apart from Mrs Cardiff and her brother James, the manager of the English bank in Bordighera.

The cousin of the Signora, who had been a witness at the wedding, is called Eugenia, and like the Signora is a beauty in her late twenties. Her father, the Signora's uncle, a soft-spoken, tender-eyed German aristocrat, who is extremely dull, but has impeccable manners and speaks perfect English as well as Italian, joins her in Bordighera.

By the second evening Eugenia, who from the start has made it clear that she is utterly appalled by the unrefined table manners of Gino Tassi's nephews, can no longer contain herself. She stomps out of the dining room during the *primo piatto*. The Signora follows her, forgetting to close the door behind her, so that everyone at the table can hear Eugenia's complaints, which unfortunately are made in Italian. She cannot sit and watch men eat like monkeys, Eugenia says, spaghetti swinging out of their mouths. It disgusts her, that's all. Nor can she listen to another greasy slurp. She will not share a table with such *selvaggi*!

Bella expects a terrible scene – humiliation followed by outrage. In fact the men from Naples turn out to be delighted by the insult, slapping the table and throwing back their heads to laugh (mouths wide open and full of food). At this moment the quiet German politely asks to be excused and goes out to the hall, where in his perfect Italian he tells Eugenia, if she doesn't gather up her manners and get back inside, he will put his fist through her face. This amuses the Neapolitans all the more and for the rest of the visit they repeat the phrase, by word or by mime, every time the shame-faced Eugenia comes within range.

With all these guests to accommodate, it had earlier been decided that Bella, Alec and Elida should give up their rooms and move to one of the hotels in town and that Edward would accompany them. As it is August, and the better hotels are booked from year to year, they settle on the Jolanda. More like a guest house, it is favoured by Czechoslovakians with enough children between them to distract Alec rather than overwhelm him. He has not taken to the wedding at all well – nor to his new papa, nor to the intrusion of guests in his house. He cringes anytime he runs into the Neapolitans, who ruffle his hair and pluck at his stomach in an attempt to tickle him. Also Eugenia, forever kissing his face and telling him how much she loves him. Since the celebrations have started in fact, Alec has been whinging a lot and has hardly come out from behind Bella's skirt.

The Jolanda suits him, with its quiet sitting rooms, and the table in the window where he can stay with his pencils and sketch pad undisturbed except for the landlady who pops in from time to time with *caramelle* and crescents of melon. Bella is happy here too: it's like being on holiday in England only with better weather. Sand in the hallway, the echo of strange voices everywhere, men drinking beer in the garden, sing-songs around the piano in the evenings with an unusually jolly Edward at the helm. It's nice having somewhere to escape to, even if it does mean using Alec's naps and shyness as a frequent excuse.

Otherwise it's been beck-and-call throughout, but at least she gets to practise her driving. Up and down the via Romano, cabbying guests to the beach, the *capo*, the train station or wherever their whims take them, in her brand new car which the Signora has managed to get on approval from a garage in Ventimiglia. A *Topolino* – a baby mouse, named for its peculiar shape and non-descript colour. Bella did try suggesting to the Signora that something a little older and a lot less shiny might be in keeping for someone who is still a novice at the driving game. But, as Edward points out, the Signora is the Signora, and will always do and hear just as she pleases.

On Friday morning of the wedding party, a telegram arrives from the American cousins.

POSITIVELY OVERJOYED. HEARTIEST *AUGURI*. SIMPLY GOT TO VIEW THAT LUCKY MAN. STOPPING OVER EN ROUTE TO SWITZERLAND. LEAVE PARIS SUNDAY. EXPECT MONDAY PM. BEST TO ALL. A & G NELSON.

At this point Edward decides now might be a good time to take his annual leave.

'But you never take annual leave, other than a weekend or two – at least not since I've been here,' Bella says when he tells her.

'Well, I'm making up for it now. Six weeks in fact. A walking tour of Germany and Austria.'

'*Six weeks?* Does the Signora know this?'

'Yes, and she's all for it. She's staying here till the end of August anyway, and she's asked Cesare to move into one of the guest rooms until I come back. Just so there's a man about – her words, not mine.'

'Cesare? Is he supposed to protect us from intruders?'

'He can always breathe on them.'

'Shut up, Edward, you're not funny. When do you go?'

'When do the Americans arrive?'

'Monday p.m., the telegram said.'

'I'm leaving Monday, as it happens – *a.m.* Shame.'

'Oh, very smart, Edward,' Bella says. 'Very smart indeed.'

But not smart enough for the American cousins, who, having had their fill of Paris, arrive two days early. Storming in on the company on Saturday evening just at the hour of the *aperitivo*, with their slinky laughs and witty asides, loud as they ever were, all gesture and cosmetics, everyone running around in their wake, until luggage, cigarette lighters, ashtrays, drinks and places at an already over-full table have all been arranged, without either having to lift a finger.

Grace has grown a little plumper and is, Bella decides, consequently dressed in a copious purple kimono, which only draws attention to the matter. Amelia, who has gone in the opposite direction, is skinnier than ever, and has obviously abandoned Katharine Hepburn and taken to styling herself on Wallis Simpson instead. She no longer has her athletic carriage and now seems to be leaning from her feet, rather than standing up on them. Between them they frighten Eugenia into a headache – making one extra place immediately available. A piano stool is brought in by one of the Neapolitans, who volunteers to sit on it himself, while his two brothers squeeze up to make room for Amelia.

The Signora's pain is written all over her face. She shows no interest in opening the wedding gift they have brought her from Paris, but simply instructs Rosa 'to put it away somewhere'. Even her new husband, who had initially been fluttering all over the cousins, senses her mood and withdraws his attentions. Edward, apart from a discreet weary roll of the eyes, keeps his dismay to himself. Bella, who tries not to gloat over his botched plans, is surprised at how pleased she is to see the American cousins again.

Not far into dinner, however, it becomes clear that there will be some sort of a scene. Amelia, who has been drinking non-stop and playing up to the Neapolitans on either side of her, has eaten nothing at all, except for some ice cream which one of them has fed her from his spoon. Every now and then her eye flicks towards Edward. The less he seems to notice her, the more agitated she becomes. Grace meanwhile has homed in on the German uncle, laughing her head off at everything he says. This seems to surprise him, as much as it does everyone else.

Throughout the meal Amelia addresses Edward on only one occasion. 'Is that water you're drinking, Edward? My God, don't tell me you *still* don't drink alcohol?'

'You know I don't, Amelia,' he says. 'I've told you often enough.'

'Well, so you have. Remind me again – why you're such a good boy?' She puts her elbow on the table, rests her chin in her hand and sends a seductive eye down-table.

'He had jaundice when he was a child,' Bella says without thinking.

Amelia widens her eyes at her. 'Oh, and what are you now – his nurse?'

'I'm only saying,' Bella mumbles. 'It damages the liver.'

'I'm sure Edward can speak up for his own liver,' Amelia says, turning back to her glass.

A short time later, just before coffee, it comes out that the cousins will have to stay in the Jolanda.

'Really?' Grace begins. 'There's no room for us here in the house? Oh my goodness. I mean to say, how mortifying – we are such a pair of nuisances. To have presumed on your hospitality – what must you think of us? Do please forgive.'

'There is nothing to forgive,' the Signora says, 'except a house that is not large enough.'

'Uh-huh. The Jolanda, you say?' Grace continues. 'Remind me, isn't that the one with the yellow sign on the corner of via what-you-call-it? Yes, I think I know it, in fact I'm certain.'

'The Jolanda is convenient at least,' the Signora says, 'and we will be taking care of the bill, naturally. You can return here on Monday. Rosa should have your old rooms ready by the afternoon.'

'Well, that's kind,' Grace says, taking a spoonful of ice cream, and playing it around her mouth, then: 'What about that interesting hotel back along the road? Hotel Angst – I've always liked the look of that, I must say. Despite its unfortunate name!'

'The Angst is booked out,' Bella tells her. 'Everywhere is except the Jolanda.'

'Oh, I think you'll find, Miss Stuart – if you forgive my saying so – that the better hotels, they often keep a V.I.P. suite in reserve in case anyone important turns up unexpectedly. Of course, I don't mean to imply that my sister and I, we are in anyway important – good heavens, no. But, given the late hour, it is quite possible that it still is available, in which case—'

'Actually,' Bella says, 'I've already booked you into the Jolanda, your luggage is in your rooms and everything.'

'But how? I mean when?' Amelia then asks her.

'Before dessert, I went out.'

'You did? Were you gone long?'

'About half an hour.'

'How extraordinary – I didn't even notice you were gone! But then I didn't even notice you were here!' Amelia bursts out laughing.

The Signora glares at Amelia. 'Is that intended as an insult to Miss Stuart?' she coldly asks.

'Why, of course not!' Amelia cries. 'As if I would insult our dear Miss Stuart.' She lifts her glass in Bella's direction. 'She knows I have nothing but the utmost for her.'

'If you mean respect, then I'm very glad to hear it,' the Signora returns.

Later on the terrace Amelia takes a final swipe at Bella. Edward has just announced that he'll be absent for the rest of their visit and shouldn't be included in their plans.

'Good heavens, Edward,' Amelia says, her speech, by now, beginning to thicken, 'we've only just arrived. Are you trying to avoid us? Where are you going anyhow?'

'On holiday.'

'Well, yes, you've said as much. But where?'

'You know – here and there, see a bit of Europe.'

'Ah, I understand now, you don't want to say where. Is it a secret? Are you afraid we might follow you or something? Is that it?'

'Not at all.'

'So where will you be going first?'

'Paris.'

'Paris? Where we've just come from in fact?'

'Ah yes – so it is.'

'And then?'

'I'll be touring around, you know.'

'Will you be alone?'

'Of course.'

'Oh sure. We believe that! Maybe you're meeting someone there. An illicit rendezvous? A chorus girl? A married woman? No? Am I wrong? Well, maybe you're taking someone along then. Oh, I bet you are. Someone we know? Miss Stuart? Is it? Is it Miss Stuart?' Amelia throws out a hard false laugh. When nobody joins in she looks surprised. 'Oh, come on,' she says. 'I'm kidding – it's obvious I am.'

Without looking to see who is on the other end of the bottle, she holds her glass out to be refilled. Then she turns to Bella. 'It's a joke. You know – a joke? Honestly, you Britishers – such stiffs.'

'Actually, I'm not British,' Bella says.

'You're not?'

'No. We only moved to London permanently when I was fourteen. I was born in Dublin. I'm Irish actually.'

'Well,' Amelia laughs. 'I wouldn't go bragging about *that* – if I were you.'

The Signora stands up. 'Miss Stuart,' she begins, 'why don't you take Alec back to the hotel now? He is looking tired. And I'm sure Edward will want to go too. It's been a long day for all. Alec, will you go to the kitchen and see if Elida is ready to leave? Oh and Miss Stuart, don't bother to come back for the American ladies. I'm sure they would like to walk. I'm sure in fact they will find the fresh air useful. Go. You too, Edward. Goodnight.'

Bella follows Edward out to the garden to wait for Elida and Alec. 'What the hell's the matter with *you*?' she asks when she sees the expression on his face. 'Anyone would think she was having a go at you all night, and not me.'

'What a vintage bitch,' he says.

'Oh well, I suppose it's my own fault really. I shouldn't have said anything. But I felt she was going to start something, you know? She's so possessive about you – are you sure nothing ever went on there?'

'Don't be so bloody stupid.'

'All right – no need to snarl. Look, she just likes a bit of target practice when she's had a few, that's all. If it hadn't been me someone else would have got it. The trick is to duck, isn't it? Get out of the firing range, like clever little Eugenia.'

'Mmm,' he says, pulling his cigarettes out of his pocket and lighting one. 'I never knew you were Irish by the way,' he continues.

'Don't really think about it much. It's so long since I've been in Dublin. Why?'

'You just never told me. That's all.'

'Why should I? It's not as if *you* ever talk about your background,' she snaps.

He shrugs. 'I just didn't know. That's all I'm saying.'

'You make it sound as if I've been keeping some sordid secret.'

'That's ridiculous. I just thought—'

'Don't tell me you're anti-Irish too!'

'Of course not,' he protests.

'Actually it would be quite funny if you were.'

'Why?'

'Well, once or twice it crossed my mind that you *might* be Irish.'

'*Really?*'

'Yes, you'd say something and I'd think—'

'Say something?'

'Oh, I don't know, once I heard you call Alec a messer. I don't think I ever heard anyone English use that expression. Other things too, from time to time, can't remember now. Oh, there was that time I found you in the old town. Now you *really* sounded Irish then.' She laughs.

'Oh, that time.'

'Well, we won't get into all that.'

'Yes, thank you, it might be nice if we didn't.'

'Maybe everyone sounds Irish when they're drunk?'

'Ah and who's being anti-Irish now?'

'It's a joke, sorry.'

'No need to apologize to me.'

'Oh Edward, why do you always have to be so…'

'What?'

'Oh, never mind. Go back inside your shell, I don't care.'

*

At the tail end of all the confusion, just after lunch on Monday, Bella's father turns up on the doorstep.

She nearly dies when she sees him. He is strange and familiar all at once, like somebody famous spotted on the street. He looks a little pale – as most new arrivals to Bordighera tend to – but fit. Younger, somehow. He is standing at the open front door, as if he is trying to decide if he should ring the bell or step into a hallway full of suitcases and shout '*hellooo*'. Or maybe follow the sound of voices and the fuss of coffee cups around to the terrace at the side of the house. Bella and Alec have just come in by the front gate, the car parked firmly on the street outside, all doors open and ready for the removal of the first lot of visitors and their luggage to the station.

He says the word 'well' about half a dozen times as he comes down the steps. 'Well. Well now. Well indeed. Well, here we are now. Well, well – and how is my little girl?'

When he says this she bursts into tears.

'No need for that. Good gracious, no need at all,' he says, taking a final step to her and giving a pat to her arm.

Alec, shocked by her tears, puts his hand into hers and scowls at her father. 'It's all right, Alec,' she says. 'This is my papa.'

'Hello, little man.' Her father leans down to shake Alec's hand, which springs behind his back and out of reach in a second.

'Will you please tell him—' her father begins.

'Oh, Alec speaks English very well. He's just a little shy.'

'No harm in that,' her father bellows. 'I used to be a little shy myself, Alec. Hard to believe, I know. In a day or so, I'm sure we'll be the best of old pals. For years to come people will talk of it, they'll say, "Remember that August back in thirty-six, eh? That Alec and Harry, what they got up to? By God, what a pair of scoundrels!"'

Behind her back she feels Alec tighten.

'You look different,' her father says to her then. 'You've had your hair cut for a start. And the suntan. Different, but my God, how well!' He looks over at Mrs Jenkins, who has been standing to one side, a few feet away. Bella has forgotten for a moment all about her father's new wife. 'Doesn't she,

177

my dear? Doesn't she look very well indeed – no, marvellous in fact! Let's make no bones about it. Continental – is that the word I'm looking for?'

'Indeed you do look marvellous,' Mrs Jenkins agrees, coming forward, hand lifted awkwardly as if it is ready to shake or hug as appropriate. Her face is flushed, her smile wide, her over-bright eye just a little shifty. Bella has to wonder how Mrs Jenkins feels about all the lies that have led up to this moment. Had she helped to construct them? Perhaps even sitting beside her father six months ago, making suggestions as he composed that letter which had obviously been intended as a gentle paving of the way:

You'll never guess who I ran into the other day – an old friend of ours, Mrs Jenkins. A very pleasant and kind woman indeed. You remember her – of course you do, she helped nurse your poor mother. Your mother, I think, was fond of her.

When Bella takes Mrs Jenkins' hand it is shaking with nerves. Feeling sorry for the poor woman then, she kisses and lightly hugs her. She kisses both her cheeks, in the continental manner; an everyday embrace in Italy, which somehow seems less intimate. Twice the kisses – half the sentiment, Bella has always thought.

'I hope you'll be very happy,' she says, wondering how she is supposed to address her father's wife.

'Well, we certainly hope so too,' Mrs Jenkins laughs, 'and please – do call me Ina.'

Bella and Alec get to like Ina Jenkins-now-Stuart and spend a lot of time in her good and undemanding company. She has an artistic hand, which pleases Alec no end, especially as she takes the time to give him a few lessons, as well as to buy him his first grown-up box of watercolours, in a proper artist's shop. Her father, although he certainly seems to enjoy looking at Signora Lami-now-Tassi, favours the American cousins when it comes to company. They are, he declares, 'the best of sports'. They in turn find him '*so* entertaining and *so* wonderfully clever', and he certainly seems to take their minds off Edward's desertion. Should they happen to run into each other in town, which they do with unusual regularity, he invites them for coffee or drinks, or if the time is right, back to the Angst for lunch where they always sit at a window table, staying right through to the other side of the siesta, and forming a lively display for anyone who happens by.

If his new wife minds all this reciprocal attention, she never lets on. Although Bella does feel when the time comes to leave for Berlin, Ina looks brighter than she has done in days.

*

On the last morning of her father's visit, Bella goes walking with him to the public gardens on via Veneto. 'I'm delighted with you, my dear,' he begins. 'I really am. And as for your mother? Well, I'm sure she wouldn't have believed how things could have turned out. You've settled very well here, they think a lot of you, you know. But if you ever want to come home. Anytime come home. Well, you know.'

'I am, as you say, happy here.'

'Just thought I'd let you know. All right for money?'

'Yes, thank you. Fine.'

'Even so. I have opened a little account in your name in London. I mean if things ever get tricky in any way, it's there for you. We are not short, Ina and I. She has her own money, as you may know, and is generous with it.'

'Oh no, really—'

'Ahaha – doesn't do to go relying too much on the Lami family, you know. Splendid as they are. Blood is blood after all and when it comes to it, they don't owe you a thing. Anyway, I will give you the bank book when we get back to the hotel.'

'Thank you, Father. That's very kind.'

'Not at all. I have also arranged a letter of credit. The same account, of course, and amount – in case you think I've gone completely soft in the

179

head. It's just in case you ever need to get your paws on the money over here, you may even need to get yourself out in a hurry. Everything seems settled now, but with his nibs on the far side of the Alps – who knows? And that other Duce chap doesn't seem to be the full shilling, either. Still, I suppose it's too easy to judge the ways of another country.'

'You used to think Mussolini was wonderful.'

'I never!'

'Yes, you did. You used to say it was just what England needed, someone to give it a good kick up the backside.'

'Good God.' He blinks good-humouredly and scratches his chin. 'Did I really?'

They stroll on, him sucking his cigar and stopping to peer at a tree now and then, tipping a leaf over, frowning at the end of a branch, as if examining a body part of one of his patients. Bella knows he is mulling over his impressions of the past few days, whatever has got stuck in his head. One by one he will draw out his conclusions until his mind is clear again.

'Where will you live when you get back to London?' she asks him then.

'Where? Well, we haven't quite decided. Probably Ina's. She feels the house in Chelsea will always be your mother's, although she has already dickied it up quite a bit.'

'Oh? What's it like?'

'Tasteful, I believe the term is – you won't know it when you see it! We could move into her house – I don't mind in the least being haunted by the late Bill Jenkins – it's not as if she has any children to object to my presence. Then again, we may quite simply start all over, buy somewhere free of all ghosts.'

'It's kind of Ina to think of Mother, all the same,' Bella says.

'And you, she's thinking of you too, you know. Indeed she is.'

'Will you go straight home after Berlin?'

'What? Not sure yet. It depends very much on Ina. We may go to Amsterdam. Return through Hull. We may try the lakes – who knows?'

'Not to Switzerland?'

'Not so far as I know – why? Ah, of course – Amelia and Grace. They've invited us to join them. Has Ina said something?'

'No. They told me. And will you? Join them, I mean.'

'No. I said we *may* do so, purely out of politeness. They are good sports, of course they are, but – do you like them by the way?'

'Sometimes,' Bella laughs.

'Yes, I know what you mean. Personally, I wouldn't trust them an inch.'

He takes off his panama hat and fans his face for a moment before handing it to Bella so he can relight his cigar.

'What will you do all day when the boy goes to school?'

'If anything there'll be more to do, bringing him to and fro, homework, all that. The Signora will be returning to Naples with her husband and it's not suitable there for Alec.'

'Why – don't they allow children in Naples?'

'I can only tell you what the Signora says.' Bella shrugs.

'And the other chap, the one off on holiday?'

'Edward?'

'Yes, I mean, what can he be at – if the boy is at school all day. Bed and board and a wage simply to teach the piano? A cushy sort of number, if you ask me. Pity I didn't learn to tinkle the old ivories myself.'

'It's never been discussed with me. And he does teach him other things, you know, mathematics and science. I think the Signora probably feels it's safer if there's a man around. We are so near the border here and well, people come and go, there's been a lot of movement lately, and she gets nervous, I suppose.'

'What's she get nervous for – she's never bloody here?'

'For Alec, Father.'

'Bit unconventional though, two single people, only a child and a housekeeper besides under the one roof. Don't read me wrong, I'm not criticizing, but—'

'He doesn't live in the house, Father. He has his own place at the back entrance, a sort of mews flat over the garage where I keep the car.'

'Ah yes, of course. You and your car what?' He gives her a nudge and a grin.

'Well, it is only on approval.'

'The Signora approves. Don't you worry – you'll get to keep your little motor.'

They come to the fountain that marks the end of the path. 'Another lap, Bella – what do you say? May as well give these old hams a stretch before they're cooped up on the train for God knows how long.' They move on. 'Still, he's fond of you, that little chap.'

'Yes. We're fond of each other.'

'He's not quite right of course. But I daresay you know that.'

Bella stops short. 'What do you mean?'

'My dear girl. Don't look so shocked. You must have noticed.'

'There's nothing the matter with him.'

'Well, it's not my field, of course. But don't you find him a little detached? A little too wary of people? Reluctant to make eye contact, for instance. To listen even? And then other times he's overfamiliar, coming straight out and saying something forward, even a little bizarre?'

'He's not used to so many strangers, that's all. It's his way of coping. When he starts school in October… And the boy scouts, you know. He needs company. That's all. Other children. He's a good little artist, he'd hardly be able to draw and paint like that if there were anything wrong with him. Ask Ina, she'll tell you how artistic he is.'

Her father looks carefully at her for a moment then takes a pull of his cigar and flips the smoke off his tongue back to the air. 'Ah, it's most likely he's just been a bit mollycoddled, probably that's what has him nervy. School will sort him out and as you say the boy scouts. A bit of rough and ready, just what a boy needs. As I've said, it's not my field. He'll grow out of it. I daresay he will.'

*

The house becomes quiet again. At the end of August the Signora and her husband move back to Naples and the thank-you cards and letters begin to arrive from the wedding guests who have finished their respective tours about Europe and are now returned to their everyday lives. Eugenia first, just back from a visit to her father's family in Dusseldorf. A large greeting card lined with red velvety rose petals: 'a thousand kisses for my adorable Alec' – who stomps off in a huff when Rosa teases him about it. The Swiss couple, thanking Bella for kindness she hadn't really shown, and inviting her to visit their house in Zurich. She had been like a daughter to them, the letter declares, puffing up what had really been no more than common courtesy into deep affection, and making her worry about how the unfortunate pair usually found themselves treated. A short girlish letter from Grace next; all snappy sentences and scattered punctuation. A sort of a jazz letter, Bella decides.

> Back in N.Y.C. Dad put Amelia to work. Get this – in his fuddiest-duddiest hotel!! A morgue practically… (to keep her out of trouble – as if – ho hum!) Lucky ol' me left to care for Mother, an invalid now, nothing much working except her complaining whine – only joking ha! Anyway. Here we both are, BORED to tears and longing for Europe. Europe! Had a note from Aunt Lami thanking us for the wedding gift – didn't say if she liked it though… Bing!!!

Then a long letter from Ina, wanting Bella to know, and please not to mind, that they have decided to live in the house in Chelsea after all, her father having all his papers and medical paraphernalia there, it just seemed to make more sense. Although the house – for so long without a woman's touch – had become a little shabby and would really need to be completely redone (with Bella's blessing of course and with no disrespect to the taste of her late mother). Bella, recalling what her father had said about the 'tasteful' improvements already carried out, is at first shocked and a little hurt by this blatant lie, but then after a while she decides not to care.

'Germany,' Ina's letter concludes, 'has been more interesting than anything else. Impressive city that Berlin is and for all the beautiful country-side afterward, the air is tense and hard-edged. Not at all like the soft warm air one finds with our friends in Italy!'

To the end of the letter her father has added a few hasty lines. Bella can imagine, now that he has a wife, he will be relieved never to have to think through, never mind write, another full letter to her or anyone else again. His few words say more than Ina's three pages.

That Führer – a certifiable nutter with too many puppets in his dangerous charge. The minute his nose sticks over the Alps, you get yourself home, girl. Hope all well with you, the boy, and that you're not causing too much havoc whizzing about Liguria in your little *topolino*. Come home or come visit – your affectionate father – The Old Goat.

Finally there is a postcard from Edward, a few illegible words, like a written mumble, sent from somewhere outside Linz and looking as if he'd been carrying it around in his pocket for weeks.

*

September and the Almansi sisters arrive, taking Alec over and leaving Bella with little to do apart from bring him to and from the beach club attached to their hotel. In between she helps Cesare in the garden, and as the Signora has made it quite clear there is no longer any need to be 'always disturbing me with domestic banalities' Bella has taken on the role of private secretary and occasional housekeeper of the Bordighera branch of the Lami/Tassi family.

Four mornings a week, she gives English lessons to Rosa and Elida, helping them with the housework to free up their time. At first Elida is horrified at the thought of Bella's hands getting dirty, but as her English improves and she begins to enjoy herself more, she gets over this. Both women prove themselves as pupils, as well as companions, giving Bella a sense of camaraderie she hasn't felt since childhood – not that, as she has to admit to herself, she'd ever really felt it then.

The summer season drags bravely on, way after there is any need for it, like an orchestra playing to an empty hall. Finally it falls away altogether. Bella loves the lull at this time of the year when Bordighera, left to its locals, long-term foreign residents, invalids and the elderly, becomes less the smart Riviera resort and more of an open-air nursing home. The air is lighter, the nights cooler, it's possible to walk a straight line on the *passeggiata* and pavements, or to get served at a café table without having to listen to a tourist quibble over a menu or bill. Or, as she has only recently come to appreciate, to drive on a Sunday without being stuck in a jam. Shopkeepers and tradesmen, relying on custom that is more difficult to woo, come back to their attentive selves. Standards rise, prices come down. All in all, Bella feels, an ideal time of the year to prepare Alec Lami to go out to the world.

And besides it might take her mind off Edward.

A few days after he is due back and no sign or word, she is beginning to doubt his return. Why should he, after all? Her father had been right – there was nothing for him here. A few piano lessons each week to a child who isn't all that interested in learning it. The company of herself, Rosa and Elida! A waste of time, never mind of a life. She used to believe he only stayed because of the Signora, that they had been lovers all along, or at least that he had been in love with her, and living in hope all these years. She had been encouraged to think this way by the jealous Amelia. Bella feels now that this had to be nonsense.

He is still young – for a man. Easy to get along with, if a little distant. Talented. Attractive to women – certainly the American cousins had thought so. And the Signora often boasted about his impeccable reference. He could make a go of it anywhere. If Edward had any sense, he would have taken his holiday money and skipped it.

One day she breaks into his room. Even while she is doing it she is deeply ashamed – although not enough to make herself stop.

The way it happens: she has just put the car in the garage after leaving Alec at the beach club and although not in any way aware of having a plan, she must have done. Because when she walks up that iron staircase at the side of the garage she has a screwdriver in her hand and when she reaches the door, without hesitation unscrews the bolt at the hinges.

Her first time inside. For all the countless occasions she has made her way down the garden path for Edward's benefit – a telephone message from the Signora; a reminder that a meal is ready after he's lost all sense of time. Maybe to bring something delivered by a shop in town: music scores he's ordered, a gramophone record, a coat that has needed altering. He has always come clattering down the stairs before she's had a chance to put so much as a foot on them. It's as if he's been on constant watch-out. Not that she's ever really expected to be asked in. It's just that he's always seemed so determined to keep her out.

She wonders now if anyone has ever been inside. Alec's lessons take place at a beautiful grand piano in the Signora's sitting room in the villa, where Edward also goes to read his newspapers and books – so long as the Signora is away. And Elida happened to mention one day that Edward prefers to clean the mews himself, coming down to the linen room once a week to exchange dirty linen for clean. She has often noticed Cesare in the evenings sitting on the steps with Edward, enjoying a quiet chat and a cigarette, while a bonfire smoulders nearby, but has no idea if even Cesare has ever been over the threshold.

The mews has one room, as well as a small bathroom; toilet, basin and hipbath and a mirror hardly big enough to hold an entire face. The main room is large and quite dark, so for a moment it seems as if the shutters are closed. It turns out to be the trees outside sopping up most of the light. A day bed against the wall. A feeble-looking card table beside it; a torch, a box of matches and an ashtray on top. An upright piano and a stool at the window overlooking the garden. There is a small wardrobe nudged to one corner. A shelf, made from a bare plank of wood and two brackets, holds a primus stove, one tin cup, one small teapot and a packet of Lipton's tea with a spoon sticking out of it. A light bulb in the centre of the ceiling with no shade. And that's it – apart from a small tin box holding shoe polishes and brushes.

She is struck by how little of himself there is in that room. Except for a few scribbled notes on the margins of music manuscripts, there is no evidence of anyone living there. Not that the mews is unkempt, but clean and neat as a prison cell. Bella is certain the Signora would have told him to take his pick from all the spare furniture in the house. Evidently he chose not to. There are no photographs, no keepsakes; not even a calendar on the wall. No past, no future – as if Edward had only been someone passing through, and in any case, had already died.

Afterwards she sits at the garden table for a while, where three years before she had sat with the American cousins listening to him play the piano. She tries to picture Edward but can't find a face or even imagine a voice. The only thing she can find is a back view caught from an upstairs window of the villa on a winter's evening that turned suddenly cold. Almost dark, it had started to rain. That peculiar Ligurian winter rain: large isolated drops for a long time, then a sudden collapse into a savage downpour. Edward walking down the path to his mews. His walk, brisk yet somehow unhurried, as if he hasn't noticed the rain, or just hasn't cared about it. Hair a little long and curled at the back like a child's. Hands in pockets, elbows sharp and determined, arms thin in shirtsleeves that the rain is beginning to stain.

*

A uniform is ordered for San Giorgio's and, after several fittings and a lot of paperwork, is finally delivered. Brown shoes, navy trousers and a very British blazer complete with a crest of San Giorgio and his dragon. A satchel and a school cap complete the look, making Alec every inch the English schoolboy, although he will have to wait another few weeks before he can play that role.

Meanwhile Bella has his photograph taken and three copies made, one for the house, one for herself and one which she sends to his mother. She wonders where it will end up – in Signor Tassi's house in Naples, or in the gallery of photographs so lovingly created by Alec's father? She wonders if that gallery still exists.

There is little or no wait for confirmation of his entry to the *Balilla*. The application for his membership is jumped at by a fawning regional *comandante* who declares it an honour to have a member of the Lami family in their legion. Another uniform – black shirt, black cap, grey shorts, grey socks, black shoes, a neckerchief the colour of azure and a perky little fez for his head. Another photograph and all that remains is for Alec to learn his oath and then take it. It's the usual guff about believing in Rome the eternal, the mother of his country. He also has to swear by the genius of Mussolini and the resurrection of the Empire. Alec loves his oath, despite his struggle to learn it, and Bella is glad Edward is not here to sneer at it.

Finally a membership card is issued in his name, signed by the *Comandante Generale di Provincia*, and Alessandro P. Lami is now part of the regime.

His first *Balilla* meeting. Bella decides they should walk rather than drive. He's been fidgety and overexcited all morning and the exercise might work it out of his system.

There will be singing and games, she reassures him – just as Rosa has earlier reassured her – marching practice and manoeuvres. Naturally, there will also be a *spuntino* break or two, for sweet treats and drinks.

Alec speculates all the way to via San Antonio on who or what he will find there, pausing at shop windows to tenderly press his neckerchief to his chest or give a cautious twist to the woggle that holds it in place, or to pat his fez without actually touching it. Each time he lets it be known, in a roundabout way, that he is thinking of and missing someone in particular.

Outside the window of Marco's shop: 'Elida says Maestro Edward will be home soon with holes in his shoes from all the walking – isn't that funny!'

When they reach the huge vetrino of Caffè dello Sport: 'Where do you think Mamma is, now this very minute? I bet she's on a train. I bet that's where she is, with Nollie. I bet that's who's with her. Nollie.'

They come to Gibelli's, where his reflection hovers over the schoolbook display. 'Do they have the same uniform for every *Balilla* in Italy? I wonder that, I do. Would they have the same one even in Torino – say for the boys who go to the school of the Almansi sisters?'

At the music shop he says nothing, but stays blinking into the glass for a while. When he turns round his eyes are moist. He has been thinking about his father, Bella is certain.

She leaves him at the door in the care of his section leader, a fat boy of about fourteen, who greets them with a Roman salute and a rattled-off fascist rhyme.

She only seems to be home a few minutes when Elida comes croaking up the stairs. Bella arrives down to a sobbing Alec in the hall, the *comandante* with a hand on his shoulder, trying to quieten him down. The chubby section leader – who turns out to be the *comandante*'s nephew – is on the other side of him, looking decidedly ashamed – whether of himself or of Alec, Bella can't be certain. They can only tell her that during manoeuvres Alec had some sort of a *crisi* and had become more and more hysterical, leaving the section leader no option but to send for the *comandante* to take him home in his car.

The *comandante* is obviously embarrassed and in a hurry to get this scene over with. His hands appear to be juggling the words as they come rushing out of his mouth. Bella has to strain very hard to translate what he is saying, but for the fact that he repeats himself so often, she may have missed the half of it.

Nothing happened. But nothing! He repeatedly insists. Nobody touched or said the smallest thing to upset that boy. It was something inside the child himself, something that erupted quite suddenly. Out of nowhere. Without warning. Maybe he isn't ready for the *Balilla*. Maybe that's it. Perhaps another time, a few years on – when he's older and has more sense. Although he is nine years old. And if by now…?

Of course he's not expelled. For God's love, of course not! A son of the Lami family – does she think they are crazy? But at the same time. For the boy's own sake. Perhaps? A doctor's certificate will excuse him from further duties. He can of course remain as a member. But in name only. They will certainly not be taking his card from him. The card is the best thing of all – it is evidence that he loves his country and his Duce. And it entitles him to free ice cream on a national holiday. Free ice cream, imagine that! Also free train travel at certain times; invitations to a little *festa* now and then. Well, maybe not every *festa*, but…?

Here he draws Bella aside and his speech at last begins to slow down. No hard feelings, eh? But the *Balilla* can't have that sort of unbecoming behaviour out on the field. If it were up to him of course – but it isn't. '*Si tratta di morale, d'onore.*' It's a question of morale, of honour, he concludes, delivering this last bit out the side of his mouth.

Bella thanks and assures him that she understands everything. She will inform the Signora of the situation immediately. By now Alec's sobs have sharpened into wheezes and she takes him upstairs to put him to bed before calling the doctor. She can hear Elida below in the hall, showing the *comandante* and his nephew to the door. Elida's voice is stretched to its limits with temper – meaning she'll probably be dumb for the next few days. How dare they show such disrespect to the Lami family? Who do they think they are? If they've forgotten, she could remind them – jumped-up peasants who can barely read or write. 'You and your pig-faced nephew,' she squawks. 'Get him out of here. Fascist *feccia* – that's all you are. Think you can rule by castor oil and the bullying of little boys.' One final '*Bastardi!*' accompanies the slam of the door.

Bella wraps the uniform in tissue, takes the woggle and puts it in a drawer for a keepsake, also the membership card, just in case it is ever needed. Everything else she gives to Rosa, who might pass it on to someone in need. The *Balilla* is never discussed again, not even behind Alec's back.

*

Edward finally returns from his holiday almost a fortnight late, and looking decidedly peaky, Bella has to remark, for someone who's been hiking around all those weeks, in the fresh mountain air.

'Ask no questions…' he sheepishly replies, and Bella guesses he's had one of his slips. She leaves him alone to come back to himself.

She has only ever seen him drunk once. That was the year she had arrived in Bordighera and long before they became friends. Rosa's husband had been dying and Bella had gone to the old town to bring supper for the family and pay her respects. She had been slightly wary about intruding, but Elida had assured her that a visit at this time would be not only welcome, but probably expected. 'Don't stay long, and recognize the moment to leave,' had been her advice.

Rosa's apartment was on the top floor of a house off the piazza della Fontana into which several other apartments had been similarly squeezed. The husband, bedridden for years, was a hugely overweight man, who seemed to be bouldered to the bed by the weight of his own flesh. Even while he still breathed, neighbours from the other apartments had been out on the landings arguing about how they would get him down four flights of stairs, never mind into a coffin.

'We'll have to wait till the flesh rots,' a woman with a bald head had finally declared, 'or else we'll have to knock the wall down.'

When Rosa heard this she had been so upset she screamed at them all to leave. She would do the *Vigilia della Morte* alone with her sons. At least they loved their father. Fat as he was. Better no prayers to accompany him to heaven than the prayers of stone-hearts and hypocrites. But the eldest son who worked for the ministry wouldn't be home on leave until morning; the second son was away in the army; the middle boy in bed with a fever. That had left only two little boys for company. Bella had not been able to leave her.

The embalmers' arrival had been perfectly timed, a few minutes after the doctor, and a few more before the priest. Two old nuns; one of them such a tiny creature that she had to climb onto a stool and kneel on the bed to reach the corpse, lifting the fleshy cowls of his chins to get at his neck with her sponge. The taller nun had set about replacing taper candles that were almost spent. Hot wax dripping on a heavily scarred hand that never seemed to flinch. She then went about the room turning pictures to the wall: Mussolini, Queen Margherita, others from the House of Savoy, and a few family portraits featuring Rosa's husband in slimmer times.

By now the two boys had fallen fast asleep, the bigger one, about ten years old, seated on a stool by the end of the death bed, slumped over, face mashed into the counterpane. The smaller one sleeping soundly in the rocking embrace of his sobbing mother. It had given the impression of the *Pietà* – as if it had been the son, and not the father, who had just died. Bella had recognized the moment to leave.

On the way downstairs she saw the priest shuffling upwards, pausing outside the door of each apartment, raising a weak hand and a weary voice in benediction, then, as they squeezed past each other on the narrow stairwell, pausing to bless her.

Bella stayed at the hall door for a time, looking out. The air was heavy and dark. She dreaded the walk home; through the *carruggi*, those high-vaulted tunnels that ran like narrow indoor streets through the town and where, even in the broadest daylight, it was dark, and even in the rainless weeks of high summer there was a smell of must, death and dirty linen.

She was considering waiting for the priest to come back down the stairs, maybe offer to go with him as far as the road – an old man might be glad of the company at that time of night, someone to carry his bag, take his elbow across the uneven cobbles. Then a door slammed at the top of the house and she felt herself jump from the inside out. Looking up, there was the priest again, this time ploughing down all the flights of stairs, banging on doors, kicking some of them, shouting and snarling as he went on his way, telling the neighbours they would burn in hell for the lack of respect they had shown to Rosa's dying husband, ordering them out of bed, up those stairs and onto their knees, to beg forgiveness from God and from Rosa. Bella slipped out the front door and into the short alleyway that led back to the piazza.

A wobble of light across the cobblestones. It ricocheted off the crumbling walls, tipped off a window, grazed on a rooftop then collapsed back to the ground. There were sounds too: metal, glass, the shift of a footstep. She decided to ignore the unreliable sway of light but to follow instead the sounds, which led her to the fountain and the milk boy already at work.

A torch in one hand, a huge enamel jug in the other, he was clumsily filling bottles, jars and billycans – whatever receptacles had been left out by local families to stay cool beneath the lip of the fountain. The boy, muttering a gleeful rosary, had obviously seen the priest in his vestments heading for Rosa's.

'*Il Grossone – è morto?*' he whispered when he'd finished his decade.

'*Sì,*' she replied (refusing to call Rosa's husband 'the fat one') '*È morto – Signor Fabbri.*'

'*Poverino,*' the boy mumbled kindly, bringing his mouth down to kiss the front of his thumb, then licking it when a drop of milk fell over his hand.

She watched him work for a while under the erratic light of his torch, milk splashing whenever an attempt to hoist the torch under his arm caused the jug to tip over. It smelled sweet and grassy – she could taste it from its scent. There was an older, sour smell too, which she took to be from the milk boy's clothes. She asked him if he would like her to hold the torch for him while he worked and he looked at the sky for a long few seconds as if deciding whether she could be trusted. Then he handed her the torch.

When the task was finished he whispered again, this time an offer to escort her back to the road, and she had been grateful that she hadn't needed to ask. He took the torch back and stuck it into his belt. Then, taking her by the hand, started to lead her along.

Into the first of the *carruggi* – not a thread of light anywhere – he spoke to her again, this time without a whisper, his voice suddenly deep. It was late, he said, for an English signora to be walking out on her own. He would take care of her, she need not be afraid. He would go with her to her house, he would see nobody jumped on her, maybe tried to kiss or fondle her, as men often did. He would protect her, all the way. She realized then the hand she was holding was not the hand of a child.

They turned right, where the *carruggio* widened and lifted, and a single lighted lantern hanging from a bracket in the wall allowed her to make him out. Short in stature, not quite a man, but near enough to it, with his Adam's apple eager and large, his skimpy facial hair, the pimples pushing to get out from under his skin. In any case, far too old to be walking around with at that hour of the night, holding hands.

She was trying to work out how she could free her hand without causing offence, when she saw something slumped in a doorway. The boy saw it too and, standing back from her, had held his hand out theatrically as if to tell her to wait until he had assessed the danger, then, laying the milk jug down, he pulled the torch like a gun from his belt and swung it to point at the slump. He clicked on the light and it bounced onto a man. A man in a heap; head down to his chest, coat hanging off him, hair flopped over his forehead.

'*È stato al bordello.*' The boy was laughing and Bella pretended not to understand. Pulling her by the sleeve he took her a little way to the corner and pointed up another narrow alleyway. An open door and a light in the window broke into the darkness.

'*Lo conosco,*' he declared.

'You know him?'

'*Sì è l'Inglese.*'

At first Bella felt she must have misunderstood; it seemed odd for an Englishman to be here, at this hour, in this state. English people only came up here in daylight, and as tourists. But then she realized that a brothel was a brothel to any man so inclined.

194

The boy wanted to leave him there. He kept saying, '*Andiamo, Signora.*'

She tried to explain. They couldn't leave him here alone, like this. But the boy was adamant. '*È pericoloso.*'

'Dangerous? Surely not that. Only drunk. *Non è pericoloso. Solo ubriaco.*'

She leaned into the drunken man. 'Excuse me,' she began, 'I know it's none of my business, but, you know, you really ought—'

The man groaned and his head rolled back slightly. Bella could hardly believe who she was looking at. 'Maestro Edward?' she said. 'Oh God.'

The boy was looking slyly at her. She walked away and then came back. She walked away again. Then she told the boy to hold the torch over the man's face.

She leaned in again. It was him. No doubt about it. Edward. Drunk. Edward known to this boy as the dangerous Englishman, a regular of the brothel, no less. She got such a fright, whatever bit of Italian she knew left her there and then. 'We must move him,' she said to the boy. 'He can't stay here.'

The milk boy shrugged.

'Let me see. All right. Oh God, how do I say it? You must help me. Help. Me. Lift. Him. *Aiuto.*'

The boy just stared at her.

'What the hell am I supposed to do now?' she asked. She gathered herself and then softly began, 'Edward. Edward? Can you hear me, Edward? It's me. Miss Stuart. Now you're going to have to try…' She took him by the chin, her hand a little shocked by the feel of his beard filling up her palm. 'Edward!' Her voice louder, sharp. Then she started to shake him. 'Edward! Wake up, for God's sake. Will you wake now. Please!'

'Ah go and fuck off,' he snarled out of his stupor. Then he hit out at her.

The boy jumped back. '*Signora! La prego. Andiamo,*' he said.

'No! We are not leaving him.' She approached him again. 'Edward, it's me. Look at me, Edward. You can't stay here. You just can't. Now, I'm going to help you get up.'

His arm flew up again, and this time caught her on the side of her face. It shocked more than hurt, ringing through her jaw. After a moment she tried again, this time giving herself enough distance to allow her to jump out of the way.

'Edward,' she began, 'I'm warning you, if you dare hit me again.'

His eyes shot open and looked straight into hers without seeing who or what they were looking at.

'Edward, it's me. Don't you know me?' she asked him. 'It's me. Anabelle Stuart.'

'Ah fuck off, leavemealone. Jaysus sake.'

Bella looked up. The boy had gone. Now what? She thought about running back for the priest, or going home for Elida or maybe calling on Cesare. But if Signora Lami ever found out about this, Edward would surely be dismissed and without a reference. Besides all that, there was Alec to consider. What would he do without his beloved Maestro?

Voices came then. The milk boy from the direction of the brothel, with a man and a woman behind him. The man big, burly, in bare feet and undervest, his head shaved to the skull, a tattoo of a swastika on his upper arm. A sailor. A German. The woman pulled a shawl over her shoulders and up onto her head. She looked nothing like the sort Bella would have expected to find in a brothel.

'English?' the German said to her.

'Yes.'

'Husband?'

'No.'

'No?'

'I mean, yes.' She thought it would make the man more likely to help. The German threw back his head and laughed.

'*Pazzo*,' the milk boy said, tapping the side of his head to indicate madness.

The German crouched down to Edward. 'Ah yes,' he said. 'Come. Is all over now, my friend. God pity you in the morning.'

Edward's arm lashed out; the German caught it and hauled him up. Edward's foot slipped as he came up and kicked the milk jug over.

'*Aiuta-mi*,' the German said to the boy, who by now had a face as white as the pool of milk spilling from his jug.

The German dragged Edward forward. Edward flopped over like a puppet, and then reared up suddenly and aimed a punch at the man. The man caught his hand and slapped Edward right in the mouth.

'No!' Bella shouted, but the German just grinned at her.

In a moment Edward was settled between the German and the milk boy. His head inclined, a bauble of blood from his mouth to his beard, arms outstretched across each of the bearer's shoulder.

'We live on via Romano,' Bella had said then.

'Forget that, lady,' the German replied.

'Oh, but please, you must.'

'Double the weight for a dead man. Triple for a drunk. It's not possible.' Then they dragged him back towards the brothel.

The woman didn't seem to want Edward to return to the brothel but when she began to protest, the German snapped at her. Bella thought he said something like – 'You took his money now take his troubles.'

The milk boy, who seemed like a child again beside the German, peeped out from under the arch of Edward's arm and told her to wait for him, he would be back to bring her safely home. Bella said that she would.

As soon as they entered the bordello, she crept away. It was almost light by then and she could find her own way home.

*

Alec starts school in October and to Bella's surprise settles in well, if a little warily. A fortnight later he comes down with a fever. Doctor Eaton, or *Dottor Inglese* as he is known to Rosa and Elida, says it's nothing to worry about: he's simply picked up a schoolboy virus – a common enough occurrence with a child who has just started school. His immune system would soon get used to the new environment. A few days in bed and he'd be fiddle-fit again.

But Alec deteriorates by the hour, his temperature soars and when Bella tries to give him a drink, he is unable to focus on the cup, his hand reaching to the right and left of it, as if the cup is dancing around. She calls for the doctor again. 'I'm afraid it's pneumonia,' he says.

It is decided not to move him to the hospital. The nurses are run off their feet as it is, with an epidemic of gastroenteritis – the last thing Alec needs. The doctor will send a private nurse instead. Nurse Willis, a very capable Scottish lady who is known for her special way with children. He himself will call every few hours. In the meantime sponge baths, and fluids – as much as they can persuade him to take. The nurse will set up a steam tent. And is there a room in the house with a ceiling fan?

'Steaming him up on account of his lungs, cooling him down again on account of his temperature – that's what it's all about now,' the doctor cheerily says, picking up his bag and leaving the room. He gets as far as the door, and turns back. 'I don't wish to be alarmist but at this point it might be as well to inform the mother, have her standing by anyway, should the worst – well, just in case.'

Edward carries Alec upstairs to the Signora's room – the closest room with a ceiling fan. His shirt is stuck to him with the sweat of Alec's fever. 'He's so hot,' Edward says, moments after he's put him down. 'It feels like I still have him here in my arms.'

While Edward goes off to change his shirt, Nurse Willis arrives. 'Alec will have to be moved again,' she announces, the second she steps into the room.

'Oh surely not?' Bella says.

'Why, look at the bed, Miss Stuart! The bed is a ridiculous size – now how am I supposed to get at the laddie? And the steam tent – are we forgetting about that? It's a tent m'dear, not a marquee!'

Edward moves him again, and again has to change his shirt. This time it's into Bella's room, which has the smallest bed in the house. It will seem strange to have people wandering around all hours of the day and night; it will make her fret a little about what they might see or surmise. And yet in some way it is a comfort too, having Alec in her room.

The Signora cannot be located. Bella tries everywhere, by telephone, and later by telegram. She is not in Sicily. 'She rarely is these days to be honest,' the English housekeeper brusquely advises. 'Try Naples – why don't you?'

'I have.'

'Well, you'll just have to try it *a-gain*, Miss Stuart. And a-gain. That's all you can do. Keep trying.'

'I have tried it again and *a-gain*. There's no answer from the house.'

'No cause to get snippy, I'm sure. What about Signor Tassi's office?'

'I don't have a telephone number.'

'Well, I do, Miss Stuart, all you have to do is ask, you know.'

The call to the office in Naples starts off well enough. Avvocato Tassi is in Germany on business, the Signora is certain to be with him, as she happens to be his client in this matter. Then Bella is connected to Tassi's private secretary, who can't resist an opportunity to show off his appalling and almost senseless English. She can't get him to switch back to Italian and in the end has to pretend to be called away, handing the phone over to Elida. 'Whatever you do,' she whispers, 'don't let him know you speak a word of English.'

There is no telephone number for the Avvocato. There is no forwarding address. He could be in Dusseldorf, or maybe Bonn. As far as the secretary is aware there are business matters to attend to in both cities, although it's not his place to question his superiors. Naturally, as soon as the signori return or make contact he will pass the message on.

Bella remembers then that Eugenia has relatives in Dusseldorf – presumably also related to the Signora. Eugenia isn't at home either but her maid manages to find the number for Dusseldorf.

Getting a call through to Germany is an ordeal. Edward and Mrs Cardiff have to go to the British Consul, who in turn has to go to the mayor of Bordighera, who then turns to a bishop in Genoa. Eventually they are allowed to skip the usual formalities, and the call is put through to Dusseldorf. After all that trouble – the relatives have moved away. Emigrated, in fact. When or where, nobody seems to know or give much of a damn.

Nurse Willis makes a little hospital ward out of Bella's room, complete with a steam tent that by now is the talk of Bordighera. All day, tubs and pots of boiling water are carted up and down the stairs by Elida, Rosa, Edward and even poor old bandy Cesare, until the corridor leading out of the kitchen begins to resemble a London alleyway in November. Neighbours have sent servants to lend a hand or have personally called with baskets of fruit he will never eat, and flowers he will never see. In one door and out the other, these gifts have been swiftly redistributed via a grateful Mrs Cardiff, to her various charities.

Bella has been excused from water duties on account of her back problems and is kept upstairs to assist Nurse Willis, whose face pops in and out of the tent like a big boiled moon and gives her little jobs to do. Bella begins to wonder if Nurse Willis has won her reputation for having a special way with children because she treats everyone just like a child, even down to the way she delegates tasks and then lavishes praise on their completion. There is no doubt she is an excellent nurse – if at times irritatingly cheerful – and that she brings a much needed air of confidence into the sickroom. However, beyond taking his temperature or checking his pulse, Alec won't have her near him. It's the same when it comes to the doctor, any lingering and he begins to grow distressed. Weak and delirious as he now is, he makes it quite clear that Bella and Edward are the only ones he will allow to wash or change him.

Nurse Willis accepts this rejection with good grace and in fact looks on it as a promising sign: 'Shows he's aware of the who's-who and what's-what!' she beams. Then, instructing them on how best to give a sponge bath and change the sweat-soaked sheets and dry him as quick as ever and leave his pores closed awhile before steaming them open again, she plucks her cigarettes out of her bag and leaves them at it while she 'pops out for a wee puff and a cup of tea'.

On the night before Alec's tenth birthday the doctor weighs the lollipop of his stethoscope in his hand and tells them the next twelve hours can go either way. 'Any luck with the mother?' he asks then and Bella feels as if he has shoved his fist through her stomach and twisted her guts.

She tries Naples again, and again. Still no sign of Avvocato and wife. And then Sicily. This time the English housekeeper is seething. 'Shoving him into a school with all sorts. I mean what's she expect? It would never 'ave done in old Signor Lami's day, I can tell you that straight off. Then she buggers off with not a word to no one. What sort is she anyway? Well, no sort of a mother, I can tell you.' There is a few seconds' silence and Bella thinks they've been disconnected. Then she realizes the English housekeeper is weeping.

'Are you all right?' she asks.

'I may never see him again. My poor little Ali Baba, my poor little lamb.'

On the way back upstairs Bella meets Elida. Elida is also crying and for one awful moment Bella thinks the worst has happened. It turns out that Edward has 'growled as a dog' at her, only because she's suggested the priest. 'Growled as a dog, Signora Stuart, and say to me – get out of here with your stupid witch talk before Alesso hear and you frighten him.'

Later that evening just after his steam bath, while they are changing his sheets, Bella on one side of the bed, Edward on the other, Alec seems to stop breathing. It's just a split second; such a short time in fact that Edward hasn't even noticed. Up to this point his breath has sounded like a tin of sewing needles being gently shaken from side to side. Now there has been that split second of silence. The steam is already on the wane and when she looks down through it, Alec is disappearing in front of her eyes. As if he is melting away with the steam. His narrow shoulders, the cage of his prominent ribs, even his thick coarse hair, all dissolving.

She is about to put down the sheet and whisper his name. But then the needles resume shivering in his throat again. Bella, saying nothing to Edward, continues her task for a few more seconds. Then a large fat sob blurts out of her mouth. It just seems to fall out of its own accord. She puts her hand out as if to catch it and shove it back in.

Edward reaches across and touches her arm. 'You go outside,' he says. 'I'll finish here.'

She shakes her head and closes her eyes. 'Is? Is he?'

'It's all right, Bella, it's all right. He's still here,' Edward says. 'He's still with us.'

*

Suddenly out of nowhere Alec improves. His temperature starts to slide towards normal, his breathing eases, the colour on his face and chest comes up, as the mottled look recedes. The doctor says, 'It's a bloody relief – I don't mind telling you.'

Nurse Willis dismantles the steam tent. Edward apologizes to Elida. Elida, through her tears, graciously accepts – after she has made a slow sign of the cross and a pointed acknowledgement to the Madonna's intervention. Rosa, who has hardly been home in a week, kisses everyone in the room including Dottor Inglese and says she is off now to see if she can find, never mind recognize, her own children.

'The crisis is over,' the doctor explains, 'but that doesn't mean he's recovered. He needs peace, quiet. Vigilance. He should sleep now for quite a bit, but the minute he opens his eyes, telephone me, no matter what time it is. If I don't hear from you I'll look in again first thing.'

Bella says she will sit with him, after all it is her room and she has more of a right to be there than anyone else. 'So go,' she says, pushing Nurse Willis and Edward to the door. 'Go. Sleep. Eat. Smoke. Get drunk. Chase each other through the streets naked. Do whatever it is that pleases you. Just leave me.'

She is light-headed with tiredness and a relief she is almost afraid to allow herself to feel. All she wants now is time on her own with Alec, a

202

chance to absorb the shock of the past few days, to monitor and accept the hope for the days to come.

Elida brings in supper, her large hand conducting a tour of the tray: ham, cheese, one or two other things on a plate. 'It's cooked *prosciutto* – not *crudo* – and soft the way you like, Signora, and a nice *caraffa* of *Rossese* to do you some good. There is the coffee pot with the English cosy to keep the warm in. And here at last is one of the peaches we preserve in September. So sweet, I can't say it.'

Bella turns off the main lights and puts a match to the night lamp. The wine goes straight to her head. She sucks on a peach and gets into her pyjamas, then changes back into her day clothes in case Alec wakes up sooner rather than later, and the room starts filling with visitors again. She pads the window seat with pillows and cushions and settles herself in. Then, afraid of getting too comfortable and dozing off, whips everything away again.

With one cushion moulded into her back Bella sits upright where she can have a permanent view of Alec. She stares at him for a while and then begins to sing. Anything that comes into her head – 'Silent Night'; an alphabet song; the dwarves song from *Snow White*; and the ditty the troops brought back from East Africa last year about the little black face looking out to sea – '*Facetta Nera*', which Alec never tires of hearing or singing himself.

A few minutes later there is a tap on the door and she opens it to Edward. 'How long have you been out there?' she asks.

'Long enough to know you're a crow.'

'Very funny. Anyway – I thought I told you to get lost.'

'Can't bloody sleep,' he begins, stepping into the room. 'I did everything you said. Had a smoke – several smokes. Then something to eat. As you know it's probably not a good idea if I get drunk. And I didn't particularly want to run through the streets naked, especially with Nurse Willis running ahead of me – she wobbles a bit, you know.'

'Does she indeed?'

'Yes. So, I thought I might as well keep you company. How is he?'

'Fine. Sleeping peacefully.'

'And his breathing?'

'Perfect.'

'Good.' He walks over and looks down at Alec. 'Ah, the colour is back. That's a good sign, isn't it?'

'Yes, Edward, that's a good sign.'

'I suppose it's all right if we talk? We won't disturb him?'

'It's fine. It might encourage him to come round actually, just to make sure he's not missing anything.'

He turns away from the bed. 'Are you eating that?' he asks, his hand already stretched towards the plate on the tray.

'I thought you had something to eat?' she says.

'Still hungry. And there's no point in wasting it – you won't eat it.'

'How do you know I won't?'

He raises his eyebrows at her, then sits into the sofa, the plate on his lap. 'So,' he begins, leaning back to rest an olive on his lips, then sucking it in. 'How come you eat so little anyway?'

'I don't eat so little.'

'You eat nothing. You're too skinny, by the way.' He spits the olive stone out onto his palm and lets it fall on the tray. 'You ought to fatten up a bit.'

'You shouldn't speak with your mouth full,' she says. 'It's very rude. And you're hardly Charles Atlas yourself, by the way.'

'True, but at least I try.' He picks up a bit of cheese, sticks it under his nose, sniffs and then eats it. 'A bit mild for my taste. Elida gets it for you specially. In fact, if she thinks you don't like something, she won't rest until she finds an alternative.'

'I have noticed, yes.'

'You're very ungrateful. Poor old Elida.'

'Oh, it's poor old Elida now? A few hours ago she was a witch.'

'Christ, don't remind me. But all that talk about limbo and weeping souls wandering about for eternity – I couldn't listen to another word.

204

Apparently, whatever the rest of us say, a *meticcio* has no chance at all on the other side.'

'A what?'

'Half-breed.'

'Because his mother is Jewish? She said that?'

'Actually no, Rosa said it. But Elida started howling for the priest then. It's just ignorance, it doesn't mean anything.'

'It means something to Alec. Jesus.'

He pulls a strip of ham up and dangles it over his open mouth.'You know, when I was in the kitchen earlier she wouldn't let me near this: "Is for Signora Stu-arta, she only like this one."' He drops it in. 'If you like it so much, how come it's still here?'

'It's not that I like it – I just hate it a bit less than the raw stuff.'

'See what I mean?' he asks, gliding a slice of roasted marrow off the plate and sucking it off his finger. 'Nothing.'

'There's a knife and fork there, Edward, please feel free to use them.'

'I like eating with my fingers.' He licks then plucks them at the napkin to dry. 'Ahh coffee – do you mind?'

'Not at all. You know, I thought my appetite had improved since I came here. My father was delighted with the weight I'd put on. I mean, you should have seen me a few years back. Then, I ate nothing. I mean really – *nothing*. I don't enjoy food, not like other people seem to – funny to end up living in a country where it means everything.'

Edward finishes the coffee, then pours her another glass of wine. The night goes by. They gossip and speculate about people they know. They laugh – at one point become almost hysterical – he is such a good mimic. The talk turns towards each other, drifts off elsewhere, then comes back again. Several times this happens. Once she sulks at something he says. Another time he tells her to mind her own business. But these are minor setbacks in a night-long conversation.

Ages after it starts, and well before it's over, she says, 'I don't think I've ever spent this long talking to anyone in my whole life. Have you?'

He shrugs. 'Maybe. In drink. When I tend to like the sound of my own voice. But never mind that – you were saying?' He wants to hear her.

At first she has little enough to give: an episode or two from a former life. Mrs Jenkins and her father behaving like sneaks – which he finds hilarious. He tells a few stories about his travels in Germany, a fight he got into one night in a town in Bavaria with a pair of Brownshirts. Having to do a flit in the middle of the night when they returned in a pack threatening to burn down the inn where he was staying.

'You fought with Brownshirts? Were you drunk?'

'Of course I was drunk.'

'How did it start?'

'I called Hitler a *Schwuler*.'

'A what?'

'A pansy.'

'Edward!'

'Your turn.' He grins.

She tells him about stealing her mother's jewels; about being unable to bring herself to visit the grave; the food she used to throw out; the cats in the garden. He listens, makes a vague comment or two, once or twice laughs.

'Now you,' she says.

Another story about drink. He was sick in a wardrobe years ago, all over a stranger's clothes. He says he was alone, but she's not sure she believes that.

'Are all your stories about drink?' she asks him.

'It's the only time anything ever happens to me.'

'Is that why you do it – to make things happen?'

'I don't know. I do it because, well, I get fed up trying not to, I suppose. The constant bloody struggle of it. I just decide to let go of the ledge.'

As the night progresses they move around the room. Yet she can't remember noticing either of them getting up to leave one place for another. She finds herself on the sofa, the next minute standing at the bed looking at Alec. Edward seems to pop up everywhere: on the window seat sitting like an Indian, then stretched out on the sofa, hands behind his head. On the floor with his back to the wall. Then standing at the door, as if he's getting ready to leave. She doesn't want him to leave. Another story.

'This one is gossip,' she says.

'That's perfectly acceptable.'

'About Amelia.'

'Even better.'

She tells him about Amelia's love bite and how she had stayed out all night. And the man Elida had caught sneaking down the stairs in the early hours of the morning.

'Naughty Amelia!'

He tells her about a heavy pass Amelia had made at him.

'How heavy?'

'Naked under the window, in the middle of the night, heavy.'

'Completely naked?'

'Well, wrapped in a blanket, but she let me know all the same.'

'Did you let her in?'

'Of course not.'

'But then you go to brothels for that sort of thing, don't you?'

'Mind your own bloody business,' he snaps.

The night light fizzles out and the darkness tightens around them. Two detached voices.

She says, 'I'll tell you a really big secret if you answer me one question.'

'How big is the secret?'

'Huge.'

'What question?'

'Are you Irish?'

'Oh Christ, not this again.'

'Oh now come on – are you?'

He doesn't answer and she presses him. 'Just tell me, I won't ask the whys or how-comes, I won't tell anyone. I just would really love to know.'

'A simple yes or no – you'd leave it at that?'

'I promise.'

'In that case yes, I am.'

'Yes?'

'Yes, I said.'

'I knew it, I knew it! From Dublin?'

'You promised that would be an end to it. But yes, Dublin.'

'All right, that's all.'

'Now I'd like to ask something – if you don't mind?'

'Yes?'

'Did you break into my room when I was away?'

'Yes. I—'

'Why?'

'I thought you weren't coming back and just wanted to see. I'm sorry.'

'That's all right. It doesn't matter. The next time I'll invite you in – that is if you're not afraid to come in.'

'I could never be afraid of you, Edward.'

He says nothing for a moment then: 'Come on, what about your huge secret then?'

Into the darkness she starts to speak. 'There was this man, this professor. From Edinburgh. He was married to my mother's cousin and was staying in our house. They were all terribly proud of him, always boasting about his brilliance and that. Anyway, I was young, a girl, only gone fourteen—' She stops then, realizing that if they can't see each other then they can't see Alec. If his condition changes how will they know? Or what if he is lying there awake now, listening to her?

Edward puts a match to the night light and when it comes back up it startles her. I'm saying too much, she thinks to herself. Then out loud to him, 'I'm saying too much.'

He replies, 'You haven't said anything yet!'

'In a while, I will. I promise. Give me a little while.'

Just before dawn she nods off. When she wakes he's there with a cup in his hand, and she remembers then that he'd gone off to make tea. She takes the cup and then says, 'All right, my secret now. The real reason we moved from Dublin to London. Ready?'

'All ears.'

*

He is so quiet when it's over, when she's finished telling her story. He waits just long enough before saying anything. Long enough for her to know that she's made a terrible mistake.

'You were only a child,' is what he finally says.

'Not really. Not so much.'

'You were fifteen.'

'Fourteen.'

'Fourteen. It wasn't your fault.'

'No?'

'No. Of course not, Bella, think about it for Christ's sake. He was the adult. He was the one who was responsible.'

'Yes, but if I hadn't gone to him. If I hadn't always been at him. You know, I was always, always. *At him.*'

'You were a bloody child. That's all there is to it.' He closes the night-long conversation.

She has told much more than she meant to tell. He has told a lot less than he seems to have done. Things may have levelled out had Alec not opened his mouth to speak, his voice dry and confused: 'Why am I in this room, and why is this room so dark?' His little voice.

It seems like only a few seconds later when the doctor arrives, the nurse soon after him; a fairground bustle breaking around the bed for what seems like age. Edward withdrawing to the rear wall. She goes back to the window seat, the curtains now open, the shutters pinned back to let in the light that no longer hurts Alec's eyes.

Bella remains there, returning Elida's occasional smile, nodding intelligently when the doctor looks over his shoulder to make a comment on Alec's condition. Each time she catches a glimpse of Alec his eyes are on her. In the course of the examination he is turned from side to side, but his eyes come straight back to her face as if they've never left it. She begins to worry that maybe he's heard something. Yet she can't remember exactly what he could have heard, the words she used, or if they were words that a child would understand. There are certain things she could not have brought herself to say to Edward, or anybody else. There are certain words she has never spoken, not even inside her own head.

*

The man in the secret. The professor from Edinburgh.

He had been invited to spend a month as a visiting professor and consultant at the hospital where her father worked. He would also be their guest during this time. Her father looked forward to the visit with boyish enthusiasm. Her mother, however, retreated into one of those gloomy moods that demoted her from barely adequate to completely incompetent hostess. In other words, got herself off the hook again.

'We shall just have to call on your Aunt Margie to step into the social breach,' her father sighed. 'Your poor mother, I'm afraid, lacks the confidence required in these matters – Professor Fallon is a man of considerable reputation and position, you know.'

Even to Bella's young mind it seemed unlikely that her mother would be daunted by the professor, her own late father having been a Master of the hospital in question, who had only narrowly missed a place on the honours list because he was regarded as occasionally seeing matters from a 'Fenian point of view'.

Her mother simply disliked having strangers in the house. She was resentful of their endless expectations and continual little intrusions. She particularly hated what her father termed as 'making the effort', and what she termed as 'chit-chat and company'.

Aunt Margaret was the woman for chit-chat and company. She was her father's youngest and only unmarried sister. Also his favourite – even if he did believe her tendency to be 'a little too well informed for her own good' was keeping her on the shelf.

Bella took one look at the distinguished professor and at fourteen years old had fallen madly in love. Years later, she still couldn't say why it should be Professor Fallon – other than he happened to arrive in the middle of what she would recall as a time of constant yearning.

For months she had been fretful and over-aware of her body, which had been pushing and shoving itself out of all proportion. Her aunts had referred to this process as 'developing' and there had been frequent remarks such as: 'I see she's beginning to develop…', 'She's still developing, then?' and, 'My goodness, she'll burst if she doesn't stop developing soon!'

Bella, by turns, had been excited and repulsed by this transformation. If she stood naked in front of the mirror and squeezed her arms together she could make a cleavage – just like one that might feature in a grown-up woman's ball gown. And if she looked down there was a growth of hair that reminded her of the chin on the pimply boy who delivered the papers. Behind this new chin, a warm sturdy butterfly was forever beating or getting ready to beat its wings. A further flock of butterflies, smaller but much hotter, seemed to be twittering away inside every nook and cranny of her body.

Her mother had given her a little talk – Bella guessed this had come about on her father's orders. A shamefaced mumbling about monthly carry-on and tender breasts – both of which Bella had already been experiencing first hand, for over a year now. There was advice about modesty, and unspecified warnings about men. There had been nothing about love and hot butterflies.

Professor Fallon was not in the least attractive. He was not even a personable man. Middle-aged, chubby-cheeked, a bald head with a clown-like tuft on each side. He wore a moustache – but no beard, which Vera, the maid, said was a sign of vanity and probably to show off that stupid-looking dimple on his chin. He had girl's eyelashes and bland eyes. For the most part his expression was surly. When Vera said there was a bit of a smell off him, Bella could not, in all honesty, disagree. Nevertheless, she thought she would die of love whenever she set eyes on him or even so much as heard his footstep in the hall.

At table he did most of the talking, usually on matters scientific or political. Sometimes he showed his artistic side by reciting long poems. When he did this her mother stared at her plate in horror. Aunt Margaret put her head to one side and gently nodded. Her father, who had long since lost enthusiasm for his guest, boyish or otherwise, looked away to the distance or continued to eat. Bella thought he had a beautiful purring voice. She said it one day to her father. 'Hasn't the professor a beautiful voice?'

'Mm,' her father replied. 'And by God does he know how to use it!'

Bella knew then her professor was considered a bore. For some reason this made her love him all the more. She became a compulsive daydreamer; exquisite little episodes running around inside her head, which never seemed to reach a conclusion. They were all about the lead-up to something indefinite, but wonderful. There would always be a passionate declaration, a surrender of sorts, of course an embrace, the very thought of which set the butterflies flapping like mad. After that, things became a little hazy and the daydream would have to go back and find another beginning.

In the end Bella imagined her way into almost believing a romance existed. She took to writing love letters. At first she had the sense to burn them as soon as they were placed in envelopes, stinking of perfume and decorated with sweethearts. When this stopped being satisfactory, she took matters a bit further. This time she cut the little love words and phrases out from the letter, and slipped them into his overcoat pocket whenever she passed it hanging on the coat stand in the hall.

She put herself in the professor's path whenever she could. On the stairs when he came out in the mornings – there she happened to be. In the garden where he took his sherry before dinner and read his newspaper, she would be waiting, often climbing out the scullery window to get to the bench before he did. Once when she knew he was giving a lecture in the College of Surgeons, she went all the way to Stephen's Green on her own and hid behind the cab shelter until he appeared. She followed him down Baggot Street and when he went into a shop and came out again, she was there, tying a coincidental shoe lace. They walked the rest of the way home together, she playing up to him all the way, precocious and coy. He saying little, but slipping her long looks from the side of his eye. It might have been funny, just a mildly embarrassing memory, were it not for how it ended.

One Sunday morning when the house was empty and Vera had slipped out to late mass, Bella went to his room. She meant no harm – just a vague desire to familiarize herself with the sort of things she might see when they were married. (The framed picture of her second cousin, his present wife, and her third cousins, his two sons, she managed to ignore.) On the locker there was a medical book, a prayer book, and a glass of cloudy water, which gave off a peculiar whiff when she lifted it to her nose. A travelling case at the side of the wardrobe showed a label with his Edinburgh address – a discovery that caused her to silently shriek with pleasure. She could send him a birthday card, and a card next Christmas! No, she could do better than that – she could follow him to Scotland! Be waiting on the corner of his street when he returned from his work at the hospital – Oh, his face when he saw her! She would try to apologize, to say, 'I know I shouldn't have but…' And he would silence her with kisses. 'Oh my darling, my darling – I thought we would never see each other again.' That's what he would say then.

The bed was still unmade, and through the window, little meadows of sunlight fell across a haphazard eiderdown. She lay down, pulling his bolster pillow into her arms and pressing it to her chest. The crumpled sheets caressed her bare legs and arms. She closed her eyes, just as the door sprang open.

As soon as she saw him standing with his hand on the doorknob staring at her, she realized the measure of her mistake. What had got into her? He was awful. An absolute horror. Everything about him was disgusting. The pyjamas had been like something under a rock, grubby and stained, when she had lifted the pillow away. The water in the glass, cloudy because his smelly false teeth had been steeping there all night. There was a stink from the pillow. She had been blind as well as stupid. And now she was in serious trouble. Her parents would be angry, and worse, much worse, ashamed. Everyone would know and talk about it. Her aunts, her other cousins – one of whom went to her school and would be sure to spread the word. It would fill up the corridors and classrooms in September; the biggest news out of everyone's news out of all the summer holidays. A snoop. A sneak. A pursuer of married men. Her teachers would get to hear about it. She might even be expelled. But first the professor would march her downstairs to wait in the study for her father's return. He would lay the notes across her father's desk, demand an explanation. He would say in his stupid Scottish voice, 'This is the work of your beloved daughter.' She could see the love words like jigsaw pieces across the walnut desk – 'kiss', 'embrace', 'tender', 'desire'.

She jumped up from the professor's bed and began a frantic show of making it. 'I'm just, I'm just,' she kept saying as she plumped the pillow and straightened the sheet. 'Making the bed. To help Vera,' she managed to add, as she moved towards the door. But he wouldn't get out of her way. 'Please,' she began, hardly able to speak with embarrassment. 'Please, professor, excuse me, please.'

'I got your notes,' he said. 'Thank you most kindly.'

'Notes? What notes? I don't know what—'

'Don't lie to me, girl. I wouldn't like you to do that, after all those nice things you said.' He caught her by the arm. She could taste and feel his dragon breath, burning on her face.

'I'm only fourteen,' she whined without knowing quite why she mentioned that.

'You should have thought of that before now, shouldn't you?'

By now her breathing was shallow and sharp, causing her breasts to heave up and down. She saw him looking at them, and knew somehow they were going to make things worse. She wished she could just cut them off and throw them away.

'Fourteen,' he said, putting his hand on one breast, so that now his hand too was lurching up and down. 'Aren't you a great big girl for your age, even so?'

He pulled her to him. Then pressed her up against the wall. The vileness of him, the spit from his mouth, the sound of his breath in her ear, his mouth snuffling at her hair.

'Would this be what you're after?' he said. 'Is this what you've been looking for? Is it? Is it?'

She was pinned to the wall by his forearm and one of his legs. A long strand of her hair was caught in the cuff button of his jacket. It tore at her head anytime she tried to move. His hand went down and slipped into the narrow space between them. She could feel his knuckles move against her stomach and after a few seconds realized he was unbuttoning his flies. He started to pull her hand down, to try to make it touch him there. She resisted. Her hand, like something on a spring, shot back and forward between them. She tried to make it smaller, less able, by clenching her fist. But as it curled her knuckles tripped off his thing. A cool-skinned thing compared to his body, which was sweaty and feverish. It was as if it had nothing to do with the rest of him; a small animal he had managed to trap.

He began rummaging at the cloth of her dress, and she wriggled as best she could under his weight. Instinctively Bella knew that no matter what, she must prevent that dress from going up. Then suddenly he stopped trying. Instead, he began pushing and shoving into her. His hand now across her mouth, he kept saying *shhh, shhh*, although she wasn't saying anything at all.

Bella thought he was going to suffocate her, she was gagging against his palm, these were her last seconds, she was going to die, there was no way she could survive another moment of it. Then he seemed to go weak in himself and his hand fell away and his eyes nearly popped out of his head. He looked like the devil. She could feel a surge of something wet on her dress. For a moment she thought he had peed on her. But it was heavier than pee and seemed to rest in an upright pool, right in the centre of her skirt. Warm, then cold.

Her mouth and hands now free, she found her breath and began to scream. She ripped her hair with her two hands to free it from the button cuff of his jacket, then pushed past him, surprised at how easily he yielded when he had been so strong a moment ago. Now it seemed as if he had no bones, only fat and skin.

She screamed her way out to the landing and to the top of the stairs. Stayed there screaming down at her mother and Aunt Margaret, who were in the hall, looking up at her, both frozen in the act of doing something – her mother pulling off gloves, Aunt Margaret removing a straw hat.

Her aunt moved first and as she came hurrying up the stairs, her eye lowered to Bella's dress. Bella looked down. It was stained and the cotton glued together in crumples and peaks. She continued to scream.

*

Her father had examined her before. The time she had fallen down the stairs and hurt her back so badly he had to bring her to hospital. When she had measles, chicken pox, scarlet fever. When she had twisted her ankle, and was stung by a wasp in the same sorry accident. When she had gastroenteritis and had vomited all over him. Whenever she was ill he had always taken care of her. He had always spoken kindly and constantly to her. His hand had always been steady.

Now, his hand was shaking and he wouldn't even look at her face. Nor would he speak to her. Any questions he had were put through Aunt Margaret (her mother had already been sedated and put to bed).

Bella couldn't really understand these second-hand questions with their heavily pronounced words that seemed to labour around in slow circles until eventually Aunt Margaret began to ignore her father and composed her own. 'Bella – now this is important. And please, darling, I promise – you are not in any trouble. But has anything like this happened before?'

'No.'

'It was the first time?'

'Yes.'

'You're absolutely certain, he never touched you – in any way touched you?'

'I'm sure.'

'Now, dear, I just need to ask you this. Did he touch you? Did he touch you, under your dress?'

'No. He tried to, but I stopped him from pulling it up.'

'Good girl. Good girl. And he definitely didn't pull it up or get any-where near your underwear?'

'No. Definitely not.'

'That's fine, dear. That's all we need to know.'

But then her father instructed Aunt Margaret to remove Bella's under-wear. Bella got a fright and folded herself up. He came at her. He told Margaret to pull her legs down and hold them open. Bella began bucking against him, sobbing.

'Please, Harry,' Aunt Margaret said. 'Is it necessary? I mean to say, the poor child.'

'Margaret, would you kindly do as I ask? I am speaking as a doctor now. Hold her down. I don't want to have to sedate her just yet, until I've had a chance to establish all the facts.'

'Look at her, Harry, please.'

'Margaret, for Christ's sake – I need to see if she's *intact*. Now will you understand and kindly do as I say?'

'But Harry. We have already established that it never happened before. You believe her, don't you?'

'Of course I believe her, but—'

'Well, look at her dress, for God's sake, Harry. Can't you see what's happened? He lost control before he had a chance. You only have to look at the dress to know she's still intact.'

There was silence for a moment, then her father pulled her dress back down over her legs. 'Very well,' he said. 'Yes. She may go now. Put her to bed, and give her this to help her sleep. Just. Just take her out of here.'

Aunt Margaret put her arm around Bella and brought her across the room. When they got to the door her father spoke.

'I won't ask, Margaret, how you, as a single woman, should know such things,' he said.

'Oh, for God's sake, Harry,' Aunt Margaret said through her teeth.

*

Doctor Eaton is speaking to Bella although it takes her a moment to hear him. 'I said – you may come over to him now, Miss Stuart.'

'Oh yes, thank you, doctor. Sorry, I was—' Bella sits on the side of the bed, puts her hand on Alec's cool forehead.

'Is it my birthday yet?' he asks.

'Yes, Alec. You were ten yesterday,' she says.

'Did I miss it?'

'You'll catch it up. Don't worry.'

Around her she hears the day starting up. There is a sound of carts and trucks passing outside on the way to the flower markets. A factory horn from Ventimiglia stabs into and rips across the belly of the sky. The back door shudders and slams as Rosa arrives. A few seconds later the furnace gives its first gurgle. The door of the bedroom gently clicks and when she looks to the wall Edward has gone.

PART SIX

Anna

DUBLIN, 1995

June

SOMETIMES I WONDER WHAT she does hear in there, if anything. I close my eyes and try to decipher it all through her ears. Can she tell the difference, say, between the uptight clatter of a hospital morning and the easier sounds of the evening wind-down? Would she know the tea lady's whine from Thelma's childish delivery? Does she recognize, maybe even dread, the brisk snarl of curtain around her bed and know that it's time for a drip to be changed, a tube to be ruthlessly inserted? Is she earwigging away while the nurses exchange gossip over her head? Does she sense the sudden charge in the atmosphere when a doctor makes a rare appearance?

And does she ever get afraid, I wonder that too, when it all goes wrong and gets out of control? As it does now and then, when something might happen, or even nothing might happen, except inside the head of a patient who suddenly and unaccountably becomes distressed. One setting off another, setting off the next. Does it upset her, all that noise and emotional chaos? Old men crying for their mammies. Old women howling over torments from the past.

I went back last week to the house on Pembroke Road and the flat where I used to live with Nonna. Dust-sheeted and stuffy, but completely unchanged since she left it for the nursing home a few years ago.

After I had a good root around, found nothing of any consequence, and put everything back the way that it was – as if Nonna would somehow find out – I walked all the way home to my own place on the far side of town. It took a good hour and a half, I think. There were angelus bells when I came out of Nonna's anyway, and when I opened the door into my flat, the lazy brass music of *Coronation Street* was coming from the telly. I can't honestly recall one step of the long walk home. Some days are like that.

The following afternoon, up in the hospital, little Nurse Blondy gave me a pat on the arm as she unlocked the ward door to let me out. 'God, you're as good,' she said. 'I mean, the way you give her so much of your time.'

I could have replied, 'I've got buckets of the stuff. What else am I going to do with it?' but I didn't like to spoil the moment.

Since breaking up with Hugh, and even more again since leaving my job a fortnight ago. Time.

When the headmistress finally got round to discussing her 'concerns' regarding my future, I couldn't have made it easier for her. 'Lack of commitment, quite simply,' she began. 'Too many excuses for too many absences, basically. You may well be having personal problems, Miss Moore, but essentially your duty lies with the students. We're talking Leaving Certificate students here. We're talking portfolio preparation. *The future of our young people.*'

To listen to her you'd think she was headmistress of Eton or Harrow and not some dive where the teachers don't know who to be more afraid of, the pupils or their parents, and where the police have to be called on a regular basis.

'Try to put yourself in my shoes,' she continued, 'then ask yourself – is it any wonder I'm having reservations with regard to renewing your contract?'

'No. God, no. No wonder at all,' I said, weak with relief as I realized the drawing I'd made of Foster hadn't surfaced after all. For over a fortnight I had lived in dread of it, sick with anxiety every time I walked into the classroom where I kept expecting to see it pinned to the blackboard, or anytime his little brother looked in my direction or there was a message waiting in the staffroom pigeonhole to say someone – in this case, the headmistress – wanted to see me.

'You must understand—'

'Oh, but I do understand, really. It's fine. I don't blame you. Indeed I don't. Well, goodbye, and good luck with the replacement. Thanks for everything.'

'But Miss Moore?'

'Look – what else am I supposed to do? You don't want me here. And to be honest I don't want to be here either.'

'You're leaving? Now, this minute? Without so much as handing in your notice?'

'My contract is nearly up anyhow.'

'But I haven't dismissed you – you do realize that? I'm simply putting you on a warning.'

'No need – I'm resigning.'

'If I could ask you to put that in writing please?' she said, obviously relieved.

'Absolutely.'

'All right then. Well, what about a reference?'

'Don't bother.'

'But where will you…? I mean how will you…?'

'Really. It's grand. I've been meaning to give up this teaching racket anyhow.'

I came straight out of her office and drove up to one of those cash-for-cars joints in Smithfield frequented by alcos and gamblers. There I exchanged my car for not all that much cash. Even though the car had nothing to do with the school – I usually walked to work anyway – it seemed the right way to finish the morning. And I suddenly wanted to be rid of all burdens. Even a car seemed overly needy; between feeding it petrol and finding it parking and sticking money into the meter on its behalf, then worrying about whether it's been stolen during the night. Besides I was running low on cash.

Walking back up Parnell Street a few minutes later, all I was able to think of was – well, thank Christ I won't have to tell Nonna anyway, won't have to listen to her trying to find ways to twist the blame away from me and back onto the headmistress. But best of all, I won't have to answer her questions with lies. Nor would that Shay Foster bastard have anything on me either. He could show the drawing wherever he liked, he could hang it up in his dive of a pub – they couldn't fire me for it anyhow. I quit while I was ahead. I felt elated for a while, although that feeling soon enough dwindled.

And so this is how, twice, sometimes even three times a week, I can go to see Nonna. By the time I walk down to Abbey Street, take the bus all the way out to Portrane, make my way up the long avenue, dish out the smokes to the two boys who will always, no matter how I vary the day or the hour, be watching and waiting on the steps for me. And, by the time I spend an hour at the bedside filling up the air between Nonna's face and mine with meaningless words she can't, in all likelihood, hear; a chat with the nurses; a trip to the smoking room, a sit-down by the bed for another short while before doing it all over again in the opposite direction, maybe stopping at the off-licence or chipper on the way home – well, that's *that* particular day more or less seen to. One seventh of a week. Gone – just like that! And I won't have minded a thing for most of it, and I won't have noticed too much either. Except that three years on, the taller of the two smoking lads no longer has such beautiful teeth.

My doctor calls it depression. A term that's too vague and self-indulgent for my liking. A malaise without just cause. I think maybe it's loss that I'm feeling. If I had to put it in a poem, that's what I'd call it anyway. 'Loss'. Last year my father, this year Hugh. You could also include my grandmother, who it turns out can't really be my grandmother but who has, in any case, always been more like my mother. So in a sense I've lost my mother again. And in another sense, I've even lost *me*.

These are the half-cocked ideas that come into my head while I'm sitting at the bed waiting for Nonna to make up her mind if she's coming or going. Or while I'm sitting, half pissed, in the darkness of my flat watching crap on the telly, and wondering if I should have one more smoke before trying for sleep, or to hell with it – why not? – open one more bottle of plonk.

I started the poem one night, I wrote on the top of a page – 'Loss' by Anna Moore. But that's as far as I got. I thought – if I write one word a day for the next six months, I could easily make up a poem. What's the big deal? One word. It doesn't seem much to ask of myself. By the time I'd finish it, Nonna would be gone. I could slip off myself then, if I wanted. I could follow her. 'Loss' by Anna No More, I decided I could call it then and chuckled ironically to myself for a few moments. Of course, before long I was crying again.

One. Word.

I have to, *have* to, get out of this place.

*

I lived with Nonna from the day my mother died until I finished college and moved to Belfast to be near, and finally get to know, my father. On and off over the years I have lived with her again.

The flat is made up of six rooms, three each side of the entrance hall, which effectively cuts Nonna's home up the middle. To the left, the kitchen, sitting room and a small bathroom. To the right, two bedrooms and another, slightly larger bathroom. Because all these rooms were once bedsitters, there are Yale locks on all the doors. To get from one side of

Nonna's flat to the other you have to cross over the hall, where, when I lived there anyway, there always seemed to be someone talking on the public phone and always letters and junk mail splattered all over the floor.

It was my childhood home – I can't remember the Belfast house where I lived before my mother died – but I never really liked Nonna's flat. The sense of living in one room at a time, brought about by having to use a hall-door key to get from one room to another. And having to remember to bring the bunch of keys every time you crossed the hall; I hated that.

The outside of the house was better. Granite steps to the front door, a small bedraggled garden; a permanent dome of mottled shadow from the huge trees on the road outside. There was a photographer's studio in the basement, which I used to imagine brought a touch of glamour to the house. For years a blown-up picture of a gawky-looking bride was stuck behind the bars of the window. As if she was in prison, Nonna sometimes said.

I loved to sit on the granite steps – the sparkle and solidity of them, the way they held the heat in summer, warming the back of my legs. I liked to watch for the bus that stopped outside the gate, waiting to see who would get off. People who lived in the flats upstairs – faces I would try to match to voices overheard talking on the phone. Or scrubbed-up customers self-consciously making for the photographer's studio. Or my father, who never came by bus anyway, but always arrived in a taxi, pockets stuffed with oil rig money.

His absence had, in a way, been worse than my mother's death. I knew he *could* come back, if he wanted. Whereas my mother could not. I also knew my mother was in heaven, but where my father was – I couldn't say. An oil rig meant nothing to an eight-year-old child. Nonna said no matter what, I should pray for them both every night. 'God bless Mammy in heaven,' was one thing. 'God bless Daddy on an oil rig,' never quite convinced, and I soon let him slip from my prayers.

I was never inside any of the other flats in the house but thanks to the public phone in the hall, I got to know everyone's business. Whenever it rang a young man who was unemployed would come clattering down the stairs in his purple flared trousers – although the calls never seemed to be for him. If he happened to be out it was my job to answer the phone and trot upstairs to knock on the relevant door. A woman on the third floor with rollers in her hair gave me a pound note one time. 'Tell him I'm out, love, there's a good girl. No – on second thoughts, tell him I've moved on.'

I came to know every brush-off, excuse and cock-and-bull story in the book, and that adults lie and find it easy to lie, especially on the phone when their faces can't be seen. I came to look on the phone as an instrument of deceit. So whenever my father called to tell me where he was, I didn't believe him. Once he rang to say he was in London and would be arriving in Dublin to see me the next day. 'Liar! *Liar!*' I had screamed down the phone at him and dropped the receiver, leaving it swinging from the cord, until his voice, condensed and slightly cartoonish, finally stopped calling my name.

Poor man, with his direct northern ways, was probably the only person I have ever known who had always given me the truth, or what little he had of it, anyway.

Once, when Nonna was having trouble with her back – lying on the floor, eyes glazed with pain and painkillers – she said, 'You're going to be beautiful, Anna, in another year or so. I hope it's not going to get in your way.'

I would have been about seventeen at the time, sitting at the dining table doing my homework. 'What are you talking about, Nonna?' I laughed, it seemed like such a personal thing for her to say.

'You should have a few pals. You know? Girlfriends – like you used to have before you started going steady with this new chap – Marty, isn't it? He's a nice boy, but you don't have to drop your friends just because a man comes knocking on the door, you know.'

I felt like saying, How come you've no pals then, if they're so bloody great? Because as long as I'd known Nonna I had only ever heard of one friend, a nurse called Dolores who phoned the odd time and whom

Nonna had once gone out in her good coat to meet. Nor had she ever really encouraged me to bring friends home. Whenever I did she became slightly peculiar, never taking her eyes off them as if she expected them to steal something. On another occasion she had said, 'Don't trust anyone, Anna, not even your best friend.' Although later she retracted that piece of advice, saying it might have been a 'bit strong'.

'You should watch those painkillers, Nonna,' I said and went back to my essay. A few minutes later I could still feel her looking up from the floor at me. '*What?*' I asked her.

'You get your looks from your grandmother,' she said.

'From you?'

'No', she laughed. 'God, no. Your other grandmother. She was a beauty.'

The next time I saw my father I asked him what his mother had looked like.

My father, brought up in a climate of suspicion, always seemed to be startled by the simplest of questions. '*My mother?* What are you askin' about *her* for?'

'I just want to know what your mother, my grandmother – looked like, that's all.'

He thought for a moment, before answering in his sharp Belfast quack, 'The bawk of a bus, if you must know.'

*

Sometimes I have these imaginary conversations with Nonna where I bombard her with questions and cheeky remarks I would never dream of saying to her face – whether asleep or awake. I say things like: 'You're trapped now, Nonna, you may as well come clean. Come out with your hands up, tell us what the hell's been going on these past fifty-odd years.'

Or I might get a little more personal. 'How could you go an entire life and still be a virgin, Nonna? I mean – the age you are and you still don't know what it's like? And that husband of yours, did he not mind having to go without? Did he leave you because of it – was that it? Did he not die in the war at all? Or did he ever even exist? And why? Why did you never tell me the truth? Did you think I would leave you if I found out we weren't really flesh and blood?'

Other times I just tell her things. Like how much I've come to hate the flat she was good enough to buy for me, with Hugh's fingerprints and stains and thoughts all over it. That I can't even be bothered to clean it, that's how much I hate it now. And what's more that I never even made all that much use of the studio. In fact, I gave it over to Hugh a long time ago when he was preparing for an exhibition and needed the extra space. And I forgot to take it back or he forgot to give it back. He hadn't even had to ask if he could use it in the first place. My idea, my insistence and, if I'm to be honest, when he accepted – my relief.

I know this would really get to her. The fact that I gave the studio away, wasted the chance, 'the talent', as she used to call it. 'You've inherited a talent, Anna, it would be a shame to waste.'

The times I've heard her say that. I had always presumed someone from my father's side had a flair for art, because my mother and my grandmother – the only other relatives known to me – had none. Nonna called it talent, I would settle for mere ability – not quite the same thing. Whatever it is, it has always seemed to matter a lot to Nonna, anyhow. When I was a child she used to fill the walls of the flat with my pictures. When I got into art college she lost the run of herself and bought a bottle of champagne. Even when I disappointed her (though not myself), by taking a job as an art teacher in an inner city school, she paid my insurance and bought me my first little car.

In these imaginary conversations I never lie to Nonna. Not like I used to do, all the time. Just for the sake of it, or just for an easy life. I used to feel bad about all those stupid lies. But not any more of course. Now that I know that all along there's been a pair of us at it.

I imagine telling her about Hugh. 'He's left me, Nonna,' I say. 'He's not coming back.'

'Is that so?' she quietly asks back.

'He's left me, Nonna, he told me there was nobody else, but that all things have a time to end.'

'Did he now, did he say that, well well?'

'Nearly six years, Nonna.'

'Six years! Was it really that long?'

'Mmm. It turns out he's gone back to his wife.'

I imagine her looking at me for a moment, measuring every word I've said, taking it all in. A slight slow nod, perhaps a pat on my hand. 'Ah well,' she says then, 'live by the sword, die by the sword – isn't it always the way?'

*

I only found out the truth about the house on Pembroke Road the first time I brought Nonna to have a look at the fancy nursing home in Chapelizod. We had spent the afternoon there and, when the grand tour was over, had come outside and sat in the car in the driveway for a while. A smitten Nonna smiling benignly through the car window at the house and its gardens. That was when she said: 'This is the one. This is the perfect place.'

I couldn't understand where she was getting such notions. It hadn't been that long since she'd bought me the flat and now here she was talking about nursing-home fees, as if she were talking in telephone numbers.

'It's lovely – isn't it?' she said. 'Don't they keep it lovely? Really though – I mean, look at that beautiful willow tree. I love the willow, I must say, despite its melancholy reputation.'

'Nonna, it doesn't matter how lovely it is. It's an outrageous price. Jesus, you could stay in the Shelbourne for that amount. How in the name of God would you be able to afford it?'

'I'll use the income from Pembroke Road.'

'The rent you save won't pay for one day in this place – surely you *must* know that.'

'I don't pay rent, I own it.'

'You bought the flat on Pembroke Road?'

'I bought the whole bloody house!' she said.

'When?'

'After the war.'

'What? What are you talking about?'

'Yes. I bought it from a German chap. You see, he'd left Germany in the thirties – he was so disgusted by the carry-on there and when it was all over he decided to go back to help out. Wasn't that very forgiving of him? A lovely man. I often wonder what happened to him after. It was very difficult to get accommodation after the war, you know. So I decided to divide the house up into flats and let them out. Then years later when your mother decided to go off and get married, I sold the little house we'd been living in and moved into one of the flats myself – where the kitchen is now. Then the bedsit beside that became available so I knocked the two of them into one. And as luck would have it, just before you came to live with me, didn't the flats across the hall become vacant? And so I took them, jigged things about a bit and, well, now do you see?'

In all the years I'd lived in Pembroke Road I'd never seen her behave like a landlady. Nor had she ever been treated like one. I couldn't remember one single tenant ever knocking on our door to complain about a leaky tap or make an excuse about late rent. The only explanation I could think of was – poor old Nonna was losing her marbles.

When we got back to Pembroke Road she tottered off to her bedroom and came back with a box of files stuffed with correspondence from a management company that for years had been taking care of the house and its tenants on her behalf. 'Now do you believe me?' she said.

I thought of all the winter afternoons I had come home from school to find her sitting in her overcoat waiting for me to appear before she'd put on a heater or put a match to the fire. Or worse, the days when she would come to walk me home through the swanky roads of Ballsbridge, her stooping under trees to pick up twigs and sticks for the fire, me ready to melt with shame. And the row of jars on the shelf in her wardrobe –

one for copper, one for silver – and how when each one was filled it would be changed to notes and stuffed into a stocking that she called a money-tuck. And when that could take no more it was transferred to what she used to call her 'little pin-money account'. Some pin money, Nonna!

I handed her back the box of files. 'And I always thought we were poor,' I said to her. 'All the time poor. I used to think Dad was tight and only spent money on ice cream and show-off outings when he came to visit once in a blue moon, that he never sent anything otherwise, that it was my fault we were always short. I used to feel so guilty about that.'

'Ah no. Your father always sent his money, every month of his working life.'

'My God, Nonna, you're a miser! That's it – isn't it?'

She shifted her shoulders defensively, her face a little pink. 'You'll be glad one day. When I'm gone and that other fella leaves you.'

'He's not going to leave me. We're getting married. I told you, as soon as the divorce comes through.'

'You'll be glad, because some day it will be all you have. But it will be all yours *to* have, Anna.'

'You've already bought me a flat, Nonna, you don't have to give me your house as well.'

'Ah, who else would I give it to?'

We both sulked quietly for a few moments, and then Nonna spoke again. 'Something I learned a long time ago, Anna.'

'What?'

'You'll never really be lost when you have your own few bob. You'll always find somewhere to go.'

*

This morning as I stand in the hall of Pembroke Road, for the second time in a week, that conversation comes back to me. You'll never be lost. And it occurs to me that for the first time in my life I am, if not entirely lost, then certainly alone. No boyfriend – if a 35-year-old woman can use that

232

term. Ever since Marty (his surname is gone now), one has replaced another. In school I was always going steady, and later in college the same. Steady – I think I used to love the word, more than the boy.

Should the boy in question, later the man in question, happen to have sisters, or mates with girlfriends, then they would become my temporary pals. Dublin, Belfast, London, Dublin again; it has always been the same scenario. Apart from Shay Foster – and I'm refusing to count him – I've never had a one night stand in my life. I've never even had to go looking. I have always been asked. And it has never, ever occurred to me to say no.

I've come back again to Pembroke Road, because I'm looking for something I didn't find last time around.

This time I linger. Nonna's flat may have remained untouched but there have been a few changes to the house itself which I only half heeded the last time I was here. The basement has long since stopped being a photographer's studio – a private flat now with matchstick blinds and a bowl of polished pebbles in the window. The garden has been flattened by tarmacadam, white lines mark out six parking places; three each side of the granite steps. A sign on the wall says 'Residents Only'. The railings have been pulled down for access. There is an intercom on the front door, which throws not only a voice upstairs, but also a televised mugshot to go with it. The single shade that used to hang over the light in the hall has been replaced by two rows of spotlights flush to the ceiling. The lino has been peeled off in favour of a varnished wooden floor. There is a plastic grey phone sitting unobtrusively on a table, in place of the big black chunk of tin that used to hang on the wall. There is still junk mail and letters for people who have moved on, scattered all over the floor.

I go into the sitting room, open the curtains, the windows. Then I come back into the hall and unlock the rest of the doors on either side, holding them back with copies of my old children's encyclopedia. I stand for a while, letting light and air stream from one room to another. The front door opens then: a man and a woman I've never seen before. Both throw me a startled look as they step into the cross draught created by all

233

the open doors and windows. A wary half nod then before they continue on up the stairs where I hear them mumble to each other, doubtlessly wondering who the hell I am.

'What are you gawking at?' I feel like saying. 'This is *my* house. Watch it now or I might just turf you out.' I have to admit, I like the feel of this small unspoken remark.

After a while I go into my old bedroom. The cerise carpet still there, darker than I remember but maybe that's down to dust. The rosette wallpaper is a bit on the faded side, a glob of Blu-tack in a few places, from long-ago posters. Everything has been tidied away into boxes. The boxes all labelled: Anna, aged 8–13. Anna, 14–18. Anna, 18–28. And finally Anna, misc.

I can't bring myself to look inside but can take a guess anyhow: toys, books, photographs, drawings and paintings I've done over the years; keepsakes Nonna couldn't bring herself to throw out.

'Ah what the fuck?' I ask myself out loud. 'What does it matter? Who she is or isn't. She loved you, didn't she? You stupid wagon – just leave her be. Forget it now.'

But I know I can't do that.

I stretch out on the bed, and for a few minutes watch the morning light on the ceiling, as I used to do, hands behind my head, thinking about this and that. The last time I was here I had gone through this flat with a fine toothcomb and found nothing unusual, just crates of useless ornaments, old clothes, books and handbags with the dry sweet smell of gone-off face powder. The general knick-knackery of a life quietly led. Yet I know it's not in Nonna's nature to throw things away. She must have left something. Somewhere.

I hear a noise then, someone on the steps outside. The snip of the letterbox and a dry shower of falling letters. I sit up and remember.

There was a letter. A couple of weeks after it had been decided to keep Nonna in Portrane. A letter from the matron of the perfect nursing home. No words of regret, no asking after her health. Just a reference to 'your grandmother's clothes and other personal items'. A simple request to remove her stuff, which, like herself, had obviously been getting in the way. It could be collected at my earliest convenience. Disgusted, I had torn the letter up in a temper and thrown it in the bin.

A few minutes later and I am down the road in the Waterloo House. The artificial darkness of a morning pub. There's an open phone directory on one side of me, a vodka and tonic on the other, and I am speaking to the matron of the nursing home. She says she's sorry but the clothes have been given away some months ago. 'It was a question of space, Miss Moore, and we hadn't heard anything from yourself, so.'

'I've been away, working in the States, I just forgot all about it.'

'Yes, I understand. However—'

'However, matron?'

'Yes, there was a box of papers and a few other things – I'm just looking at a note of it here in the book we keep for unclaimed items – now, that would be up in the attic. If you could give me a few hours or better even a few days?'

'I'll be there this afternoon,' I say.

*

By the time I reach St Ita's the hospital day is all but over. 'Oh God. You're *really* late today,' Thelma squeals as she opens the door to the ward.

'I know. Had a few things to do first. No change I suppose?'

'Never is. I'm off for a smoke – comin'?'

'I'll follow you, Thelma,' I say, 'just want to say hello to herself.'

'S.B. – wha'?' Thelma laughs softly as she always does since she first heard me call Nonna this name.

'That's right, Sleeping Beauty.'

It's not yet seven o'clock but the blinds are drawn in the ward, and the night light is on and someone down the far end of the room is quietly wailing for God.

I take my seat. There's a new arrival in the next bed where Mrs Clarke used to be. I don't look at the face, but can tell it belongs to another mover and shaker; constant fingers plucking on the downturn of the sheet and feet hard at it under the bedspread.

And there's Nonna, statue-still, out for the count, and not coming back to me anytime soon. I decide to go for it.

'I'm not going to read to you today, Nonna, because I want to talk to you instead. I mean properly talk.'

I take off my coat, fold it behind my chair and lean in: 'Listen, I've been thinking a lot about Pembroke Road lately. Actually, I've been over to see it, last week, and again today. And I noticed that you haven't rented out our old flat or done it up either. It hasn't been touched since you left it. Then it dawned on me, Nonna, that maybe you kept it like that, well – for me. In case I needed it or that. And I hope I'm right, Nonna, because I do. Need it, I mean. So.'

I wait a moment or two, get up and rearrange the top of her locker, pour myself a glass of water and sit back down again.

'You see the problem is, Nonna, because none of us know – not me, the doctors, God, probably not even yourself – how long you're going to stay in there, wherever you are, well, I've got to make the decision. And I've decided. Yes. I've definitely decided. That I'm going to sublet my place on North Great George's, maybe even sell it after a while, and move back into Pembroke Road. Until I can decide what to do with my life. I hope that's OK now with you. I don't want to be presumptuous and I'll have to take it that you don't mind. But. Well, I just need to do *something*. Put one leg over the fence, as you used to say. Hope the rest of me follows, eh?' I feel my throat tighten and so I drink more water and then slowly continue.

'I think. I think it will make me better, if I live someplace else. I'm not sick or anything, not in the usual sense. But – I still need to get better. If I go home, Nonna – you know?' I'm crying a little now, and I can see the flinty glint of eyeball from the patient in the bed next door, watching me. I wipe my eyes with my hand and stand up.

'By the way, Nonna, I collected a few things belonging to you today from that nursing home, remember that place? Now, I don't want you worrying. What I find, I find. I won't care or fuss about it. I promise. I won't think any less of you or anyone else. I'll let you know how I get on, eh, Nonna? I'll let you know that.'

I put the glass back, take a baby brush out of the mouth of the locker, and fix Nonna's hair, which though thinning is still thick enough. In this light its colour is shocking white.

God, that bloody smoking room. It's empty when I go in and gratefully I sit down. I choose a wooden stool, rather than one of those armchairs that start me scratching the minute I look at them. There's a coffee table with a selection of old Sunday supplements or out-of-date housewifey magazines, which used to amuse me, but which I no longer read since opening a page and finding a big lump of phlegm embedded into a knitting pattern. The cushions on the armchairs show bulges of orange foam through the flowery stretch-nylon covers. They have curved wooden arms with most of the varnish scraped off by names that have come and gone over the years: Pete. Jeannie. Mairead. Turlough. Milly. Aine. Jonathan. There is a heart carved into one, with '*I luv ?*' written in it. A child of Prague with his young head on old shoulders stands on the window ledge. And there's a J.F. Kennedy plate on the wall that makes him look as if he has Down's Syndrome. The ashtray is stuffed with cigarette ends; more are spread over the upside-down lid of an old biscuit tin on the floor. It stinks in here; you could scrape the nicotine off the walls.

I'm halfway through my cigarette and thinking about getting up to go when Thelma comes in carrying one of those lopsided trays made in the arts and craft class, with three mugs of tea on it, and one bun on a plate. The bun is for me. Thelma insists. She's already had four. But the staff nurse said it was all right. Mr Carroll will never eat them anyway and she doesn't want them left hanging around in case they bring in more mice.

The owner of the third mug then struggles in behind Thelma. And I see it's Mona, the aptly named tea lady. Mona's son is collecting her after work and it's getting dark and looking like rain, so I take her offer of a lift as far as the bus stop in Portrane. Even the way she makes this offer sounds like a lament. Then she pulls a single cigarette out of her overall pocket, plumps it into shape and lights it up. And she's off: her feet are bleedin' killin' her, the neck as stiff as a board. Her next-door neighbour has cancer. 'Doesn't even smoke, I wouldn't mind.' Mona says this as if it's an unfair world that the neighbour has cancer and she hasn't – after all the trouble she's gone to puffing on her forty a day.

Thelma tuts with sympathy and makes little heartfelt suggestions to ease Mona's hardships:

'A hot-water bottle! I hear that's great for a sore neck.'

'A basin of salty water – that's the man for the feet.'

'Do you know now what you should do – put honey in your tea! You'll never feel tired again.'

But Mona is not interested in Thelma or her prescriptions. 'Do you know what it is?' Mona says to me. 'There's days I do be that knackered I swear I could climb into bed with one of them loonies out there, and not care if I never get up out of it again.' She takes a pull of smoke, then darts a look at me. 'Oh God, sorry, love, I'm sorry. No offence.'

'You're grand,' I say.

'No change with your poor granny?' she asks me then, putting one cigarette out while accepting a fresh one from me.

I shake my head.

'God love her all the same. Doesn't be a peep out of her these days.'

'Not a dickie bird!' Thelma confirms.

'And she was a great one there for a while, yapping on like I don't know what – wasn't she, Thel?'

'Oh yea.'

'She'd be going goodo there before she'd the stroke.' She leans over, tips me on the arm, casting a vague wink and a twitch of her lips towards Thelma as if warning me to say nothing right now. 'That other business. I have to tell you, I thought that was a bloody disgrace. I mean how that happened, it's beyond the beyond. Do you know what I mean?'

'Rabbitin' on,' Thelma says. 'So she was, S.B. Rabbitin.'

'Ah no,' Mona says. 'Not always. Be fair now. You could have the odd conversation with her like. Sometimes she used to even speak Eyetalian.'

'Yea?' I say.

'Ask me how I know that, go on, ask me.'

'How do you know that, Mona?'

'Didn't I used to work in Macari's. The chipper on the Malahide Road?'

'Right.'

'She's not Eyetalian but – is she?'

'No. She lived there for a while, when she was younger.'

'Ahhhh, that explains it. Handy little number it was, working in the chipper. But me ankles like, with all that standing. And I usedn't be able to breathe, the steam and that you know, brings on me asthma.'

'I can imagine.'

Thelma touches the tray. 'You never ate your bun,' she says to me.

'You know, I'm not really hungry, Thelma – would you like it?'

'All right.'

'Ah, ah, fatso,' Mona says. 'I thought you were cutting down? Ten Ton Tessie, if you don't start watching it, you. Do you hear me now?' Then she looks over at me again. 'Do you know what I often meant to ask you?'

'What?'

'Who's Alec?'

'Alec?'

'Is he your little brother?'

'No. Why?'

'Well, I reckoned he's a kid anyhow. She used to be on about him some-times. You know the way they do. Askin' after people you wouldn't know. But you don't like to be ignoring them either and so you humour them along a bit.'

'What sort of things would she say?'

'Ah you know – just little bits of things while I'd be cleaning around the bed and that. Where's Alec? she might go. And then I might say, Ah, he'll be back now shortly in a minute. And then she'd say, Is he with Edward? And then I'd say, Do you know what? I think he is. Havin' a lesson? And then I'd say, Oh, he is. Piano or tennis? would be the next thing she'd want to know. And I'd say, God, I couldn't tell you that now but it'll be over soon enough anyhow. And she'd say, He won't do his algebra, do you know that? And I'd go, Isn't he the little divil not doin' his algebra? Wait'n I get him, I'll give him a good smack for himself I will. And she'd go, Ah no, you're not to smack him, you'll only hurt him. And I'd say, Ah of course I wouldn't smack him, I'm only jokin' you. He's too good to smack. And she'd say, He's a good boy. Then I'd say, Ah God he is, sure everyone knows that he's the best boy. And she be delighted with herself then and off she'd go back to sleep.'

We say nothing then, waiting on Mona's son to arrive. Thelma spluttering away on her bun. Mona lighting another cigarette and smoking it as if it were her last.

PART SEVEN

Bella

BORDIGHERA, 1938

September

BELLA COMES BACK THROUGH the garden and the overripe air that marks the start of an Indian summer. Through the open kitchen door there's a back view of Elida still preparing food, most of which will have to be thrown in the bin or hauled up to Sister Assumpta's orphanage fund. When Bella left earlier to have coffee with Edward, Elida had been squinting at small curls of pasta and stabbing them with something on the end of a pin. Now she is punching her fist into a large lump of dough.

Bella considers leaving the coffee tray on the windowsill and sidling past, but knows Elida, with the eyes in the back of her head, will be certain to spot her. The kitchen so stifling, Bella stays in the doorway, where at least she can feel the air on her back.

'Your letters,' Elida begins without turning around, 'I leave for you in the chair of the hall.'

'Thanks. I got them. *On* the chair *in* the hall. I'm going out now, Elida.'

'To where?'

'The old town, see what's happened to Rosa – it's been almost a week. I'll give you a hand later. Cesare will be here at eleven anyhow and Edward will be down shortly to move the crib. By the way, he doesn't think there's a chance the Signora will make it today. Trains cancelled or late. Long delays all over the country, it seems. He's been complaining his morning papers haven't arrived.'

'Is not your business to give me a hand.'

'Oh, don't be so prim, Elida. You know I don't mind in the least.'

'The Signora would not approve.'

'Well, let's not tell her then.'

'That Rosa,' Elida says. 'Unreliable. Lazy. What do you expect from Genoa?'

Bella comes into the kitchen and puts the tray on the table. 'She's not from Genoa, Elida, her father is.'

'Same thing.'

'She could be ill.'

'Why not send a message then?'

'Maybe she has no one to send.'

'She's has her five fat ugly sons.' Elida picks up the dough and slaps it like a face, from side to side, then drops it. 'I tell you what happen. More money what happen. Now her big shot son get for her the job.'

'What job?'

'Fascist uniform mistress.'

'Hardly that! It's just a bit of mending and cleaning and it's never stopped her from coming to work before.'

'They are all the same these *Genovese* – thinking only of this.' Elida lifts one hand, rubs her thumb into her first two fingers. 'Will you take the car?' she asks.

'Not much point with all these parades, the roads will be impossible. And I'm fed up being stopped and questioned every five minutes.'

'Is the fault of so many strangers in town.'

'It's a holiday resort, Elida, there are always strangers in town.'

'These are different strangers.'

Bella goes to the drawer in the kitchen cupboard and begins searching through.

'Will you be back for lunch?' Elida asks her after a few moments.

'Doubt it. I've to collect Alec's new school blazer and I want to see if the bangle I bought for the Signora's new baby is back from the engraver's. Leah, it's a lovely name – don't you think?'

'But not an Italian name.'

'It's the Signora's name. Have you seen my purse, Elida?'

'Top shelf, on the right, as always.'

Bella finds her purse and stuffs it into her pocket.

'I'll pick up Alec on the way back – he's hardly had a wink all night, thinking about the musical picnic today. The Almansi girls have tambourines *and* a recorder, he's brought his harmonica. They're calling themselves the Beach Blues Trio. God help any sun-worshippers. Anyway, I'm off. See you later, Elida.'

Elida follows her out to the door, wiping her hands on her pinny. 'Will you go to the office of the *Prefettura*?'

'If I've time, why?'

'I see the letter.'

'It's only a reminder to have my documents verified, nothing to worry about.'

'I think.'

'You think what, Elida?'

'Nothing. But maybe speak to the Signora first.'

'Why?'

'The *Prefettura*, they don't just want to know about you. Also this house – who lives here, why, how long, this and that – you know? The Signora, she always change her mind so much. And better to wait until you have one story only.'

'All right. A day or so won't make a difference. Anyway, I best get—'

'Wait until later, please, Signora Bella, it's too hot for you now.'

'Really, Elida you're in an odd mood today – what's the matter?'

'Nothing, is so hot.'

'Elida, I have just had coffee in the garden and believe me it's not

245

half as hot outside there as it is in this kitchen. God – how can you breathe?'

'Crazy heat for September,' Elida mournfully agrees.

Elida walks with her out to the garden, her big face reddened with worry, heat and exertion. There are caps of flour dust on her elbow and nose, a pulp of tomato sauce under her heart, a stain of plum juice on her lips. She looks, as she always does when she comes out of the kitchen, as if she's coming away from a fight. She pushes her voice at Bella. 'I hope they don't think they are coming here again.'

'Who?'

'The American misses – I see the letter.'

'Well, of course you did! Don't worry, Elida. People are trying to get out of Europe, not into it.'

'There's no rooms for them. With the Signora and the bambina and if she brings with her any of that Sicilian band of—'

'I'm sure it will be just the baby.'

'And the new husband, don't forget that one.'

'He won't be arriving till next week. I told you this already. And Elida, we could stop calling him the new husband, his name is Signor Tassi – they have been married two years, you know.'

'*Un napoletano.*' Elida closes her eyes and blows through her teeth. 'A woman who could have marry anyone. And what about that English housekeeper, her – I suppose she will arrive with her face on her feet?'

'My God, Elida, is there anyone you like?'

'I like you, Signora,' Elida says, patting her on the cheek.

Bella moves towards the gate. 'Please stop worrying. And by the way, the letter from America? It's from Grace wondering if we've heard anything from Amelia. She's in Berlin it seems.'

'Why?'

'Who knows with Amelia? And before you ask – the other two letters? One is from my father telling me to come home at once – which I have no intention of doing, regardless of whether Hitler invades Czechoslovakia.

The other is from the Signora postmarked three weeks ago so whatever it says will no longer matter.'

'Your letters are your own private affairs, Signora.' Elida sniffs. 'And make sure you eat lunch.'

'I will.'

'Make sure you do. But not in La Marita. Those Venetians – they don't know how to cook. Only poison.'

'*Ciao*, Elida.'

But Elida is not finished yet. 'Signora Stuart?'

Bella turns back.

'Up there,' Elida says, pointing her finger towards the old city. 'Up there in the *città alta*, they wear each other's trousers.'

Bella laughs. 'What's that supposed to mean?'

'If Rosa is sick, they all know it. Someone would come tell us by now.'

*

Bella steps out onto via Romano. Heat that would skin you alive. Along the pathway, placed at intervals, there are benches under trees. Far down the road one solitary old man, the picture of peace, sits in a snooze opposite the Hotel Angst. To have to trudge all the way up to the old town now, leave the merciful shade of via Romano behind, turn onto the spiral road; round and round, up and up, further and further from the sea's constant breeze. Her mind starts to jiggle with second thoughts.

She could always leave the matter of Rosa for later when the air has cooled down, sit on one of these benches and finish reading her letters instead, feel the shade glide like a silk slip over her face, throat, arms. Or. She could go down to the centre, have an iced coffee in the Caffè delle Onde, sit among the elite shoppers, with their small ridiculous dogs and fragile parcels of pastries. Read the letters there. Or. Stroll down to the seafront, throw a sly eye over Alec and the Almansi girls, then into Bar Atu; the brush of the sea breeze as she reads, the flimsy overseas pages in her hand trying to slip off back to Sicily, England, America. Or she could tear the wretched things into confetti, fling them over a wall; not bother to read them at all.

A bicycle bell clucks behind her. She turns to see the water salesman on his way back up to the mineral springs at Madonna della Ruota. Big purple face breathing sharp and slow as a carpenter's saw. The tremble of bottles all around him; dangling in nets from the handlebars, crossbar, his wrists and around his neck. He passes and she reads the familiar, if unfortunate, sign on his back: '*Aqua della Madonna*'.

Bella folds the letters and shoves them into her dress pocket, then crosses to the other side of the road.

From a side road that leads up to the *colli*, a large group of middle-aged hikers pour out. She stops while they pass. Brawny and pink, moist faces beaming, knapsacks hoisted on backs. They are holding their alpenstock at the ready although the rough ground is well behind them now. Germans; more this year than ever. The visitor columns in the newspaper are crammed with Herrs, Fraus, Von this and Von that. Herd-like, they continue to cross her path, hearty nods and eager grins, until it occurs to one man to call halt and, arm graciously extended, he invites her to pass.

The road takes a bend. On her left, the rising walls of the villas: Vera, Valentina, Cordelia. A little further on Villa Capella, a sign on the gate: 'Oranges, sweet and bitter. Apply the gardener's house.' Across the way on the corner is Luzzati's old café. The '*In Vendita*' notice has finally been taken down. The café sign on the ground, sun-faded and cracked. A ladder leans against the outside wall, and from inside comes the dull determined sounds of reinvention: hammers, saws, planks of wood being dragged across bare floors. Through the murky curtainless windows she sees men in overalls drift.

A workman comes out holding a large framed picture in his hand. She crosses the road to ask him if he knows where the Luzzatis have gone.

'*Non so.*' He shrugs.

'*Sono tornati a Trieste?*' she asks him.

'*Non lo so, Signora.*'

A voice from inside the shop suggests, '*America?*'

'*Ah sì.*' The man with the picture in his hand is suddenly certain. '*Sì, sì, America. Certo. Tutta la famiglia è andata in America.*'

He adds the picture to the stack already resting on the wheel of his truck. It is a large red poster-picture of a dancing clown eating a bowl of spaghetti. It used to hang in the corner above a table where she often sat, looking up sometimes from the book by her plate, to relieve the strain in her neck. Even after she had become friendly with Mrs Cardiff and they had taken to joining each other for dinner, she would still find herself glancing up at it. She knows this picture as well as she knows the view from her own room. Bella thinks about asking him if she could buy it, but he has gone back inside before she can decide if she wants it at all.

Under the ladder buckets of paint are covered with lace to keep the flies at bay. The lace torn from a communion dress or maybe a veil. Beside it an ormolu vase holds a quartet of damp paintbrushes. Two silver-service knives, smeared with paint, lie on the ground. In the back of the van a plump hunting dog, tongue pulsing against the dirty glass of the window, a glitter of sweat on his fur. Bella stands for a moment and considers all this. What Mrs Cardiff would call 'the small everyday brutalities of Italian life'.

She turns to cross back. The road, so long from left to right and as far as the eye can see, is deserted. Bella notices the amount of houses that have remained vacant this summer, houses that would usually have been taken by English holidaymakers. Even the Villa Cordelia is silent, a long thick chain and lock dangling from its gate, behind which a tangle of garden shows. For years it had been rented by an extended English family. The father, a peer of the realm. Grandmothers, uncles, aunts, children who behaved like savages, throwing water bombs over the wall. They had caught her father slap on the head two summers ago. He had called to complain but had been given short shrift for his trouble. Later he had written a letter to the English *Riviera Times*. 'One expects more,' he had said, 'from British children.'

A small orange Fiat turns out of a driveway and judders off towards the high road like a piece of fruit on wheels. From the opposite direction a cart returning from the San Remo market appears, baskets of unsold flowers and swaddles of palms roped in at the back. A woman drives the mule on, one foot on the rim of a smaller basket to keep it from toppling over. As it passes Bella sees there's a baby inside. The woman looks old enough to be the child's grandmother, but her heavy breasts and the stain on her blouse show that she's not. The cart and the Fiat pass each other with an exchange of rattles and jangles. Then the road is empty and silent again.

She follows the curve into via Pineta. Above is the pine garden where she promises herself a little rest, higher again is the old town, the *città alta*. Looking down to the right – a shuffle of terracotta rooftops all the way to the centre and the seafront. She hears the first stirring of the parade below, sees the stragglers emerge from their different angles. Unaware of each other, yet behaving like each other – berets pressed into heads, Sam Browne belts adjusted across chests, feet lifting to buff a shoe on the back of a leg before rushing to catch up, slip in, without drawing notice.

At the newspaper kiosk a van is parked. A man swinging low from the hips unloads bundles to the ground; another man flicks his knife through the twine that holds them together. She reminds herself to stop on the way back for Edward's newspapers. Under the curved half-wall of the gent's latrine a pair of lower legs dressed in green linen gingerly slips into position.

Bella places her hand on the rail in the centre of the first stair alley, already hot to the touch. She braces herself for the climb. Her shoes suck on her feet; the cloth of her dress pastes itself to her legs.

A few moments later she slips into the pine garden, where she stands with her hand for a while against the giant Indian fig tree, gently gasping for air. The Luzzatis come into her head again. The Day of the Faithful – was that the last time she had spoken to them? The café had closed soon after and about a year after that again, the For Sale sign had gone up. She had spotted them through the window a few times, but they never seemed to come out. Once she had even tried knocking on the door.

Regaining her breath Bella wanders through the rockeries, passing the punier spits of water until she finds a good healthy rope of it, which she breaks with the cup of her hand. It fills and she sucks the water up, taking pleasure in the sound it gives her, the privacy in here that allows it. In the distance the band is warming up. Notes rub, bump, scrap off each other, jostle for a moment, then suddenly catch. Finally a tune stumbles into shape. Now voices. '*Siamo l'eterna gioventù, che conquista l'avvenire.* We are the eternal youth, who will conquer the future.

Now on a bench, surrounded by umbrella pines, chestnuts, all sorts of trees set close to each other. It's like sitting in a room with walls made of shadow. Baubles of sunlight prowl outside. She can see downhill, a thin weave of ocean through the pines and on the verge of the via Pineta, bunches of aloe and agave, their long arms extended, like octopuses trying to crawl back to the sea.

Bella closes her eyes and sees the Luzzatis. She does not for one moment believe they have gone to America.

*

The Day of the Faithful. An unusually cold day for Liguria, it had been, a day of startling December light. She had thought it might be a bit of fun for Alec, breakfast in town and then off for a look at the proceedings. Edward would have none of it. A farce without comedy, he had called it. Married women queuing for hours to donate their gold wedding rings to Mussolini's African campaign. Then receiving a steel band in its place and muttering a coy oath of fidelity on the exchange – 'as if he was marrying the whole stock and breed of them'.

She could remember walking down to the centre that morning and the tired faces of workmen who had been up all night hooking up loud-speakers so that the speeches from Rome could be heard all over town.

Queues since dawn. Unbelievable crowds. They had come from all over, people who hadn't been seen in years; peasants in old-fashioned suits from four valleys away, dowagers in furs who preferred to remove their jewellery slowly and in full public view rather than bring it along in a bag. Everyone anxious to throw in their lot. Or to be seen throwing in their lot, anyhow. There had been something joyless about the atmosphere, a sense of barely controlled panic. Bella had noticed this at once.

'It's very squeezy, Signora,' Alec said as they came near the church and peered into the pack. He seemed a little shaky and pale.

'Yes, isn't it, Alec? Would you like to go home? I know I would. Let's do that – shall we? Let's just get out of here, go home and annoy Maestro Edward. Maybe we can play cards. Make toast at the fire – would you like that?'

As they turned to go back they saw Luzzati pushing to get through. On a day that was meant to be only for women, with men as spectators on the side. A day that was only for wedding rings. He couldn't make himself stay away, even though he had already donated a considerable amount during the previous weeks, as everyone seemed to have done, except for Signora Lami.

The newspapers published details of all contributions and Luzzati had underlined his name and donations in red, then hung the cuttings on the café wall, alongside a framed copy of his letter praising the regime that had been published in the *Popolo* newspaper.

Now here he was again, humping a bolster pillowcase on his back, looking like a thief in a child's book. Bits of candlesticks poking out of the top, bumps of other things showing through the cloth. He was shouting at the women to get out of his way. Demanding the record-keeper write every item down so it could be printed in the newspaper for all to read. People, without looking at him, stepped aside.

Bella would never forget the face of this usually serene man, emptying the pillowcase out, the sound of the items clanging onto the ground. His wife, coatless and shivering, was standing halfway up the street, twisting this way and that, as if quite literally she didn't know which way to turn. Bella took her arm and led her back towards their café. The poor woman had tears pouring down her face. '*È impazzito, Signora*,' she said to Bella, '*a causa di Trieste*.'

Eventually Bella managed to get out of Signora Luzzati why her husband had 'gone mad'. His brother's shop in Trieste had been broken into, his nephew beaten up. They were scrawling the synagogue with words the old lady could not bring herself to say.

Bella knew so much about the Luzzatis – that the Signora had a touch of lumbago, that he had a morbid fear of the sea and couldn't even walk along the promenade, how they had moved to Bordighera to retire and had ended up buying the café. How they had first met years ago in the dentist's surgery in Trieste where their son and five grandchildren still lived, that he had been engaged to someone else at the time – there had been a scandal and talk of a lawsuit. All that. Yet until the Day of the Faithful she had no idea that the Luzzatis were Jews.

*

She wakes with a start, head swaying from her neck, jerks back and takes a soft crack against the bark of a tree. Her neck. Bella curls her hand over it and squeezes the ache. A dream is still whispering in her head – something from the past. 'What was it about?' she asks herself out loud, the mild shock of her own voice bringing her fully awake. She is in the pine garden, yes. Where she had stopped for a rest on the way to see Rosa.

The bells of the midday angelus wander up from the Nervia and Roya valleys. Churches she may have seen on Sunday outings, churches she may never see as long as she lives – she listens to them all now. Down in the centre of Bordighera the peals are more rounded as if they are being weighed on the palm of a hand. Loudest at her back they come from the old town and the church of Maria Maddalena.

Bella scratches her arm where the mosquitoes have taken advantage of her sleeping absence. She tells herself to get up and go. But she is still a little tired and the noonday heat holds her down. The smell of Sister Assumpta's orphanage soup rolls on and off the air. Brewed out of local donations: kitchen gardens, restaurants, shops, farms. Bella sniffs a guess at this week's surplus – cabbage and *salumi*.

The last toll of the angelus shivers then dies and she can hear now, through the long pines, a sound of passing voices. Two men, possibly three. Occasional phrases slip out of their deep dull rumble: '*Difesa della razza.*' '*La questione ebraica.*' '*Demografia.*' '*Manifesto.*' Words she's been hearing more and more, and is sick of hearing more and more, these past weeks. Defence of the race; the Jewish debate; demography; manifesto.

They will pass, like so many other notions and fads have passed since she first came here. This is not Germany – this is Italy, she reminds herself, yet again. Bella stands, stretches her arms over her head, pushes them against a non-existent weight, then leaves the garden.

The old town is full of pre-lunch activity on piazza del Popolo and all the narrow streets leading into it. Women on last-minute errands press past each other in shop doorways. Street pedlars, returned from the parade, congregate around the shade of the clock tower portico and begin removing themselves from their trays like horses coming out of harness. In front of the church, men stand around in tidy groups of two or three. From the widow's bench, five soft-leathery faces stare out.

Outside the café the three small tables are taken. Two men in a mumble over a jug of wine. At the next table a young priest sips his *aperitivo* under a wide-brimmed hat and reads the newspaper, pausing sometimes to make notes on the margin or to underline a phrase. At the last table a municipal official smokes a pipe and glares angrily at his plate of *bruschetta*. A boy in uniform sits on the church step eating a half moon of melon as if he is using it to wash his face.

She can hear the beads on shop doors rattle and drop like Japanese fans; and the roll and grind of handcart wheels across the cobbles; and the suck of the boy on the melon. She can hear everything except voices – there is a surprising absence of those.

The sound of a thud. When she lifts her eyes to it Bella finds herself looking straight at the window of Rosa's long kitchen – the window she knows to overlook the church and this square. It is shut. For a moment it

254

seems the curtain has shifted, and a brief shadow falls over the lace. Bella lifts her hand to wave, but sees after all there is no one.

A few steps around by the side of the church into piazza Fontana, the smell of the orphanage soup becoming suddenly keen. She can hear the voices of children singing grace before lunch. Bella looks at the fountain and thinks of the milk boy – a milkman now, with full beard and two small children, always careful to ignore her whenever their paths happen to cross.

A woman leans over the fountain; darts of water dancing into a tin bucket resting on the stoop. The baker, outside his shop, swishes a broom across a small area of ground. Over his door a crick-necked Madonna peeps out of her flour-dusted niche. Bella can see now, the windows on the other side of Rosa's apartment which run the length of the house are also unpromisingly shut.

She crosses the piazza, returns the woman's tired half greeting, thanks the baker for his '*buona pranzo*' although she doubts she'll bother with lunch today.

Now in the house where Rosa lives. Up dim flights of stairs, past food smells and clattering kitchens. The doors of the apartments on each return are all open, giving a steamy wedge of daylight that helps her to follow the way to the top of the house. But when she gets to Rosa's the door is shut tight. She decides to knock even so.

She knocks again. 'Rosa?' she says. '*Sono io* – Signora Stuart.'

On the landing below, a footstep. A voice calls up. Bella looks down and recognizes the bald woman who insulted Rosa's dying husband five years ago. The woman comes up a few stairs and stops, then asks if she's looking for Rosa.

'*Sì – cerco Signora Fabbri*,' Bella confirms.

'*C'è. Di sicuro.*' She is there. Definitely. The bald woman is gleeful, like a spiteful child telling a tale. That door was open not five minutes ago, she declares. Give it a good bang. The woman forms a fist and thumps the air in case Bella has failed to understand her. Then she climbs the last few stairs to stand beside Bella outside Rosa's door. She begins to jeer through the keyhole. '*Rosa Fabbri? Ci sei? So che ci sei. Apri la porta.*'

Bella would just as soon go now. Let Rosa pretend not to be at home, if that's what she wants. But the neighbour will not be satisfied until Rosa is thoroughly mortified. She thumps the door again.

'*Stia tranquilla. Non importa,*' Bella says and turns to go.

The woman catches her by the arm, her grip gypsy-firm. Bella watches as she flattens her other hand and bashes it off the door. She sees now the woman also lacks eyebrows and eyelashes. She remembers they call her *La Testa Nuda*, and wonders how she came to be that way.

Slowly the door opens a crack, and a red-faced Rosa peeps through. 'I am sorry, Signora Stuart,' Rosa begins in her careful English.

'Why should you be sorry?' Bella asks her.

Rosa shakes her head but doesn't reply.

'Are you ill, Rosa?'

Rosa shakes her head again.

'Is everything all right? Your sons, they are—?'

Rosa nods, biting her lip.

Bella stands waiting. Now and then she throws a deliberate glance at the neighbour to let Rosa know they're not alone.

'Won't you let me in, Rosa?' she whispers after a moment. 'Nothing can be that bad, surely?'

Rosa opens the door. As soon as Bella is in, she closes it again. The neighbour shouts on the other side, words Bella can't make out.

'*Zitta.*' Rosa snarls back through the keyhole. '*Puttana pelata.*'

'Excuse me, Signora,' Rosa says, angelically, as if she has not just called her neighbour a bald-headed whore.

The air in the apartment feels tight and hot like a greenhouse. Bella sees this is because Rosa has been ironing and all the windows are closed. There is a pillar of white shirts stacked on the table and in the little room that leads off the kitchen, rows of black uniforms hang from rails. There is a dry musty odour of pressed cloth, and an acrid waft of old sweat on warmed cotton. Bella notes the electric iron she gave to Rosa when Signora Lami brought the latest model from Switzerland and declared this one to be obsolete.

'Rosa – may I ask you for a glass of water? It's so warm.'

'Oh *scusa*, *Signora*. I'm so sorry. Of course, one moment. One moment.' On the way to the water jug, Rosa goes around and opens all the windows.

The room where the uniforms hang is small, the size of the pantry in Villa Lami, kept dark to protect cloth from the sun. The rails that cross it from wall to wall are from a time when Rosa's husband was a travelling salesman of men's suits. Military uniforms now fidget and sway in the new breeze the opened windows have admitted. She can see the black shapes of shoulders, arms, legs. The glint of a button or epaulette when they give a slight turn like headless soldiers at ease.

Rosa hands Bella a glass of water then removes a stack of shirts from a chair for Bella to sit down.

'I've been worried about you, Rosa,' she begins.

'Yes.'

'I just wanted to see if—'

'I know. I'm sorry. They are all in the centre for lunch after the parade so I have nothing but fruit to offer. Please excuse me.'

'Rosa, really, I didn't expect lunch. To be honest I should have been here an hour ago but I stopped in the pine garden and, well, fell asleep.'

Rosa gives a small smile, then goes to the sideboard and pulls out a bowl of apricots and grapes. 'I have some cheese, Signora – if you like?'

'No, I'm fine, the fruit is plenty, it's too hot to eat, really.'

Rosa comes back and sits down beside her. 'I did not know what to do, Signora Stuart. So instead I do nothing. But now you are here.'

'Yes. I am.'

'It's my son, Signora. Alberto – you know, who works for the Ministry of the Interior?'

'Has something happened to Alberto?'

'No. He is well. But he has the new promotion I tell you about? Now he works for Demorazza – I think it's the name.'

'Demorazza?'

'The new department for the problems of race.'

'Oh.'

'He says no more I cannot work for the Lami house.'

'Why does he say that?'

'Signora, you must know this already.'

'I don't.'

'But it is in all the newspapers, on the radio news too. Please, Signora, don't make me say it.'

'Edward didn't get the papers today, they were late. I'm supposed to bring them back. And I haven't heard the news, I've been out.'

'My son, he know this for many weeks. He say first wait, things could change. I try to tell you before.'

'Yes, but you only said there *could* be problems, nothing definite.'

'Now is definite. So I must not go again to Villa Lami.'

'I still don't understand.'

Rosa begins to cry.

'Oh Rosa,' Bella says. 'Tell me. We're friends – are we not friends?'

Rosa nods. 'The race laws. They have come true, Signora.'

'The race laws? Oh God. I thought they were just another rumour because of the manifesto.'

'Alberto says the manifesto is the scientific proof these laws are necessary. Now they are here. They are the law.'

'I see.'

'Alberto says it better to stop working for the Lami family before the law comes to the public. I write a letter to the Signora and tell her already.'

'There will be a way around these silly laws, Rosa, wait and see. They'll all be forgotten by this time next month.'

'No, Signora.'

Bella plucks an apricot from its pile and begins to roll it between her palms. She waits for Rosa to explain.

'She is a Jew. I am an Aryan. It is the law, Signora. No Aryan can work as the servant of a Jew. Alberto says. Only the other way around from now on.'

'So is Alberto suggesting that Signora Tassi should come and work for you then?' Bella snaps.

Rosa glances at her, then looks away. 'I don't want to leave Villa Lami,' she continues. 'I need the work. Because Alberto is promoted he goes to Roma, he is the only one who brings real money to the house. And the Signora is always good to me.'

'Yes. I see how it is now. Do you know, Rosa, what the other laws are?'

'You must read for yourself.'

'Do you have the paper?'

'No. My son Dario, he take it.'

'Please tell me. The newspaper kiosks will be closed now.'

'I remember the one for schools because I am thinking of Alessandro. No more Jews teaching in schools and universities. No more Jewish influence over Aryan children.' Rosa pauses and looks down at her hands. 'Or no more going to school, Signora. Alessandro will not be allowed in the school.'

'But that's absurd. Apart from anything else he's Catholic, like his father.'

'Only bloodlines will be important now, Signora. And the Jew it comes from the side of the mother. Alberto say is called contamination.'

'But to take a child's education! It's too much. It can't be right. You *must* be mistaken.' Bella stands up. Rosa pulls at her wrist to make her sit down again.

'There is no mistake. I swear that to you.'

'After all he said about protecting the Jews! He'll never get away with it, surely not?'

'He is il Duce, Signora.'

Bella looks down at the apricot in her hand, then replaces it in the punnet. 'He is a monster,' she says.

'Please don't speak that way, Signora,' Rosa quietly says. 'If anyone hear.' She waits for a moment. 'There are other laws also, I don't remember now. There will be more ones after. They will keep coming. My son is certain.'

'Yes, yes. That's all right. I can't hear any more now. I can't. Please. I must go.'

'I try to tell you. You would not listen, Signora, you would not.'

'Even if I had listened, Rosa, what difference would it make now?' Bella says.

Rosa comes with her to the door and puts her hand over Bella's. Her eyes are hazy from crying. 'We are still friends, Signora?'

'I have to find Alec,' she says.

Bella runs, the sound of her footsteps over the empty piazza like slow sardonic applause. She tells herself to think only of Alec. Nothing of what Rosa has said, either now or before. Nothing that has been said by anyone, anywhere, over the past months or weeks. Half-heard rumours, or words almost read. *Nothing.* She cannot allow her mind to go beyond Alec. Not five minutes into the future. Until he is beside her, holding her hand, until the door of the Villa Lami is shut firmly behind them. Alec.

She turns into the long, vaulted *carruggio* of via Bastoni. The light of dusk inside. From the eaves the constant smug gurgle of pigeons then a frenzied implosion as Bella rushes inside. Something swoops down through the darkness and skims past her ears. She can feel the agitation of the air on her face as it whips by. Bella screams and folds herself down. Then turning she catches a glimpse of the bird bursting through an arch of sunlight.

She comes out at the porta Sottana, stands for a moment and looks down all the scales of its steps. Beyond the Roman palms, the cobbled roofscape below, the tower of Santa Teresa, the beneficent sea.

Behind her, on the far side of the old town wall, she hears the tinkle and bleat of goats browsing. A washing line over her head purrs on the afternoon breeze. There is a tin plate of cat food outside a door, a blue-bottle nosing around the rim. A woman's voice calls out, 'Mimi! Mi-*mi*!' and a young black cat pounces from a ground-floor window.

'It is nothing,' she says to herself, pressing her hand into her heart to slow down the beats. A lot of hot air. Of course it will pass. What was I thinking of, getting myself all worked up like this? Bella gives a short dismissive laugh, then begins her return down the steps.

Back on via Pineta she sees Mrs Cardiff rounding the bend, the Australian teacher whose name she can't recall, waddling by her side. Mrs Cardiff begins speaking to her while still yards away and although Bella can't yet hear, she can tell by the bluster of movement that all the reassurances she's been feeding herself on the way down the steps have been in vain. Bella knows her stoic friend is not easily given to the excessive gesture or word.

She walks into the downpour of Mrs Cardiff's voice. 'Oh, Miss Stuart! Miss Stuart. What a terrible, terrible business. A disgrace, no less. Goodness knows we've been expecting the worst since Austria. And with all this carry-on with Czechoslovakia we might well get the war we've been expecting. But these laws? They have come as a bolt, a complete and utter – you remember Miss Norris, of course.'

'Yes, of course, Miss Norris,' Bella says.

'What are we to make of it, Miss Stuart?' Miss Norris asks.

'I've only just found out actually,' Bella says. 'I mean, I'm not even sure what to think. Mrs Cardiff, you'll have to excuse me but I need to find Alec. I don't want him hearing this from anyone else.'

'But Alec is at home, my dear. Edward fetched him as soon as he heard the news. We met them at the beach. He already knows.'

'Was he all right?'

'Well, you know Alec, dear – but yes, he seemed fine. Those two chums of his were quite hysterical though, they had so been looking forward to going to their new school, it seems. Of course now? Anyway, I thought we should have to call the doctor at one point. Particularly the one with the shorter hair. Little…'

'Martha? Oh the poor girls.'

'Their father came and took them away. They are leaving the hotel, if they've not already left.'

'Oh surely not – they've only just started their holiday!'

'Well, Jews, you see,' Miss Norris says with a wise nod of the head. 'They say before long they won't be allowed to share the same resort.'

'Where have you heard such a thing?' Bella demands.

'Um. I can't remember now.'

Mrs Cardiff takes Bella's arm. 'Why don't we sit for a minute, you're looking a little peaky, dear. In fact, why don't you join us for coffee – do.'

'No, thank you. I really should—'

'Edward has everything in hand. And if you don't mind my saying it would be better for Alec if you were to compose yourself a little before seeing him – am I not right, Miss Norris?'

'Oh dear me, yes,' Miss Norris agrees.

'Do come with us – shall we go to Concetti's? At least in there we can talk in peace, no one will understand a word we say.'

A few minutes later they are in Concetti's, a bar Bella knows only by the view through its ever-opened doors. A girl, not much older than Alec, ushers them past a group of hairy-capped fishermen, behind a curtain to a small room at the side. Mrs Cardiff orders *caffè corretto*, insisting a shot of brandy will do them all good.

'Actually, I wouldn't mind a little nibble,' Miss Norris says. 'I missed lunch, you see, on account of all the excitement.'

'Of course,' Mrs Cardiff says and asks the girl to bring some panini.

'I knew there had to be something up,' Miss Norris says then, 'when they issued us with that magazine! You know, the Defence of the Race thing – have you seen it, Miss Stuart?'

'No. I'm afraid not.'

'Oh, what an appalling thing it is. All against the Jews. Not one good word to say about them. I mean everyone has their good points, after all. A copy was sent to all educationalists – teachers, librarians, and so forth – with instructions to read and promote its opinions. That was a few weeks ago, the start of August in fact, and I remember saying to myself at the time, well, what's all this *really* about I wonder?'

'Miss Norris, I don't have the slightest idea what you're talking about,' Bella says. 'I don't mean to sound rude but…'

'Oh, you don't! And even if you did I'd never blame you, Miss Stuart. You're bound to be more upset than most.'

Bella looks at her.

'Mrs Cardiff has been telling me about your Signora being…' she takes a quick look around and speaks the word like an unsavoury secret, 'of the Jewish persuasion. Well, your job could be in jeopardy, after all. And even if it's not – how is she going to pay you? She won't be allowed to own land, you know, or businesses or anything like that. They'll take all her lolly too.'

'Oh, now really, Miss Norris,' Mrs Cardiff says. 'Let's not get ahead of ourselves.'

'Well,' says Miss Norris, 'of course, not *yet*. But sooner than later, they'll be as poor as the rest of us – I mean some of the rest of us.'

'Do you have a newspaper?' Bella asks Mrs Cardiff. 'I want to read these laws, I simply cannot believe them until I do. I need to see them with my own eyes.'

'You need to go back to London, that's what you need, my dear. And I tell you that as your sincerest friend. Go now. Today, if you can.'

'But that's ridiculous, Mrs Cardiff, what about Alec? The Signora? I can't just… I wouldn't want to.'

'Yes, I do understand the fix you're in, but just the same.'

'Good job she's not a foreign one.'

'I'm sorry, Miss Norris?' Bella asks.

The girl comes back under the curtain with the coffee and a plate of panini and lays them on the table.

'*Grazie*,' Mrs Cardiff says.

'*Prego, Signora.*'

As soon as she leaves Miss Norris continues. 'They're expelling all foreign Jews.' Then she picks up a panino and looks inside. 'I do miss butter, they're so terribly dry without, don't you think?'

'Oh yes,' Mrs Cardiff agrees. 'Why not go and ask for some, Miss Norris?'

'Ought I?'

'By all means. And have her fetch you a nice cake. The cakes are always good here. And would you mind terribly if I asked you to bring some water back? Ice too? Am I being a terrific nuisance?'

'Of course not. You leave it up to me.'

*

Mrs Cardiff waits a moment. 'Of course, you probably don't know, dear, but indeed they are going to expel all foreign Jews. I didn't like to say in front of Miss Norris, but...?'

'The Signora is German.'

'Quite.'

'They can't just give her the boot – surely?'

'It seems they can. Well, she'll have six months to clear the decks. And she will, you know, otherwise she can kiss goodbye to her money. James says there'll be a terrible job getting funds out in any event. Mussolini won't want that sort of cash drain leaving the country. The flight of hard currency, they're calling it.'

'James?' Bella asks.

'Yes, dear, my brother – he works in the bank? The manager.'

'Of course. I'm not thinking.'

'Well, apparently a few weeks ago the department of finance requested information on all Jewish accounts. I mean to say – really!'

'You never told me that.'

'I didn't know until this morning! Anyway, the General Director instructed the banks not to break client confidentiality. But how long will they get away with that – I ask you? Finish your coffee, dear. Alec is an Italian citizen of course, so for the moment he is safe but, well, she'll hardly leave him behind?'

'But his father is a Catholic. *He* is—'

'It won't make any difference, it appears.'

'But this can't be happening,' Bella says. 'How can it be?'

'Oh, my dear girl – now you're as white as. Here, eat one of these ghastly things.' She lifts the plate of panini to Bella and leans into her. 'I am sorry I let slip about the Signora. Caught unawares, I'm afraid. Probably best not to say too much more to her. Australian – did you know?'

'I'm glad you sent her out, I felt like slapping her.'

'Of course you did.' Mrs Cardiff sighs. 'I'm going to smoke, dear. Do you mind?'

Bella waits for Mrs Cardiff to fish around her wool and needles and to pull out a pack of cigarettes. 'Now,' she continues as she lights one, 'you must put a call through to your father, that's what you must do at once. Tell him you want to go home. But say nothing else, give him no information whatsoever over the telephone. He'll think it's to do with all this fuss with Czechoslovakia and that, understandably you're afraid of war. You can spill all the beans you like as soon as you arrive in London. Trust me. That's my advice and it's coming from a good source, let me tell you. I'm to leave tomorrow. James will have to stay on at the bank for a bit but—'

'Tomorrow? Already – is that really necessary?'

'Of course it is! Don't you see what's happening? He's doing this to appease that Hitler thug. And let me say this, Anabelle, Hitler at least waited a few years before he took his diabolic ideas out on Jewish children. They weren't pulled out of school immediately, you know. Whereas Mussolini has plunged straight at them. If you saw those two little girls today. And the Italians supposed to be so fond of children!'

Mrs Cardiff finishes her cigarette and, coughing a little, looks at Bella through watered eyes. 'It will ruin Mussolini in the eyes of every civilized country. But he doesn't care and why should he? He has his chum. They're going in together, you mark these words, Miss Stuart. Nazism is on the doorstep.'

'Oh, but Mrs Cardiff. This is not Germany. This is Italy.'

Mrs Cardiff sighs and pats Bella's hand. 'Anabelle, this may be the last chance we have to speak, so I'll be frank. I know you, like most people, think that rules in Italy are made, if not to be broken, then certainly bent. But not this time. And please don't presume that Bordighera is Italy because it's not.'

'It's hardly Timbuktu!'

'Bordighera is a pretty seaside resort, an all-year resort, where people start to believe they are on endless holiday. If you want to see the real Italy, go to Rome, Bologna or Trieste indeed, where you can be sure there will be those gloating at today's news and eyeing up all they have envied for so long: Jewish homes, jobs, land. I wish you well, my dear, whatever your decision. I will contact your father – no, even if you tell me I mustn't – I *will* as soon as I get back to London. One last word of advice, change all your money to sterling. Go to James, he'll sort you out, that way at least when you come to your senses you'll be prepared because the lira will be of no use soon enough – *shhh* now, here she is – ah, Miss Norris! There you are, at last. We were beginning to wonder. Unfortunately, Miss Stuart is just about to leave. You have the butter I see. Well done.'

*

When she gets home Alec is in the bath. Elida, crossing the landing with an armful of towels, pauses to throw a complaint over the banisters – Edward has brought the poor child home from the beach, coated in sand 'like he is a *cotoletta alla milanese*.' It is clear by Elida's face that she hasn't yet heard the news.

'Hadn't time to dry him,' Edward mutters then pushes her into the kitchen where he makes tea and begins to tell her what happened.

He'd been wrestling with the crib half the morning and ended up having to carry it, piece by piece, into the Signora's bedroom, the size of the bloody thing like a garden shed. He'd decided to wait for Cesare to give him a hand and so went out onto the terrace to have a smoke and see if there was any sign of him. Edward never got to light the smoke because when he looked down the old man was there already, and he knew at once that something was off. Cesare was standing, hands hanging, back to the garden, nose to the wall.

Edward called to him – no response. Then after a moment sent down a whistle. Cesare turned, looked at him for a moment, then nodded. Edward nodded back. 'It was,' he tells Bella, 'like an acknowledgement of some sort between us.'

When Edward came down Cesare pulled the newspaper out of his pocket and handed it to him. '*Siamo fottuti*,' he said.

'What does that mean?' Bella asks.

'Literally?'

'Yes.'

'We're fucked.'

'Oh, I see.'

Edward continues. 'Down on the beach the news spread, I suppose like it always does, from group to group – if you remember how we heard about Spain? Or Vienna? – and I must have arrived just after it had. At least, when I came out of the *sottopassaggio* there was the usual noise – you know, that manic seaside quacking – but as I began to walk along the *passeggiata* the silence seemed to roll ahead of me.

'By the time I got to the Parigi all I could hear were the gulls and the sea. I stood at the railing scouring the beach for Alec. Bit by bit people started to talk again. Amongst themselves first, but then they began to break from their groups, get up and cross the beach to speak to each other. By now the newspapers had come through and paperboys were running up and down the promenade or trudging over the sand shouting, "*La Difesa della razza!*" And something about new racial laws.

'I don't think anyone knew what to do or how to take it. Most were shocked, I'd say. Naturally, this being Italy it didn't take too long for opinions to form. From what I could pick up the general consensus seemed to be – if he's doing this to the Jews he's rowing in with Hitler, and if he's rowing in with Hitler we're headed for war.

'I finally spotted Alec and the girls. They were standing a few feet away from a family group, listening to a man reading aloud from the paper. As I got near I could hear his voice, full of approval, announcing the law to ban Jewish children from school. Lina was standing with a ball wedged between her ankles listening to him. Then she began to sob. The other one…?'

'Martha.'

'Martha, she skipped the tears and went straight into screaming.'

'And Alec?'

'Alec just stood there looking at them.'

'He said nothing?'

'Not a squeak. Then Mrs Cardiff came along and that fat lump she sometimes has with her.'

'Miss Norris.'

'Yes. They scooped up his beach things, handed them to me and shooed the pair of us off. I took him home while they looked after the girls. And well, here we are, I suppose.'

*

It takes an age to get Alec settled that night. He neither eats nor says much during dinner and only agrees to go to bed at all after Edward telephones the station and puts the *capo* on to personally confirm there will be no more trains before morning. He can then stop waiting for his mother and new baby sister to arrive.

For a time they hear him up in his room, playing his harmonica. At first he plays in a non-stop tuneless block, then gaps begin to appear that gradually expand into silence.

Bella goes up to his room, prises the harmonica out of his hand, shakes the spit out and wipes it dry. Then she folds Alec's legs, stiffened with sleep, under the covers. She sits on the side of the bed for a few moments and watches him. His lips roughened by overuse of the instrument, his limbs longer and bonier than they seemed to be yesterday. Ironically, now that all the baby softness and cuteness has gone from his body he seems vulnerable. Even in his sleep, he looks awkward and incompetent for an eleven-year-old boy.

Bella stands up, checks everything on his bedside table is as he likes it: flask of water, flash lamp should he waken frightened, the tennis ball autographed by the Italian champion six months ago in Monte Carlo that Alec has been carrying around as his *portafortuna* ever since. Behind all this stands a framed photograph taken in the garden this time last year, with the Almansi girls prancing about in bare feet. There is a postcard, stuck in the bottom corner of the frame, sent by his mother when he first started school, telling him how handsome he had looked in his new uniform. Finally, an old pair of gold spectacles once belonging to Signor Lami and which Alec has recently taken to keeping near his bed so 'Papa can watch over me'. A notion Bella finds just a little disconcerting.

She pulls a jar of petroleum jelly from a shelf over the bed, dips her little finger in and gently dabs it along the chapped rim of his lips.

Later, just as she is going upstairs to bed, the sound of the telephone smashes into the house. Bella watches from the stairs while Elida approaches the phone as if she's expecting a bite from it. She tries to catch the gist of the call by the shift of expressions on Elida's face; now alarmed, now puzzled, finally annoyed. '*Da Vienna*,' she tuts, holding the receiver to Bella as she comes down the last few stairs.

'*Vienna?*' she says. 'The Signora's in Vienna?'

But Elida has already gone to the house phone to call Edward up from the mews.

It turns out to be a drunken Amelia. Bella can hardly understand what she's saying. It's as if she's speaking with her mouth full of toffee. In the background there are the hysterical strains of an *orchestrina* that's asking too much of itself, and the surge and fall of drunken voices, possibly German.

'I can't hear you, Amelia,' she shouts down the phone. 'I'm sorry I just can't—'

The noise suddenly cuts. 'Forgota close door.'

'Yes, that's better.'

'Look, the thing is, well. I'm in a – you know – fix. The problem. The problem is I can't get out of Vienna.' Amelia starts to laugh.

'I thought you were supposed to be in Berlin?'

'Well, I would be! I would be! Let me tell you *right* now. I would, if I could be, if I could. But they won't let me back in. I'm not kidding. This place is. Gonetahell. That's what. Last time with Grace, it was so. Now. It's a tragedy, that's what. Poor old Vienna. Can't see the buildings for swastikas hanging from every window. The whole damn town overrun with German soldiers. People shrieking "*Heil Hitler*" at each other like maniacs in the streets, every shop you go into, every bar, even the babies are doing it. All over. I mean, *shrie-eeeking*. It's more Nazi than Berlin, for chrissake! I want. I want out of here, Miss Stuart. But they won't allow it! Not unless someone whaddayacall vouches for me. They won't even let me home to the States. I mean, come on! Anyway who cares? I don't wanna go to the States, much rather come visit with you instead. That'd be OK. Wouldn't that be OK? It'd be fun. Like it used to be fun. You, me, Edward, whatshisname Alec. Trouble is, I need Aunt Lami to – you know, whatever. To vouch for me – I thought maybe with that special thing going on between Germany and Italy. If that husband of hers, that Tassi husband lawyer guy, could – you know? And she's got her share of contacts, you can bet on that, Miss Stuart. How are you anyhow? How is Bordighera?'

'Well, I'm—'

'Get her to do that for me, would you? Aunt Lami, tell her I'm in a fix, you know. Talk her round, the way only you can, there's a sweetheart. I tried calling her but—'

'Amelia, I'm sorry but I can't—'

'You can't?'

'The thing is I won't be—'

'You won't?'

'No, what I mean is. Amelia – are you still there?' Bella asks after a few silent seconds.

'Lemme get this clear in my mind – did you just say you won't? Is that what you just said?'

'You see, the problem is—'

'The problem is?'

'It's just not possible.'

Bella listens for a moment to the sounds of Amelia organizing a cigarette: click, suck and blow. Then as if the cigarette has sobered her up, her voice returns almost clear and certainly cold. 'Now you listen to me, Miss Stuart.'

'I am listening, Amelia, if you'd just let me explain.'

'Do you have any idea what could happen to me here? I've lost my papers – don't you see? They were stolen actually, if you must know. Without papers I could be goddamn anyone. I could be a fucking Jew. Do you know what's happening to Jews right now in Vienna? Let me speak with Edward.'

'You don't understand, Amelia.'

'What I don't understand, Miss Stuart, is just who the hell you think you are?'

'Amelia, please.'

'You know something – I'm really not all that surprised if it comes to it. I mean, you've pretty much always had it in for me. Always been something of a bitch quite frankly. Oh sure, you're all sweetie-pie and shiny-shoes when it suits you, but you've never fooled me, you know. She's warned you off, hasn't she? Your precious Sig-nora. She's told you to say you don't know where she is. Well, you go tell her from me that if she doesn't help me, she'll be sorrier than she knows how. Because I have the read on her. And I know.'

'You know what, Amelia?'

'I know what she's been taking out of Germany and Italy. Drip, drip, drip. And you can tell her from me that's my uncle's money. Money she no longer has any right to, by the way. You tell her that now. You go tell her that right now, from me.'

'I promise, she really isn't here.'

'Let me speak with Edward.'

'Amelia, I'm simply trying to—'

'I want Edward – are you *deaf* as well as dumb?'

'Please, if you would just listen—' but then Edward is beside her pulling the phone from her hand.

'Ah, Amelia,' he says. 'Yes, it's me, yes, indeed. Oh dear, dear, how terrible. I see, yes. Do you know – she's not here – oh, but let's not talk about her. I can help you just as well. Now, where are you staying? Well, that's not too bad, eh, that's hardly a prison cell now, is it? From what I hear that's the best in Vienna. But didn't you have to leave your papers at reception when you checked in? Oh I see, you took them back when you went to the bank. Well, did you go back to the bank and see if you'd left them there? Ah, a nightclub. Yes, well I agree, they're most likely gone. Never mind, we'll sort it all out. Yes, of course we will. Now what I want you to do – listen to me, Amelia, are you listening? Go back to the hotel. Oh, you're there now – excellent. Well, I want you to go to your room. Yes now. No, don't even say goodnight to your lovely friends, just go to your room. I'm sure they are, yes. We'll get you out of there before you know it. Now, it could take a few days. That's right, right, right. Just stay put, have them send whatever you want up to the room. Me? Well, you wouldn't know, Amelia, I might very well do. Yes, I'm sure I would love it there. Yes. Splendid. Now what room, did you say? Oh now, Amelia, let's concentrate on one thing at a time, eh? Up to bed with you now. Well yes, that is a shame. I'll get onto it straight away. Promise, absolutely. Don't worry about the Signora, I'll organize everything. Goodbye. Yes. I won't let you down. Night night. You too, you too.' He puts down the phone. 'She was on far too long – I hope no one was listening in.'

'What's happened?' Bella asks.

'Do you have an address for Grace? Write it down for me, would you? I'll be back soon.'

'Where are you going?'

'To send a telegram.'

'But what about Amelia?'

'Don't you think we've enough to worry about? I'll send a telegram, her father can rescue her.'

'But what did she say?'

'She's lost her papers, has no money, Tassi's office has been refusing to accept her calls – I think we should do the same from now on. Oh, and she's keeping the bed warm for me.'

Bella and Edward look at each other and laugh. Elida tuts and closes her eyes in disgust. Then Edward says, 'I was thinking maybe I'll move into the house, for a night or so, until the Signora shows up at any rate – what do you think?'

'Oh. I'm sure that would be fine,' Bella says. 'What do you think, Elida, it should be fine? I don't think the Signora would mind – would she?'

'I don't care what the Signora say,' Elida says, clasping her hands. 'If it make it more safe for us all.'

*

Every day seems to bring more bad news. The wider world coming in through the radio: Hitler, Czechoslovakia; every move another move towards war.

A few days after the race laws are published they hear on the radio that all French officers have been recalled from leave.

'Meaning what?' she asks Edward.

'The French are preparing for war.'

Then nearer to home a letter arrives from Alec's school: 'Kindly note

273

that following instructions from the *Ministero dell'Educazione Nazionale*, there is no longer a place available for the abovementioned pupil in the forthcoming term.'

Even though she has read the laws, several times, in several newspapers, and has listened to them being endlessly discussed (if rarely criticized) on the radio, Bella can still hardly believe it. After all the time he has put into that school; all the hours fretting and fussing about uniforms and books, the daily struggles with homework and friendships, the small occasional triumph. Up and down that San Remo Road, knowing every stone, sweep and turn of it, every pillar and shopfront to be passed on the way. And the same thing every morning as they came into the centre, Alec pointing to his landmark of the dome on the Russian church and shouting out, 'Almost there. Almost there! Only four minutes thirty seconds minimum, to five minutes at the very maximum, more. Punctuality excellent! Alec Lami. *Brav-is-simo!*'

And this is what it all amounts to in the end – a 'To Whom it May Concern' few lines-and-a-bit typed in the middle of the page, as if the secretary had been trying to take the mean look off a few morsels.

She has to ask Edward to take Alec for the afternoon because she can't bring herself to look the child in the face. She is that upset she almost misses the handwritten note slipped into the back of the envelope.

Miss Stuart – It might be worthwhile applying to the Demorazza for Alec to be considered for *discriminato* status. I'm not sure what this means yet, but gather it may allow exemptions in certain cases. It's worth a shot anyhow. Please tell him we send our best. I don't have to tell you how simply awful we all feel about this. Let us hope and pray it blows over soon.

The note is unsigned, but probably from Alec's geography teacher Miss McHugh who has always been fond of him, despite his indifference to her subject. Bella is grateful anyhow for the comfort it brings and keeps it in her handbag to glance at now and then. At least someone, somewhere, might actually care about their predicament.

Every now and then they ask each other what should they do? And the answer is always the same – 'Let's give it another day or so – see if the Signora shows up.'

*

Meanwhile her letters and messages for the missing Signora continue to pile up, including calls from two different bank managers as well as a notice to attend the Commune Registrar for the *stato di famiglia* certificate. Elida informs them it's compulsory now, every family has to have its status confirmed and ready to produce at any given moment: for enrolment in school or the *Balilla*, to avail of free milk. Even at the other end of the scale, to take part in the regatta or go out on a pleasure cruise. A friend of her neighbour's cousin's uncle has the letter E printed on hers.

'E?' Bella asks. 'Why E?'

'For *ebreo* – status of Jew.'

Then a few days later, another letter, this time addressed to Bella, equally dreaded but also expected, from the *Prefettura* of the police. She is having breakfast with Edward, as they have done since he moved from the mews into the house, him reading the morning papers, her going through the morning's post, Alec absent but traceable by the occasional drawl of his harmonica throughout the house and garden. Even with all this worry and uncertainty, as she opens the letter with an unsteady hand, Bella is aware that it warms her a little to see Edward across from her, leaning back in his chair, relaxed and manly, his long hand coming around the newspaper to grasp the width of the cup, while she half listens to the items he occasionally reads out, and he half responds to whatever she might say. Since Edward moved from the mews to the house there has been this sense of companionship – the sort a married couple might enjoy and, as she occasionally reminds herself, probably the nearest she'll ever get to the experience.

The letter is in fact an order to appear before the federal committee on Friday, 30 September, with all her documentation to date and in order. The hearing will require her to explain why she has failed to have her documents verified despite reminders, and also to decide if her future is in Italy. Should she fail to appear an immediate deportation order would be issued against her.

'Oh God – not this. Not this *now*, on top of everything else!'

Edward doesn't seem to have heard her. She is about to slide the letter across the table to him, when something occurs to her.

'Edward?'

'Mmm?'

'Haven't you had anything from the *Prefettura* yet?'

'Who?'

'The *Prefettura* of the police, or the federal secretary even – haven't they been in touch with you yet?'

'No. Not yet.'

'Nothing at all? Not even a notice to verify your documents?'

'I've been here longer than you.'

'What difference does that make? Edward, are you listening to me, don't you think it's odd, I mean? You filled out the census form in August, didn't you, so really there ought to have – *Edward*?'

He puts down the paper and looks across the table at her. 'The British fleet has just been mobilized,' he says.

*

For days they've been keeping to the house and garden and Alec has finally stopped asking why. Not that this self-imposed exile has been discussed or agreed between them; it has simply become easier not to go out.

Days in the garden, trying to make more of it – picnics in a different corner each time, badminton at a makeshift court set up by Edward. Alec, sitting on the rim of a forgotten pond that Cesare has revived and filled with fresh water, splashing his legs or playing with boats. Everything is about keeping him distracted, his mind off questions and away from dark corners. But there are days when nothing can please him. Not talk of building a tree house; nor of getting a puppy; not even the ping-pong ball battle they staged one evening, which only set him off sulking and crying.

Only the postman calls now, or the ice man, who is related to Elida and is, according to her lights, *discretissimo*. Even so, Bella has noticed, he never goes away from the kitchen without a bag of something or other swinging not so *discretamente* out of his hand.

One day Bella asks Elida how much longer she thinks she'll stay working for the Signora.

'It's only work if you take money. So if I don't take money, only food and a bed, then I don't get paid so I don't work really but stay as a guest in the house who just help.'

'But you can't work for nothing.'

'I have nowhere else to go, Signora,' Elida quietly says.

'You could look for another job.'

'So many others like me also suddenly must look for another job.'

'The authorities know you're here, Elida. They know where everyone is now since the census. How long do you think you'll get away with it?'

Elida folds her big fists. 'Until they come drag me away.'

*

Elida has stopped putting in grocery orders over the phone for delivery. She says she won't run the risk of being refused Jewish credit. Instead she goes out herself, counting the money from a box in the steel-plate safe, and filling it full of receipts on her return.

Carting two big basketfuls back up the road each morning, she brings home along with the fruit and the meat more and more worrying snippets. On the posters outside the market Elida has read: 'Those names *failing* to appear on the list below must relinquish their party card.' Or: 'Those names *not* published in next Saturday's newspaper must *not* enrol for the coming school year and need *not* apply to renew their *Balilla* membership.'

Elida hates these indirect hits. 'At least when Hitler stabs you,' she fumes, 'he sticks it in your belly where you can see the hand that is holding the knife.'

She keeps them up to the minute on the comings and goings in Bordighera. Most classical concerts are cancelled, she says, only German musicians seem willing to travel. But Vizzali–Marini, the dancing duo, continue to shine – tonight's demonstration in the Kursaal will be of 'The Lambeth Walk'.

She often complains that there are more and more military on the streets every day. Or that the town is full of suspicious types pretending to be holidaymakers; one eye on the border, the other on your purse. Or that greedy grabbers are already starting to hoard – today she could only get five packets of Nazionali cigarettes for the Maestro and six kilos of sugar, which means they now have only twenty.

'In the name of God, Elida, why do we need twenty kilos of sugar?'

'Signora, in wartime everything is currency.'

She reports on shop conversations. Private whispers over the counter. Or free-for-all rants involving customers and staff. Today's gripe – the new French law banning Italians without a visa, even for a day trip, even for an hour. *Disgrazia* – is what they are saying. Italian workers losing jobs because of delays at the border. One woman in the queue of the *tabaccheria* said her son got the sack because he was three hours late for his work in Villefranche. And when a man at the back of the shop said they only wanted an excuse to get rid of him anyway, because he's Italian – voice by voice, the whole packed shop had agreed.

In the pharmacy Elida heard someone tell the assistant that there are signs up in the shops in Rome. The signs don't say '*Juden Nicht Begrüßen*', or '*Juden Verboten*', like in Germany, but '*Negozio Ariano*'. Aryan shop.

'Another back-stab,' Elida snarls, clutching her metaphorical knife.

'Oh God, Elida! Tell us something nice for a change, something *hopeful*,' Bella pleads when she hears this last piece of news.

'The olives are starting to ripen, Signora. They are laying olive cloths all over the ground.'

*

Her father actually telephones. Even down the line, behind the voices of English and Italian telephonists, she can feel him simmer with rage.

'They'll be pipping me in a minute or two,' he growls as he comes on, 'so I'll keep this brief. Your Mrs Cardiff has been to see me on her way to Northumberland and I must say I am appalled not to mention utterly ashamed by the total disregard you have for those with your best interest at heart. And safety, I might add. Do you know this very morning our prime minister has issued a warning to Germany to stay out of Czechoslovakia? Do you imagine for one moment that warning will be heeded? And do you have any idea of the possible consequences? Ina and I are getting ready to leave London, when – rather than should – the need arise, but we will be staying in the country with her sister. I will leave the details here on my study desk, Mrs Carter has the spare keys, but let me tell you now, Bella, that I will expect to see you at your haste either in London or at Ina's sister's house. Old as I am, I would be prepared to go over there to you this minute and personally drag you home were it not for the fact that the Home Office has curtailed travel to the continent. I hope I've made myself clear in this matter and I certainly don't expect to have to repeat this call.'

The pips sound and he hangs up the telephone, before she has a chance to say a word in her defence, or any word at all.

*

There is an electric storm one afternoon, about halfway into the month. Big bruisers of hailstones first, hammering against the windows and battering down on the garden. Then only rain. No wind or thunder. A sky snagged with eerie light. Under this relentless downpour everything in the garden gleams. Half-mesmerized, she sits with Alec looking out a window in his mother's sitting room.

Until Edward sticks his head around the door to announce he is going out. 'There's someone I've been meaning to talk to,' he says. 'This would be a good time to go.'

'You'll be soaked. Should I drive you?'

'No. Stay here with Alec.'

'We could all go,' she begins. 'It means we'd at least…'

He looks at her, waiting. And for a moment she pictures them cosy in the car, the wheels pressing into long swills of water, the shushing windscreen wipers. She sees the blur of premature light from cafés and bars and a sudden pair of brave feet splashing across an otherwise deserted street. The rain hopping off the ground with such force, and bouncing off the bonnet of the car, straight back to the sky, as if it's raining in both directions. She feels if they could only do that, get into the car and keep driving and driving through rain.

'Well?' he says.

'What I mean to say, Edward, is, we could get out of the house for a while, you know, but because we'd be in the car, there'd be no need to worry about meeting anyone, saying the wrong thing. That's what I mean.'

'No. Best if you two stay here,' Edward says.

A few minutes later Bella gets up. 'Alec, I'll be back,' she says.

'Where—?'

'Just popping down to the kitchen for an apple – would you like one?'

'Yes please.'

She stands at her bedroom window, watching the spike of Edward's black brolly bob down the lane towards the town centre. Bella is assaulted by thoughts of the worst, the fact that she has started to doubt him. Supposing he doesn't come back? Supposing there's somebody waiting at the end of the lane to drive him away? Or worse, he starts drinking? What if she is left here alone? Left to make all the decisions. And how can she make the smallest decision without knowing what has already been done, or said, by the Signora, or what she may yet have up her sleeve? And now Edward disappearing into a haze of rain, not saying who he is going to see, or where or when he'll be back, or if.

She notices the shape of the postman then, sleek as a seal at the garden gate. Bella slips off her shoes and runs downstairs. She opens the front door and the postman peers in at her through a veil of rain.

'*O che brutto tempo!*' she says and invites him to step inside, maybe have a coffee to help him on his way. But the postman says he'll carry on, that at his age he finds temporary comfort worse than no comfort at all.

He fumbles under the fall of his sou'wester cloak and she asks him how long he's been postman to this house. He smiles under a thick white moustache. '*Da tanti anni, Signora,*' he explains. Since he was a boy when he used to come with his uncle, the postman before him. He had always loved coming to the Villa Lami, he tells her, the old Signora would give him something sweet from her pocket. *Gentilissima.* She did her own gardening, he adds, as if this is a fact that still bemuses him.

He produces two letters and she asks him if he has anything for the mews.

'*Scusi, Signora?*'

'*La casetta in fondo al giardino? Il garage? Signor King? Edward King?*'

He looks at her blankly, as if he doesn't know who or what she is talking about. Then he smiles again and takes a step back into the rain.

When she comes back to Alec he is at the table, teasing a pencil across a page. She walks the length of the Signora's sitting room where lately they seem to spend so much time. As if there is no other room in the house. The most private anyway, even with all the lights on, it remains hidden from the street. The piano is here, and a few days ago she had Cesare move the wireless and gramophone down from the library. They have started to eat dinner here, now that the evenings are darkening and Elida says it's easier to have only one fire to light. Bella believes she just finds it easier to eat with them in here, as equals, rather than downstairs in the dining room with its association of servant and served.

They eat, then play cards, listen to the gramophone or to Edward play the piano. After Alec has his bath they allow him to lie on the sofa in his pyjamas until he falls asleep and Edward carries him to bed. They can listen to the radio in peace then, fussing through wavelengths and un-recognizable languages, until they find a speech or news item they can understand. Everybody is making speeches these days. It irritates her the way Edward cocks his ear closer to Russia or Hungary, as if any moment it's all going to start making sense. But then lately she has noticed many things about Edward annoy her.

Bella leans over Alec and looks down at his drawing. 'Oh, that looks good. What is it?'

'It's a dragon. It *will* be a dragon. I saw it in the sky. Where's my apple, Miss Bella? Did you forget?'

'Oh sorry, yes I did.'

'It doesn't matter very much anyway,' he says, and looks as if he's going to cry.

'Alec? It's only a silly apple and it will only take a minute to go back down, you know.'

'No. I no longer want it. I really no longer do.'

She watches him for a moment. 'If you change your mind, just tell me.'

'Mmm,' Alec says but already he is being pulled down into his picture and is starting to forget the apple.

Bella goes to the sofa, lies on it, fixing one cushion under her back, another under her neck so she can watch him work – the movement of his hand and forearm, the way he brushes the hair on one side of his head with the harmonica or taps himself on the forehead with it or nuzzles it against his lips at intervals to make a short discordant blare. The smudge of charcoal on his cheek, the rise of colour behind it as the picture takes shape and he becomes more excited, the tip of his pinkie slipping up his nostril for a sly pick.

'All right, Alec?'

He turns to her and smiles.

'Good boy,' she says, and for a few seconds they stay looking at each other.

She must have dropped off because she wakes to hear the harmonica blasting through the room. Then Alec's voice, peevish: 'When, I said, *when*?'

He's still sitting there at the table, in the same way, nothing altered except for the bloom of dark colour all over his page. Bella pulls herself out of the comfort of her snooze. It's still raining. 'When what, Alec?' she asks.

'When am I going back to school?' He is whining now. It's the same question he asks at least twice a day. Usually, she tells him that start of term has been postponed because repairs are being carried out on the roof of the school. This morning when he asked, he had looked carefully at her mouth, as though examining each word to come out of it, and Bella knew then he no longer believed her.

The afternoon of the September storm, she decides – in so far as it's possible anyway – not to tell any more lies to Alec.

'How old are you now, Alec?' she asks, sitting up.

'You know how old I am.'

'Yes, but tell me anyway.'

'Do you mean now this minute, or next month on my birthday?'

'Now.'

He drops his pencil, sends it rolling amongst the crayons and charcoals with a short impatient sigh. '*O Dio!*' he says. '*Undici.* Eleven. *Onze. Elf.* Nine and two makes me. So does ten and one.'

'I was hoping you'd be old enough to tell something important to, but if you're going to be a cheeky-boots.'

'No,' he whispers. 'I'm not a cheeky-boots. I'm a big boy.'

'Alec, these are things I'm not really sure about myself, never mind if I should be telling you – but.' She pats the sofa and he comes and sits beside her.

When she's finished he says, 'So the boys in the *Balilla* were right then?'

'What boys?'

'The fat one, the *comandante*'s nephew, and his friends, you remember when they take me home from the *Balilla*?'

'Yes. So they did say something to you then?'

'No. It was only about two weeks ago. The last time I go to tennis I saw them on my way home. And he say, "*Ah, il piccolo ebreo da Villa Lami.*"'

'The little Jew from Villa Lami?'

'Yes. Then they run after me, all singing together, "*Il piccolo ebreo da Villa Lami, Villa Lami, Villa Lami!*" But then they see Edward at the top of the road and they stop and go the other way.'

'Alec, why didn't you tell me this?'

'I don't know, Miss Bella. Am I a Jew then?'

'Sort of, I suppose. Part of you anyhow.'

'Papa's part?'

'No.'

'Well, that's all right then because I want to be like Papa.'

'But you are like your Papa, in so many ways. It makes no difference to the boy you are, really, Alec, it's just something some people get worked up about.'

'Why?'

'I don't know, to be honest. So they can find someone to blame, someone different to themselves.'

'Blame for what?'

'I don't know.'

'But I go to holy mass now. I say my prayers. I'm not different now.'

'Well, yes, darling, of course. You know, this will pass in a while and all seem very silly. But just the same, we have to be careful. That's why I'm telling you because I want you to understand. I want to keep you safe.'

'Why hasn't Mamma come?'

'Probably because she wants to keep you safe too.'

'But am I not safe?'

'Of course you are.'

'Yes, of course I am!' he shouts and jumps up from the sofa. 'I am safe here with you and Cesare and Maestro Edward and Elida!'

'You're as safe as houses.'

'I'm as safe as *all* the houses in Bordighera! Imperia! Liguria! Italia! Libya and the colonies of the *Egeo*!'

'Shh, shh, calm down, Alec. Sit down. Come. You are safe. Absolutely safe.'

Alec puts his head on her shoulder and they look out at the rain for a while. Then he sits up. 'If Il Duce doesn't like the Jews, then they must be very bad.'

'But Alec, you know Martha and Lina Almansi are Jews. Your mamma is a Jew.'

'Oh yes, of course, that's right.' He frowns.

Later when Bella is passing his room, her eye falls on his bedside table. An absence. The photograph of the Almansi girls, along with his mother's postcard, has disappeared, and she is sorry now not to have stuck to her lies.

*

Her days are solid with hours. Hours that won't lessen no matter how much she chips at them. So that a day can seem like a week, a week as long as a month, and she can hardly believe it's still only September. Other hours seem to slip through the cracks of the day, so she can't remember how they were spent, or what date they belonged to, or even the name of that day.

She decides to keep note, to write the day and date on top of a notebook page every morning. To keep, not a diary but a reference of some sort: an incident that has occurred or perhaps a small household task carried out. A pin to keep the day in its place.

She has come to dread her own bed, lying in the dark listening for danger in every bat squeak or palm shudder out in the garden. It's been that way since Elida came home with Signora Codoni's story. Signora Codoni, who lives at the far end of via Romano, had recently returned after three months abroad to find a middle-aged Austrian couple living in her garden shed. She called the police to remove them, but the military had arrived instead. They were so brutal the gentle Signora had felt heartily sorry for the poor Austrians. After all, they had known her house was empty but had slept in the shed just the same. They had taken nothing apart from some fruit and vegetables from the garden, which would have rotted anyway. The Signora had tried to say she'd changed her mind, the Austrians could stay after all. But of course it was too late, the soldiers had been determined to have them.

When Elida tells them the story of Signora Codoni, Edward puts an extra bolt on the back gate and ringlets of barbed wire along the back wall. Then he nails up the door of the mews and the garage.

'There now,' he says. 'Fort bloody Knox. A wasp wouldn't find its way in there.'

But Bella can't stop thinking about desperate men with starving eyes, living like wolves in the bottom of the garden.

She sleeps in snatches now; usually when there's someone nearby. Afternoon naps in the garden while Alec swings in the hammock or swishes his legs in the pond. Or at night when Alec has gone up to bed and she slips into the warmth he's left on the sofa, pretending to read, while Edward sits at the piano and pretends not to notice she's fallen asleep.

One morning she wakes early, with a cover thrown over her and Edward asleep on an armchair across the way. It occurs to her then that they've been sleeping together, in the same room – if not the same bed. His arm hanging over the side of the chair, his hand barely touching a newspaper that has slipped onto the floor. He looks different. Almost dead. That completed sort of peace. In stillness his face seems more definite; skin paler, hair darker. He has a softer, fuller mouth. Her eyes keep returning to the mouth. Her mind, half asleep, starts to drift and for a moment she sees herself getting up and going to the mouth, touching it first, then kissing it. She sees herself sitting up on his lap, putting one arm around his neck, one hand on his chest, lifting it sometimes to touch his beard, face, hair. Then just as she is about to conjure up his part in the scenario, Edward – the real Edward – shifts in the chair, turning his head from side to side, stretching one leg. Bella is up and out of the room before he has time to finish the movement or, worse still, open his eyes.

After that she makes sure to wake while the notes from the piano are still floating in the background. Chopin sometimes, more often Satie, some mildly mournful piece anyhow that drives her up the wall and at the same time puts her to sleep. She always, no matter how tired she feels, makes sure she hears herself say, 'Well, I'm off up now, goodnight.'

'Yes. Goodnight now. Sleep well.'

They speak to each other like strangers.

*

One day Cesare stops coming. Edward comes into the kitchen to tell them – he doesn't say how he knows. Later she will put it in her notebook: 'Friday, 23 September 1938. Cesare not coming again.'

The day will be marked by larger events. Hitler reneging on his agreement with Chamberlain. German troops moving near the Czecho-slovakian border. French troops heading towards Alsace. Edward will spend most of that day rushing to and from the radio to report on the latest broadcast, the latest step towards disaster, until she shouts at him, 'I don't bloody care, Edward. Just leave me alone. Just leave me!'

None of these events will go into her notebook. It is enough for one day that Cesare has left them.

Sometime that evening she finds Elida on the front step, weeping. Bella sits with her and thinks about Cesare in the garden. Always there, as if he were part of it, familiar and sturdy as one of those trees. Never without a work tool in his hand. She tries to imagine him, as Edward had described, the day the race laws were published, standing with his arms hanging, his back turned to the garden. Idle for once. His bandy legs like the maw of a bridge over a hump of scorched grass, or a flowerbed squeezed with flawless petals, each one coaxed and cared for, by him.

Elida can't stop weeping for Cesare. Bella, overwhelmed by a sense of abandonment, puts her arm around her and envies Elida her tears. *Siamo fottuti*, she thinks.

*

Two nights after Cesare leaves them, Edward calls her back as she is about to go to bed.

'You know, we can't just stay here like this for ever,' he says. 'We can't just wait for them to come knocking on the door.'

'You must do as you wish,' she answers, 'but I'll be staying with Alec. Don't let us interfere with your plans.'

He looks startled, as if she has just hit him, which is what she wants to do and how she wants him to feel. 'You think I would—?' he begins but she can't listen.

'Why do you never get any letters?' she asks him.

'*What?*'

'You heard me. Why does the postman never have anything for you?'

'What's that got to do with anything?'

'Nothing. I just want you to know, I've noticed.'

'Well, bully for you!'

'You didn't put your name on the census forms – did you? Anyway, don't bother to answer, I don't care to be honest. Really. Leave Bordighera. Go, if you're going,' she says.

'You're not going to rile me, Bella.' he says.

'No. You never do get riled, Edward – do you? I mean never. What sort of a man never gets angry or even annoyed?'

'One that never gets letters?' he suggests.

'Only a dog lives his life so resignedly.' She pushes past him out of the room.

*

She wakes before full light and looks down at Alec lying beside her, finally quiet, after hours of jigging around the bed like a fish on dry land. He had come to her room about midnight complaining that the air in his own room was filling up with *mostri*.

'There aren't any monsters in Liguria, Alec.'

'There are! Little tiny ones, so small and ugly you can only see them in the dark. They travel on cake stands made out of bones.'

'Cake stands – goodness!'

'Yes, and they come through the dark at you so slow, and they turn like this and this and I can see them on all the plates, hundreds of them trying to reach me and eat me all up. With blood and goo on their mouths, and their fingers so long and—'

'All right, all right,' she had said, pulling back the blanket and secretly glad to have the company of his wiry little body even if it did mean being kicked for most of the night.

Wide awake now, and still not quite light, she is fed up worrying about Alec, the Signora, Edward. Edward, Edward. All this wondering and waiting. She decides to get up and make tea.

Bella stands at the sink and folds back one shutter. It could be the end or the start of a day. A low grey mist strokes through the garden like cigarette smoke in a nightclub and she thinks of Amelia again, and wonders what happened and why they have heard no more from her.

There's a wheelbarrow stuffed with compost leaning on the orchard wall. She sees a pile of ornamental rocks, empty flowerpot stacks, seed trays, a watering can. Other things too that she can't quite make out – remnants of Cesare's unfinished business. Maybe she could follow them like clues until she has worked out what his intentions had been. Maybe that could be today's distraction.

289

She thinks about making tea again, goes through the necessary steps in her mind's eye. The kettle, still regarded with suspicion by Elida, will be stuffed out of sight in the back of a cupboard, the tea caddy and milk out in the pantry as well as the matches to light the gas, the sugar in the press behind her. She will have to switch on the electric light to gather everything, and just for now prefers the kitchen in this drab, early morning dusk.

Even while she is thinking about the tea, an impression is forming in her head. There is somebody in the kitchen with her. There, over her right shoulder. A presence. It could be her imagination or it could be someone gone mad with hunger and ready to kill her. The longer she stares out the window, the more she can feel it behind her. Eventually, she takes a step to her left, prepares to make a screaming dart for the door.

'Don't.' A voice softly behind her. 'Hushush now.'

Somehow Bella manages to hold the scream.

The voice belongs to a woman. After a few seconds it speaks again. 'Everything is perfectly fine. When you turn you will know me. Turn.' The words come out tentatively, as if the speaker is feeding them to her bit by bit. 'Yes, that's all right, now. You may. Yes, yes. Very good.'

Something about it reminds her of Signora Tassi, but she knows it's not the Signora's voice. Bella turns. And the woman stands; thin, tall, one hand raised, which she gently presses on the air as if to bat away any possibility of a scream. The face with its peculiar forehead seems to have floated upwards and Bella is reminded of a marionette show; white face standing alone against a black background. There is a rustle of her dress, something rattles. Bella's eye follows the sound – crystals. A rosary entwined around the little finger and falling from the wrist.

'You know me?' the nun says, sitting back down. 'Please.' She gestures for Bella to sit, as if it's her kitchen, her table.

Bella shakes her head and finds the word. 'No.'

The nun says, 'Think.'

'I'm afraid not. No.'

'Miss Stuart, you are not *thinking*.' There is a glint to her voice, as if it's a game. 'By the way, I am so glad you have come down. I would have not liked to go up the stairs and search the rooms in case I disturb all the household.'

'You are not Italian?' Bella says.

'No. I am German. You still don't recognize me?' A short laugh hops out, and she raps her hands gently on the table.

Bella shakes her head.

'All right then, I shall hint you. Sicily – there is my hint.'

'Oh yes, of course.'

'I am Sorella Ursula.'

'The house in Sicily, I should have known.' Bella puts her hand over her chest, feels the words exhale as if she is pressing them out. 'I am so sorry but you frightened the life out of me. How did you get in?'

'A key, of course.'

'Oh? Is the Signora—?'

'No. She cannot just now, I am afraid.'

'Sister, I must tell you, we are in a terrible state here and so worried about the Signora. We don't know what to do or where to go. Not only that but I'm to attend the federal secretary's office next week and—'

The nun lifts her hand again. 'Please,' she says. 'I cannot hear all this now. But soon perhaps there will be no need to worry about these matters. I want you to come with me, Miss Stuart. You and also Edward. Now. If you can wake him perhaps?'

'To see the Signora?'

'If you would only wake Edward and we will go then.'

'What about Alec?'

'Leave him with Elida.'

'I'll have to tell her.'

'Of course. You may write her a message. There is no need for her concern; you will be back by evening. On plenty of time for dinner. Tell her that now. But no more.'

'I can't take the car, sister, they've stopped car insurance for foreigners – mine has just run out.'

'There is a car already waiting. Come, we must hurry. Wear dark clothes, a black coat, if you have it. Tell this to Edward also.'

*

They come out of Villa Lami, to find a large black car waiting a little way up the road, engine running. As they approach, the doors open from the inside; passenger door first, then the two at the rear. Bella tries to catch Edward's eye as Sorella Ursula ushers him into the front, but he will not return her look.

She sits in the back behind the driver, a priest. The nun beside her. Before they have even settled in, the car begins to move off. There are no introductions and the priest says nothing.

The car moves along via Romano, deserted but for a lone *cacciatore*, trudging along in his hunter's clothes, rifle on shoulder, dog at heel. Then a little further on, at the first flank of trees in the winter garden, she sees her old friend the milk-boy-now-man lift his head to watch them drive by.

They turn onto the coast road into full sudden light twitching all over the sea between Capo Verde and Capo Nero, and flinching across the backs of greenhouses and glass chests on the surrounding hillsides. She notes the priest wince and then lift his hand to snap down the overhead sun visor.

Just before San Remo they run into a traffic jam: flower carts, lorries, a truckful of big-buttocked pumpkins. Passengers who have alighted from their vehicles strut up and down, craning their necks towards the cause of the delay and gesturing complaints at each other. The priest hits the heels of his hands off the rim of the steering wheel and then thumps the horn. Sorella Ursula looks up from her rosary.

On the cart in front a man stands to his full height, ankle-deep in carnations. He turns, sees this impatience belongs to a priest and respectfully removes his cap. The priest lifts his shoulders and hands in query, rolls down the window and sticks out his head, first shouting at, then listening to, the man. The car fills up with the smell of flowers, damp earth and the sea.

The priest begins rolling the window back, then at the last minute pauses to stick his hand out to deliver a cursory blessing to the man on the cart. The man lowers his head in gratitude. The priest pinches and then pulls on his nose. '*Un blocco stradale,*' he mumbles, then sneezes, releasing a silvery snot-spray onto his hand, the dashboard and part of Edward's shoulder.

'A road block,' Sorella Ursula explains, and Bella says, 'Yes, I know.'

Moments later, from behind the row of flower carts, two black uniforms appear. They see the priest and walk over to the car. The window is down again, this time the priest is all personality; laughing, joking, telling them there's no need to apologize, everyone has his duty all the more in these troubled days, but unfortunately this morning his happens to be a concelebrated mass in Imperia. He gestures helplessly but good-humouredly to heaven.

'*Scusi, Padre.*' One soldier bows. '*Un momento prego.*'

The other one walks around the car and looks in the window. Sorella Ursula smiles and gives him a little wave.

'*Lei ha documenti, Padre?*' the man at the window asks.

'*Documenti? Ma certo.*'

'*Li hanno tutti?*' he asks then, his finger moving in a circle to include all the occupants of the car.

'*Certamente,*' the priest assures him, adding that they are all attached to the same convent. He reaches to his inside pocket and asks if the soldier would care to see them.

The man is almost insulted. '*No, no, Padre, va bene così. Prego.*' He begins waving them out of the queue while the other soldier clears the path of people.

The priest positions the car partly over the grass verge so he can get it past the queue of traffic.

'*Dica una piccola preghiera per me, Padre?*' the soldier asks as the car moves away.

The priest replies that he will say a prayer, for him, his comrades and his family. They salute, then he drives the car away at a slant.

Edward, who has been looking straight ahead, now turns towards the sea. Bella notices the colour has drained from his face.

They leave the main road and begin to climb. Miles of nowhere. There are moments when she longs to break the silence, but is reluctant to start, or worse have the responsibility of keeping up, a conversation. She looks out the window where mountains made out of forest have stamped out the sky.

The car twists on. They pass a cone-shaped shepherd's refuge and, further along, a stubby votive chapel. Green light wraps around the car as it passes in and out of a pine grove. Finally a long straight dirt road leads through the gateway of a monastery.

The sky reappears. Farmland all around. The slow white hides of cattle on the lower fields. Further away, a row of monks, bent to the land like brown moths edging up a wall. She sees an olive mill, a two-bay barn. On a stool surrounded by baskets, an old monk sits in the shade, testing peaches between the twist of his hands.

A young Indian monk rushes out to greet them, hardly more than a boy. He dances about the car, waiting to take it over, barely able to keep the grin off his face. The priest drops the keys into his open hand then walks off without a word, the hem of his cassock slapping his ankles, his feet whipping dust out of the ground. The monk ushers the remaining passengers out, nodding and chuckling silently to himself, then hops in and the car moves off, bouncing and clucking around to the side of the house. Bella feels the slightly chilled air of a higher altitude settle over her face.

Sorella Ursula leads them up several flights of stairs to a large corner room. A row of arched windows cut into two right-angled walls. On the back wall of the room, a large brown crucifix. There is a table, two chairs, a broken lectern pushed to one side. Sorella Ursula says she will send breakfast up.

Somewhere the chanting of monks. Bella goes to a window and looks down. The crescent of a sleeping dog in the centre of a courtyard. Across two rows of chairs, long strands of spaghetti are draped over broom handles, left in the sunshine to dry. A monk appears out of the shadows. The dog stands, stretches and skulks off. The monk begins to test the spaghetti, section by section, lifting it like a long silk fringe onto the back of his hand, settling it back into place, lifting again.

'What do you say to all this, Edward?' she asks him.

When he doesn't answer she turns to look at him. He is sitting on one of the chairs, legs stretched out and feet crossed at the ankles. Hands in pockets, collar up, coat tucked around his legs. He is obviously cold and still a little pale. Whatever he might be feeling, Bella knows she won't find it written on his face.

She crosses to a window on the other wall. A cemetery below. The graves, stacked over each other, are slotted into a wall, like a great big filing cabinet for the dead, she thinks. On the front panel of each one, a photograph of the occupant, also a votive and a small vase of flowers. A monk, leisurely, plump, pushes a work trolley, which holds a box, a basket of flowers, a large jug. For a while Bella watches him move from grave to grave, and is soothed by his practical method of work. She recalls the first time she saw one of these cemeteries. The night train from Nice, and her first time crossing into Italy. She had no idea what she was looking at but had believed it to be some sort of a message shaped by lit candles on the side of a hill. Half letters of half words that were on the verge of turning into a phrase – she had presumed the wind had blown out the rest of the candles. Desperately, she had wanted to make sense of it, childishly treating it like some sort of an omen, moving from window to window along the corridor, until the train had passed by.

'Edward, I'm sorry,' she says to the window. 'I'm really sorry I've been so awful lately, and to you in particular. I don't know why I have been, but

I am really sorry. I don't want to make excuses but I'm so afraid of everything; of being sent back, of what's going to happen, to Alec, the Signora. You, I suppose.'

He still doesn't reply and she turns again.

'Edward? Won't you say something?'

'Such as?'

'Anything – I don't care what. But please talk to me.'

'Woof woof,' he says and almost smiles.

The young monk brings in a tray rattling with coffee, plates of focaccia and apple fried cake, and they sit politely over it like children in a strange house. They don't say much about anything; a comment on the saltiness of the focaccia, the overwhelming sweetness of the cake. Sometimes they point out sounds to each other. Voices in a nearby room that for some reason they decide can't belong to the monks. Bella thinks she hears a cat. Edward says it's a baby.

'How would you know?' she asks him.

'Where I come from, the one thing you were always certain to hear, day or night, was a baby bawling.'

'Where was that, Edward?'

'Oh, in the centre of the city. My father was a publican. I suppose you could say we lived over the shop.'

'So he wasn't a music teacher?'

'No, that was just a story for the Lamis, you know?'

'Did you have brothers and sisters?'

'One sister but she died.'

'Oh, that must have been awful for you.'

'We didn't get on. Didn't like each other much, if at all. I don't remember her well.'

'Do you know what I remember most about Dublin?' she says.

'What?'

'Ducks. Ducks and the smell of coffee – a softer coffee smell than you get here. Once a week my father would take me out and we always went to feed the ducks in Stephen's Green, then into a café.'

'I think of – I don't know; the markets, I suppose. The smell of fish. The river, the Four Courts, prisoners shouting down to relatives on the street from the Bridewell cells.'

It's so rare to have a conversation like this, the two of them talking about their respective pasts. Even more unusual for Edward to mention anything of his former life. She would give anything to have it continue, but the monk is back by now, picking up the tray and beckoning them to follow.

In another room there is a fire in the grate, a table laid with linen and silver, and the remnants of what appears to have been a substantial meal is being cleared away by two elderly monks. Sorella Ursula stands to greet them. Through the half-open door of an anteroom come the voices of men. A few seconds later another nun enters, with a baby in her arms. Edward nudges Bella.

'Is the Signora here?' she asks.

Sorella Ursula shakes her head. 'We won't be seeing the Signora today. Please take a seat.'

'Oh, I'm really sorry to hear that,' Bella says. 'I wish you'd tell us where she is. Can't you please at least tell us that?'

'Please, Signora Stuart,' Sorella Ursula says. 'Signor Tassi is here now.'

Tassi comes in from the anteroom followed by another, much taller man. He hardly looks like the Tassi they know, the holiday Tassi of bright clothes and beaming demeanour. He's dressed in a dark business suit and his expression is sombre. He shakes hands with them both, but doesn't kiss them, and this is unusual too. '*Vi presento introdurre un avvocato Inglese – che parlerà per me.*'

'*Perchè parlerà per Lei?*' Edward asks him.

The English lawyer answers. 'I am not speaking *for* him, but instead of him. This is a very complicated business and we don't want any misunderstandings. I am Signora Tassi's lawyer and I act solely on her behalf, as I have done since she was Signora Lami. It's best if I don't introduce myself fully – beyond how do you do – please do sit down.'

Out of a large attaché case the lawyer begins pulling files and brown packets and pressing them down on the table. He pauses to brush a few crumbs from the linen cloth, then begins to arrange his papers.

Bella turns to Sorella Ursula then Tassi, but it's clear that neither of them intends to look at her. She takes her seat; Edward sits a few feet away from her. 'No,' she blurts out then. 'No. I don't like this.' She turns directly to Gino Tassi. '*Signor Tassi – Dov'è la signora?*' she asks him. '*Dov'è la madre di Alessandro?*'

The lawyer sighs through his nose. 'Miss Stuart, you do better to speak directly to me. I can assure you the Signora is safe. I have instructions from her, for you and your colleague – Mr King – isn't it?'

'Yes,' Edward confirms.

'These instructions are to be handed over only if you agree to help her. Do you understand? I will go through everything with you first, then you may decide. If you find yourselves unable to help the Signora, you may go, and she asks only that you keep this meeting to yourselves. If you do agree, then I will take you through the steps in greater detail. Don't worry, all will be clear soon enough. Now if I may begin – Miss Stuart? Mr King?'

He waits for them to agree.

'Very well then. As you know the Signora is in a somewhat precarious situation at the moment. Not just here in Italy but also in Germany where she has many business interests. I understand you are already aware that the Signora is not an Italian citizen and is also of the Jewish persuasion. In light of the recent race laws, along with other events, it has become clear to the Signora that she can no longer remain in Italy. She has already been given notice to leave. Measures have also been taken to seize certain assets as well as to prevent her from taking money out of the country. What concerns the Signora is the safety and well-being of her children.

'You mean the safety and well-being of her money!' Edward says and Bella is shocked at this unexpected outburst.

'You are of course entitled to your opinion, Mr King, but without money she can hardly take care of her children, not in this climate for certain. If I may continue—'

'Yes,' Bella says. 'But what about loopholes, you know, all the *Discriminato* business?'

'There has been talk of loopholes through use of the *Discriminato* clause, and certainly the Vatican is bringing pressure regarding the children of mixed marriages. But by and large these loopholes are all too vague and open to constant change, not to mention corruption and blackmail – something the Signora does not intend to involve herself in. The fact remains she will not be allowed *Discriminato* status in any event, and even if her children are, they will still be regarded as second-class citizens and have very few rights. Besides, as we now know, the situation in Germany regarding Jews makes no exceptions and the Signora is naturally concerned that Italy may well follow Hitler's example in due course, particularly if there is a war.'

Gino Tassi comes out of his corner and walks to the nun who is holding his baby. He goes to lift the child from her arms, and Bella notes the nun won't let go until Sorella Ursula nods her permission. Then Tassi lifts the baby and goes back to the corner, the bundle in his arms close to his face.

The lawyer continues. 'What the Signora would like you to do, that is, both of you to do, is to take the children with you to London.'

'London!' Edward asks. 'Is she mad?'

'She would like you to take them to your father's house, Miss Stuart, and keep them there for her, until she is in a position to follow.'

'Well, I don't think that sounds like such a bad idea, Edward,' Bella says. 'I think we should listen, at least. I'm probably going to be turfed out after the hearing next week at the federal secretary's office – so?'

Edward ignores her and addresses the lawyer. 'How are we supposed to do that? I mean, with all these travel restrictions and regulations – how the hell are we supposed to smuggle two Italian children out of Italy?'

'I'm coming to that, Mr King. The Signora has it all arranged.'

'Yes, well, she would have!'

The lawyer puts his hand under the first package and raises it slightly. 'This envelope first. You will travel as a family, husband, wife, son and new baby. There are papers in here for an Italian family of that description taking a holiday in Nice.'

'Nice?' Edward says. 'France is far too risky, I know – we live close to the border, we see people being dragged back every day of the week. Why not just Genoa and sail straight to Southampton?'

'Even riskier, I'm afraid. You will be travelling on false papers, Mr King. To leave Italy as an Italian family bound for England will cause suspicion. There's a far better chance of success the other way. And we have looked into all the possibilities on your behalf, you know.'

'Oh, how kind,' Edward sneers and Bella says, 'Edward! Will you please just listen?'

'Thank you, Miss Stuart,' the lawyer says and continues. 'There are two sets of papers. One presenting you as an Italian family going for a holiday to Nice. I repeat, all the visas, documentation, passports, etc. have been taken care of – although we still need to take your photographs, but that's a small matter which can be organized here. You are booked into an hotel for one week.'

'A week in Nice? Why waste all that time?'

'Of course, you won't stay for the week, Mr King. You will have in your possession a letter confirming your reservation for a week. This can be shown at the border and can be verified with a telephone call. When you get to the hotel you will indeed register. Then the next day, as if you are simply going on an outing – you leave Nice. Leave a suitcase in the hotel, clothes in the cupboard and so forth, so as not to arouse suspicion. Then discard, better still burn, whatever Italian documentation you have. Go to the train station and catch the train to Paris and from there to Calais. Now you will be using this envelope.' He lifts up the next package.

'This time an English family, returning from holiday in France. There is a receipt from the Bristol Hotel in Nice, showing an English address, which corresponds with that on your papers. To be perfectly honest, the second set of papers is unlikely to pass muster in England nor would they on an English ship – they are certainly not as authentic as I would have liked, but no matter, once you are on English soil, all that can be sorted out. Your father, Miss Stuart, may be called on to identify you. I will give you a telephone number where a colleague of mine may be contacted, should the need arise.

'So that's the bones of it. The important thing is that we get you *into* France. Once there it will be easy to travel as an English family, the French being sympathetic to the English just now and the next few days will see so much confusion at train stations with everyone trying to bolt, you shouldn't stand out too much. Should you agree, there are several details to go over.'

'Hold on a second,' Edward begins. 'I have a question, *if* you don't mind.'

'That's what I'm here for, Mr King.'

'What happens if we're caught?'

'Well, that depends on where you're caught.'

'I mean here, in Italy.'

'The answer is, I don't know. The Italian papers are authentic – that is, they are not forgeries but were purchased from an actual family. However, you will be committing a serious crime and will be treated accordingly. My information is that the government is setting up internment centres until they decide what to do with those detained at the frontiers. There is also the possibility of being sent to a *confino*, that is sent off to live in the remotest of areas for a long period of time, where there are very few comforts, if any.'

'Yes, thank you,' Edward says, 'I know what a *confino* means.'

'Naturally, we would do all we could to get you out, but these laws are at an early stage, and who knows how far Mussolini tends to take them. As I've already said, if you are caught in England, the matter is not so serious; the worst that will happen is a few days' detention while the authorities ascertain your real identity and are satisfied that you are not a spy, or some such.'

'I see,' Edward says.

'I should add that it will mean leaving Italy tomorrow. I will give you some time now to talk matters over and make your decision.'

'How long?' Edward asks.

'Half an hour. I'm afraid I need to know before returning to Berlin, which I must do as soon as possible.' Edward abruptly stands up. The lawyer ignores him. 'And there is something else. The Signora would like me to ask you to carry a sum of money, along with some jewellery. This is not my idea, nor do I particularly advise it, but she feels it may come in handy for your own use, or indeed for her use when she arrives in London. At the moment they are carrying out random searches at the border, but this time next week it will be a fine toothcomb for anyone leaving the country. So it's your risk to take, and your decision to make.' The lawyer begins to repack his attaché case.

Bella is quietly weeping. After a moment Sorella Ursula hands her a hanky. 'I'm sorry, sister,' she says.

'It's very understandable. Naturally, you are afraid.'

'No, it's not so much that. Not even that. I don't want to go simply. I just never really saw myself leaving Italy, not like this. Not ever, I suppose.'

Edward looks over at Tassi. '*E Lei? Non ha niente da dire?*' he asks.

Gino Tassi makes no reply, kisses his baby and places her back in the arms of the nun. He lightly squeezes Bella's shoulder as he passes for the door.

*

They get back towards evening. The priest drops them on the far side of Bordighera leaving a good half-hour walk back to Villa Lami.

Sorella Ursula explains, 'It is better if you walk from here, as if you are on an evening stroll. Tomorrow morning at half past six, I will come for you. Miss Stuart, please have Alec ready, and remember – prepare the baggage to seem like an authentic holiday. But for no more than one week.'

'Yes, sister, I know. You told me.'

'Yes, I did. Bring a bucket and spade, that sort of thing. And I know I told you that too, but I want to be certain – you understand?'

'Yes.'

'You will not be taking the train from Bordighera where you are certain to be recognized, but we will drive you to a station further up the coast near where your papers say you live. This means of course that the train will travel back through Bordighera so be sure Alec makes no comment and keep him away from the window in case he is recognized. I will bring the baby tomorrow along with all her needs, also your documents and photographs which will be ready by then. I think that's everything now. Yes, I am certain. Oh, and don't forget your wedding rings. The steel band for Italy like a good fascist wife. Later the gold.'

'Yes, sister.'

'The gold was the Signora's from her first marriage – I told you that, yes. She thinks it will bring you luck.'

'I don't know the first thing about looking after a baby,' Bella says.

'You will learn and improve as you go along. Like all new mothers – eh? Like I have done in fact this past fortnight. Oh, and most important – your own papers. If you will both leave them in an envelope in the house for me, perhaps in your room, Miss Stuart. I will fetch them in a few days and send them on to you in due course. In case you are searched – you understand. You don't want to have to explain who are Mr King and Miss Stuart on top of everything else. Goodness, no!'

They get out of the car and Sorella Ursula rolls down the window. 'By the way, you must say nothing to Elida.'

'Not even goodbye?'

'No.'

'Please, sister. She's my friend.'

'I'm sorry, Miss Stuart, but it must be the way. In these times we can trust no one. Not even our best friend.'

They walk in silence towards San Ampeglio. Early evening and an indolent sea. Edward keeps his face turned away. Bella decides it's probably best anyhow if they don't speak for a while. Her mind could do with a pause. All they're expected to remember. All they still have to do. And here's Edward meanwhile, quietly sulking, as he seems to have been doing for so much of the day.

They cross the road and the church shows its head over the coast wall, roof peak and belfry. Behind it the ornate slab of the casino stretches towards the promenade. She can see the copper sway of the church bell but the ocean has sucked away any sound of its ringing. Down on the shingle beach: evening bathers on the rocks. A fishing line shimmers. The head of a diver smashes a hole in the water, leaving a deep white ruffle behind.

Bella looks across to the other side of the road. The plinth for the long-disputed statue of Queen Margherita has finally been put in place. A shrine of flowers set out around it. She wonders how many more squabbles there will be before the statue itself arrives, then with a shock realizes she may never know, or even get to see it. She is about to say as much to Edward but then decides not to bother.

Edward so angry with the lawyer; hurling obstacles and objections at every word that came out of his mouth. As if he'd been determined from the start to knock the plan flat out. And then so quiet over lunch. Mostly smoking. For once she'd eaten more than he – tiny white beans, knuckles of soft dark meat, cake made of chestnuts squelching with sugar. Even if she can't seem to hold on to the details on her phoney papers, she can remember all this. The address somewhere in Imperia. Oneglia – is it? Or is that the name of the road, via Oneglia? The children's names – Alberto and Edda, good fascist names. Edda after Edda Mussolini. Alberto is at least convenient for Alec.

As for the English identity papers? All she can remember now is her name is Rose, her husband is James and that they're supposed to be a family from Bournemouth – spelled incorrectly as Burnmouth.

Edward so rude to Sorella Ursula. After they had finally given their answer and she had taken them downstairs and led them through cloisters and an ambulatory into the monastery barber. A proper barber chair where one pinkish head, freshly tonsured, was being merrily spanked with cologne. Nearby a beaming monk whipped up a bowl of froth and cast an eye over Edward's beard. But Edward had refused him the pleasure.

'I think it would be best,' Sister Ursula had advised.

'What difference does it make?' Edward snapped at her.

'It will attract less attention. It's less…'

'Less what?'

'Less Jewish, I suppose is what I mean,' she had quietly replied.

Edward had turned on his heels. 'We either get this photograph taken as I am, or not at all.' He had stomped off then, back through the cloisters, Sorella Ursula trotting meekly behind him.

So much for not getting riled! Bella glances at his face again as they cross the road towards the centre of Bordighera. Back to himself – back to nothing.

They take the narrow route behind the Hotel Parigi and the backstage preparations for this evening's dance. Waiters in shirtsleeves pass back and forth behind open French doors. Further along, through a small square window, a pair of hands arranges flowers. Outside, a band unloads instruments from a van. A woman, a guest, with a towel turbaned onto her head comes out onto a first-floor balcony and frowns at the sky. They cut across the piazza.

'Would you mind?' she begins. 'Would you mind, if we walked a little way through town. I'd just like—'

'Of course,' Edward says.

'Unless you want to…?'

'No, this way is fine.'

'You know, Edward, we may as well accept it – we really don't have a choice. I mean, we can't stay here, we can't leave Alec and—'

Edward nods and walks a little ahead.

Shadows of last-minute shoppers and children stiff in new uniforms.

Strollers, just like they're pretending to be, talking about *aperitivi*. Outside the Terrasanta church there is a scatter of scarlet petals from an earlier wedding. A tram waddles towards them, they wait for it to pass, then a motorbike with a sidecar.

'Hard to believe,' she begins to say, but then stops.

Outside Gabrielli's, a woman shouts impatient instructions through the glass at an assistant in the window. '*Questo, sì, sì, questo. No! No! Non quello, questo!*'

Edward leans over the woman and raps angrily on the window. '*Questo!*' He stabs his finger at the glass, pointing to a china bowl. The woman in the street stares up at him, open-mouthed. The woman in the window nods a wary thanks.

Bella says it again as they turn right into via Roberto. 'Hard to believe, Edward, that this is our last day here.'

'Yes.'

'So sudden. Isn't it – so sudden?'

They stop. Edward lights a cigarette. They are outside the tennis racket factory. The smell of wood and oil and paint through the open doors. Bella looks past him, at a view of the workshop interior. Splashes of soft light everywhere, on the pale wood of the workbenches and floors, the curve and turn of the rackets, the pegs where the frames hang all the way up the walls. She allows her eyes to stare for a moment. Then the man who made Alec's last racket comes to the door, carrying a stack of tennis presses. He gives her a nod and smile of recognition. The smile that she returns feels heavy on her face.

'Yes,' Edward says as if replying to something she has asked, although she can't recall what that was.

They continue up the hill towards via Romano, and she begins to notice the amount of birds. Telegraph poles are studded with them and all over the rooftops and gutter rims more and more seem to be squeezing themselves in. A man walking towards them twists his neck to look back at the sky, raises his hands and laughs. '*L'invasione delle rondini.*'

'What are they?' she asks Edward, lifting her voice against their increasing din.

'Swallows. Going south.'

The nearer they get to via Romano, the greater the amount of birds, until the sky over the Hotel Hesperia is just one huge black trembling patch. The noise. A deafening rant of metallic squeaks and flapping wings. People are coming out of houses and hotels to look at the sky. A little boy ducks down onto his hunkers and lays his two hands flat over his ears. A woman opens her double windows and the ticking hedge of hysterical birds on her balconette explodes and scatters. She sees the woman's mouth shape into first a scream, then laughter.

They walk through the noise until eventually it starts to thin and they can hear themselves again.

Bella tries a lighter approach. 'You know, I will release you from your marriage ties as soon as we get to London. I mean, if that's what's worrying you.'

She notices he's only just finished one cigarette and is already fishing for another.

Outside the Bicknell Library, he stops and lights it. 'Bella,' he says.

'Yes?' She closes her eyes.

'I can't.'

'You can't what?' she asks, although in her heart she already knows.

'I just can't.'

After a moment he speaks again. 'Please, don't ask me why. But I can't risk going back into England. Certainly not on those bloody papers.'

She looks up and down the road, then at him, then away.

He says, 'The best I can do is – maybe see you over the border but as soon as, I'd have to leave you. Not even as far as Nice. Perhaps Menton or maybe Monte Carlo.'

Bella tries to speak but nothing will come past the sick feeling in her stomach.

He takes another pull of the cigarette then throws it to the ground where he twists his foot over it. 'I am sorry, Bella, and I wish it was otherwise but I just can't take the risk. You see, I did something, a long time ago. I know you've guessed there was something. And I don't want to tell you what it is, but it's enough that you understand the moment I put my foot on English soil, I've had it.' He runs his hands through his hair.

'I thought you were Irish.'

'Ireland, England, it's all the same when it comes to this sort of thing.'

She nods and bites into her lip.

'For Christ's sake. There's nothing I can do about it.' He raises his voice suddenly and she jumps. 'I mean, that's even if we get as far as England. Did you see the Italian papers they have for me? Did you see what they've put down as my profession, my job?' He has her by the upper arms now and she shakes her head. 'A carpenter, that's what.'

Bella blinks at him.

'A carpenter, Bella. For fuck's sake, look at my hands.'

He drops his grip and shows his hands, smoother, whiter than her own.

'They are so stupid,' he says quietly. 'They haven't a fucking clue. A carpenter and his family travelling first class to Nice to stay in a hotel for a week. Jesus! Talk about looking for attention. Anyway, it doesn't matter because once I get to England – that's it.'

He reaches out to take her arm and she takes a step back.

'Please. I can't tell you how sorry. How—'

Bella feels her head repeatedly nod. 'Coward,' she says then and leaves him.

*

Coward. She nurses the word in her head all evening. As she tries to pack without Elida noticing. As she roots out all the jolly paraphernalia: swimming costumes and beach toys, sun hats and anything with a seaside stripe that happens to be in the house. Whatever it takes to convince the authorities that they are hip-hip-hooray holidaymakers. *Coward.* The word burns on and off her mind like a neon light, as she attempts to reassure Elida.

'Please tell me, Signora, what is the matter?'

'Nothing! Elida. Really.'

'Where you were all day?'

'I will tell you, Elida, in a day or two. Promise. You'll know everything by then. But it's nothing for you to worry about now.'

'Were you crying?'

'I was not!' And it crosses her mind more than once that she would have been better off had they decided to dress Elida up as a husband to go with her instead. Elida's hard-working hands would have been more convincing than the lily-whites on that. *Coward*. The word bounces off the walls of the room, and goes silently screeching through the house.

She says no to dinner and asks Elida to look after Alec and put him to bed. Then she goes to her room. First she writes a letter to Elida explaining matters, insofar as she can do, and telling her to stay here in the house for as long as she wishes or as long as it remains safe to do so, also to use whatever money remains that she finds in the house, to keep herself going. She finishes by asking Elida to hold on to the envelope with all her documents until Sorella Ursula comes to collect it. Then she promises to telephone as soon as she can and signs off the letter to her friend.

Bella then removes piles of magazines and linen from the bottom of her wardrobe and takes out a box, which she lays on her bed. She pulls out the money-tucks – these days made from men's long merino wool stockings; sturdy yet light. Bella drops them on the bed, picks out the ones full of lire and, pinning the letter to Elida onto one of them, slips them under her pillowcase, where she knows by next washday Elida's hand will find them.

She writes Edward a note next, digging the pen into the paper so hard it makes a tear and she has to start again, this time forcing herself to calm down, then printing her message in a careful, lighter hand. She thanks him for his kind offer to go as far as Menton or Monte Carlo and says that she's decided to go it alone. Coolly she wishes him the best with whatever he decides to do and whatever direction he happens to take.

She goes upstairs and puts the letter under his door.

Coming back to her room she lifts two suitcases onto the bed, begins to arrange money-tucks full of English money around the edges of their bases, then disguises them with piles of clothes and toys. She wraps a diamond tiara in a nightdress and packs it in, then stuffs four diamond rings into the toes of shoes. She closes the suitcases, straps them up and slides them in behind the door. Bella then takes her mother's old green alligator-skin travel bag out of the cupboard and, tilting it to the light, cuts an incision into the lining. She wraps a diamond necklace and bracelet belonging to Signora Tassi in a silk handkerchief along with a coil of pearls and three rings belonging to her mother. She works them into the hole and stitches it up. Pressing the last three money-tucks into the travel bag she stuffs it up with a few remaining bits and pieces belonging to Alec: his pyjamas, a pair of plimsoles, a sketchbook, a tennis sweater, a bucket and spade. Then she puts it with the cases behind the door all ready for tomorrow.

Bella locks her bedroom door behind her, then goes upstairs to Edward's room and walks straight in. He is by the window reading her letter. 'Do you mean this?' he asks.

'It's better if I say my husband has been delayed in work and I decided to take the holiday anyway rather than disappoint Alec or Alberto as I must now call him. I can say you – I mean he – will join us at the weekend. Also that your, I mean his, boss paid for a first-class train because he felt bad about postponing your holiday. It won't matter so much when it comes to leaving France or entering England. In any case, I'll think of something.'

'You seem to be taking it all very well,' Edward says.

'Yes I am – don't you think?'

'You're sure you're—'

'Oh please, don't give it another thought.'

He looks at her carefully. 'I see.'

'Do you, Edward? Do you see?' She walks across the room and slaps him across the face.

310

Even in the blindness of her temper, his head seems surprisingly light as if she could have, with a bit more effort, whacked it away from his neck. She tries it again.

'Leaving me on my own with two children.' Her voice is dry but still not raised.

'I'm sorry,' he says.

'You could have told them. You could have said it there and then, in front of that lawyer, in front of Tassi. Given them a chance to come up with something else. Coward. I hope you get whatever you deserve. I hope they catch you and that whatever you've done is so bad, they hang you.'

'Yes,' he says. 'It is. They will.'

She goes to the door, opens it, takes a step out and in a matter of seconds loses all of her composure. When she comes back to him she's crying. 'I don't even know one end of a bloody baby from the other.' This time she punches him on the arm. 'You never cared tuppence for me, Edward.'

'I did. I do.'

'Never enough to trust me. Never enough to allow me to get to know you. Every time you shut the door in my face. You never cared. And I cared, and you've always known it. You're a coward, that's what you are, after all. A bloody lousy coward. Whatever it is that you've done, I wouldn't have minded. I wouldn't have minded in the least – if only you had trusted me.'

'You would have minded,' he says. 'Bella, you would.'

She hits him again, this time repeatedly on the chest and head. 'You bastard, you lousy bastard. I hate you.'

She throws herself at him and now she's down on the floor with him. Still hitting him, not sure if he's hitting her back or if she's hitting herself. Hitting each other, then kissing each other, sucking and biting lumps out of faces, necks, arms. She is clutching his hair and he's pulling at her clothes and she's tearing at his beard. She is drowning and he's on top of her. And she wants to kill him, and she wants him to kill her back, but more than that, she wants him to do whatever he does with the whores he visits in brothels. There are sounds shared between: breaths, grunts, sobs. And she can hear the words, 'This changes nothing, it changes nothing,' over and over and she thinks it might be her voice that's speaking.

Then somewhere outside of them there's another sort of screaming and Edward is rising into the air and falling away from her and her arms are lifting to drag him back down to her, and she's screaming, 'Leave him! Leave him!'

Alec sobbing in the doorway. Elida barking like a bereft goose. 'Maestro Edward! What are you doing to her? What are you doing to her? *Basta, basta, basta.*'

Bella looks down and sees her dress is opened and torn, the skirt of it up around her hips. She tries to catch her breath. 'Elida. It's all right. Really, it's all right.'

She gets up. At the door she looks back at Edward. His back is to the wall, head bent, hair fallen over his forehead, shirt open and hanging to one side, hands pressed down on his legs. He looks up at her through his hair, breathless.

'It changes nothing,' she says.

*

The priest lets himself into the hall the next morning and she watches from the kitchen while he picks up the luggage she has hauled down the stairs in the middle of the night. He beckons, and she follows, dragging a still sleepy Alec behind her. When she gets to the gate Bella stops to take one last look at Villa Lami. She sees Elida standing in her nightgown at an upstairs window. They look at each other for a moment, then Bella blows a kiss and Elida nods and smiles to show she understands.

In the back of the car Sorella Ursula waits, the baby in a Moses basket beside her. She tells Alec to sit on the other side of the basket. 'Come, Alec, see your new sister.'

Alec peeps into the bundle and nods. 'Which part of her is the Jew part?' he asks.

Sorella Ursula looks over his head at Bella.

'What's her name – is it Leah?' Alec asks then.

'Oh no. It's Edda, like il Duce's daughter.'

'Then is she not a Jew?' he asks. 'But that's not fair! Why do I have to be one, and she is not?'

'I'm sorry, sister.' Bella begins taking her place beside Alec. 'I had a little talk with him a few days ago about why he couldn't go back to school, and ever since he's been going on non-stop about what's Jewish and not.'

'Alec,' the Sorella says, 'you must not say that word again.'

'You see?' he says to Bella. 'I told you it was bad to be a Jew. That's why il Duce doesn't like them.' Then he turns and sulks out the window.

'I haven't explained things properly to him yet, where we are going or how,' Bella says. 'I thought we could use the car journey to do that.'

'Of course,' Sorella Ursula says, then looks out the back window. 'Where's Edward?'

Bella shakes her head.

'He's not coming? He has changed his heart?'

'His mind.'

The nun makes a move for the door.

'It's no use, sister, he left late last night. He could be anywhere by now. But it's fine. We'll manage, really. I have it all worked out.'

'It's too dangerous.'

'Oh, sister, what choice do we have?'

The priest has turned and is resting his elbow across the back of the seat looking at Sorella Ursula. After a few second she nods and the car moves away.

Somewhere after San Stefano they turn into a quiet side road so that Sorella Ursula can give her a quick lesson in changing and feeding the baby. 'Everything you need is in this bag,' she says, 'also the envelopes with your papers. The Italian papers are in this side pocket here so you can easily put your hand to them. The English papers for the next part of the journey are hidden under all the things for the baby, at the bottom of the bag. Also the money we spoke about. Now – I have put a little something in the bottle to keep baby asleep for some time so you shouldn't have to worry until you get to France. Hopefully there won't be too much of a delay at the frontier near Ventimiglia.'

'Hopefully,' Bella agrees.

*

They pull up at the side of a small country station. A porter, who looks as if he's been expecting them, rushes forward and the priest gets out of the car to have a word. Bella takes the Moses basket from Sorella Ursula, then the baby bag. She tells the porter she'll keep the alligator bag with her, but then finds after all she can't manage it along with everything else. In the end she gives it to Alec to carry. They walk into the station, Alec tilted to one side by the weight of the bag. She does not say goodbye or look back.

Ten minutes to go before the train.

She sits on the end of a bench away from the other passengers. Alec stands beside her, keeping a watch for the train.

'Remember all we said in the car? In a minute we're going to stop speaking English. Will you be able do that, keep it up until tomorrow?'

'What time tomorrow?'

'Well, it depends, but I'll give you plenty of notice. You call me Mamma and I call you Alberto. If anyone speaks – don't answer. I'll say you're shy and answer for you.'

Alec smiles, liking the game.

'And I'm going to have to leave you in charge of this bag. This was my mamma's bag and for now anyway it's yours. Look, it's made out of an alligator.'

'An alligator! Where's his teeth?'

'The dentist took them out,' Bella says and Alec laughs.

'Are my things in it?'

'Actually yes, some of your things are in there. So you must carry it on and off the train, and keep a good eye on it at all times.'

'Should I put my *portafortuna* in it?'

'If you like – where is it?'

'In my pocket – here.'

Bella takes the tennis ball from him and slips it into the bag.

He cups his hand over her ear. 'May I play my harmonica on the train?' His voice drifts into her head. 'May I? *Please*.'

'No, Alec, it will only annoy people. And we want to be invisible – remember?'

'I mean silently play it. You know, like pretend.'

She whispers back down into his ear, 'All right then, but only pretend playing. Absolutely no sound.'

He lifts his shoulder and stretches his neck at her whisper.

'Tickly?'

'Yes.'

'And no questions about Maestro Edward.'

'Signora Bella – why were you fighting?'

'Aha, what did I just say?'

'Oh yes, I forgot.'

'One more thing – you must say nothing when we come into Bordighera station. You must act as if you've never seen it before.'

'Why?'

'Because we don't want anyone to know we live there. We are pretending to be from a place called Oneglia. Oh Alec, wait till you see where we're going! It will be such a surprise. A wonderful surprise. You won't believe it until you see it. Your eyes will pop out of your head! But you must be patient or it will never happen. All right?'

'All right.'

'One, two, three,' Bella begins. '*Allora, solo Italiano – d'accordo?*'

'*D'accordo!*'

Two minutes to go.

'*Andiamo,*' she says and stands as the signal post drops.

They find their carriage, the luggage already racked and the porter the priest had earlier spoken to waiting in the corridor to guide them in. He tells them they can pull down the blind if they don't want to be disturbed although it will be quiet enough until San Remo. After that, he says, dipping his knees and throwing his head back, hands up – the train will be crazy. Like a hive full of bees. '*Un alveare d'api!*' He makes a buzzing noise as he takes the bag from Alec and swings it overhead.

Alec laughs. '*Questa è la mia valigia – solo per me,*' he says proudly, watching the bag being jostled into place.

'*Che bravo!*' the porter says, then winks and leaves them.

Alec sits opposite her. '*Mamma?*' he says.

'*Sì, figlio mio?*'

'*Niente.*' He grins.

The train begins to move and Alec picks up his comic book. He seems happy enough, now and then heeling the riser under his seat, or lifting his head to look out the window or getting up to take a peep into the basket at the baby.

'*Ciao, Edda,*' he whispers. '*È carina – non è vero, Mamma?*'

'*Sì, è vero.*'

She is hopeful that today will be one of his better days.

A few minutes later the porter returns. '*Mi dispiace Signora,*' he says, joining his hands as if to beg forgiveness. Bella sees there's a man in uniform behind him. Her mind turns white. The porter is explaining something she can't even try to understand, all she can think about is the uniform out in the corridor.

Until Alec stands up. '*No! È la mia valigia.*' He is pointing to the alligator bag and she realizes then that the porter has been telling them that all luggage must be labelled and checked into the baggage car. A new rule, he is very sorry.

'*Non c'è problema*,' Bella says. The other man steps in and she sees it's only the inspector after all, the *capotreno*.

'*Uno, due, tre – ci sono tre valigie, Signora, vero?*' he asks her.

'*Sì, tre.*'

He sits beside her, pulls a pen from his breast pocket and leaning the labels against a raised thigh begins, '*Allora – nome, cognome?*'

'*Non è guisto!* Alec whines. '*È la mia!*' He folds his arms and flings himself back down on the seat with an angry little bounce.

The porter explains they are going to write his name on a label and put it on the bag so everyone will know it belongs to him. No one will touch it, he promises.

'*Mi chiamo Anna Magrini*,' she says.

'*Da?*'

'*Via Torino, Oneglia.*'

Now the *capotreno* is asking if her husband is not with her.

'*Sta lavorando in questo momento – ci raggiunge più tardi.*'

He begins rolling one hand, unfortunate men, always working, always having to come along later. The women have it easy enough. He smiles and tells her he's only joking, then looks at Alec. '*E il tuo nome, Signor Bravo?*'

Alec presses his lips together and looks over at Bella with two startled eyes.

'*Alberto Magrini*,' she says. '*Mio figlio.*'

The *capotreno* ties the labels on the two suitcases and the alligator bag. When he turns around he notices the baby bag on the seat beside her.

'*E questa, Signora?*'

'*Cose per la bambina, anche per il viaggio.*' She opens the bag to show baby bottles and nappies. Fruit and panini.

He nods, takes an admiring look at the baby, tells Alec to be a good boy for his mamma, then apologizes for taking their bags but with so many illegals smuggling money out of the country – what can be done? He wishes them, '*Buon viaggio e buone vacanze*,' then signals for the porter to take out the luggage.

When they are gone Alec looks at her with sheepish eyes and she knows he is worried that he's let her down. She smiles to let him know that everything is fine, then reaching into the end of the Moses basket wipes the sweat from her palm on a fold of the baby's eiderdown.

The train pushes on. *Contadini* with crates of fruit and vegetables to sell in the markets, farm labourers and flower pickers on their way to work. As the morning progresses each station becomes brighter and busier, each delay that little longer. The sun is beginning to warm the windows. The shape of the passengers changes. Now office workers and schoolchildren, women with shopping baskets, old men on the way to funerals. Everything so normal, people chatting, smiling; children running out of waiting rooms shouting, '*Arriva il treno!*' Men leaning on counters in station cafés, throwing back a last-minute espresso. She begins to think how ridiculous all this is, to be here on the Milan to Paris train, pretending to be Italian, smuggling two children out of the country. Diamonds sewn into the lining of her bag, for God's sake! This is Italy, after all. These are children – who could possibly want to harm them?

She begins to seriously consider getting off at Bordighera, returning to Villa Lami. She could pay a visit to the British Consul, find a lawyer for the hearing, put in a call to her father for advice. She could do all she should have done in the first place and forget about this foolish charade.

San Stefano station. A young priest comes to the door of the carriage and asks if she could endure two of his pupils, just as far as Taggia. The school inspector arrives today, the priest explains, and these *birbanti* need to look over their homework, the train so full and noisy. '*Molte distrazioni – prego, Signora, per cortesia?*'

'*Certo, Padre*,' Bella agrees, not knowing how to refuse his kind eyes.

The schoolboys duck under the priest's arm, throw a Roman salute her way and sit down beside Alec. As they sit, Alec rises. He takes a place next to Bella.

The priest stays out in the corridor, opens his newspaper and leans against the glass in the compartment door. One of the boys takes out a book and opens it – *Il primo libro del fascista*. He begins reading aloud: 'Guidelines for the Treatment of Jews'. He reads each rule then closes his eyes and repeats it until he knows it off by heart. The other boy pushes his finger along the lines in the book and whispers the words disconnectedly as if he hasn't a clue what they're supposed to mean. So this is their homework. She feels Alec fidget beside her. He takes out his harmonica and mashes it into his lips.

Bella looks away. Out in the corridor, the priest catches her eye and smiles. She nods and makes an effort to smile back. He turns to the side, leaving the front page in her sight. She reads a headline: 'FRANCIA E INGHILTERRA RICHIAMANO TRUPPE'. France and England recall troops.

He shakes the paper out, turns it so the back page is now on view and she can see what appear to be columns of advertisements from Italians denying they are Jews. 'LA FAMIGLIA TREVISI NON È CONTAMINATA! – the Trevesi family is not contaminated!

She abandons all thoughts of getting off at Bordighera.

*

Taggia station. The boys thank her on the way out and salute again. The priest steps in to say goodbye, leans into the Moses basket to lay his hand on the baby's head and then moves to touch Alec. Alec folds himself into the corner.

'*È timido, Padre, scusi,*' she says.

*

Now San Remo. Smartly dressed women appear through the steam; travelling suits, hats and high heels. Anxious faces – obviously in a hurry to get away. Around them hotel porters fuss. Men in sports jackets carrying bags of fruit and magazines come and go from the *Informazioni* window.

A good twenty minutes' delay. The compartment is beginning to feel like they're being cooked inside a casserole dish. Alec takes off his jacket and begins whinging for his *portafortuna*.

She sees a group of middle-aged women, stout shoes and sketch pads under-elbow, form an orderly queue behind a drawing master and climb onto the train. Bella recognizes them as English Dots, making a point of *not* being flustered or feeling compelled to go anywhere. She tells Alec to pull down the reserved blind on the door of their compartment so they can remain alone and undisturbed.

The early start is beginning to show in his eyes. She tells him the *portafortuna* will keep the bag safe, then tells him to lie down. 'No!' he argues, but they have barely left the station when his head and his eyelids begin to yoyo in time with the train. He slides down, lays his head on the seat and sleeps. Bella stands for a moment and stretches out her back.

*

Ospedaletti. Just one stop away from Bordighera. She hopes Alec will stay asleep as far as the checkpoint at least. But then a bicker of English voices breaks out in the corridor. One high-pitched woman: 'And not even a bloody seat to be had. Honestly, Peter, you're such a bore, we might have stayed one more night, it's not as if rotten Hitler is going to come and per-sonally drag us out of our beds, after all we did pay for it and how! It's supposed to be our honeymoon. If this is what—'

'Oh, do shut up, Audrey. Your voice is piercing my head!'

'*Well*, I can't believe—'

The voices are cut by the shudder and slam of the connecting door to the neighbouring carriage. Alec's eyes open and he sits back up. Bordighera. He stays with his forehead butted into the window, gazing out through the blurts of steam.

'*Ricorda-ti, Alberto?*' she warns. '*Silencio.*'

He nods tiredly against the glass and for a moment it looks as if he's about to slip back down into sleep. But then he's jumping up and down and gasping out the window. His head jerks around and looks at her. She signals for him to be quiet and stay out of sight. But he looks back to the window, craning his neck, pressing his face against the glass. Any second she expects him to start shouting that this is Bordighera and they are home.

She sees the English Dots follow their drawing master out of the station. Bella stands up and pulls him away from the window. Alec's face is flushed, his eyes wide awake. '*L'ho visto! L'ho visto!*'

'Yes, I know it's Bordighera, now for goodness sake sit down and be quiet.'

Alec looks shocked. '*Hai parlato in Inglese!*' he chides, which surprises her, as she had felt sure he had forgotten their little game. The door of the carriage opens behind her.

'*Sì, sì,*' Alec shouts. '*L'ho visto, l'ho visto!*'

Bella looks around as Edward steps into the carriage. 'Sorry I'm late, dear,' he says.

She can't bring herself to look at him and turns her face away to the window. Her heart is so loud she feels sure he can hear it. Edward nudges her.

'Look at me,' he says.

'No.' She can see the imprint of his face behind hers on the glass of the window, the side of her face resting under his beard.

'Look at me, Bella.'

'No.'

She waits until the train begins to warm up.

'Will you be getting off at Menton?' she asks after a moment.

'No.'

'Monte Carlo then?'

'No. Not Monte Carlo.'

'Oh? How far are you going?'

He says, 'All the way – if I'm allowed.'

Edward is beside her. She tries not to remember last night, what she said or almost did. Her feelings switch one second to the next; now shame, now regret, now not giving the slightest damn beyond wondering how soon they can do it again, this time to the finish. Then elation because he has risked so much for them, followed by – for the very same reason – fear.

'The thing is—' he begins, but she puts her hand up to stop him.

'Let's just get through today, Edward.'

'You're right. Of course.' He throws his knapsack onto the rack. 'How's the baby?'

'Edda – you mean?'

'Yes. Edda.'

'Drugged, actually.' Bella turns around but doesn't quite look at him yet.

'Scandalous!' he says. 'What have you done to her?'

'Not me, Sorella Ursula. Just to give me a start, I suppose.'

'Well, I can help you now. If you show me how.'

'Actually, I wouldn't mind a stretch. My back has been at me.'

'Off you go.'

'Do you want to come with me, Alec?'

'No!' Alec pouts.

'What's the matter, Allo?' Edward asks him.

'You ruin our game. We won't get the surprise now. Because you make us speak English.'

'Ah, scusa mi, Allo, sono un papà stupido,' Edward says.

'You're not my Papa.'

'Only for the game, Al. After that I'll just be your friend again.'

'And you fight last night with Signora Bella and I don't love you now any more.'

'She fought with me! She's quite rough you know. I'm badly bruised. Ought to be a law against it.'

'I'll be back soon,' Bella mutters and ducks out.

She sways up the corridor clutching on to the rail, bumping past or dancing against oncoming passengers. Finally she finds herself alone outside the lavatory on a clanking floor between carriages. A sweet cool breeze crosses from the open windows on both sides. She dips her head out the sea-side window. The start of the promenade ambles by; just a distant glimpse of the roof on the Kursaal now, and a clumsy glint from the one-man band as he totters down to his usual post. She comes back to the middle.

Now leaving Bordighera, really leaving it. The sea on her left, the last stretch of town on her right, the hillside rising behind it. Between its rocks and its olive groves, its light, numerous balconies, there is always that dark green hillside. She looks down through the gap in the floor, watches Italy slip away under her feet.

When she comes back to the carriage Alec is standing face to the window, his reflection like a little ghost looking back at her. Edward has taken off his coat and, sleeves rolled up, is turning a penknife over the peel of an orange.

'See, Allo,' he says, 'not a nick.' He holds the bare orange up and drops the twirl of peel onto a handkerchief.

Alec turns around. 'Where are we?'

'Near Ventimiglia, the frontier.'

Out in the corridor the voice of a conductor is pacing. '*Documenti!*' it calls. '*Documenti!*'

Bella takes the envelope from the side pocket of the baby bag. She pulls out the papers and quickly arranges them. The papers that will take them out of Italy first: certificate of family status, passports, workbook for her husband, the carpenter Marco Magrini. Beneath them the papers that will take them into France: *carte de tourisme*, visas. Between the two lots she places the letter to the hotel, which may be useful in both cases. She knows it's unlikely that the Sorella would have forgotten anything, but checks it all again anyway, then hands the papers to Edward, so he can do all the showing and talking.

'I think we should put the reserved blinds back up,' he says, 'or they might think we have something to hide.'

'As if!' Bella says, releasing the cord, revealing an empty corridor.

He parts the segments of the orange and lays them on top of the curled peel on the hanky, then puts it carefully on the seat beside Alec. The train begins to slow down.

'Well, here goes,' Edward says.

Alec picks up his harmonica.

Blackshirts all over the platform. *Polizia di frontiera* with guns to their shoulders. Small groups of people being led this way and that. There is a long, low, flat-roofed building parallel to the train where officials pass in and out. Through one of its windows she sees the open mouth of a suitcase, hands rummaging through. Further down the building a queue bends through an open door.

The train comes to a complete stop and a line of officials approaches, then divides into shorter lines to stand before each door. Bella feels the carriage rock as they climb on.

The *capotreno* comes back to clip their tickets. '*Ahh il marito!*' he begins when he sees Edward, but as two officials push in behind him, he hands the tickets back without another word.

The first official is all chat, looking in at the baby, asking her name and going, '*Ah che bella.*' The other official just stands there. Out in the corridor soldiers pass by.

Bella notices Alec's eyes are beginning to flutter. He runs the harmonica over his lips, backwards and forwards, again and again.

The official goes through the papers, pausing to ask a question or make a comment at each one: '*Vacanze? Bellissimo. A Nizza? Mi piace Nizza. Solo per una settimana?*'

'*Sì.*' Edward smiles.

'*Un po d'aria fresca per i bambini, eh?*'

Edward agrees.

The official hands back the papers, then his eye catches sight of Alec gnawing his lips on the harmonica. He puts a hand to his ear and says, '*Allora, Maestro? Non posso sentire la musica.*' He laughs, delighted with his joke.

Alec drops the harmonica with fright. Bella is horrified to see squirts of blood along his chapped lips. She pulls a hanky from her sleeve. '*Vieni qui, a Mamma*,' she says.

But Alec won't move.

The custom official looks at him for a moment then picks up the harmonica and hands it to him.

Alec puts his hands behind his back and shakes his head.

Bella stands up and takes it instead. '*Grazie, Signore. È molto timido.*'

The customs official nods, then sullenly wishes them *buon viaggio* and closes the door behind him.

'Jesus,' Edward says.

Alec starts crying. '*Mi scappa cacca.*'

'Oh, Alec, I asked you if you wanted to go just a little while ago. Can't you wait?'

'*È diarrea. Penso.*'

'Diarrhoea! Oh no, Alec.'

'*Mi dispiace.*'

'It's all right, Alec,' she says. 'Be a big boy now, we just have to think.'

'I'll take him,' Edward says.

'No. He can't go while the train is stationary, the toilets are all locked. Wait till the train moves again.'

'He can't wait – look at him. They've checked us already, Bella. We'll be fine. Listen, they've already moved on to the next carriage. We're through. I can't bloody believe it, but we're through. Ventimiglia station is only down the way, we'll be back in a few minutes.'

'Yes, but what if they don't let you back on?'

'Of course they will. Tell you what, I'll bring our tickets, just in case.'

'Yes. I suppose so,' Bella agrees.

Edward removes their tickets from the stack and hands the French visas and *carte de tourisme* back to Bella.

'Come on, Al, lets go.'

Alec shakes his head and looks at Bella.

'It's all right, Alec,' Edward says. 'It's safe now.' He lays one hand on top of Alec's head and guides him through the door. The other hand he places on the top of Bella's arm. '*Fra poco, Bella*,' he says.

Bella looks out the window. Everything outside appears to be moving at a faster pace now. The queue at the door to the customs office is considerably shorter, the crowd on the platform greatly diminished. She can think of only one reason for this spurt of rare Italian efficiency – a glance at her watch confirms it – almost time for lunch. Out in the corridor she sees first-class passengers who have been already cleared beginning to stream along the corridor to the restaurant car. They speak lightly to each other as they go, in the easy manner of the English upper-crust tourist.

Her head turns back towards the window of the train; her gaze falls upon the soldier standing at the door of the room where earlier she had seen the hands rummaging through a suitcase. Inside the room, an official is talking to a man sitting in the shadows. She sees papers being passed one to the other.

The next time she looks at her watch, ten minutes has gone by. She reminds herself that Alec's nervy bouts of diarrhoea can take quite a while. She watches a man get off the train and go to the newspaper stand. A woman walks up the platform fixing her skirt as if she's just come back from the station lavatory. She stops, opens a compact and bares her teeth.

Bella presumes Edward is still in the main station building. Maybe he slipped in for a coffee there, but she can't believe he would delay in these circumstances. The man comes back from the newspaper stand, flipping the paper under his arm, and jumps back onto the train. The woman closes the compact and also climbs on a little further down. Fifteen minutes – where are they? By now the stream of people in the corridor for the restaurant car has slowed to a queue.

The baby distracts her with a whimper. 'Shh, shhh,' Bella soothes and sits down beside her, watching the little mouth open and close. Bella lowers her face into the deep sour smell of a dirty nappy. She decides to be prepared, going through the baby bag: nappies, pins, petroleum jelly, olive oil packed to one side. On the other side there's a tin of dried baby milk, two empty feeding bottles, two more already made up. She pulls the smaller bottle out just in case, along with a few things she'll need to change the nappy.

As she lifts her head from the bag her eye falls on the soldier at the door again. He is beckoning at someone further up the platform to hurry along. The soldier takes a few steps forward, beckons again a little more forcefully; this time he leaves the door unattended for a few seconds. A gap. For a terrible moment she thinks she might have seen Alec in the room. Bella stands and goes to the window, but the soldier has returned to his place now and no matter how much she tries, she can't see behind him.

The baby whimpers again. Then falls quiet again. Bella turns to look at her. When she comes back to the window she sees the soldier moving aside to allow two men into the office. One man is the porter from earlier on, the other a soldier. The porter is carrying her mother's green alligator travel bag.

For a few seconds she dies. Her heart, mind, body, everything stops. Until Alec comes into sight to take a seat at the table. The bag lands in front of him. She sees an official sit down beside Alec, laughing and joking, tossing his hair. The official stands then to open the bag. Alec's hand goes in and pulls out his *portafortuna*, holding it up for the official to see.

Bella tries not to panic. Her hands hit off each other as she goes back to the Moses basket, slides it off the seat, in her hurry knocking the baby bag onto the floor. There's a tumble of clothes and the thud of a jar; the tin of baby food rolls, then stops. The envelope with the false English papers flops out on the floor. The envelope with the money follows. The baby starts crying.

'Sshh,' Bella says. 'Oh God. Don't do that. Don't cry. Don't. Not *now*.'

She lifts the baby out of the basket and into her arms, rocking her a little. This only seems to make the baby worse. Bella stoops to the floor to pick up the envelopes, the baby balanced over one knee. She is aware that she's beginning to attract attention from the queue for the restaurant car. She begins stuffing things back into the bag with her free hand.

The train rumbles beneath her. Bella throws the bag onto the seat, unsteadily gets a hold of the baby in her arms, then gets herself back onto her feet. She can feel the engines struggle and fuss. She grabs the baby bag and makes a rush for the door.

She hears the stutter of the warning bell, the lengthy screech of a whistle. 'No!' she shouts out and turns to look out the window. The platform is moving. She jumps at the window, bangs her fist against the glass, shouting for Edward and Alec, for the soldier in the doorway, for the old man passing by, pushing a bicycle, for the woman closing up the newsstand. Anyone who might heed her. She rushes back to the door of the compartment, begins tugging on the door handle. The whistle screeches again. She knows she is sobbing now and that her behaviour is startling people in the queue who are avoiding her eyes and looking at each other instead.

The baby cries louder. A violent tremble coming up from its tiny bootees. Bella feels it vibrate through her arms into her body. She sobs back at it, 'Stop. Can't you just stop?'

Eventually a young couple step out, the woman first, followed by the man. The woman tries to open the door from the corridor side.

'Let go of the handle,' the woman shouts in at her. 'I can't open the door unless you let go of the handle.' Then to the man, 'The poor thing doesn't seem to understand what I'm saying. I wonder where she's from, maybe we should see if we can find someone who speaks her language.' She looks up the corridor as if she's hoping a linguist will step out of the queue.

Bella is frantically nodding: I do understand, I do. But she can't seem to let go of the handle and she can't seem to speak.

The train stumbles forward and she almost loses her grip on the baby. She feels herself jerk, puts her hand out to stop herself falling, and then a pain like a knife stabs into and scores up her spine. Bella falters and falls back on the seat.

The door opens and the couple come in. They look at her, and then at each other. Bella tries to get up, but the pain in her back won't allow it. By now the baby is hysterical, her skin almost purple and there's one fat vein on the side of her head like a pulsing worm. Bella hears the word '*permesso*' echo along the corridor.

The woman asks where she's from, but Bella can't catch her breath to reply.

'I believe. You may. Be holding. The Baby. Too. Tightly?' the woman says slowly and loudly. Then, turning to her husband, 'Oughtn't we see if we can get a doctor? How do you say doctor in French – would you say that's what she is?'

'I have no idea,' the husband says, 'on either count. You best get that child away from her though before she squeezes the poor thing to death. She's obviously not right in the head.'

'Stop the train,' Bella says.

'Oh, you're English, thank goodness for that,' the woman says, while at the same time throwing a scornful look at her husband.

'Please. Stop. Please stop the train, the emergency cord, over there – see. I can't. Can't get up. I must get off. I have to.'

'Would you like me to take the baby?' the woman asks. 'You do seem in rather a state.'

The word '*permesso*' comes closer now and Bella looks up to see the crowd of English tourists part and the porter push his way through. He closes the door behind him.

'*Prego, Signora, tranquilla, stia tranquilla.*'

She is shouting now. 'No! I will not be *tranquilla*. You gave them… the bag. I saw you give. Give them. *La valigia. Perché? Perché?*'

'*No, no, no. Signora, che cosa fa? Allora, attenzione alla bambina.*' He gestures towards the baby.

'I want to be with them, I want to go with *them*. Take the baby, please take the baby and let me go. I don't know this baby. I don't want it. I don't bloody want it! That woman there said she will take the baby.'

She holds the baby out but can't seem to loosen her grip. Bella hears her own voice wailing over and over, 'I'm not able, I'm not able.'

The porter kneels down and holds her arms while the train takes up more speed, pushing faster and faster. Slowly he prises the screaming baby from her hands. The woman takes the baby from Bella while he continues to hold her down. '*Niente da fare, Signora. È troppo tardi, Signora. Stia tranquilla, stia tranquilla. È troppo tardi, troppo tardi.*' It's too late. Too late, too late.

LONDON

SHE REMEMBERS THE TAXI and crossing London in the web of first light. Every moment of the journey in fact, as far as the checkpoint near Ventimiglia; the long, low building with the soldier at the door and shadows through the window she can't bring herself to name. It's the rest of the journey, the countless hours that have taken her from there – through Paris, Calais, Dover – to here, a guest house off the Bayswater Road. That part is not always clear in her head.

She knows she was looked after; the honeymoon couple, the nurse and of course the porter. Later there would be the guest house owner. Without their help she would never have managed. The English passengers in first class too, who had all, in their own quiet way, colluded. And that somehow she had passed safely through the checkpoint on the French side and, even more astonishingly, managed to get through English customs without a hitch. Although this may have been down to her dodgy papers being slipped in with those of the English party.

The newly wed couple – not that young after all. The man's name, Peter. The woman – a pillbox hat with a demi-veil of lace, sharp-nosed and pretty beneath it – Audrey. Frilled cuffs on her blouse, a little jacket, gloves. She kept looking at and touching her clothes. There had been an air of self-congratulation about the way she did that, as if no one else could have quite carried off such an outfit. The nurse, a far plainer woman, had materialized out of nowhere. Dolores. She had been making her way home after a stint of private nursing in Venice, getting out before Europe blew up in her face, she said, then told them she was Irish, from Dublin. Bella hadn't bothered to mention the connection.

The nurse had taken charge of the baby then given Bella a pill. 'Don't ask,' she said as she dropped it onto her palm, with a mischievous gleam in her eye. Not that Bella had any intention of asking. Arsenic, for all she had cared.

The man, Peter, had brought her a brandy and told her to rest. 'I'll keep her company,' the nurse said, 'while I feed the baby. What's her name by the way?'

'Katherine,' Bella had said, thinking it best to go with the name on the English papers.

'Kay or a Sea?' she asked then. And Bella hadn't known what she meant. 'Spelling?'

'K,' she had said, taking what would turn out to be a lucky guess.

The sound of the baby tutting on the bottle, loud and alien.

Not far into France, she had looked down through the window on the outskirts of a town. A circus tent surrounded by a field. Acrobats and a tightrope walker practising out of doors. And the music of Satie had flooded into her head. The way it had been flooding into the Signora's sitting room over the past weeks.

She could hear one particular piece then – the one she had heard, her first day in Bordighera, having tea with the American cousins. And she could see, too, the Almansi sisters dancing around to it, barefoot in the garden. Even though there could have been no music that day – Edward was the one who had taken the photograph. And besides, the Almansi girls always danced to their own little made-up songs.

'Gymnopédie,' he had said it was called when she'd finally got around to asking him. He had been impressed that she could recognize it from a distance of five years – '*Gymnopédie*' – and had laughed because she thought he had said – 'Jim Nobody'.

Later in the restaurant car the couple had helped her decide what to do, voices low to the table. The woman had removed her gloves and was working the knife over the butter, flicking off smuts then swiping them off the side of a napkin already speckled with soot.

Bella couldn't always hear what they were saying. There was so much else besides. The smell of the brandy. The crockery chattering like teeth. The hard dry sobs coiled in her chest that were itching to get out. Across the table she exchanged answers for questions as best she could. The woman's small mouth never stopped moving. And the music of Satie played on and off in her head; so she could think of nothing else then except his music, his peculiar titles, what they might possibly mean, as the train pounded and shrieked through tunnels, on and off, on and off. Black to unyielding blue.

She must have given them a story they liked, devising it as she went along. Enough truth to scaffold the lies or to make them want to risk helping her. Clearly she had said she was married because they had used the words 'your husband' on more than one occasion – and there was the Signora's wedding band. And she must have mentioned her father because they knew she was going to Chelsea. Whatever else had been part of the story, Bella has long since forgotten.

'Look – why not just stick with us?' the woman had said, obviously growing bored. 'Stick with us and we'll see you safely to your father's doorstep in Chelsea. All agreed? Marvellous! Not another word about it now. Well, thank heaven that's settled. Shall we have a little drinkie-poo, on the strength of it? Another brandy? Why not!'

Bella had agreed. There was really nothing else she could do.

When they returned to the compartment Dolores had been reading a magazine, the baby tucked up in the Moses basket.

'Oh good,' Audrey said. 'You've tidied the child away.' Then she sat down and beamed. 'Well now – isn't this cosy?'

Bella, leaning into the corner by the window, pretended to be asleep. Behind her closed eyes she held an imprint of the compartment: the outline of the couple, the nurse, the curve of the Moses basket. On the overhead rack, the shape of Edward's knapsack that he had bought for his walking trip two years ago and Alec's harmonica tucked into the top of the baby bag, his comic book in among the neat pile of magazines that had been arranged by Dolores on top of the fold-down table. She could taste the orange and orange peel in the bin, for a moment thought she was going to be sick.

Audrey started talking about Venice. A voice that could pass under a door. 'I was there myself, of course. Several times. I must say I don't see what all the fuss is about. Quite frankly I find it damp and, well – morbid.'

'Well, it is Venice,' Dolores mumbled.

'Why, of course! But really, don't you think it's rather much, you know – *overdone*?'

'And don't *you* think you ought to pipe down for a bit?' her husband said then. 'Can't you see they're both sleeping?'

'Oh bugger off, Peter,' Audrey snapped back. 'Why do you always have to make a point of being so bloody considerate?'

At some stage the porter came in to say he was sorry. '*Mi dispiace, mi dispiace, mi dispiace.*'

And Bella felt if there had been a gun nearby she could have easily shot him in the face. He said he'd be getting off soon to take the return train back to Italy. Then he begged her to allow him to change the tags on the luggage using the name on her English papers. '*Le due altre,*' he explained when she looked blindly at him. The two other suitcases. She had forgotten they were still out in the baggage car.

He went on to swear he had done the best he could under the circumstances. The authorities had the man and the boy, nothing would have changed that. Besides, the man with the beard had encouraged him to pretend there was only himself and the boy. '*Siamo in due,*' il barbuto had said, and the porter had simply backed him up. At least she was

334

safe, also the baby. '*Mi dispiace, mi dispiace.*'

He had given them the bag because the officials had asked him to bring the luggage from the train. He had to give them something – one bag at least.

He hadn't realized it would be so incriminating – a child's bag after all? He would telephone the *Padre* as soon as he got back to Italy tomorrow, ask him to send a message for her anywhere she cared to name. The *Padre* would fix everything, she would see. '*Mi dispiace, dispiace, dispiace.*'

'*A Villa Lami,*' she said, closing her eyes again. '*Si puo lasciare un messaggio a Villa Lami.*'

Her companions were impressed with her command of the language, their eyes following every word, mouth to mouth. But she sensed they were a little less forthcoming for a while after the porter had left. As if they couldn't, no matter how much they wanted to, quite trust anyone who could speak a language other than English, so well.

*

They changed trains in Paris. The English holidaymakers surrounding her like a movable wall as they passed through checkpoints and platform barriers. Hours to kill before the next train. Dolores went off to see the Eiffel Tower, Audrey to take a tour of the shops. Bella stayed where Peter left her, in a corner of a café near the station.

Frenchmen staring at a wireless set, some standing in a semicircle around it, others twisting out of their chairs and leaning back towards it. Behind the steady voice of the translator she could hear Hitler's manic screeching and the men in the café sometimes shouting angry comments at the radio. Sometimes falling silent.

At a nearby table two red-haired English women, about to join the train, argued about the departure time, then argued about the exchange rate, then argued about the luggage. One freckly arm, wobbling with rage as it tried to keep a fly from a cake. 'Nothin' short of disgustin', that's what it is, bleedin' flies everywhere.'

Peter had gone off to make inquiries. When he came back he said there was no point in trying to put a telephone call through to Italy. 'Best wait till we've the boat journey behind us and we're back on home ground – eh, old girl?' he said, and promised to help her when she started to cry.

*

She was asleep when the train drew into Waterloo station, but knew the moment she opened her eyes, they were back in London; everyone over-dressed, in the sense of too many, rather than too lavish, clothes.

Through the window she could see people asleep on benches or lying on coats on the ground, standing in queues at ticket windows or stuffed into doorways of waiting rooms. There were makeshift canteen counters set up by the wall; women in crossover pinnys and nets in their hair, splashing out Bovril and tea. Posters pleading for calm. And a sign that said, 'Children for Evacuation. No parents beyond this point.'

All over the concourse, a criss-cross of movement. Sailors with duffle-bags, young men in new khaki. Nurses in navy-blue cloaks. Women dragging children behind them. In the middle of it all, one old lady, muffled up to the ears in fur, stood like a stem to the current.

Bella stepped down from the train, into a clamour of English voices that seemed, to her ear, jagged, ugly and utterly foreign.

By the time they came through the station it was almost morning. Peter went off to try for a taxi, Audrey to the lavatory to freshen up. Bella waited with Dolores on the corner, the Moses basket weighed between them. Dolores pressed a piece of paper into her hand with her address in Dublin on it. 'In case,' she said. 'Just in case.'

In silence they watched the evacuee children arrive. Poor children on foot accompanied by overly chirpy mothers pushing prams full of luggage. Across the street, children of substance popped down from coach buses, one neat small suitcase each and one tweed-suited teacher per orderly queue, calling out names from a roll book while keen hand after keen hand shot up in response. Girls in felt hats and double-breasted coats. Boys – she tried not to notice. Although one or two strays managed to slip into her view just long enough to show a belted gabardine, and a cap moulded into the perfect shape of a young boy's head.

'Rich or poor it makes no difference,' Dolores remarked. 'They either cry or they don't – did you notice that?' And Bella said no, she had not.

In the taxi she suddenly decided she couldn't go to Chelsea, couldn't face all the questions, the fuss. Even if her father had already left for the country, she still couldn't bear to face the empty house with Mrs Jenkins' 'tasteful stamp' all over it.

'What day is this?' she asked, all innocence.

'It's Wednesday – isn't it? The twenty-eighth.'

'Oh dear, I'm sorry, I just wasn't thinking. You see, the thing is, my father works in a hospital in Birmingham on Tuesday and Wednesday, he won't be home until tomorrow night. I had forgotten all about it.'

'But didn't you say you had a stepmother or something?' Audrey asked.

'Yes, but she always goes with him and I'm afraid I don't have a key.'

'You mean, there's absolutely *nobody* there? You don't have a maid?' Audrey sounded worried.

'Yes, but she's a daily. Today's her day off.'

'Oh. Couldn't we just go to her house and fetch the key?'

'She'd be asleep, I couldn't disturb her at this hour.'

'But where will you *go*?' Audrey, by now barely able to keep the panic from her voice.

'A guest house or a small hotel would be perfect,' Bella said.

And Peter said he knew just the place.

*

The owner of the guest house insists on liking her, lending her a pram that once belonged to her granddaughter, and heating up a bottle for the baby now known as Katherine.

She says it's a pity to have overslept breakfast, though given the circumstances, quite forgivable. 'I mean, travelling all night, with a war snapping at your heels? Can't have been easy, my love.'

Then she makes the 'breakfast girl' – who looks about seventy – go back into the kitchen just as the poor weary woman is about to put on her coat and go home. 'Tea and toast for our guest, and try to be smart about it, there's a good girl.'

She tells Bella they had kidneys earlier, lovely and fresh, 'All gone now, what a shame.' And Bella feels grateful for small mercies.

Another 'girl', named Judy, also quite elderly, is sent off to wash and polish the pram.

The owner says her name is Mrs Mains. She calls Bella the name on the English identity papers. Then tells her all about Mr Chamberlain's speech last night.

'Not looking good – is it now, Mrs Barrett?' she concludes. 'Not looking good at all.'

'No, Mrs Mains,' Bella has to agree. 'It certainly is not.'

'Here, why not let me give the little one her bottle whilst you have your tea?'

'Well, if you're sure you don't mind?'

Mrs Mains feeds the baby, and at the same mildly interrogates Bella, who in turn watches and learns from Mrs Main's baby-feeding technique, while at the same time tries to remember the advice Peter had given her in the early hours of this morning. Bella was not, at any rate, to mention Italy. *Terra Non Grata*, Peter had called it. 'Best not tell anyone, really, until we know the lie of the land. I'll think of something for Mainsy. You just rub along with it.'

'And Peter was saying your hubby's still in Paris?' Mrs Mains begins.

'Yes, that's right, he sent us on ahead of him, wants us to be safe, you know, just in case.'

'Course he does, my love. You'll be missing him, I daresay. And Peter was saying he works in the embassy?'

'That's right.'

'Oh now! A clerk he was saying?'

'Mmm.'

'Oh well. At least you've got your lovely little *bay-bee*, eh? Let's be thankful for that much anyway. I don't know when we last had a kiddie in this house. And we must look after her for her *da-ddee* now, we must keep her safe at all costs. Gas masks first and foremost. Well, the embassy – I *am* honoured.'

'He's just a clerk, really.'

'Oh, we get chaps from the civil service here all the time, the bowler brigade, I call them. The foreign office too on occasion. But it's not the same – is it? The French embassy. And in Paris. Well, now.'

A short while later Bella blunders the pram down the garden path, aware of how clumsy she must seem. The wheels lodge into the cracks in the paving, the carriage of the pram jams in the garden gate and Mrs Mains stands watching from the steps of the house.

'All right, my dear?'

'Yes. It's just a little different to the one I'm used to,' Bella says, no longer surprised at how the lies just seem to fall out of her mouth.

She turns onto the Bayswater Road. The streets muddled with people and traffic. It's a London she doesn't quite recognize. Everywhere sandbags. Men dragging them off the back of lorries; horses pulling them along on carts; people moulding them into walls of buildings and around the plinths of monuments. Another truckload staggers around another corner. As if the whole of London is to be upholstered by nightfall.

Bella tightens her grip on the handlebar; her knuckles white and hard as pebbles – no matter how much she squeezes, the shake remains in her hands. She glances at the stranger in the pram and dismisses the urge to abandon it.

Through Lancaster Gate. Into Hyde Park, a hefty draught of horse manure. She pulls in behind a group, pram-pushers and pedestrians already paused to give way to the Ladies Riding Club hack.

In front of her two nannies chatter: 'All little chaps, don't you see?

Hitler, five six if that. Musso five nothing, and as for that Italian king, well, they say he's a midget!'

'Do you mean a proper midget? Like in a circus and that?'

'Oh yes, just so.'

'Trying to prove themselves – if you ask me, and I—'

The thuds and snorts of the passing horses beat the rest of her comments into submission.

Bella follows behind the two nannies, drawn by the solid shape of them, their sense of purpose, the sure way they handle their prams. On North Carriage Drive they are joined by another.

Over the treetops, out on the street, workmen crawl along rooftops. A constant sound of tapping hammers from the direction of Park Lane. She sees sheets of galvanized iron edging over the upper windows of hotels and houses. Through trees, the red smear of a passing bus.

There's a brief worry that someone might look down from a top deck and know her. If not here in the park, then later on, out in the street. She is only beginning to realize now how close she is to Chelsea and the hospital where her father still occasionally works. And she is not sure if she wants to be seen just yet – if at all. But then who would know her in this cream, French-cut coat and these Italian shoes? And who would ever place her behind a pram? Her own father wouldn't think to look twice, not that he would still be in London with all this going on.

She looks down at her clothes, resolves to buy something more English first chance she gets. Blend, she thinks, blend.

Bella steps up closer behind the drably dressed nannies, but finds after all that this makes her more obvious, not less. She breaks away.

All over the park lawns are being carved into trenches; mounds of yellowish earth along the rims. A head pops up out of the ground, then a spade. Along the lines it makes a pattern: head, then spade. Head, then spade. The bite of shovel and pick.

Just off the path, a congregation of onlookers. A glint of silver against the mass of dark greenery. Bella moves closer, finds a viewpoint between the shoulders of two men and watches an anti-aircraft gun swing into position. On Speakers' Corner voices are howling, one more hysterical than the next.

*

She doesn't recognize Peter at first and wonders why this man in a bowler hat and pinstripes should be standing grinning at her. He looks younger in his old man's attire, almost clownish.

He tells her he's very pleased to see her and asks how she's getting along with Mrs Mains.

'Oh, very well, she couldn't be nicer. In fact I'm thinking of staying on a bit longer. I didn't like to say in front of everyone but you know, my father will have already gone to the country to his new wife's family and I don't really, you know…'

'No need to explain. Stay as long as you like, until you know what's what, that's my advice. She's not a bad old bird, Mrs Mains. Keeps a good house, I'm told.'

She asks him how Audrey is feeling after the long journey.

'Oh, you know.' He smiles and grimaces childishly, like she's his teacher and not his wife. 'Bit peeved at my going back to work so soon, but I thought, well, everybody's got to do their bit, you know. She wanted to complete the honeymoon by going on outings. I mean – outings! What did you have in mind, I said to her – filling gunnysacks with sand in Whitby Bay? Anyway, we've had the most frightful row.'

He walks slightly ahead, talking back to her, one hand on the hood of the pram. Whenever they have to cross a road, he comes back to the handle and guides it over.

'Now – it goes without saying, Mrs Barrett, that you will be listened in on, so I'll just run through a few guidelines to avoid your being disconnected. Thankfully this person you are telephoning speaks English, because any spouting off in a foreign language and chop-chop, I'm afraid. Please *don't* use any foreign-sounding names and try to make your

341

questions as ordinary as possible. I suggest you make out that you're calling your mother who is on holiday. Obviously you are going to have to get your meaning across, just be careful of how you do it. I'm sure I don't need to tell you this is a very great favour. And a once-off. Also, I shan't be able to stay with you. Oh, and you will have no more than a minute or two. We are this close to war you know.'

'Yes, Peter, I understand. Thank you, I can't tell you—'

'Oh well, never mind all that,' he says, bringing her in through a gate marked 'Deliveries' and crossing a yard to an office building with steps to a steel door. He comes round to take over the pram, hauling it up the steps.

'A chap called Fred will take care of you. He's sneaking you in. Now he's going to stay in the room so be warned, if you say anything even vaguely incriminating he'll cut you off to save his own skin.' He opens the door and reverses the pram into a hallway.

'You're quite the expert with that thing,' Bella remarks.

'Oh yes! Tell the truth, Audrey is not my first. Third, in fact. I'm an old hand really. One child first time around. Two the next. Some people never learn, what?'

He waits for a moment, then lowers his voice. 'Now. I've already slipped a ten bobber to our friend, so don't you go giving him any more. Please – it was my pleasure.' He blocks her hand when it reaches for her handbag. 'Ah, there he is now, the shifty little bugger. Well, good luck, Mrs Barrett. I really hope everything works out.'

'Thank you, Peter, and please give Audrey my regards.'

'I will,' he says and grimaces again.

*

She can hardly hear Elida, her voice so frail and tight from trying to hold back the tears. Bella decides to jump straight in, and hopefully give Elida a chance to catch on.

'Mother! How lovely to talk to you. How's the holiday going? Hope it's not too warm for you. Oh, your poor throat still sore then? Never mind, don't speak. So how are the boys? Are they back from Monday's fishing trip yet? You'll never guess who we met on the train? That piano chap, can't think of his name, anyway he's gone fishing too. Isn't that nice? So they're still out then?'

'Nobody is here, no,' Elida cautiously croaks.

'Oh, Mother – what a pity about your not being well, you should stay in the good weather as long as you can – promise me now? Don't go anywhere until you're well again. And what about that aunt of mine – I suppose she's out shopping as usual. Has she even telephoned to say what time she'll be back for lunch? No? Now let's see what news this end... Oh yes, that nice friend of Ursula's said he might be in touch. Such an interesting man. Do you know the one I mean? He works with her. Tall, handsome, dark; all that. We have friends in common you know – did he call at all looking for me?'

'Yes. This morning.'

'Lovely! Did he mention if he'd news of any of the old gang?'

'He has no news but hopes soon.'

'Oh, ask him to drop me a line sometime, would you? I'd love to hear from him. No, I'm not staying at home – the builders are in. I'm with a friend.'

Fred looks up from the racing page of his newspaper, catches her eye and taps his watch.

'Well, Mother, I must go. I'm off now to the post office in Portman Square – I said the P-O-R-T-M-A-N – to fetch letters for that nice lady I'm helping out. Ursula introduced us, yes, she's English all right. From Bournemouth, I believe. Has a little baby girl – ask Ursula, she'll tell you all about it. Hasn't made up her mind to come or to go, so for the moment her letters go to the *Portman* Square. By the way, that little parcel I left? Don't give it to Ursula after all but put it away safe for me somewhere, would you? Until I decide what to do. I'm afraid those children of hers will get their hands on it and you know what they're like!'

343

Fred has folded his newspaper under his arm and is rapping his knuckles on the desk now.

'Yes, darling, I've got to go now. Yes, I have to really. You take care and tell that family of mine I miss them and to write. I'll try again soon. I'm thinking of you always. I'll see you very, very soon.'

She puts down the phone on Elida's sobs.

Fred waits a few seconds and says, 'Look, I'm really going to have to ask you to go. I'm sorry but... I really am.'

'Yes. Yes. Just give me a minute – would you? I'm afraid I'm not feeling all that well.'

Bella wipes her eyes and goes to her bag. She takes out a ten-shilling note. 'I wonder. I wonder if you'd mind, I mean, if I could ask you to take the pram back down the steps for me?'

Fred takes the note and does as she asks.

*

When she gets back to the guest house she tells Mrs Mains she has a headache.

'Exhaustion, my love. Everything's catching up on you, I shouldn't wonder.'

She wears herself out, all that afternoon and well into the night, her ribs ache and the walls of her throat swell up from the strain of crying. Even after it seems there's not a drop of water left in her body, it jolts on regardless, for another hour or so, like a car that's run out of petrol.

The following evening Mrs Mains invites her into the private parlour for a listen to the wireless. They drink cocoa. Mrs Mains knits and prattles away. Bella nods, occasionally mutters something agreeable while desperately trying to hear what the radio broadcast is saying. Mrs Mains talks like someone who, despite long periods of practice, is still not used to living alone and can't help but take full advantage of a new pair of ears. Bella tries not to scream.

It's probably one of the most important items Bella has ever heard come out of a radio, Chamberlain returning from Munich saying there won't be a war after all. Yet the news has to weave through and duck under Mrs Mains' anecdotes and opinions in general.

Sometimes the voices appear to mingle. So that it seems as if Mr Chamberlain has a daughter out in Australia named Alice, and it's Mrs Mains who has just come back from Munich.

'Peace for our time,' she hears the man on the broadcast say.

'Peace for our time,' Mrs Mains repeats with a sigh. 'Well, let's see how long that lasts!'

'You think not?'

'I tell you what I think, I think that Chamberlain is a right doormat, is what. They ought to have sent that Anthony Eden, he's man enough for the job.'

'At least there won't be a war.'

'Oh, I don't know. Call me gloomy but. We've got a right few Jewish refugees come in lately – you must have noticed, dear, London's crawling with them. More coming in every day. The landlady of the Avon guest house down the road was telling me only yesterday that her house is jammers with them. Some of the stories! Germans, Austrians, Hungarians, all sorts, she's got a few Eyetalians coming in the next few weeks, Frenchies too. Well, it can't go on. It can't really. Someone will have to put a stop to that Hitler.'

'You're not hopeful then?'

'The government's been expecting it all along. No reason to stop expecting it now.' She puts down her knitting and leans towards Bella. 'Put it this way, Mrs Barrett, did you never wonder how so many gas masks should be ready so quickly? I mean thousands and thousands?'

'Well, I suppose.'

'It's the interval, darling, that's all. We can't see it, but everything is still going on behind the curtains. They'll come up again, soon as we're ready. Anyway, what was I saying?'

What she was saying was that Alice had married beneath her.

345

'Oh yes. Unlike her mum, who went up – I did. I make no bones about it. Hence this lovely house, long may it stand. And I've made a fair living out of it, in its time. Though I don't stretch myself too much these days, a few lifers, as I call them, the occasional pass-through that Peter might throw my way. But our Alice? She's got nothing to fall back on. Someone who works on a ranch is what she's got. A cowboy or whatever they call the Australian equivalent.'

*

The crisis in Munich blows up, then blows over. Every day she wakes and thinks today she will go to Chelsea. She gets the baby ready, has her small breakfast and leaves the house before Mrs Mains has a chance to pounce. She walks the legs off herself, the wheels off the pram. She moves through a London where, for a few days anyhow, everything seems to be happening in reverse.

Evacuees come out of train stations and climb back onto coach buses. In parks, scars begin to settle over refilled trenches. Sandbags, damp and fat as slugs from the rain, are removed, leaving rooftops and walls looking raw and deserted.

She goes into one of the new American milk bars when it's time to feed the baby. Or a Lyons Corner House café whenever a nappy needs changing. For a day or two after Munich she hears strangers everywhere having the same loud, long conversations. She hears the small uncertain silences in between sentences.

She learns how to cry in public. Looking into shop windows on Oxford Street, or standing outside picture houses studying photographic stills, or sheltering under the trees in the Strand watching the traffic and picking black taxis out of the shoal.

Late afternoon she returns to Kensington Gardens, where she wanders around or sits on a bench staring at the dusk tighten around her. Until the all-out whistle smashes her thoughts and it's time to go back to Mrs Mains. The next morning she will think about Chelsea again. There is always something else to be done. Something more urgent. Usually something to buy, and Bella is often glad she took Mrs Cardiff's advice to change her money to sterling. She goes to Smith's to buy a book about babies; how to feed, change and wean them. Then she has to buy all the things the book tells her a well-minded baby needs. Another day is spent buying a charcoal-grey suit and black overcoat that Mrs Mains says makes her look like a widow. 'You don't want to go putting the mockers on your old man now do you, my love?'

The day after she buys her new black coat she goes into a second-hand shop to give away her continental clothes and finds herself in a queue of refugees who are selling the coats off their backs. She tries to tell the assistant that she doesn't want any money, that she's not selling, but giving the clothes away. The stupid woman insists on bargaining anyway, speaking slowly and loudly into her face. In the end Bella just leaves, giving the bag of clothes to a little black-eyed girl who is sitting on the kerb outside the shop, waiting for her mother.

She is frequently in queues these days, and usually surrounded by refugees. In the poste restante line or at the international telephone exchange. She probably looks like one herself by now: a furtive look over a shoulder; a face with a fading suntan; a reluctance to answer when spoken to; a jump, barely contained, if someone comes too close on the street.

The first few times she checks for a letter she is cautious, asking only that the name Barrett be checked. Then, as it becomes more widely accepted that the war is off, and the man behind the counter grows more disinterested, she chances her other names: Magrini and Stuart. But it doesn't matter which name she gives him, he always come back empty-handed.

Two weeks since she's arrived and there's no trouble putting a call through to Bordighera. The crisis is over, the threat of war has passed. Her heart starts to thump even before she's told which number booth she should go into. The light springs on, she pulls the door behind her, tucks the baby into her arms and picks up the receiver.

Bella listens to the phone ringing into Villa Lami. She imagines it crashing into the silence of the hall. Spreading out to the rooms that lead off it: kitchen, pantry, dining room, cloakroom. She follows its course up the first flight of stairs, the Signora's sitting room and bedroom. Weaker on the second flight up; barely audible by the time it gets to the library, her room, Alec's. She hears it roll towards the windows and French doors in an attempt to slip through and tumble down over the terraces, into the garden. But she knows by now the windows are shuttered, the sound of the telephone is trapped inside the house, away from the garden, the street, the gate.

'I'm sorry, madam, there's no reply from that number, try again later.'

'Yes, thank you, I will.'

A few days later she does it again; sits and waits and listens and follows. It's like sending her own heartbeat through the empty house.

Mrs Mains has stopped asking questions or passing remarks, even for something as obvious as the lack of a phone call or letter from a husband in Paris. She lets it be known that Bella will always be welcome, without pinning her down to a date or a large, upfront payment. She offers to provide meals even though she doesn't normally run an 'all-in' house, but Bella says she prefers to eat out. She can't do enough when it comes to the baby; insisting the sink downstairs be used to wash out the nappies, dragging out an old ham pot to boil them in first and allowing her kitchen to be turned into a bunting of steaming nappies. She even suggests babysitting anytime Bella fancies a bit of time on her own. 'The pictures maybe or someone perhaps you might care to visit?'

'No, thank you, Mrs Mains, I'd rather stay with the baby.'

'Just as you please, my love.'

She shows kindness after kindness, in return only asks for an hour or two's company in the evenings, and every day Bella dislikes her a little bit more.

At the end of October Mrs Mains moves her to a room at the top of the house. She tells Bella it will be much better up there; what has to be endured in extra stairs will be compensated by privacy. There's even a gas ring in case she wants to make herself a cup of tea or heat little Katherine's bottle. Like her own little flat, that's what it will be. The reason she wants to move Bella is that she has decided to open her house to refugees. Mrs Mains has already had a word with her remaining long-term guests and is very glad to say they have no objections. She wants to have it all up and running by Christmas. There'll be furniture to move, partitions to put up, a temporary kitchen to allow these people to eat.

'Not everyone can afford to nosh out every day, you know,' she says and Bella wonders if she's taking a dig at her.

'My husband was a Jew – you didn't know that, Mrs B, did you? Oh yes. He didn't bother with all the palaver, skullcaps and synagogues and so forth, but he was a Jew just the same. Just think of it, if our Alice had married a European instead of her Australian cowboy, she could be living out there in Europe somewhere; Germany, Austria, Czechoslovakia, Italy, even France. Anything could happen really. Her being a halfo–halfo.'

The room at the top is a large converted attic. Four and a half flights up, its windows give over rooftops and distant black trees. It holds a double brass bed and two singles, as well as a cot. Mrs Mains says the singles will be shifted downstairs for her refugees as soon as their rooms are ready but the cot of course will do for Katherine, who will have grown out of her Moses basket before they know it. There's a bathroom next door with a geyser in good working order and a walk-in storage cupboard beside it, where, one day when Bella is out, Mrs Mains has the 'girls' move all her luggage, including the two suitcases which have remained strapped up and packed since her arrival.

When she comes back to the house Judy is in the hallway holding her lower back like a pregnant septuagenarian and resentfully glaring.

Bella looks out the window of her new quarters and sees brown foggy days. She sees the flutter of torchlights on street corners and phantoms groping their way along by the railings. She sees skies that stay on the same low wattage all day. She feels a sun that blinds, but gives little warmth. She feels rain that seeps into her bones.

One day in the post office the man behind the counter says, 'I think you may have struck oil today.'

She knows his face so well by now, the spots around his mouth, the inner pink rim of his eyes. She's surprised when she hears him speak with a phlegmy Liverpool accent. This is all she can think about as he goes behind the counter and returns with an envelope – how unexpected his accent is.

The envelope is addressed to Mrs Barrett and has been posted in London. There is nothing inside, only an address in Pimlico.

*

Bella knocks at a door in a cul de sac off the Pimlico Road. There's a sign in the window – 'Catholic Mission Closed Until Further Notice'. A nun comes out and helps her bring the pram into the hall, then through a side door into a dingy brown room; two kitchen chairs and one long table at the wall piled with religious pamphlets.

The nun then invites her to sit down. 'I'd offer tea,' she continues, 'but we're all packed up – I'm off to India tomorrow, this place is to close down.'

Bella nods.

The nun smiles. 'Would you like to smoke? We have an ashtray.'

'No, sister, I'm fine.'

The nun takes the seat opposite and lays her hands on her lap. 'How is the child?' she asks.

'Very well.'

'You've been able to manage?'

'Yes,' Bella says.

'Good. Now, Mrs Barrett, the reason you are here.' The nun shuffles her seat a little closer to Bella. 'We have had word from our sister convent in Italy, have in fact been asked to pass a message to you. I'm presuming you will know and understand what it means.'

'Yes, sister.'

She smiles again. 'Now, it appears that the woman you work for…'

'Signora Ta—'

'I don't know her name and it's probably best not to tell me, after all our sisters are still in Italy and the less we know, the fewer lies we have to tell.'

'Yes, of course,' Bella says.

The nun resumes. 'The woman has still not been located although it is almost certain that she is in Germany.'

'Oh. And the boy?'

'The boy and the man were both detained. The boy is, so far as we know, in an orphanage for Jewish children.'

Bella presses a fingernail into her wrist. 'Where?'

'It doesn't matter where – he could in any case be moved to another orphanage.'

'Where?' she asks again.

'Mrs Barrett, may I ask about your own papers? That is to say, your original papers?'

'I left them in Bordighera, as I was told to do. They're to be sent to me in due course.'

'It's just that the maid there said she couldn't find them.'

'Oh? Well, I don't have them.'

'You must understand there is no possible way you can return to Italy.'

Bella nods.

'You have committed a serious crime, travelling on false papers, taking a child from the country, not to mention money and other valuables. You will be arrested before you get down from the train. No matter which papers you use. Do I make myself clear? You will put yourself and the baby at risk. *And* you will also jeopardize whatever steps have already been taken to help the boy.'

'Yes, I see, sister.'

The nun waits for a moment. 'The man who was with you was also arrested, although we understand he is to be sent to the south of Italy where he is to be detained indefinitely.'

'To *confino*?'

'*Confino* – is that the name of a place?'

'No, it's a sort of Italian exile to a remote place, usually in the south. The conditions are not – well, some say it's worse than prison.'

'In that case, yes, it is *confino*. Would you like a drink of water, Mrs Barrett?'

'No, thank you.'

'You have a choice. You may give the baby to me and I can see that she is taken care of in one of our convents here, that is until such a time as her mother reappears. Or…'

'Or?'

'Are you sure I can't get you a glass of water? You're very pale.'

'No, sister. Honestly.'

'Or you can keep the baby, but only if you agree to go to your father's house where we can find you, when we need to do so.'

Bella reaches out and holds the handlebar of the pram. She feels it rock and slightly squeal under her hand. 'Yes, I'll do that.'

'Which, Mrs Barrett?'

'I'll go to my father's house.'

'If you're sure? It is quite a responsibility looking after someone else's child.'

'Yes, I am sure.'

'Very well. I'll need your father's address, Mrs Barrett. I'm afraid we don't have it. As your employer is missing and your papers were unavailable.'

'Of course, yes.'

Bella stands up. 'Will he be all right?'

'The boy?'

'Yes. Will they take care of him?'

'Oh, I'm sure—'

'You see, he's very, he's a little nervous, not too good with strangers and—'

'I'm sure they'll treat him kindly, Mrs Barrett.'

'Thank you, sister.'

'The address, Mrs Barrett? Your father's address?'

'Oh goodness, yes of course. I'm sorry.'

The nun puts a piece of paper and a pen on the table. Bella notices then the red crescent mark from her fingernail is embedded into her wrist. Yet her hand as she writes is rock steady. She is careful not to hesitate, not even for a second.

'There you are, sister,' she says, holding out the paper.

The nun smiles and accepts the false address.

*

In a downstairs room Gracie Fields is yelling out of a radio. From the house next door comes the yap of a highly strung dog. Bella stands at the window in her room, breathless from her journey up the stairs; the weight of the baby in her arms, and the weight of fear in her chest. And she hears that too: her breath, the dog, Gracie Fields, her fear, louder and louder.

Soon the baby will wake. Gradually Bella calms herself, turns from the window and washes her face. She lays the baby on a towel on the bed and opens the nappy to a sharp, warm smell of ammonia. The skin on the scrawny little backside is raw. Bella folds the nappy into itself and puts it in a basin on the floor. Then she opens the baby book and begins to follow step-by-step instructions: washing, drying, plastering with cream, squirting clumsy puffs of talcum powder on what is referred to as 'the area'.

Intent on this task she doesn't notice the baby has woken until she happens to glance up and find her little eyes watching her.

'What?' she says. 'What are you looking at?'

At the sound of her voice the baby begins kicking her arms and legs. At first she moves slowly; deep, concentrated movements. The longer Bella looks at her the more force and speed she uses, until it looks as if she's running for her life.

Bella holds one tiny foot in the palm of her hand, feels it push and push again. For the first time she really looks at this baby: Alec's half-sister, the Signora's daughter. This Italian, half-Jewish child lying on the bed watching her.

Bella stands up and goes to the mirror. Her skin, tinged a slight yellow, almost back to its old pasty self. She sees her father's green eyes in a face that might have been pretty but somehow never quite was. It's her mother's face now: thin, hard, worried. It shows every day of its thirty-seven years, and perhaps a deal more.

'I will never be married,' she says to it. 'I will never have my own child.'

Behind her, through the mirror, the baby croons away to herself, still joyously waving her arms and legs.

Bella goes back to the child, dresses, reswaddles her, leaving the hands free, before putting her into the big bed. She tidies everything away, washes her hands, then gets in beside the baby. She knows now if she goes home to Chelsea her father will make her do the right thing, give up this baby. And even if he can be persuaded to let the baby stay on, one day a knock will come on the door. And even if it doesn't, she will always, always be waiting.

There is a winter chill in the darkening room, the coils on the electric fire beam orange onto the rug. Outside on the street she can hear the giddy chatter of trainee typists coming from the Pitman's college down the road. Further out is the purr of traffic on the Bayswater Road. A gate clicks out on the street.

When she looks down again the child is sucking the thumb of one hand, and has laid the other hand on Bella's shoulder. A baby gesture that means nothing, but there is something companionable about it, something reassuring and comical.

'Oh, Katherine,' Bella says, and kisses her on the forehead.

A few seconds later, the baby is asleep.

It grows dark and Bella gets up and puts on the light. She goes out to the landing, pulls all the luggage from the walk-in cupboard, hauls the two full suitcases up onto one of the single beds, unstraps them, then pushes their lids back.

The first sight comes as a shock: seaside stripes, Alec's bent plimsoles, his brand new tennis sweater still wrapped in tissue with the name of the shop, *Farini di Bordighera*, printed on it. Bella snaps the lid down and has to sit for a few moments on the corner of the bed with her back to the suitcases. Her mind is dazzled with grief. She waits for a while, then gets up and empties both cases.

Now she is moving. Deciding what can and cannot be taken as she goes along, she hears her voice say, 'Yes. No. Yes. No. No. No. Yes.' Two separate piles begin to grow. Whenever she comes across a money-tuck she puts it on the double bed beside the baby. She doesn't stop until the larger of the suitcases is refilled, restrapped and dragged back out to the cupboard.

She comes back to the room and sees, behind a hedge of money-tucks, the shape of the sleeping baby.

Much later, after Katherine has woken again, been fed and put down for the night. After she has spent her hour with Mrs Mains, told her she has decided to go home to Bournemouth and asked for permission to leave one of the suitcases for a more convenient time. After she has said her goodbyes, drunk her cocoa, said her goodbyes again – she comes back to the attic room and opens Edward's knapsack.

Her hand goes over his few possessions: shirts, collars, underwear, socks, cigarettes. She removes nothing, except for one silver sea horse from a pair of cufflinks and a long page with writing on it that she comes across almost by accident, folded into an inside pocket. It's the letter she wrote to him on her last night in Bordighera on Signora Tassi's handmade Amalfi paper. She unfolds it and sees he's written a reply on the back of the page. She has never seen so much of his writing at once. Every inch of the page has been used, starting at the top and bringing it right down to the bottom and his initial. She goes back to the top and wonders why his letter should begin mid-sentence, until turning over the page she finds his first words there, his 'My dearest Bella' starting his letter, where she had ended hers.

DUBLIN, 1940

June

SHE IS IN WOOLWORTHS in Dublin when she hears that Italy has joined Hitler in the war against the allies. It's the day before Katherine's second birthday and she has brought her into the shop hoping the child will light on something that can be bought behind her back and given to her next day as a surprise. But she is two years old and everything surprises her.

They have just come from feeding the ducks in Stephen's Green, Katherine trying to get into the pond to force-feed the bread to the unfortunate creatures. In the end Bella had to lure her out of the green and down Grafton Street with the promise of sweeties.

Katherine, now overtired, is having a last spurt of energy. She runs up and down the aisles of Woolworths, pointing at rubber dolls, train sets, ashtrays, kettles, egg cups and holy statues. Everything is bestowed with equal love and admiration. It's a quiet time in the shop, shortly after the lunch hour, and the June heat is keeping customers away. One pregnant woman at the sweet counter, one old man peering at wallets, two young girls giggling over hair ribbons.

The sales assistants are getting a kick out of Katherine. She is a funny, outgoing child, tearing up and down the shop, singing her little head off, throwing her arms open to anyone willing to catch her, coming back sometimes to slap her hand on Bella's skirt before running off again.

'You have your hands full there.' The older assistant smiles and Bella smiles back and says, 'That's for sure.'

'Go on,' the younger assistant is saying to Katherine. 'Give us an oul song there and I'll give you a choccie.'

Katherine is screaming out a primitive rendition of 'Baa Baa Black Sheep' when the manager comes back from his late lunch and announces the news.

'Well, that's Italy in,' he says, striding through the shop, newspaper under his arm. 'That's Italy in the war. That's the Eyetalians for you now.'

'With Hitler, sir?' the young assistant asks.

'Who else, Bridget? Who else now would you think would be up to Mussolini's mark? The wonder is he contained himself this long.'

Her legs go from under her when she hears the manager's news, and all the things she has put out of her mind come screaming back into it. The Signora in Germany. Alec in a Jewish orphanage. Edward. The pregnant woman clutches her bag of sweets and walks over to ask if she's all right. The old man looks up from his wallets. The older assistant tells the younger one to bring out a chair. Katherine comes tearing down the shop, lays her curly head on Bella's lap, nuzzles it there for a second. 'Mammy,' she says, then scuttles off again.

The manager calls out for someone to bring a glass of water.

Edward's Letter

Villa Lami, Bordighera
26 September 1938

Edward,
Thank you for your kind offer to go with us as far as Menton or even Monte Carlo. However, I have decided to go it alone. I will take my chances with the children.

    Whatever direction you decide to take, I wish you all the luck you deserve.

B.

My dearest Bella,
I am writing this letter in the hope that you will never have to read it. Because if it's in your hand now, it means something will have gone badly wrong. As you know by now, I decided to go with you after all. In any case, my things are on the bed ready to be packed and I'm here at my desk, writing this letter, instead of in a bar,

hugging a bottle. It's the middle of the night and soon I will leave Villa L. There are arrangements I've made, which now must be cancelled. I am laughing to myself – *at* myself rather, that after all these years I should come to this. But I can't leave you alone, not with Alec the way he is, and a baby on top of everything else. I have to try. And I promise I will try. These past few hours I've been thinking about what you said, that I never trusted you enough to let you get to know me, and that when it came to it I always closed the door in your face. Well, if you want to know, if it makes you believe I do care for you.

In that case – my parents. They started with a bargain – her fine English artistic ways in exchange for his money. In the end both found themselves tricked. My mother was a minor opera singer who, along with notions of grandeur, had an insatiable need for endless disputes with colleagues and short-lived friends. A prima donna who would never be more than a *terza*. My father, for all his coarseness, was weak in these matters, and for years backed her up against his better judgement. I hated him for that, but realize now he had no choice. He had to convince himself that her outrages were somehow justified, or face the fact of her mental instability. Perhaps I've inherited that! Later his weakness soured into resentment, against me mostly, the child most like her, the one sent to an English boarding school in the hope that I might become even more like her! He made no bones about it. I was a waster, and probably not even his. Louise (my sister) his pride and joy. And yet I can't blame my parents for me. And it's a sad state of affairs when we can't even blame our own parents.

Back to us. You are reading this letter and something has happened, most likely to me. Either I have been lifted, or I have decided that it has become too dangerous to carry on and have left you somewhere. In the middle of the night or when you least expect it, I have slithered off, leaving this letter behind where you may find

362

it. You see, that's the thing, when it comes right down to it, I will save my own skin. Above all else, I will do that. And for this reason I know I don't love you and I feel that's what you want now, that's what you expect, after last night. What nearly happened. My saying this will cut your pride to the quick, but it's too late now for the usual rules of engagement, and besides we know each other too well for such games. I don't believe it's in my nature to love. Or to sacrifice myself to love anyway. It's simply not there. If it's any consolation I have come close with you, or as close to it as someone like me can do. And you have been my friend, Bella. You have always been that. In many ways, this is stronger than any romantic love could ever hope to be. If you feel any regret for me, any sense of loss, I can tell you how to cure it – find out about me – believe me, it will soon get you over it. I left Dublin in 1924 on 5 August. Go to the newspaper archive in the library, you will find all you need to know.

Wherever I am, whether taken, or by my own free will, rest assured I am thinking of you. My dear, brave Bella, my friend. I am thinking of you and Alec and the baby, wishing you safe and well and wishing I were a different sort of man.

Think badly of me. I deserve it.

E.

PART EIGHT

Anna

1995

August

NONNA DIED WITHOUT FUSS at four in the morning; not an unusual hour, it seems, for old people to 'snuff it', as she might have put it herself. The phone rang into my dream in the dead of night just as I was standing in the back of a rush-hour bus. 'Excuse me,' I kept saying to the standing-room-only passengers, 'can you let me through please? Can you let me through? That's the phone ringing now, to tell me my grandmother has died.' I had been shoving and pushing to get through the crowd, the sweat running off me, and it had all seemed so normal. Then I woke up, the duvet over my face.

Of course, it had to be Bunty. 'At least she's not suffering anymore,' she said.

'Well, thank you for letting me know,' I calmly replied. 'Thank you for that now.'

'It was very peaceful, Anna, she went in her sleep.'

And I felt like saying, 'She's hasn't opened her eyes in months, how the fuck else was she going to go – roller blading?'

'Oh yes, that's good to know, thank you again.'

'You'll be in touch about—?'

'Yes, yes. I'll give you a call tomorrow. I mean later on, today.'

'I'm presuming you won't want her buried in the hospital cemetery?'

'No.'

'That you'll be making your own arrangements?'

'Yes.'

'I'll put her in the mortuary so.'

'Yes, if you wouldn't mind. Goodbye.'

I put down the phone and decided to get under the shower. I'd been back living in Pembroke Road since the beginning of the summer and still hadn't fully reacquainted myself with the moods of the house, like the fact that the immersion needed to be on at least twenty minutes for the miracle of hot water to occur. And so at around five o'clock on a chilly morning in late July, on learning that I had just lost the last member of my family, the only person in fact with whom I had any sort of a relationship, I found myself gasping and gibbering under an ice-cold shower. I don't know why, but it had seemed the only thing to do at the time, and getting warm afterwards at least gave me something to do.

A while later I was skinning the back of my legs on the heat of a full-blast radiator, drinking tea and chain-smoking, my mouth chasing the trembling butt between my fingertips like a baby going after a nipple. It was bright by then and I stayed listening to the household shifting above me. The clatter of a toilet roll holder, the flush of a toilet, feet crossing floors, a rattle of clothes hangers, a television breakfast show. Another flushing chain. Each tenant in their own secretive little corner, imagining themselves to be private. I made myself another cup of tea, this time adding a tot of whiskey, wrapped myself in a duvet and crawled into the corner of the sofa.

Upstairs, the door of flat number three opened and I followed the footsteps down the stairs, through the hall and out of the house. Then the car; a beep to open it, a thud to close it, and a rev or two to take it away. A few seconds later, the next tenant – flat number six; a heavier step, taking slightly longer to come downstairs, but more or less the same routine. And for a moment I felt that maybe I should be telling someone. Maybe the next time I heard a step on the stair I should waddle out in my duvet and stop someone in the hall and say, 'Excuse me, just thought you might like to know – the woman who owns this house? Well, she's just died.'

But then I thought, To hell with it, they wouldn't know who I was talking about anyway. And besides, I was the woman who owned this house now.

*

We buried her from Haddington Road church. I say we – there were other people present but there was no one with me, as such. Not enough to turn *me* into a *we*, anyhow. Still, I was glad that such things still existed as old ladies and First Fridays, otherwise it might have been even bleaker. In that near-empty cave of a church.

When I arrived Bunty was already standing in the porch. I nearly died when I saw her there. She was with two others from the hospital: a little ginger-bob junior nurse I knew vaguely and a slender brown man with soft chocolate eyes whom I'd never seen before in my life. A male nurse – a term Nonna used to hate because she said it always had her expecting Dick Emery or one of those chaps off the English telly to come prancing along.

As I walked into the church I noticed another woman, about my age, sitting on the left, halfway up the aisle. It took me a few seconds to twig it was Melanie Connors, a girl who was in my class at school. I'd heard from another ex-classmate, recently met in the doctor's waiting room, that Melanie had fallen on rough times and had taken to going to the funerals of anyone she half knew or had heard of. On the make apparently: a funeral always being a good spot for free drinks and a bit of company or even to tap a few quid from the bereaved, which, according to report-backs, wasn't beyond her either.

As the priest began to run through the funeral rites, his voice fluttering in and out of pockets of empty space, I kept thinking about Melanie

369

and what she was up to back there, and how out of the hour or so that day in the doctor's waiting room, gossiping about old schoolmates – the engineer who had gone out to Africa, the solicitor who had recently been on the news, the mousy one who had run off and left her husband and kids – it had been Melanie, taking her chances at the funerals of strangers, who had stolen the show. Even so, I pretended not to know her on the way up the aisle, and by the time the coffin was hoisted back down on the undertakers' shoulders, she'd gone. Melanie, clearly no fool, wasn't about to waste her time on a funeral of such paltry promise.

The three nurses ended up coming to the cemetery with me. I got the feeling they hadn't intended to go any further than the mass but had changed their minds on realizing that the few old biddies posted here and there along the church benches, like counters on an abacus, had nothing to do with me, and that otherwise I would be burying my grandmother on my own. And so Bunty insisted on paying off the taxi I had waiting outside and we all went together in her Fiat Punto car.

The traffic was slow on the Harold's Cross road and we found ourselves stuck in behind another funeral so well attended, the hearse was no longer in view. I watched with envy as each car slipped out of the line and over the road into the cemetery. Faces through glass, stony or weeping; drifts of cigarette smoke whiffling out the gap of a car window or up through a sunroof; a last-minute butt flick out onto the road. Then it was our turn: Nonna's hearse, followed by its pathetic one-car cortège.

As the gate of Mount Jerome came into sight I saw an elderly lady standing near the flower stall, nonchalantly leaning on a Zimmer frame as if it were a garden fence. For every second or third car that came her way she lifted her hand in a halt and said something in through the passenger window. She allowed Nonna's hearse to pass undisturbed, blessing herself as it did, then stopped us.

'Do you mind if I ask the name of the deceased?' she said.

'Barrett,' I replied.

'Barrett? Oh, thank God for that. I thought I was after missing her.'

Nurse Bunty put her into the car and the male nurse gave up his seat and offered to follow the car on foot.

The old lady turned out to be Dolores and I was appalled to have forgotten all about Nonna's only friend. I apologized over and over, until Dolores more or less told me to shut up. She had read the announcement in the paper, she said, and was dismayed to see the mass was in Haddington Road because she would never have made it that far and was fecked if she'd pay one of those robbing taxi men to take her there, but then luckily enough she had continued to read on down the death notice and was thrilled then to find, after all, that the burial would be here, in Mount Jerome, because she only lived down the road, a manageable distance for someone who travelled by Zimmer frame. 'All the same,' she finished by saying, 'isn't the weather terrible disappointing for this time of the year?'

Nonna had been dead to me for some months. Dead, if still breathing. And realistically I should have been prepared. I'd often heard mourners say the likes of, 'I can't believe I'll never speak to so-and-so again,' or 'I can't bear the idea of never hearing so-and-so's voice again.' But I had grown used to the lack of communication. I had grown used to the absence of her. So why was I crying from the pit of my stomach, making a show of myself in front of Dolores and the three nurses? Why was I hurling tears after the coffin as it fumbled like a rusty elevator going all the way down?

Everyone so kind to me: hankies, shoulder pats, a little hug, an arm to link. And all the while I kept thinking – I wish they'd all just fuck off home and leave me alone.

Afterwards we went in for a drink. Dolores came as far as the pub, but disappeared while I was in the toilet. 'Where is she?' I whined when I came back out and found her gone. 'Did she not leave a number, did she not even leave an address?'

'Ah, she was tired, God love her, ' Nurse Bunty said.

I sulked over a whiskey or two, then forgot about Dolores as the conversation came round to Nonna.

I told them all the registrar had said about Nonna never having given birth. Then I told them all about the stuff I had found in the box in the nursing home storeroom.

'Oh my God!' Bunty said. 'It's obvious, she was Jewish. She had to be. Rose Barrett – would that be a Jewish name? I mean, come on – two sets of identity papers? Just before the Second World War? And do you know what that means – we've probably just buried her in the wrong graveyard!'

'Or she could have been a spy maybe!' ginger-bob suggested.

'Oh, such intrigue!' the male nurse, a Bengali named Dilip, deliciously beamed.

*

For a week or so after the funeral I played with Nonna's effects, placing everything of possible interest on the table and making notes on my little finds. Trying to get the clues to follow each other – it kept me going, I suppose. It put in an evening.

I would gather my cigarettes, lighter, ashtray, glass of wine or whiskey, depending on what form I was in, a pen and paper. And off I'd go. The box contained of two sets of identity papers. One set, obviously Italian, in the name of Magrini: husband, wife, a boy called Alfredo or Alberto – the writing was slightly frayed, so I couldn't really tell – and a baby named Edda. The other set was English in the name of Barrett, which was Nonna's name. Mrs Rose Barrett, husband James Barrett, also naming a boy, John, and a baby, Katherine – my mother's name.

The address was in Burnmouth. I had never heard Nonna mention such a place, nor anyone named John.

On both sets of papers, including a *carte de tourisme* for France, there was a place for photographs. But every photograph had been removed.

There were a few other items in Nonna's box of tricks besides the identity papers. A silver harmonica and an old comic book in Italian. I found a letter from a hotel in Nice addressed to Signor Magrini. And a receipt from another hotel in Nice made out to Mr Barrett. These were all dated in and around the end of September 1938. Finally, I found a letter. I suppose you could say, two letters in one.

The letter had been written in a place called Bordighera, or at least the name Bordighera was printed on top and the name of a house or hotel maybe – Villa Lami. It was addressed to someone called Edward and sent from someone who signed off as B. A reply using the same paper was written to someone called Bella. Alec was mentioned in the letter. The same name that Mona the tea lady had said Nonna used to sometimes mention when she was rambling in her mind.

I looked down my list, adding the suggestions the nurses had made.

MAGRINI

Father – Marco
Mother – Anna (am I called after her?)
Son – Alfredo or Alberto
Daughter – Edda

BARRETT

Father – James (Nonna's husband)
Mother – Rose (Nonna) (Jewish?)
Son – John (?)
Daughter – Katherine (my mother)
Who is Alec? Who is Bella? Who is Edward?

*

A few days after the funeral I called the solicitor. Nonna's man had retired a long time ago and I was put on to a younger and less personable version.

He thought I was just being greedy. 'I'm about to send you a letter, Miss Moore,' he said, 'to ask you to make an appointment for the reading of the will. The week after next, I thought perhaps might—. You do realize what with probate and so forth it could be some time before—?'

'Oh yes, that's fine, but I just wondered if you could tell me if there would be any surprises.'

'Surprises, Miss Moore?'

'Yes, like have any funny names turned up?'

'Funny names, Miss Moore?'

'Any names, other than mine, is what I mean.'

'You're the sole benefactor. Your name and the name of the executor – a Mrs Dolores Purcell, I believe, if you give me a moment I could check. I don't have her address but I have a telephone number, my secretary was just going to give her a—'

'No. That's all right. I'll phone again about the appointment, bye now.'

'Would you like me to enclose a copy?'

'A copy?'

'A copy of the will, Miss Moore.'

'If you want to.'

*

It was easy enough to track Dolores down. I went back to Mount Jerome, imagined how far I'd get on a Zimmer frame, decided the answer was not far at all, and then went into the nearest corner shop.

'A woman in a red raincoat,' I began to explain to a blank face behind the counter. 'She has a fringe of white hair and black glasses. She wears runners.'

'A lot of oulones around here would fit that description, love, including meself, except I don't have a red coat.'

'She has a Zimmer frame and her name is Dolores.'

'Ah Dolores! Why didn't you just say so? She lives there.'

I turned around. 'Where?'

'There, look out there, there she is now.' The woman came around the counter, stuck her arm out the door of her shop and pointed across the narrow side street where Dolores, framed in a mantilla of white curtain netting, was frantically waving.

'I hope you don't mind?' I began as Dolores shuffled back from the front door to let me in.

'Ah, not at all, not all, come in. Save me having to phone you up.'

'Were you going to?'

'Of course I was.'

'Because you heard from the solicitor?'

'Oh that, and reasons besides.'

I was only in the door when she turned me around and sent me like a child back over to the shop, two fifty-pence pieces pressed firmly into my hand to pay for two cakes.

'Oh, there's no need really, Dolores,' I began.

'Sure we have to have cake with our coffee, Anna,' she said, looking at me as if I were half mad.

'All right, but let me pay for them.'

'It's my house. Don't embarrass me now just because I haven't the use of me legs.'

She made coffee in an espresso pot and showed me her little garden. While the coffee brewed I was brought around plant to plant, like a visitor being introduced at a family wedding. Then she sent me inside for a tray she had set when I was at the shops. We sat at her garden table.

'Nice coffee, Dolores. And I love the cups and saucers.'

'Isn't it? I can't stand that oul instant muck. Since Italy, all those years ago, I'll only drink the good stuff. I bought the cups in Brown Thomas. In the sale. Cost an arm and a leg even so.'

'Oh. You were in Italy?'

'Only for six months but it doesn't take long to get to you. It spoils some people for life, you know – in a good way, I mean. So, Anna, what have you got to say to me?'

I told her all about the box; the papers, the harmonica, the comic. Then I threw out my Jewish theory, and on a lighter note the suggestion that

Nonna had been a spy. Finally I showed her the papers, which I had brought along, as well as the letter addressed to Bella. When she'd finished reading it, I asked if she knew or had heard of anyone by that name.

'Mmm,' Dolores said, shaking her head, 'but now that could be just a term of endearment. *Bella* meaning beautiful in Italian, and they use it sort of affectionately you know. You don't even have to be beautiful, just beloved. Or at least? Do you know what you do now, before we go any further – go up to my old room at the top of the stairs, a door straight in front of you, and in the end of the wardrobe you'll see this big square handbag, a tan-coloured, old-fashioned yoke. Bring it down to me.'

'You don't recognize the writing – no?' I asked her.

'No. I mean it's hard to say, it's print isn't it? Could be anyone.'

'Yes, that's what I thought. I don't think it was Nonna's but as you say. Anyway I'll get the bag.'

When I got back Dolores was smoking. 'Show,' she said and I gave her the bag. 'Anna, I should tell you first off, I didn't know your granny all that well. Certainly not in Italy, just in case you're expecting anything. I met her on the train going out of Italy, her and the baby – that'd be your mammy. She was in trouble. That's all I knew, and so me and this other couple, well, we wanted to help her, without being too involved, you know. We all thought war was a matter of days away, nobody doubted it really. And you have to help your own in time of war. But now, Anna, I'd have to say, I'm not sure I believed everything your granny said, even then, to be honest. But I pitied her, you know. I pitied her.'

'So you didn't know her in Italy at all?' I try not to show my disappointment.'

'No. But there could well be something in your Jewish theory though, because that Mussolini was only after bringing out the anti-Jew laws and Jews were making a run for it from all over Italy. As for your spy theory? Don't make me laugh. She wasn't cool enough to be a spy. If you'd seen her the first time I did, you'd know what I mean.'

'What about here, when you used to meet her here, did she ever say anything, you know?'

'No. It was missus this, missus that. Neither of us got too personal. But now I do remember this one time – and if she was Jewish, this might make sense – I met her in Wynne's Hotel for tea, and while we were waiting on the girl to bring the tray I happened to mention something about a programme I'd seen on the telly a few nights previous regarding the Italian Jews and how so many thousands of them had been rounded up and sent to the German camps after the occupation – you know?'

'I'm afraid I don't know a lot about Italy and the Second World War.'

'Well, the way it was, the Italians were in with the Jerries for a couple of years, then they changed over to the Allies. That made them enemies. So Germany occupied Italy, and first thing went after the Jews – are you with me now?'

'Sort of.'

'Anyway, I happened to mention this to your granny and how a few thousand of the Italian Jews had been rounded up and sent off to these camps where they died. Well, you want to have seen her. One minute she was grand, and the next minute she's this pain in her stomach and has to go home. Not a biscuit, not even a sup of tea had passed her lips. So. There you are. Just thought I'd mention it. Do you know whose bag this is?'

'Hers, I suppose?'

'That's right. She gave it to me to mind for her, a good few year ago now.'

'Do you know what's in it?' I asked.

'Ah yes, I do know. Even though I said I wouldn't look – not that she asked me to promise – but, well, to be honest, the older you get the nosier you become, and the less point there seems to be in keeping secrets. It was so long since I'd seen her, I thought she was dead. Anyway, it's yours now. Here, take a look at this.'

The first thing she pulled out was a bank book in the name of Anabelle Stuart. The opening balance was in the amount of five hundred sterling, the date the account had been opened was 1936. The bank was in London.

'Who's Anabelle Stuart?'

Dolores shoved her cigarette into the corner of her mouth and closed one eye. She poked her finger at the name on the bank book, and then back at the letter. 'Bella – Anabelle? Short for? Ah, who knows? I'd never have even thought of it but you showed me the letter. Tell you what but, five hundred quid – now that was worth a right few bob then. And here – this mean anything?'

Dolores handed me a silver sea horse. 'What is it – an earring?' I asked.

'No. A cufflink. Only the one, mind.'

The last thing in the bag was an envelope. She put out her cigarette, opened it and emptied it onto the table. A group of small passport-size photographs slipped out. The missing photographs from the identity papers.

'Well, there you are now,' Dolores said as we pieced them together and studied the official stamps on each one. 'Same faces, different names and nationalities. One set obviously has to be false. What do you make of that now?'

'The woman is her. I'm sure of it.'

'It certainly is.'

'The man – I don't know.'

'Me neither. Would it be your grandfather?'

'I don't know. I never saw a picture of him.'

'Go away?'

'No. And there's no picture of the boy.'

'No,' Dolores echoed. 'No picture of the boy.'

*

Dolores phoned me about a week later. 'Do you know what I'm only after remembering?' she said, as I picked up the phone.

'What?'

'The harmonica. There was a harmonica in the compartment on the train. She said it belonged to the boy. But later when she'd calmed down a bit and I questioned her further about it, she didn't answer me.'

'Right. But there was only her and the baby on the train?'

'She insisted the husband had been arrested at the border. I don't know, I only ever saw your granny and your baby mother. And the only time she mentioned the boy was with the harmonica. Here – did you ever find out about your man?'

'What man?'

'Him in the letter. Did you go to the library, find out what he did?'

'No. I might wait for a while before I do. But listen, I'm thinking of going over there, to Italy.'

'Good for you, Anna! Where will you go?'

'To Bordighera, you know, the town that's in the address on the letter? Because I was thinking, as you said, it's obvious that one set of those papers has to be false. But the letter seems real, doesn't it? I mean, why forge a letter like that and why say those things in it? Anyway, I was going to give you a call to say goodbye.'

'Well, good luck to you.'

'I don't really know why I'm going or what I'll find there, but.'

'Ah, you'll always find something.'

'You take care, Dolores. Will I write, let you know how I get on?'

'If you feel like it.'

'Well, I'll see you when I get back anyway, tell you all about it.'

'When you get back? Sure I'll be well dead by then,' she said and cackled like a witch down the phone.

*

I may have a fever; my head is banging and my throat sand-dry. The nightdress is stuck to me and there's a sweat-moist patch on the bed where I lie. I don't know this room; high, narrow, shaft-like. Except for a diagonal ladder of light leaning against one wall and falling across the bottom corner of the bed, the room is in darkness. Overhead a ceiling fan huffs.

From the street, a chaos of sounds. Car doors, beeping horns, the on-and-off rev of motorbike engines. Music. I hear muffled car stereos and the raw insistence of a ghetto blaster. Further away, a broader more cohesive sound – a disco or maybe a live band playing. There is something belligerent about all these different factions of sound; beating, thumping, punching out at each other. I feel like an innocent bystander caught up in a mob fight.

After a moment I begin to hear laughter. The laughter is young, but not childish. And voices. The voices: foreign. I sit up, suddenly wide awake, and hear myself say, 'That's right. Jesus, that's right – I'm *here*.'

The shutters creak back. Stepping out onto a balcony hardly big enough to hold one pair of feet, I remember that I'm on the fifth and topmost floor of a hotel called *Centrale*. Across the way, the train station where I arrived a few hours ago, worn out after my misguided plan to arrive in Bordighera as Nonna might have arrived, more than sixty years ago, down through France on a train. Too excited to sleep for the first part of the journey, too exhausted to stay awake for the latter. The train sucking me into its rhythm and knocking me out. It was only chance that made me open my eyes, as the wheels squawked up alongside a sign that said 'Bordighera'.

I test the balcony railing – sturdier than it looks – then, leaning on it, look down. The middle of the square is pooled with light beamed out from the headlamps of parked cars and scooters. People everywhere, mostly young or at least energetic enough to deserve to be young; bare limbs and light, well-cut clothes. A scooter slips in and out of the crowd and a head of thick black hair on the pillion sways into a spray of silver light. Another scooter arrives, then another. Brown arms wave goodbye or hello. Kisses are exchanged, first in greeting then farewell, often a matter of seconds between the coming and going. The air is convulsed with music that seems much less offensive now. It's like a makeshift, open-air, drive-in nightclub. Couples smooch close together, others bob in a circle. Over to the side two boys show off their break-dancing skills. On the outer edge of the square tall palm trees in the shadows look down like dowagers; like me.

I hold my wrist out to the light and look at my watch – past one o'clock in the morning and I wonder if the whole town is like this, and if it's always like this. I hear a wolf whistle and my eye automatically follows it down to a young man, maybe eighteen or nineteen years old, sitting sideways on the back of a parked scooter, his fingers stuck in his mouth. He whistles again then waves up at me.

'*Ciao, Bella*,' he calls. I look down at my bit of a nightie and what amounts to most of my legs. Then jumping back into the room I shove over the shutters, mortified, but far from displeased.

A few minutes later I come downstairs in search of something to eat and there's nobody in the small foyer. A voice rattles out of a radio somewhere and a television flickers through the crack of a half-opened door marked '*Privato*'. There's a handbag sitting on a chair and a large ring of keys lies just an arm-stretch over the reception desk, including a key with my own room number on it. The entire front of the hotel is opened out onto a terrace – white plastic furniture under a green striped canopy, which in turn opens out onto the square. Most of my money is upstairs, my passport, the brown envelope of Nonna clues. But I'm too hungry and excited to worry about any of that now.

Turning away from the bright-light action of the hotel square, I take a short street that leads to a crossroads where a bar on one corner shows light.

It's an ordinary little bar; a few tables out on the narrow pavement of a busy main street, a few tables inside, only one of which is occupied by a middle-aged couple sitting over two small glasses of wine and a plate of thick pizza cut into squares. The couple stare intently into one another's eyes and hold hands as if they're about to start arm-wrestling. Outside an old man sits, nothing on his table at all but pipe, pouch, matches and ashtray. He holds a newspaper up to his face, over which he sends an occasional wandering eye.

I know how to say *panini*. This is how I put in the time on the journey over, learning scenes from a phrase book. Although the only scene I recall now is the bar scene, and out of that, only the words *panini* and *prego*.

An elderly lady with a squashed brown face stares out over the cash register. Another one in her late fifties sweeps cigarette butts across a floor that appears to be used as one huge open-plan ashtray. A man comes out to serve me, wearing a grey silk suit and a sleek silver-tipped moustache.

There is one panino in the glass case on the counter. A puny thing with what looks like a squeeze of white wax peeping out of the slit. I point to it and say, '*Panini.*' The old lady looks up from the cash register. I add, '*Prego.*' Then point to a bottle of beer.

The man in the grey suit starts talking to me and I go into a mild panic, shaking my head to let him know I've exhausted my vocabulary.

He says, '*Inglese?*' Then tries, '*Americana?*' And I shake my head again before remembering how to say *Irlandese*.

'*Ah Olandese. Hamsterdam?*' he suggests.

'No. Ireland. *Irlanda?* Dublin? *Dublino?*'

The woman with the sweeping brush says, '*Irlanda. Irlanda, vicino a Inghilterra,*' and for some reason the way she says it makes me understand that she's his wife.

'*Ah Irlandese! Che bella! Mamma,*' the man says to the old lady, who has left the cash register and come down the counter to serve me. '*La signora è Irlandese.*'

'*Bellissima!*' Mamma declares and I notice her hand veer away from the glass case where the lone panino cowers like the last brown mouse in the cage. She digs under the counter and begins to pull things from a press: bread, a brick of cheese, an arm of salami.

'*Bella Irlanda per una bella signora,*' the man says, practically swooning, his hands lifted out towards me in abject admiration. His wife at the sweeping brush catches my eye, and gently rolls hers to heaven.

The man guides me out to the pavement and, with a maître d's flourish, serves me my beer. His mother comes out with a fresh panino, a plate of pizza squares, rolls of salami, a bowl of olives, a bowl of crisps. She begins yapping away about Ireland. I smile a bit, frown a bit. Then she stops, pats my arm as if to say, It's all right, I know you don't understand a word I say, but I wanted to say it anyhow. Then she goes inside and resettles her squashy face back over the cash register.

By now, I realize the clue that relies on the name Bella is not going to get me too far. I eat my sandwich and watch the late night traffic of flash cars skim past my nose.

Later I find my way to the promenade and twice walk the length of it. It's past two in the morning – not that you'd notice. There's a fifties-style bar with a curved outdoor counter, another bar further along; neat rows of tables and chairs and a man with a microphone in hand, crooning through and around them. I come to a playground; children still playing. A jaded granny on a bench tries not to nod off while her hyperactive grandchild mills up and down a slide. I pass grass verges, flowerbeds, benches, palm trees, a pavilion. Stalls selling jewellery and knick-knacks, and a black man, the tallest man I've ever seen, in full yellow robes selling handbags spread out at his feet.

I notice odd things as I walk along, like the amount of adults eating ice cream, and the amount of children who are still up and about, although a few casualties are beginning to show: a toddler flaked out over a father's shoulder, another child over the side of the buggy as if rigor mortis has just set in. And how everyone seems to stare at each other, old people on benches, younger ones perched on the railings by the sea, those in the centre walking along; everyone openly gawking at everyone else. And how nobody's drunk. I notice that too.

I step to the right to avoid two roller bladers winging their way towards me. Then I stay with the sea. Looking down the beach back towards

France; umbrellas, furled for the night, stand in troops behind their individual beach clubs. Pubs and restaurants extend into the water on stilts. A queue of people at a nightclub down the way disappear under a canopy beaded with Hollywood lights.

I come to the end of the promenade and a few small hotels. I stop at one called Parigi. A ball has rolled from a pile of plastic toys at the top of the steps. I bring it back up and replace it. The hotel is closed for the night. Through the glass door I can see the foyer: dark wood and marble glazed with dimmed light. It's quiet down here at this end of the promenade, so quiet I can hear the sea. I study the tariff list pinned to the door but can't make sense out of the sums of lire. So I write it down to work out later, along with the hotel's name and telephone number.

The road slants up, the beach goes down. I continue on towards a small church that has a tower like a chimney pot jutting over the sea wall. I light a cigarette, sit on the wall, look out for a while at a black luscious sea. To the east a port of boats and small yachts fidget and jiggle, beyond that a headland stuffed with the lights of another town. Across the way, solid and square, is a statue of a queen that I take to be Victoria.

Next morning sound gets me again. Sweeter, softer, but no less intrusive than the racket from the night before. Every fifteen minutes it wakes me up, this recurrent conversation of bells. In the hour between dawn light and daylight, I lie, until my ear finally stops expecting, and allows me to go back to sleep.

*

It's only since I've arrived here that I realize how little I know about Nonna, how seldom I've actually considered her life. Now everywhere I go I think of her. I imagine her sitting on this bench; queuing in that shop; walking along this street in the shade of these trees. I wonder what she'd think of the constant slog of traffic moving down the main street, or the outrageously expensive boutiques and fabric shops it passes on the way. Was every second shop in town a hairdresser's or beautician's then, as it is now – the way in an Irish town every second shop is a pub? And did women go out to breakfast dolled up to the nines, as if they've already been up for hours at the mirror? And was the shop that sells nothing but seashells here in her time? Or the holy shop, staffed by pretty nuns in cream habits, which appears to sell only statues of angels?

Was her favourite street the corso d'Italia – clean, bright, tree-lined; restaurants discreet to a woman on her own? Not that she would have been on her own.

Or did she, like I do, prefer the old town, dusted in dirty-apricot light, a cut of clean blue from sky or sea when least expected, at the end of an archway or a gap between buildings. And houses that browbeat each other in shadow where unseen families throw down to the passer-by the small symphonies of their everyday lives: the clearing of dishes, the slapping of a child, the argument that could easily end in sex.

I wonder how my private little Nonna coped with being looked at all the time, and being greeted by kisses and all the touching that the Italians seem to do – after five years she would have earned her share of that! And the food – how did she put up with so much food? The presence of it everywhere: shop windows, restaurant terraces – the smells of cooking arriving out of nowhere on this and that breeze. And I wonder if Italy spoiled her, like Dolores said it did to some, or if it gave her the sustenance she may have needed for the rest of her quietly turbulent days.

But most of all I wonder what she would think of me, wandering around staring at everything, like an amnesiac searching for memories that belong to somebody else.

One day I go to the old town and see perfectly respectable men hanging around in groups talking. And I remember a day in North Great George's street when she had been unfazed by the gurriers hanging around at the corner and had told me off for fussing. Another time I'm surrounded by German accents in a café, and a day from my childhood comes back to me, when, on a bus on the way out to Dún Laoghaire, a group of German tourists got on and Nonna, becoming more and more agitated, finally had to get off. Later I had pestered her to tell me why. 'Ah nothing,' she said, 'I'd a headache listening to them. They give me a headache, that's all.'

I walk on the promenade on a navy-blue night, with the stars sharp as new screws, and I think about how many times her feet went this way and if it was at this hour, on a night such as this, and who walked with her then, or if she walked alone.

*

The girl in the library tells me that many villas changed their name after the war. Some were converted into apartments, others were locked up and never returned to. Often they were left to crumble.

'A war, you know?' She shrugs and smiles.

She speaks English and is glad of a chance to practise, or a chance to work at all. The library is quiet at this time of the year, she says. Nobody comes now. Not even students. Her name is Maddalena. 'Like the church in the old town,' she says and asks if I've seen it. I tell her yes, but haven't gone in yet. She smiles and says she's never been inside herself, that she's not from Bordighera anyway, not even from Liguria but another region, a small town in Piemonte. She only came here because she thought every-one would speak English, but they don't. It is her dream to some day work in London.

Maddalena thinks Lami must be the name of the family who owned the villa. In those days, she says, villas were often named for their owners, although she knows no one by that name herself. She goes off to check in the telephone book and some sort of register, also to make one or two phone calls.

While I wait I pace about. It's a small enough library, made entirely of wood; floors, mezzanine, shelves, railing, steps. I can hear Maddalena talking on the telephone in the background and the name Lami which she spells out – 'Elleh. Ah. Emmeh. Ee – sì, Lami.'

She comes back shaking her head. 'Sorry.' Then she tells me I should walk up and down via Romana as most of the villas in Bordighera are here. I should also check the pillars because even if the house is called something else now, there may still be a trace of the original name.

'If the stone is strong enough,' she says, 'the name never fades absolutely.'

And so I put in an afternoon of searching pillars, villa by villa, up and down a very long via Romana, like someone not right in the head. There are hotels and guest houses with bright seaside names on signs over doors, but a different name clearly carved into their pillars. There are large houses transformed into apartment blocks with electric gates and intercom buttons, but pillars nonetheless bearing a name that once had meant something to someone. There are no end of beautiful private houses with gardens of Eden behind high ornate gates held up by scrubbed pillars that sparkle in the sunlight. There is an old soldier's home that once was the residence of a Queen Margherita. I pull a fringe of ivy back from a forehead of ancient stone and find Villa Torino cut into it. I find derelict villas named for long-ago brides: Cora, Paulina, Cordelia. I even find one forlorn edifice on the edge of what has become a small building site, its head knocked off and brackets of a gate still wedged, like thorns, into its side.

Late afternoon and I stop and sit on a bench under the trees for a rest and a smoke. There's an old man on another bench up the road, and two old ladies yakking on a corner, and I think how easy it would be if I could speak Italian or if this was an Irish town where I could say, 'Did you ever hear tell of a family called Lami living along here?' and would probably be told what they had for their tea of a Tuesday. Then I finish my smoke, pull myself back into the heat and start over.

Just before sunset I stand at a huge shell of a burnt-out hotel. The sun in its last forceful moments is pushing a blast of light onto the hotel's decaying façade. The windows are sockets of darkness, the ironwork rusted, the temporary yellow on the walls almost blinding. Below all this, the gardens, dense and black with overgrowth. Yet even this desolate place has something written on its pillars – the aptly named Hotel Angst.

I come back into town taking a short cut down a leafy laneway between two villas. At the end of the slope the wall on my left turns on the corner. A faded narrow pathway runs alongside it, and I can see about half-way down what appears to be a bricked-up door, over it a ring of rusted barbed wire. I stand for a moment and consider taking the pathway, but then a young couple appear from the opposite direction. They are pushing a bicycle between them, now and then leaning over the crossbar to kiss or touch. They would have to separate and stand aside to let me pass, and so I remain on the straight path back into town.

*

The next morning I go back to Maddalena, as she told me to do, in case she managed to find anything of interest. I tell her about my failed venture on via Romana and she laughs when she hears how I checked every single pillar on the road, then says, 'Ahh, what a pity but here are other suggestions.' She hands me a list. '*And* we have found something in a newspaper that could be interesting for you. My colleague, he bring it now.'

While we wait I glance at her list: tennis club, bridge club, Anglican church, old people's home.

'Thanks, Maddalena, these are good ideas.'

'Yes,' she agrees then asks me if I am staying long in Bordighera. I tell her I don't know. That I'm moving to the Hotel Parigi today for a week or so and then I'll make up my mind.

'You don't have to be back?'

'No. Not in the least.'

'Not for work?'

'No.'

'Not for nobody?'

'No.'

'Oh. Well, if you decide to stay, perhaps for a month or two anyway, tell me. I know a very nice apartment near the tennis club. I think you will like it. It's better than the hotel, I think. And less money.'

'Yes. I'll keep that in mind.'

'You can invite people for coffee.'

'People?'

'Me!' she laughs. 'And whoever else, of course, you make into friends. We can teach each other, English, Italian. We can help each other – no?'

'Oh,' I say, a little surprised by this unexpected friendliness. 'Yes, why not?'

'Why not!' Maddalena says. '*Perché non!*' she adds, her finger raised like a teacher, as if the lessons have already begun.

A man comes out carrying a large leather-bound book in his arms. One leg moves a little heavily and his head leans slightly to one side. I think he may be disabled. When he reaches the table he holds on to the book and behind his glasses his eyes blink nervously. He begins to speak to Maddalena, and although I can't understand a word I can sense his awkwardness. Absurdly I feel as if I'm eavesdropping and so look away, down at my list, or over the walls of the library.

After a while Maddalena stops to introduce us. 'This is my colleague, Emilio,' and he turns to me for a second and nods before looking away. Maddalena begins to explain, 'Emilio heard us talk yesterday about the family Lami and when he goes home last night he asks his mamma if she have heard of them. He say that she can remember *her* mamma telling her something.'

'Really?' I wait, while Emilio gives another few sentences to Maddalena.

'His grandmother told to his mother that there was a family living here once called Lami, but his mother she can't remember where they live exactly. And now his grandmother, she is dead so we cannot ask.'

Maddalena looks back up at Emilio, who has removed his glasses to wipe them clean. He is getting into his stride now, speeding up his little story, and going at it with more confidence.

'He say that the story is the signora of the family was very beautiful and that she was a Jew and that they…' She turns back and asks Emilio a question. I cannot believe it takes so many Italian sentences to make up so few English words.

Maddalena comes back to me. 'They say she die in the concentration camp of Buchenwald like the granddaughter of our Queen Margherita, Princess Mafalda, who also died there, although obviously she was not a Jew. That is all he know but can try to find out more for you.' Emilio is looking at me now, nodding morosely.

'Oh no,' I say. 'The poor woman. That's terrible.'

Maddalena frowns. 'Yes, there are many such terrible stories from the time of the war.'

Emilio begins to speak again as he lays the book down on the table. Maddalena puts her hand on the cover of the book and then pauses. 'He says, his mother remembers talk of a man. He came after the war, and stayed in the Lami house because he used to work for the family. But the funny thing is he didn't live in the house, even though it was empty, but in the garage at the end of the garden.'

'What happened to him?' I ask.

'Nobody knows. Maybe went away. Maybe died. His mother only remember that he was a very sick man.'

Maddalena goes back to the book and carefully lifts the cover. 'Old newspapers,' she says. 'This one we find is interesting for you. She lifts and settles the flimsy pages and stops at a newspaper dated August 1936. A photograph.

It's a group picture of well-dressed people standing in two rows at what seems to be the port. I squint in and attempt to read the caption beneath it. Maddalena helps me. 'Here a couple, just back out of honeymoon,' she says. 'This woman and this man beside her. She is very beautiful – yes?' Carefully she points with the tip of her little finger as if her index finger might bruise the face.

'Yes,' I say. 'She is.'

'Do you see what her name is?' Maddalena goes to a drawer at the side of the table and takes out a magnifying glass. 'Look.' She draws the glass along the caption. 'This woman is Signora Lami and she has married in France, this man Signor Tassi.' Maddalena moves the magnifying glass in and out and the woman's face grows and shrinks. 'It is the second marriage for her, I think.'

'Why?'

'Because it say here that she is celebrating with her son, family and friends at Villa Lami. This has to be the son here. This boy.'

'Does it give his name?'

'No. And there are no other names written down, only the bride and groom. I don't know why.'

I take the glass in my hand and look at the boy standing to the left of the bride. I watch his face, slightly turned towards his right shoulder, expand in the glass. Like his mother he is good-looking although he doesn't really resemble her. One by one I go over the rest of the party. Another beautiful woman stands beside the boy; next to her is an older, distinguished-looking man. On the far side of the groom there are three men, one fattish and middle-aged, the others could be his sons. These are all dark, like the groom. On the back row a middle-aged man and a woman smile out like Cheshire cats. Behind the bride is another man and woman although their faces are a little blurred. There is a gap of a few feet in the back row until the last woman who is standing right behind the boy. She is wearing a half-brimmed hat but her face shows well enough beneath it. Her hand is on the boy's shoulder. It is as if she had moved over and left the gap in the back row so she could place her hand on him. They are the only two in the picture to make any contact. Even the bride and groom stand separate to each other.

'Does she look familiar?' Maddalena asks.

'Who?' I say.

'Signora Lami – does she look familiar?'

'No.'

I put down the magnifying glass and stand up. 'Maddalena, I'd like to go outside for a few minutes.'

'You are OK?'

'Yes, yes. I just want to have a cigarette. Can you leave this here?'

'*Certo*,' she says, frowning at the brown flakes that have fallen away from the old newspaper pages, then brushing them under the table.

I go outside into the shaded arcade with its pelmet of thick mauve flowers. I light a cigarette and sit on a stone bench. It is almost lunchtime and the street outside gives few sounds. There is only the occasional drone of a Vespa or the murmur of a passing car. I can hear insects close by, but can't see any, and I can taste the heavy scent of flowers on the edge of my cigarette smoke.

I think about the group in the picture. The man, slightly blurred, standing behind the bride – could easily be the same man in the picture found in Nonna's old handbag. The boy could easily be the missing boy: Alfredo or Alberto or John. I think about the hand on his shoulder and who it belongs to. I need a few moments' absence before going back in. But I am almost certain, it has to be Nonna. Her hand stretched out to comfort. It is the only thing that makes sense to me now. Finding her like this, trapped in a moment from the past. A moment that fits perfectly with the rest of her life. A woman with a half-hidden face. A woman in the back of a photograph.